The Last Iceni

Ronald Haines

Published by Haines Communications, 2022.

THE LAST ICENI

First edition. January 20, 2022.

Copyright © 2022 Ronald Haines.

ISBN: 978-1637860076

Written by Ronald Haines.

Table of Contents

Chapter One: Ceridwen

"Father," Ceridwen forced a pseudo serious tone into her voice while she gathered her raven hair into a thick cascade down her back. "Kelpie say's I can't marry Donogh because," she leaned forward and placed her left ear against her horse's neck. "Yes?" She said, nuzzling into it. "I see." Ceridwen's blue eyes peeked up at her father over Kelpie's gray mane before she sat up again with a flourish to announce, "Because we always beat him and his horse every time we race."

"I understand he's to be on the Ordovices' team for the Beltaine race." Conwyn released a smile as he turned to his daughter. "Perhaps he's getting better."

Conwyn had always been fond of Donogh and enjoyed the tease at Ceridwen's expense. The riders from most teams were either tribal kings or their children and to them it was a ceremonial position, but the Iceni differed in that they always sent their best riders regardless of social status. The Iceni therefore always won at Beltaine each year, cementing their unquestioned renown as horse masters. Ceridwen had recently tried out for this prestigious team and had ridden well, but since she refused to ride Kelpie through the river like the others, she lost too much time going over the bridge and ended up in the middle of the pack instead being of one of the first three. Unlike other horses, Kelpie wasn't an animal to remain mounted on while traversing water.

"He is smart, though," Ceridwen conceded.

"Indeed, he is." The teeth from the right side of his mouth shone through Conwyn's full red beard. "And he's to be trained as a druid. That's no small honor."

Conwyn slowly twisted his head back over his right shoulder to check on the cart following them. "One day," he continued, turning back to his daughter, "you could be queen of the Ordovices."

"But I'm Iceni," she teasingly protested, straightening up and nudging Kelpie two lengths ahead and out of earshot of the rest of their party. "Besides," she called back, "a queen has to be responsible for other people."

"True," Conwyn trotted up to her side. "But you'll find that comes anyway," he smiled, "once you have children."

"Oh, that's not going to be for a very long, long time." Ceridwen's hair swirled from side to side. "If at all."

"We'll see."

"Right..." Ceridwen's voice froze at the sound of a twig snapping from the underbrush just behind them. Conwyn instantly turned his horse and reared it up on its hind legs as the swarm of arrows thudded down around them. "Swords," was his single shout. He drew Glynu, his own oversized iron sword and, brandishing it over his head in his right hand, immediately bore down on the band of Trinovantes emerging from the trees closest to the cart. Trinovantes weren't true Briton Celts but Belagics from Gaul who had migrated to Britannia a hundred years prior. This was a cowardly attack, typical of their kind.

The four vassals immediately jumped down from the cart and drew the swords that Conwyn had given them prior to the trip. "Far better to die in battle than to be captured," Conwyn had always warned, and they were ready to fight. Ceridwen turned Kelpie in a tight semicircle and dug in her heels in an attempt to catch up to her father when the second volley hit. Blood spewing from its neck from a bolt though its carotid, Conwyn's horse stumbled and dropped dead. Conwyn was thrown to the ground, his sword flying away in one direction as he rolled to absorb the fall in another. Everything around Ceridwen was happening so quickly yet her own actions seemed so sluggish and ineffective. In spite of the sounds of battle surrounding her, the loudest sound she heard was from her own open-mouthed breathing. She galloped toward Glynu but as she leaned to retrieve it, left arm and leg wrapped tightly around Kelpie's neck, the sudden pain of an arrow in her side caused her to lose her grip. Falling from Kelpie, her only thought was to recover Glynu and return it to her father. Landing awkwardly on the ground, she rolled over, gulped a breath to recover from the shock, and then desperately began to crawl toward the sword. Conwyn meanwhile staggered to his feet, drew his dagger from its scabbard and leaped on the assailant bearing down on Ceridwen, yelling and knocking him to the ground while simultaneously slicing his throat. Immediately, three of his accomplices ran over to join in the fray. Ceridwen lunged for the sword quickly took the hilt in both hands and rolled over, clutching it in earnest, while she turned to look toward where the Trinovantes and her father were fighting. She watched in horror as Conwyn spat out blood due to a sword protruding from his belly yet having already dispatched two of his newest attackers. She opened her mouth to scream but the sound she heard instead was the scream of the remaining Trinovantes as her father brought him down, driving a dagger into his chest as they fell to the ground together. There was still movement close by. Ceridwen lay flat on the ground with Glynu firmly in her right hand while she felt for the source of her pain with her left and quickly located the arrow stuck in her tunic. The tip was half an inch deep into her upper right side and made jagged cuts into her flesh every time she moved. Carefully placing the sword on the grass, she reached for her dagger and cut through the leather ties of her tunic then simultaneously pulled the arrow away from her breast while rolling over to remove the garment it was stuck into. She gritted her teeth to remain silent, and then desperately grabbed Glynu once again. That last movement attracted the enemy, but as the Trinovantes' shadow fell over her, she summoned the strength to scramble up on one knee. The pain from her wound gave her focus; she swung the heavy sword into the side of her opponent, throwing him to the ground as a spray of hot blood hit her face. It tasted like metal. Using Glynu as a crutch, she staggered to her feet and with one stab impaled the moaning Trinovantes, leaning with all her weight on the hilt until he finished writhing beneath her. Satisfied that he was finished, she pulled back on Glynu but it was stuck. She leaned back, straining and pulling, but it wouldn't budge and her efforts only forced more blood out of her wound. Near panic, she put her foot on the fallen body for leverage and, screaming to offset the pain in her breast, somehow managed to withdrew the sword. She immediately spun around, panting and holding it as hard as she could in her trembling hands. No one there, she staggered toward the cart. The packages were intact but the entire party was dead, sprawled across the ground along with the five slain attackers and the mangled bodies of three horses. Hair matted and her right side throbbing and drenched, she struggled to keep the tip of the heavy sword off the ground as she turned in a complete circle, panting through her clenched teeth as she determined that all was indeed clear. Then, staggering and dragging the sword, she made her way to where her father's body was still lying next to his victim, the hilt of his dagger still clutched in his fist. His head was upturned to the sky and his gray eyes, even in death, were still as wide and defiant as she's always known them. Falling to her knees next to him, she reached out to touch his face and forced a smile. "It was a good death, Conwyn," she said quietly, trying desperately to speak with authority. Her face nevertheless shuddered uncontrollably with her words and, unable to contain it any longer, she collapsed to the ground, wailing.

The sun had about set when she regained consciousness. Aware of something moving in the shadows close to the tree line, she made an attempt to whistle for Kelpie but the distress from her wound deprived her of sound. The object near the trees, a wolf, was certainly watching her, waiting for darkness. Clenching her teeth, Ceridwen stretched her right arm out, pushing her fingers until she was able to grasp the sword, then pulled it to her side and used it to help her up onto her left knee. Straining to focus her eyes on the wolf, the animal seemed to disappear in her blurred vision, but there were faint sounds from that direction. She struggled to her feet and slid Glynu in front of her, the hilt firm in her two clenched, trembling fists and its tip barely above the ground. "Come on, then," she panted at what now appeared to be a figure moving directly at her.

"Ceridwen," said a familiar voice. "It's all right."

"Llyn?" She kept her grip on the heavy sword until she could be certain, but as soon as he was close enough for her to clearly make out the druid she dropped Glynu and ran to up him. "Oh, Llyn." She threw her arms around his neck and gripped tightly in order to remain upright. "It was horrible." She took a deep breath. "And father is dead."

Llyn hugged her silently for several minutes then slowly broke free by first patting her back. "I'm on my way to speak to the Iceni council," he said. "It's fortunate I came across you. What's happened here?"

"He's dead." Ceridwen repeated as her face contorted again. Head shuddering rapidly from side to side she quickly grabbed the Druid's hand and pulled him across the field to where her father lay. "Look."

They stood together over Conwyn's body until Ceridwen composed herself enough to be able to speak. Llyn asked her to describe the ambush then walked over to the cart, surveying the scene and nodding, chin in his right hand. "This is completely intolerable," he began. "It began a few weeks after the last solstice when the Trinovantes began sending raiding parties north into Iceni territory, going into the villages and taking peasants to sell as slaves." His hand savagely caressed his chin as he spoke. "And now it's escalated into this."

"What about the non aggression pact?" Ceridwen asked. "Doesn't King Cunobelin forbid this?"

"Indeed!" Llyn released his chin and nodded. "And the fact he hasn't acted on it is most troubling. I've known him for years and it's unlike him to tolerate any sort of disorder. The last thing he wants to do is give the Romans any hint of instability in Britannia." He sat on a fallen crate and patted a spot next to him.

"Could it be he wants to appease them by sending more slaves?" Ceridwen asked as she joined him.

"Unlikely. Cunobelin allows a minimum slave trade to keep the Romans appeased but he really doesn't like it. Camulodunum's main exports to Rome are jewelry and tin and hunting dogs. Not our people." Llyn slapped his thighs and stood up. "But enough of that, which is the Trinovantes that you dispatched?"

"The body's over there." Ceridwen dragged Glynu, its tip digging into the earth behind her as she walked, to the corpse of her fallen assailant. "This is the one I killed." Her voice was devoid of expression.

"Then you know what you must do now." Llyn's words were rhetorical. The pain of lifting the weight of Glynu somehow expressed itself as a smile on Ceridwen's face as she held the sword in her clenched fists and raised it above her head. She stood upright, feet slightly apart, and studied the corpse. A streak of already dried blood extended from the half open mouth all the way down the cheek. The right arm lay extended while the left was contorted beneath the body. The torso had no movement, no breathing. She had killed. Ceridwen screamed as loud as she was able, then swung Glynu down onto the neck and severed the head. It rolled and stopped against her feet. Right hand tightly around the hilt of the sword for support, she reached down with her left and without hesitation intertwined her fingers into the mass of scraggly brown hair. Slowly and deliberately, she picked up the head and held it aloft to take in the detail. One eye was closed and the other crusted over. The nose seemed disjointed and the lower lip was sagging beneath its own weight. Ceridwen's own lips finally parted into a satisfied display of white teeth, her blue eyes transformed into a vibrant gray, and then, after a silent minute, she simply tossed the head aside.

Llyn took care of the bodies while Ceridwen made up a poultice and, after applying it to her wound, succumbed to an herb induced sleep. When she awoke it was already mid-morning and time to leave for Venta Icenorum, the Iceni capital city.

Llyn drove the cart and Ceridwen rode Kelpie alongside. Her breathing was controlled and she was grinding her teeth. "Why do the Romans need slaves anyhow?" She finally blurted out. "Surely they can afford to employ free people?"

"Rome is a culture more different than you can imagine," Llyn replied in a professorial manner. "Slaves are property. The rich own hundreds of them to do all of the work while they enjoy the pleasures of citizenship. Rome was built by slaves. They have a great demand for them and get them from all over the world."

"Why would anybody allow themselves to be a slave?"

"Most of them don't come about it by choice, as evidenced by the Trinovantes raiding parties. Peasants are easily trained and if a slave were to run away, they'd be horribly tortured to death as an example to the others. For the most part, slaves are well fed and cared for so it's not a bad life at all for them to serve in a Roman household." Llyn cocked his head to the left and raised his right eyebrow. "Those that refuse to comply, typically people like captured enemies, are put to work rowing galleys or sent to the arena."

"What's the arena?" Ceridwen swung her head around and glared with her still gray eyes.

"That's where they hold the games, my girl." Llyn squeezed the edges of his mouth up toward his eyes. "Gladiatorial combat to entertain the citizens of Rome."

"Absurd," Ceridwen snorted. "And these Romans consider themselves civilized?"

"They consider themselves," Llyn rocked back and forth, his expression flattened, "to be the rulers of the world."

"Well, they don't rule Britannia."

Llyn smiled at Ceridwen's defiant outburst. "No, they don't," he agreed. "But that's mostly due to Cunobelin's resolve, keeping the peace between the tribes, which," Llyn aggressively rubbed his bearded chin, "brings me to the reason for being here in Iceni territory. Your King Anted has appealed to the Druids for permission to make war against the Trinovantes."

Llyn slowly licked his lips. The three Iceni kings, Anted, Aesu and Saenu, along with Conwyn and other minor kings who made up the Iceni council, had authority over all internal activities but there could be no war without Druid authorization. He had been sent to them charged with the responsibility to, at least temporarily, defuse a very volatile situation. Already the Iceni had sent warriors to protect southern Iceni towns and they were understandably anxious to take the offensive but, without authorization, were banned from crossing into Trinovantes lands. After what had just happened he knew that he had very little time before major conflict arose, even without a formal declaration of war.

"Will you be granting us permission for war, Llyn? After them murdering my father it's surely just." Ceridwen leaned forward and patted Glynu which was in its rightful position around Kelpie's neck. "Trinovantes are dogs."

"War between the tribes is counterproductive to the Druid goals of forging Britannia into a single nation, Ceridwen, and I'm at odds as to why Cunobelin is permitting this escalating tension. Before any decision of war is reached I need to know what's going on in Camulodunum." He rubbed the back of his neck with his right hand.

"Anted's not unreasonable and, considering what's at stake, I'm confident that I can convince the Iceni to hold off for a month, until the feast of Beltaine. This will give me the chance to travel to the Trinovantes capitol city, meet with King Cunobelin and attempt to resolve things peacefully."

"That would probably be for the best." Ceridwen murmured as she mentally grappled with how her life had so suddenly changed. This coming summer was to have been an exciting time for her, the time when she and the other fourteen year old girls were to begin training in the use of a sword, but yesterday's events had already advanced her years ahead of them to warrior status. She would even now have to accept some responsibility for her people; her father's death meant that she would take his place on the war council.

Chapter Two: Beltaine

While the Iceni party was jubilant as they made their way to Camulodunum for the Beltaine festivities, they were also heavily armed with hounds and handlers both leading the procession as well as bringing up the rear. Despite assurances from Camulodunum by way of Llyn for safe passage through Trinovantes territory, they were taking no chances. Ceridwen rode toward the front of the column with twenty other warriors. Glynu, hers now by birthright, was sheathed and strapped to Kelpie's neck, just in front of Ceridwen's left leg in a position ready to be drawn. For weeks she'd been practicing dismounting while handling the heavy sword but had yet to perfect the effortless-looking Iceni technique and had mostly found herself lying flat on the ground after each attempt. She'd grow into it; Celtic iron swords were just too heavy for her right now. Her tall body simply needed to fill out a little more.

She looked behind at the column of carts and wagons flanked by three chariots on each side. This was a major market opportunity and the artisans were bringing cartloads of highly-prized jewelry and clothing. Insatiable Roman demand for Iceni work had more than tripled its value in the past year and the merchants in Camulodunum were eager to acquire as much as possible. It was to be both an exciting and profitable Beltaine for the Iceni.

Andarta, Ceridwen's closest friend, was moving up the side of the column on her horse. If it weren't for her red hair, equally as long and full as Ceridwen's, the girls could pass for twins. "Hey there Ceri," she called out and rode up alongside her. "Excited about seeing Donogh again?"

Ceridwen twisted her mouth and blushed slightly as she was reminded of the carnal relationship she had recently developed with Donogh. While they had been childhood friends and innocently played together since the age of six, the past session on Mon, the Druid Island where children of the Briton aristocracy were schooled, saw their friendship grow to incorporate new, sensual aspects. Donogh regaled her with his insightful poetry and they shared the long walks and swims as they always had done, but now they were enjoying each other's company like never before. He was almost perfect, yet one thing about him really bothered her. It was something she couldn't speak of since it reflected so strangely on her that no one would ever understand. Donogh was so much stronger than she was physically, yet in their most tender times, those intimate moments that they spent alone, he was always so annoyingly gentle with her. Always! It was if she might break. It was so demeaning. She'd teasingly bite or scratch and once even dug her nails into his flesh in an attempt to unbridle raw lust, but he either refused or was unable to give in to his deepest, or, more to the point, her darkest passions. An attempted discussion around this subject with Andarta clearly suggested that he was quite normal, however, so after feigningly laughing it off, Ceridwen decided it best to keep her "unnatural" thoughts to herself. Especially since chances were that she would end up marrying Donogh. It was a good match since he was favored amongst the Ordovices to succeed his father as king. The problem was simply hers and she'd just have to learn to live with it. Clearly, if a king couldn't meet her dark desires then they weren't to be satisfied anywhere. Besides, Ceridwen's mouth wrinkled involuntarily as she continued to reminisce, Donogh wasn't without conventional attributes. In fact he was vastly superior to anyone in her village.

"And you'll have plenty of time to spend alone with Prasutagus, won't you, Andarta?" Ceridwen replied with a sideways grin. "I take it you've been keeping up on your pomegranate?" For young Iceni women the introduction of this contraceptive fruit was, perhaps, one of the greatest benefits to have emerged from their tribe's reluctant inclusion in overseas trade.

"How's the wound?" Andarta neatly avoided the question. "Doesn't all this riding bother it?"

"No problem at all." Ceridwen put her hand to her breast and gently caressed the still tender, raised skin. "It's going to leave quite a scar, though."

"You were lucky, Ceri. I still can't believe you were able to wield that thing," she nodded toward Glynu, "never mind make a kill with it."

"Llyn says that when your emotions run high enough, you have almost unlimited strength. I believe it too." She patted the hilt of the sword. "I suppose that's what happens to warriors in battle."

"I'm not sure I'm so anxious to experience that firsthand," Andarta confessed quietly. "I could see myself throwing a spear or driving a chariot, but to be that close to someone, to see their face as you try to kill them." She shook her head. "I don't know. I'd have to be incredibly angry or something."

"That rage becomes the source of your strength. The Druids teach how to focus passions and bend them to your will. Llyn told me we'll begin to learn about that next year, but that it takes at least ten years to master it."

"Still, I suppose it is a natural response. Look at what happens when a boar is cornered, or how a bear acts when it's protecting its young." Andarta pushed the fingers of her right hand across the top of her head, intertwining them into her hair as she spoke.

"Let's hope we don't have to put that to a test on this trip." Ceridwen pointed to the three square-cut marker stones by the side of the road. "We're on Trinovantes land now."

The Catuvellauni capital, Camulodunum, was actually in the heart of Trinovantes territory. After King Cunobelin had annexed it so many years before, he decided that the main city of the Britons should also be the major trade center. He built his lavish wooden palace in the center of town and over the years as the population soared, it became the focal point for every major festival and a gathering place for all of the tribes, Belagic and Briton. Cunobelin would personally preside over every festival, a tradition that was to make this one particularly difficult for his sons, Togodumnus and Caractacus. Their first inclination was to attempt to conceal their father's illness and bluff it out, but the fact that the Iceni council had demanded an audience made that impossible. Llyn, having been in the city for several days, had advised the princes as to their best course of action and had promised to stand with them when the delegation arrived.

"Thank goodness you're here," Togodumnus nervously exclaimed, leaping to his feet as Llyn entered the throne room. "Have the Iceni arrived yet?"

"Caractacus is welcoming them into the palace courtyard as we speak," Llyn answered, slightly raising the corners of his mouth as he spoke. "Are you ready for their council to assemble? It's best that we don't delay."

Togodumnus took a deep breath. "As ready as I'm going to be. Let's go."

Togodumnus and Llyn walked outside through the main palace door and stood at the top of the steps together. Togodumnus generally welcomed the Iceni royalty, and then Llyn called out the names of the war council, inviting each of them to approach. "King Anted and Prince Prasutagus."

Togodumnus greeted them individually as they climbed the stairs, first firmly shaking Anted's burly forearm while looking directly into his deep set eyes then eagerly taking his son's hand. Prasutagus was tall, over six feet, almost as tall as Togodumnus himself. They assembled behind him and Llyn continued the role call. "King Aesu, King Saenu," then, after they were up the stairs, he finally called out, "Princess Ceridwen."

She ascended the stairs looking straight ahead. Flitting her blue eyes from side to side she wishing that Andarta could also have been here, but this meeting was only for members of the war council. Certainly, Ceridwen had been to the palace before but always in the background and she was feeling more than a little overwhelmed until Llyn shook her forearm and grabbed her shoulder. "You now take Conwyn's place," he reassured her.

Once the Iceni council was seated at the circular table in the palace war room along with Llyn, Caractacus, and Togodumnus, the guards began to close the large wooden doors.

"Wait." Anted called to them, then turned to Llyn. "We're here to see Cunobelin. Where is he?"

"That question," said Llyn, his palm raised slightly and nodding for the guards to resume, "will be answered first."

The doors closed with a boom. The room was silent, all eyes focused on Llyn. "King Cunobelin lies dying in the next room."

"And the Trinovantes are running rampant," Saenu blurted out, smoothing his scraggly gray hair with both hands. Llyn turned suddenly and glared at him. "And you'll respect the rules of this room, Saenu."

Llyn went on the explain Cunobelin's stroke, how his eldest son Adminus had attempted to bring in a Roman legion to conduct a coup, and how Caractacus had taken the Catuvellauni army, outmaneuvered him, and driven him out of the country. "But," he looked up, his unflinching eyes scanning the seven faces sitting at the table, "several renegade Trinovantes took advantage of the army being away to engage in slaving raids on the Iceni. Most of the offenders died at the hands of Conwyn and Ceridwen." He turned to his right. "Togodumnus, please address us."

The tall, well dressed man poised his hands together on the table. "First," Togodumnus began, "let me offer sincere apologies to the Iceni and condolences to Ceridwen for the loss of her father. Conwyn will be missed." All eyes on her, Ceridwen bit her upper lip to retain her composure. "Second, tomorrow I shall make the declaration to the tribes that there is to be no more trading in our people. Britannia will no longer supply the Romans with slaves."

"Ha!" Anted gripped the edge of the table as he leaned over it. "And by what authority do you assume the power of King of the Britons while Cunobelin still lives?"

"By the rule of regency, King Anted. With Adminus gone, I'm the eldest son and can therefore carry out his wishes while he's infirm."

"So it's the will of Cunobelin that there be no more slave trade, is it?" Anted leaned back into his seat and laughed at the ceiling before suddenly lurching forward again. "He's permitted it for thirty years."

"Tolerated, Anted. Only tolerated." Togodumnus held his ground. "Father put up with it in order to keep an active level of trading with the Romans. He knew that as long as we provided a market for their goods with enough to trade back they'll leave us alone and for years it was the slave trade that kept the balance. Now that Rome's demanding more jewelry and clothing, the likes of what the Iceni bring to trade, we can buy more than enough of their spices and wine without trading in slaves. They're getting all they need now from Germania anyway." He wiped the back of his hand across his mouth while continuing to stare at the Iceni king. "Father was pragmatic," Togodumnus leaned toward the center of the table and forcefully placed his fist in front of himself, "so yes, this is Cunobelin's will." He slowly turned his head, scanning each face in the room. "With the Catuvellauni army back from Cantium and slave trading no longer an option," he continued, easing back into his chair, "I can give you complete assurance that the Iceni will have no more trouble with the Trinovantes."

Anted nodded thoughtfully. "Regent Togodumnus has both explained the extraordinary events that enabled the Trinovantes incursions and given his assurance that it will happen no more," he said, speaking to no one in particular. He suddenly turned his head to his right. "Aesu, speak," he demanded.

Aesu, who up to this time had been sitting attentively and stroking his cropped beard, suddenly became animated, deliberately taking his hand from his chin and slapping it flat on the table in front of him. "We have no desire for war with the Trinovantes, other than to prevent their raids. If Togodumnus can control them, then I am satisfied." Aesu looked directly at Anted as he spoke, as if no one else were in the room. Anted then turned to Saenu.

"Trinovantes are Belagic scum, they know no better," Saenu snarled as he looked up at Togodumnus. "But as long as the Catuvellauni can keep them in line, then the Iceni won't have to."

"Ceridwen." Anted turned to address her. "Speak your mind and hold nothing back. All will be decided here and you're the most aggrieved amongst us." He continued his eye lock and conveyed a slight smile of encouragement to her.

She spoke back directly to him. "They took our people and sold them into slavery. They ambushed us and killed my father. I wanted nothing more than revenge. But, Saenu is right; Trinovantes are Belagics, not Britons. Their actions underlie what they are, but as long as they're kept in line, I'll be content." She swallowed and quickly glanced around the room, then shoved herself back into her seat.

Anted made a rapid nod in her direction and loudly exhaled "Llyn." He addressed the Druid across the table. "The Iceni hereby withdraw their petition to make war on the Trinovantes."

"Very good," Llyn nodded as he spoke. "The Druids applaud the wisdom of the Iceni council."

Togodumnus stood up and nodded to the guards to open the door. "We shall eat together," he announced. "Come," he beckoned. "Roast flesh and the finest Roman wines await us."

As the group proceeded down the hallway Ceridwen sensed someone immediately behind her and a voice whispered, "So, the Iceni feel they are superior to the Belagics?"

Ceridwen turned rapidly to see who spoke and found herself face-to-face with a smiling Caractacus. Shorter than his brother, he was still an imposing figure. While Togodumnus cropped his hair and dressed for court, Caractacus wore his field leather and, although his straw colored hair was neat, it was still long like the rest of the warriors.

"Feel?" she answered defiantly.

Caractacus laughed. "They've lived in Britannia for a hundred years. If we're to make this a united nation, we'll have to do a better job of accepting them."

"Then they'd better start acting like Britons or we'll have to drive them back to Gaul." Ceridwen answered with a half smile. "How do you see them?"

"I've lived amongst the Trinovantes for years and, for the most part, they're just like the rest of us. The Cantium, too. Now," he winked, "the Atrebates."

"So, Caractacus," Llyn interrupted and patted him on the back. "What do you think of our Ceridwen?"

"Well, she's feisty and opinionated," Caractacus stroked his smooth chin as he spoke. "But she impressed me in council, setting aside her anger for the benefit of all." He nodded at her. "You'll make a fine queen of the Ordovices one day."

Ceridwen contorted her mouth as her eyes flicked between the two men, unsure what to say.

"Donogh is my nephew after all," Caractacus added in an attempt to alleviate her quizzical look. "He talks about you all the time."

"Incessantly," Llyn added with a friendly laugh. "We decided that Donogh is to spend the rest of the season here with his uncle. Since Caractacus is one of the few people to ever complete Druid training and then return to aristocratic life, time spent with him will give Donogh some good perspective."

"You're—" Ceridwen was aghast. Caractacus was one of the most well-known warriors in all of Britannia and a renowned military leader, as well as being married with three children. "You're a Druid?"

"Indeed he is," Llyn chimed in. "The first of what we hope will be many more placed securely in the ruling classes. Each kingdom in the combined nation of Britannia will have fully-educated people running them." He turned to Ceridwen. "Donogh has the aptitude for Druid training and he's also in line to be king of the Ordovices."

"What of the Trinovantes?" Ceridwen asked. "What about the other Belagic tribes? How do they fit in?"

"Well," Caractacus responded, speaking slowly. "The Trinovantes and Cantium are already under our control, so there's no reason for them to even have a king, is there?"

Ceridwen liked his answer. She also wanted to know where Donogh was.

"Ceri!"

Ceridwen beamed instantly at the sound of a familiar voice and rapidly scanned the crowd of people around her trying to pick him out when he tapped her on the left shoulder. "Donogh," she shouted excitedly as she quickly turned and wrapped her arms around his neck, the momentum enabling him to pick her of her feet and whirl her around.

"I'm so sorry to hear about your father," he said, then tipped his head back causing her hands to slide onto his shoulders. Her blue eyes half closed.

She smiled awkwardly at him. "Thanks." She began to look down but, not wanting to show any weakness, caught herself and sprung her head back up. "He protected me and killed his attackers. He died a good death," she said firmly, then quickly changed the subject with, "I'm so pleased to see you."

"But no kiss?" Donogh teased.

Ceridwen immediately reached up, grabbed the sides of his face and pulled his lips down hard onto hers. Donogh's arms enveloped her even more tightly, pressing her body to full contact with his as he eagerly responded to her persistent tongue with his own. He continued his embrace long after their lips parted and stood silently while Ceridwen snuggled the side of her face into the nape of his neck, emitting only a barely perceptible murmuring.

"Let's go for a walk along the seafront," Donogh suggested once his ability to speak had returned. "Get away from the crowds for a while."

They ran hand-in-hand away from the stalls and crowds of the Beltaine market to the edge of Camulodunum, up the hill to the north, and were soon walking in the meadow overlooking the waves breaking onto the rocks below. Donogh nodded his head toward a solitary oak tree in the distance. "Without your horse, you don't stand a chance of beating me in a race to that tree," he said.

Ceridwen immediately started running. "We'll see about that," she called out as Donogh started after her. With his longer legs, he easily caught up with her and ran alongside her, matching her pace for a while, before finally pushing ahead and tossing himself at the base of the tree to watch as she came running up. "So what do I win, Ceri?" he asked.

Ceridwen stood in front of him and silently reached behind her neck. She unfastened the leather tie and slowly pulled it out of the series of eyelets down her back causing her dress to slide off her shoulders and float to the ground around her feet. "What would you like, Donogh?" she asked coyly.

Donogh looked first at the dress around her ankles, then slowly moved his eyes up her naked frame, squinting at but not turning away from the newly forming scar occupying most of the outside of her apple-sized right breast, up past her neck, her mouth, until he made contact again with her wide open blue eyes. He reached out his right hand and, without breaking eye contact, took her left hand in it and eased her down beside him. His left hand went to her forehead to push the wisp of stray black hair back from her face and he gently kissed her cheek, her neck. She leaned into him as his head moved down further, first caressing her shoulder with his lips, then her forearm, then the wound. She closed her eyes and leaned her head back slightly, her mouth partly open as Donogh kissed every part of it, then ran his tongue up the full length. He looked up at her face then back down to her right breast, kissing it in entirety and ending with special attention to the firming nipple. Encouraged by her purring he pulled her face-up across his lap and proceeded to use his mouth to caress her left breast in the same manner before tracing a line between them with the tip of his tongue all the way up, up her neck, over her chin and into her open mouth. Her hands pushed his shirt up as they kissed and they broke apart only for the moment necessary to pull it off over his head before lying side-by-side on the ground and resuming.

Donogh's bracae were soon kicked off and the two of them rolled across the grass entwined together until they came to rest with him on top. Ceridwen clasped her legs tightly around his waist and dug her fingernails into his back as he thrust into her, faster and faster as the pain on his back intensified. Suddenly she pulled him down and wrapped her mouth around his left shoulder, sucking on it, then slid her parted lips down his front and, holding onto him firmly, pushed her teeth into his chest. Donogh gasped, pressed his teeth together and arched his head up, pushing fully inside her in satisfaction while she trembled beneath him. They remained frozen in that position until Ceridwen's jaws slowly released Donogh's flesh and he sank to the ground next to her. They lay there, at first waiting until their breathing resumed, then just to be together.

Finally Ceridwen leaned up on one arm and grinned at Donogh. "You can hurt me too if you want," she said, rocking her body from side to side. "Want to?" She bared her teeth and bit into the right side of her lower lip.

"You know I could never hurt you, Ceri."

Ceridwen huffed, pushed away, slapped backwards onto the ground, and tightly folded her arms across her breasts, but Donogh didn't notice. Instead, he was reaching over his right shoulder to feel the scratches on his back. He then stared at his bloody left hand, "Although you probably deserve it," he muttered.

Ceridwen mentally overrode her frustration, reached out for his hand, and examined the blood smeared on it. "Do I?" She murmured seductively while kissing the tip of his middle finger then, still holding his hand close to her lips, she stared up at him. Without budging her blue gray eyes she ran her chin from the center of his hand up his index finger, engulfed the tip of it with her lips and sucked it all the way into her mouth. Even though he would never be the sexual beast she craved, Ceridwen would still enjoy Donogh as best she could.

Following the meeting with the Iceni public acknowledgment of Cunobelin's illness was made inevitable and Togodumnus made the formal announcement that he was stepping in as regent. An immediate procession in and out of the master bedchamber followed as the kings of each tribe, already in Camulodunum for the festival, demanded confirmation that the king was still alive. So long as Togodumnus was simply regent acting on behalf of Cunobelin, there was no way for any of them to challenge the ban on slaving since they had all sworn allegiance to the old king. If Cunobelin were to die, however, Togodumnus would have to obtain new oaths of allegiance from each of the tribal chiefs in order to hold the country together. Although a couple of them grumbled, the only one that openly complained about the slaving ban was King Verica of the Atrebates. Occupying most of the land along the southern coast, the Atrebates were in a powerful strategic position. They had used that fact over the years to gain concessions from Cunobelin. Concessions unavailable to the other tribes; principally to conduct an active, separate slave trade with the Romans by raiding the weaker Belagic tribes to their west. This new decree was to have a severe impact on the Atrebates commerce.

When Verica took his turn to view Cunobelin, he leaned across the bed and put his face close to the pillow. "You speak the truth, Togodumnus," he said. "The old king still breathes." He stood up and looked earnestly at Togodumnus and Caractacus. "We're not craftsmen and we don't have the Catuvellauni skill at training hounds. Cunobelin never objected to our trade in the past. Surely he would grant an exception for the Atrebates."

"The decree is clear," Caractacus jumped in before Togodumnus was able to respond. "No one shall deal in slaves in Camulodunum. Not Briton, not Belagic, not even the Atrebates." He glared at Verica. "No discussion."

"Then in Camulodunum it shall be as you wish." Verica looked down in a slight bow and left the room.

"Deftly done, Brother," Togodumnus said quietly once Verica was out of earshot. "I was ready to force the issue but you gave him an out. Llyn would be proud of you."

"It plays to our advantage," Caractacus answered, a huge self-satisfied smile appearing on his face.

Chapter Three: Marek

Rome hadn't changed at all in the two years that Marek had served with the auxiliaries and for days after his return from Germania, he moped about the city, revisiting familiar haunts, while deciding his next move. The family spice importing business seemed his only real option but his thoughts continued to remain with the frontier, which made him most unsettled with city life. He envied those officers, retired from military service, who were set up with villas in occupied territories and maintained thriving enterprises coordinating supplies and trade between the local populations and the army. As far as he was concerned, that was the best of all worlds, the freedom of living on the fringe of society yet enjoying the benefits of civilized life.

"But what civilized woman would want to live like that?" his father asked when Marek described his vision of the ideal life. "Those men always marry the locals. Surely you wouldn't want a stinking, unkempt barbarian in your bed every night, would you?" The old man smiled and put his slender arm around his son's broad shoulders. Their conversations invariably led to Marek taking a wife and settling down. "You're in your twenties now and you've had your adventure. You'll soon realize that life in Rome is the best in the world."

"For citizens," Marek added, scratching the right side of his head through his trimmed, brown hair. He'd experienced racism first hand from the legionnaires.

"Mm, that's true, but I've found it even more so for wealthy merchants."

"Wealthy?" Marek's eyebrows rose.

"It's not at all like it was when you left a couple of years ago." Marek's father wagged his crooked index finger in front of his sun tanned nose. "When you left we were simply making a good living, but Roman demand for perfume and face color is ravenous." He pulled up his hand into a fist. "And we've been able to capitalize on it. With our contacts back home in Egypt and money from a couple of local investors we've become rich; rich enough to be included in society. Wealth, as you'll see, seems to have a wonderful way of overriding the fact that you're foreign."

Over the next several weeks Marek did, indeed, see as he was introduced to senators and other men of influence around town, joining them for opulent meals and lavish parties. According to these prominent citizens, there was unlimited wealth and opportunity for merchants like him in that Rome's taste for the goods of other countries was insatiable. It was also very easy; Marek's work of overseeing the books took no more than a few hours a day and many days were completely free. Slaves did all of the work of stocking and dealing with the customers. He was able to enjoy long rides in the countryside, feel the wind against his tan face as he and his expatriate horse galloped with the same abandon they had enjoyed years ago in their homeland. He'd never been any desire to return to Egypt, though. The promise of adventure always lay ahead of him, not behind. After a month in Rome, however, he had started to realize that perhaps he could become accustomed to a life of privilege. Maybe he would grow out of his desire for a life on the frontier, as his father insisted he would, as he became more and more acclimated to the pleasures of the imperial city. Occasional business trips back to Egypt might even satisfy his need for travel and diminish the allure of the frontier altogether. However, six weeks after Marek had returned to Rome, the fourteenth legion paraded back into the city, freshly returned from Germania. Business ceased as the soldiers went by and the townspeople ignored their mundane day to day activities to line the streets and cheer the legionnaires and their officers. As he watched them, Marek's mind immediately reverted back to his days in the field as an auxiliary and he wondered how he could ever have entertained such a preposterous idea as settling in Rome. He had served an exemplary tour as an auxiliary, a horseman, in a turmae attached to the fourteenth and had risen to the rank of duplicarius. His commander, Ostorius, had told him that if he were a Roman citizen he'd certainly be an officer, but since Marek was an Egyptian there had been no chance of that happening. At least, that was the way it was before Claudius became emperor. Now, actively incorporating the elite from throughout the empire into Roman affairs was one of the new emperor's major initiatives and he had decided to begin with the army.

The news that select foreigners were to be allowed military rank was of particular interest to the legates and tribunes of the legions. They immediately realized that the auxiliaries would be an excellent recruiting grounds for potential officers; especially important now since a big part of Claudius' plans were to expand and modernize the army. Because Ostorius had always held the auxiliary horsemen in high esteem it was quite logical, once Claudius' edict was announced, to give him the assignment of building a strong cavalry for the fourteenth legion and the title of praefectus, or cavalry commander, was added to his title of tribune. Right away Ostorius realized that he needed to establish a strong officer corps so the first action in his new role had better be to locate those auxiliaries who had demonstrated leadership potential in the past campaigns. He quickly sought out Marek at his family's store on the other side of the city and spied him sitting behind a desk toward the back, clearly deeply occupied by whatever it was that he was working on. "How's the spice business, Marek?" Ostorius boomed broadly then burst out laughing, adding, "that's no place for a solider."

Marek, instantly recognizing the voice of his old mentor, tossed his quill aside and enthusiastically pushed his chair back from the desk. "Ostorius," he called out, rapidly scurrying to the front of the store to clasp the burly career soldier's forearm. Like most Romans he stood a head shorter than Marek, but unlike most of them he had Marek's respect. "What brings you down to the business section?"

"I came to see how you were doing, my lad. Let's go have some wine and you can fill me in."

They sat at a corner table and Marek ordered bread, dates, and a pitcher of wine.

"I'm pleased to see you're still looking fit, Marek. No wife?" Ostorius asked.

"No." Marek half smiled as he shook his head. "I don't think Roman women are my type. They're too pretentious, too caught up with fashion."

"What about companionship?" Ostorius flashed his upper teeth. "You know."

"They're all too delicate. They insist on perfumes and soft couches and, umm, let's just say they consider me a bit rough."

"Ah, you miss frontier sex, do you?" Ostorius gulped a draught of wine. "But you've got brothels and slaves here. What's wrong with them?"

"It's not the same, Ostorius. They don't resist. Oh, they'll play along but," he looked around then leaned across the table and whispered, "They really won't try to hurt you."

Ostorius leaned back in raucous laugher and nodded his head. "I hear you, Marek. Ah, it's good to know that Rome hasn't tamed you. In fact, with that in mind, I've come with a proposition. I take it you've heard about the emperor's decree to expand the legions?" Ostorius took another swig of his wine.

"I have. Is it true that cavalry is going to be considered a regular army division?"

"Yes, it is true. And I'm to build the cavalry for the fourteenth."

"How many men will you need?"

"Well, let's see." Ostorius looked up at the ceiling and pretended to count on his fingers. "Each legion is to have 32 alae," he looked at Marek. "That's a wing made up of sixteen turmae," then averted his eyes back to the ceiling, "so with 32 troopers to each turmae that's a total of 1,000 men and horses."

"Whew," Marek whistled. He tore a piece of bread from the loaf but simply held it in his hand, gesturing with it. "That's quite a recruiting job Ostorius."

"You're the first person I thought of, Marek. You'd do the legion proud."

"Another two years in the field as an eques alaris?" He tossed the bread back onto the plate, picked up a date and tapped it on his lower lip. "I don't know. There's no question that I enjoyed my time in the auxiliaries, but there's no future in it." He bit the end off the date.

"How does sixteen years service at full pay sound to you? And I'll start you as a decurion in charge of your own turmae."

"An officer? You can do that?" Marek took the half eaten date away from his mouth and dropped in on the plate in front of him. "How?"

"Claudius' decree calls for opening up the officer ranks to all men worthy of it." Ostorius leaned over the table and clamped his hand onto Marek's shoulder. "Legionnaires and cavalrymen will come from all corners of the empire," he said. The fingers of his sword hand also conveyed his enthusiasm. "This is an opportunity of a lifetime, Marek. As an officer, you'll be considered a Roman citizen and after your sixteen years you'll be offered a villa in the provinces if you'd be willing to spend the next four in reserve." He spread a scroll on the table in front of Marek. "This is your commission, signed by legate Titus—and here," the tip of his index finger jabbed the bottom of the parchment, "by Emperor Claudius himself."

The scroll rolled itself up again so Marek took it in both hands, his left held it in place while his eager right unrolled it downwards, trembling slightly while he slowly read and absorbed it. "This is what I've dreamed of, Ostorius."

"Then all you need do is sign it and you'll have that dream." Ostorius produced another scroll. "And this copy is for you to keep. Sign your allegiance to Rome and prepare yourself for adventure and profit. That is," he leaned back in his chair and spread his arms, "unless you'd rather remain in Rome as a spice merchant."

Marek instantly called for the attending servant to bring a quill and ink.

"Before you sign, I should tell you that you'll right away report to the legion's base at Moguntiacum where for the next three months you'll go through regular legionnaire training. All the action you've seen so far has been on horseback but you'll also need to learn how to fight on foot. It's pretty grueling training."

"Trying to scare me off, Ostorius?"

"I'm just being honest about it. In the new army the cavalry will double as foot soldiers if needs be."

"I understand." Marek eagerly reached for the quill that had just been placed on the table. "Are there any actions forthcoming?"

"We'll see," Ostorius said as he watched Marek sign. "But I have a suspicion that you won't be disappointed in the least in that regard."

"There are rumors on the streets that Claudius wants to invade Britannia." Marek studied Ostorius' well fed face in hopes of a reaction but even the praefectus' bushy eyebrows remained noncommittal. Still, Marek persisted. "I'd like to think he'll have a better plan than Caligula."

"If Claudius does decide to make that commitment," Ostorius said, the right side of his mouth slightly upturned, "you can be assured it will be well-planned indeed. If I were you, I'd just make sure I'd trained my troops well, just in case."

"I hear of newly-discovered tribes in the north of Britannia that have equality of the sexes," Marek added, licking the inside of his teeth. "That there are women that fight and own land."

"I've heard that too. They're the ancient Briton tribes, quite unlike the Belagic Celts along the coast that Julius Caesar encountered."

"All I know about them is through the traders. It's said they're warrior races, though, and that the women go into battle alongside the men."

"They sound like your sort of women, eh, Marek?"

"You never know." Marek rubbed the late afternoon stubble on his chin. Certainly the women he'd met to date in Rome were not.

Chapter Four: Claudius

"Why are Romans the masters of the world?" Claudius asked out loud as he stood in the center of the Curia addressing the senate. "Are Romans inherently better than people from other nations?" He scanned the faces of the senators as he spoke. After the turbulence of the past few years under the Emperor Caligula, Claudius knew he had to be careful, but sound reasoning was never a tool employed by his predecessor. "Yes," he continued, "Romans are better, but it's not due to their birth. It's due to Rome's superior technology and culture." The edges of his mouth curled upwards as more than a few of the senators nodded. He had them now.

"It follows, then, that the educated classes of other lands, once exposed to our culture and technology, benefit greatly, just as Romans themselves." He moved his right hand up and down slowly as he spoke. "Since we've opened these opportunities to them," he paused for an extended moment, "think how they could become even more useful members of our society if they had a voice in its governance. Think of the alternative military techniques they could provide to our legions. Think about how they could bring different perspective to our debates here in the senate as we chart the future course of the empire." He stopped moving his hand and clenched it into a fist. "The empire is comprised of people from many nations. I propose that our leadership, just as we now allow our citizenship and our armies, be permitted to reflect that."

Claudius easily answered their questions, taking the opportunity each time to accuse those who still clung to the racist ideology that only a pure Roman should be a citizen as holding back the future of the empire. His leadership style was to ensure that the senate was aware of, and hopefully understood, his plans prior to his making them a decree in order to both let the senators absorb them and to flush out any potential discontent beforehand. This approach had worked admirably so far in that his two previous edicts, to allow foreigners both the ability to become citizens and to achieve military rank, had been implemented smoothly. Confident, he saw no reason that this third aspect of his grand plan shouldn't follow. Logical arguments from an intellectual, as opposed to reason starved dictates of the previous emperor, clearly endeared him to the majority. He just had to ensure that he always maintained that majority.

After thanking them for their attention, Claudius left the senate to continue its debate in his absence. Narcissus, his secretary, was waiting outside, his fingers intertwined across his slender lower abdomen. "Was there any unanticipated opposition?" He leaned forward and turned his head to the right as he spoke but still remained half a foot taller than the emperor.

"No opposition at all." Claudius moved his jaw to the right revealing his full set of teeth. "Just the questions we prepared for."

"How many do you think might be influenced back by Seneca?" Narcissus's black eyebrows tightened on his pale forehead. "He's probably already planning to meet separately with the key senators as we speak."

"Planning," Claudius pursed his lips as the two men strolled, "oh, he most certainly will be." He stopped walking, gripped his secretary's shoulder with his right and looked up into Narcissus' pale blue eyes. "But Seneca won't want to act until after he meets with me tonight." He released his grip and resumed walking. "You know, since I wrote that book on Cicero, Seneca's been accusing me of being a republican."

"There's a lot to be said for a republic," Narcissus added. As the emperor's closest confidant he enjoyed the privilege of speaking openly. In fact, Claudius insisted on it, wanting to avail himself of the full attributes of the Druid's keen mind. All the same, Claudius appeared to grow taller as his eyes widened.

"Or, more appropriately, decentralized government," Narcissus added calmly. He waited until the emperor had unlocked his mouth before adding, "With a singular head of state, of course."

"Of course." An uncontrolled smile moves across the emperor's face. "He'll first try to change my mind, though. Seneca will. It's funny really since he was born in Gaul and now he's one of Rome's most prominent citizens. You'd think he'd be sympathetic to this cause."

"He came to Rome at an early age and probably doesn't even remember anything prior to that. I suspect he feels he's not contaminated like someone actually living in the provinces."

"More likely he just doesn't want competition from other people who can think. He knows how easily senators are influenced; he's so often swayed them to his point of view." Claudius punched his right fist into his open left hand and held it there. "Most of them are happy to just be in the senate and don't let their minds stray to anything more than that. There's so much potential for new ideas and new opportunities, yet they'll timidly hang on to the status quo." He swung his head up to make eye contact with his secretary. "We need more leaders, Narcissus, but the way it is now, the only place you find Roman leadership is in the military. We need people who can make decisions. People who aren't afraid of change. We need to pull in the princes from out of the provinces. Oh, we'll wake the senate up all right."

Later that afternoon Agrippina, Claudius' favorite niece, came by requesting an audience with him. He had already instructed that she was to be immediately shown in. With her bother Caligula now dead she was free to return to Rome, but she was broke. When her husband, Gnaeus Domitus, died right before her exile, Caligula had denied her inheritance and absconded with Domitus' wealth for his own use. She had been reduced to working as a sponge diver since in order to survive.

Agrippina rushed into the room; arms outstretched and enveloped her uncle with them, giving him a big hug. "It's so good to be back in Rome," she said, holding onto him tightly, her perfectly made up face resting on his left shoulder, "But I need a new husband, Uncle." She leaned her head back and parted her red lips. "A rich one."

"And knowing you, I suspect you already have some unsuspecting soul picked out, don't you?" He beckoned to the couch and they sat down side by side.

"I do!" She nodded. "But he's not at all unsuspecting; he's absolutely infatuated with me. But," she looked down at her hands, wringing them together, "there is a problem."

"What could possibly be standing in the way of your snagging a man infatuated with you?" Claudius asked jovially.

"His wife." Agrippina's mouth slid sideways.

Claudius furrowed his forehead. "Who is this poor fellow?" he asked. "Do I know him?"

"Oh, you do. It's Gaius Sallustius Crispus Passienus."

"You aim high, my dear. He's one of the wealthiest men in Rome."

"I know, but he's so unhappy in his marriage. Would you do us a favor, Uncle?" She cocked her head to the left which somehow seemed to enlarge her eyes. "He's too old-fashioned to ask for a divorce on his own so I need you to tell him to divorce his wife and marry me." She took Claudius' right hand up in hers and kissed it. "That way he'll be able to tell his wife that the emperor made him. Please?"

"He really is unhappy with his wife?"

"Terribly. And I'll make things so much better for him." She brushed Claudius' hand against her left cheek, her eyes not leaving his. "Besides, as the emperor's niece I need to be well-placed in society, don't I?"

Claudius retrieved his hand, raised it to her forehead, and brushed back the lock of perfectly styled auburn hair that had fallen over her face. "It's going to be wonderful having you back in Rome, Agrippina," he said, sliding his arm around her shoulder and coaxing her closer to his side. She slid her head onto his chest while he stroked her hair. "You have to stay awhile, have some wine and take something to eat while I consider your request." His hand slid down to her neck, which he began to massage while simultaneously straightening his right arm, pushing her head towards his lap. He leaned back into the couch and parted his legs. "Perhaps I'll speak to him tomorrow," he said. "Provided you're a good niece for your uncle."

After Agrippina left, Claudius spent the remainder of the afternoon alone at his desk until Seneca came by for their appointment. The two men enjoyed a cordial meal together and were relaxing with after dinner wine before they began the discussion of Claudius' impending decree: a proclamation that would not only open up Roman citizenship to select members of the far reaches of the empire but, even more contemptuous to people of Seneca's ilk, would also allow them rank and even the ability to be elected to the senate. Seneca had always vehemently opposed expanding the rules of citizenship and the subject had been the source of friendly disagreement between him and Claudius for the past ten plus years, but the idea of foreigners in the senate was more than he could tolerate. Tonight was to be his latest and most fervid appeal to try, in his mind, to stop Claudius from destroying the very fabric of the empire.

"You and I have debated this for years, my old friend, and we're each well-acquainted with the other's point of view," Claudius said, indicating his unwillingness to further entertain Seneca's thoughts on the subject. "The difference in our positions now, however," Claudius leaned toward Seneca with a half smile on his face, "is that I'm emperor and if you openly disagree with me after I've made a decree you face the prospect of death."

"If my martyrdom can serve to save Rome from your polluting its very essence with monotheists and barbarians, to prevent the legions from being overrun by Nubians and Egyptians, then so be it." Seneca glared directly back.

Claudius leaned back and laughed towards the ceiling. "I've no desire to see you dead, you old goat," he sputtered out, leaning forward and shaking his head. He suddenly went silent and pointed his index finger directly at Seneca's chin. "But you've made it eminently clear that I can't have you in Rome either." He stood up. "So I'm having you banished."

"You can't simply banish me for insurrection, Claudius. It's a capitol offense. If you persist in making this horrendous idea of yours the law I promise I'll do everything in my power to turn the senate against you. If you want to stop me, you'll have no choice but to execute me." He set his chin. "It's the law."

Claudius reached into his desk, removed a scroll and handed it to him. "You're absolutely correct. About the law, that is."

Claudius watched as Seneca untied the scroll and began to read. "As you can see, your banishment isn't for insurrection. It's for adultery. Adultery with a member of the ruling household of all things. My niece, no less." Claudius beamed, opening his mouth in fake horror. "I'm appalled, Seneca," he said, flopping the back of his right wrist on his forehead as if he were an actor on stage. "A man of your age and standing."

Seneca stared at the scroll in silence for several minutes then slowly moved his head back and forth. He licked his lips and swallowed hard. "Well played, Claudius." His voice was barely audible.

"You're banished to Corsica where you can focus on your financial interests. Besides, I understand your import business is doing very well anyway so time spent there will no doubt be good for you." Claudius refilled their goblets as he spoke in friendly tones. "The internal affairs of Rome are no longer your concern." He quaffed half of his drink and used his chin to gesture the scroll being crumpled in Seneca's hand. "So drink your wine, Seneca. You leave before daybreak."

With Seneca now gone from Rome, Claudius had little trouble bending the few potentially dissident senators to his will and made his general declaration with the full support and backing of the entire senate just a week later. Delighted with his political victories he intended to spend the next few years concentrating on interviewing foreign dignitaries for inclusion into the senate, but it was to be an entirely different group of foreigners that would come to demand his focus.

Narcissus answered the familiar knock at the door of the villa with a hearty, "Good afternoon, Adminius," and beckoned the Cantium prince inside.

"Is Claudius available?" Adminius asked urgently. "I must speak to both of you at once."

Narcissus went to the office, announced the visitor to the emperor and, after receiving an affirmative nod, motioned Adminius in. The three men sat together around Claudius' desk.

"I just received word that Cunobelin has died," Adminius told them. "This means that my brother Togodumnus is now officially the

king and the only treaties he has in place are with the Trinovantes
and the Cantium, the tribes that he and Caractacus directly control.
If they aren't able to re-establish treaties quickly with the other tribes
then trade will be severely affected. It's time to act."

"It's my understanding that Rome established a non-aggression
pact between the tribes years ago." Claudius said. "Why should
Cunobelin's passing have any effect on that?"

"Because Celtic contracts are between people, not states,"
Narcissus answered. "Adminius is right, this could be very disruptive.
There's been a growing tension between Camulodunum and the
Atrebates and it's well-known that Caractacus has had crossed words
with King Verica on numerous occasions."

"Use this opportunity to take Britannia before my brothers can
pull the tribes together," Adminius said excitedly. "Make it a Roman
province and secure the trade. I can arrange for landing sites in
Cantium for your troops. Most of the Cantii are pro-Roman and I
have many loyal followers there."

"And put you back on the Cantium throne, I suppose?" Claudius
queried.

"Why not? There'd be no doubts regarding my allegiance."

Claudius turned to Narcissus. "Where will the Druids stand?"
he asked.

"They'll assist Togodumnus and Caractacus in securing the
allegiances of the Briton tribes. Probably the Atrebates too," he
added, chin in his right hand. "If the Catuvellauni and the Atrebates
make a pact to secure the island it will make an invasion very
difficult. This will, no doubt, be the Druid's goal."

Claudius turned back to Adminius. "You're confident you can
slip back into Cantium and establish landing sites?"

"I am."

"Then do it." Claudius eased back into his chair. "We can't afford
disruption in trade from Britannia and if we do this right we could

end up significantly increasing it." He drummed his fingertips on the edge of his desk. "Narcissus," he said, "find me an able commander."

Chapter Five: Allegiance

Since Venta Icenorum was less than a day's ride from Toftrees, Ceridwen decided to make the journey alone and enjoy the freedom to ride Kelpie at speeds that even the best Iceni warriors would have had difficulty keeping up with. For most of the trip, she rode along the bank of the River Wensum so the fast riding also made it easier for her to keep control of her highly-spirited mount. As a result, by mid-afternoon she'd already arrived at the capital city and was making her way through the busy streets to the palace when she saw her best friend milling through a pile of fabrics at a vendor's stall. "Andarta!" she called out and quickly dismounted. "I'm surprised to see you here."

"Ceri!" Andarta put the fabric down, politely thanked the vendor, and then turned back. "Since my father had to come to the city, I thought I'd come along and do some shopping. Blyth came too, although I have no idea where he is at the moment." She gave Ceridwen a hug. "I'll walk with you to the palace."

"You mean to tell me you didn't come here to see Prasutagus?" Ceridwen teased.

"Well..." Andarta could no longer control the edges of her mouth and both girls giggled together.

"Have you seen him yet?" Ceridwen managed to ask between chuckles.

"Not yet. We only arrived this morning and he's been with his father preparing for the meeting. He doesn't even know I'm here." Andarta peered over Ceridwen's shoulder. "You came alone?"

"It's only a short trip for me. Besides, I can take care of myself."

"Ah, so you've figured out how to draw your sword without falling off your horse, have you?"

"It took three months, but yes. And the bruises are starting to finally fade." She rubbed her right thigh. "I understand now why sword training comes last; these things are heavy."

"I know. I'm looking forward to completely getting away from weapons when we go back to Mon after Lughnasad."

"I'm looking forward to Mon, too." Ceridwen licked her top teeth.

"I'll bet, although after last year Devyn said he's going to do his best to keep you and Donogh apart."

"Actually, I'm hoping to see Donogh sooner than that, when the council goes down to Camulodunum. He's staying with Caractacus again this summer. He's learning to be a warrior Druid too."

"That's an interesting mix, you know; it seems almost contradictory." Andarta nodded slowly then pointed ahead. "Well, there's the palace, Ceri. Good luck."

"Thanks." Ceridwen jumped back up on Kelpie's back and trotted to the main entrance.

Stable hands rushed out, taking Kelpie away to a stall as soon as she had removed her sword from the strap around his neck. She bucked the belt, shifted it so Glynu hung at her left side, and proceeded up the steps.

Prasutagus was the first to greet her as she entered the palace. "Aesu and Saenu are already here," he told her as they walked to the meeting room. "Blyth's here too. He and I are to be permitted to sit in."

"Then I'll be able to congratulate both of you for your success in the Beltaine race. First and second," she nodded, "very impressive."

Prasutagus tried to conceal his pride as he opened the door for her. "If you'd have been willing to ride your horse through the river instead of taking the bridge, you'd have beaten us all in the trials and no doubt won Beltaine, Ceri," he said. "Maybe next year?"

"Next year we might run faster," she said as they walked into the hall. "But I won't be riding Kelpie through the water."

Only Ceridwen knew the reason she kept Kelpie away from water, and she became thoughtful as they walked to the meeting, recalling how she and her horse had met. She had been attending school on Mon and wandered off one afternoon to walk the beach alone, as she often did. Suddenly, a large, white stallion came galloping through the surf and stopped directly in front of her. More curious than afraid, she walked up to it. The horse lowered his head and she reached out and ran her hand across his smooth neck. "Where did you come from?" she asked calmly, placing a hand on each side of his neck as the horse nuzzled against her cheek. She stepped closer to him, her hands moving across his prominent withers, the ridge where his neck met his back, and after feeling the powerful muscles of his neck and shoulders she felt a compulsion. She had to ride him. Stepping back she ran her hands up both sides of his neck, down the sides of his head and cupped his muzzle, then leaned forward to share breath. The Iceni were renowned horse people, and she knew this would make them friends. The horse made no complaint. "May I ride you?" she asked softly, and then slid up his left side and onto his back. The horse first walked slowly up the beach and Ceridwen positioned her knees against his shoulders and lay across his neck, wrapping her arms around it, whispering instructions into the horse's velvet ear to move faster. She felt his muscles pulse against the inside of her thighs as he increased speed, and within minutes of pulsing gallop she closed her eyes, rocking in time with the horse's undulations until she screamed out the most intense orgasm she had ever experienced. Fortunately for her, she had a quick recovery. The horse was heading back down the beach and was only a few lengths away from re-entering the surf. She leaped off but held tightly onto his mane with both hands, digging her heels into the sand while expecting him to resist her. Instead, he just stopped. "You're a Kelpie," she panted in astonishment, her excitement overriding any fear she may have had about what had nearly happened. "You're a Kelpie, and I've caught you."

"Ah, here's Ceridwen." Anted immediately came over to greet her as she and Prasutagus entered the room. "The meeting's not scheduled to begin yet, but since we're all here..." He gestured to the table and, as soon as everyone was seated, Anted began. "Cunobelin's death requires us to decide if we wish for the Iceni to continue our 30-year-old pact with the Catuvellauni by recognizing Togodumnus as the new king of Britannia. We are then to immediately proceed to Camulodunum with our decision."

"Do we know if the Romans will recognize him?" Saenu asked. "Trade depends on it."

"I understand that such a designation is automatic for the Romans, Saenu," Anted responded, "although I can't understand how, but there's no question there about continuation of the trade that our people have come to enjoy."

"They're a funny lot, these Romans, aren't they," Aesu shook his head. "What do they do, make treaties with buildings?"

The men in the room guffawed.

"I mean, everybody's different. Do they really think that a son will behave exactly like his father? I've even heard that sometimes the next emperor isn't even from the same bloodline."

"They do indeed have strange customs," Anted said. "But since Rome won't be an issue for us, how do you feel about Togodumnus?"

"Oh, I like him. I vote yes."

"He moved quickly to subdue the slave traders and he's true to his word in that he keeps the Belagics in check," Ceridwen added. "I say yes also."

Anted looked across the table. "What do you say Saenu?"

"I agree. He's done well as regent. I vote yes."

"As do I," Anted added. "It's settled then. We'll leave for Camulodunum in the morning and take him the approval of the Iceni."

As children of kings Prasutagus, Blyth, and Andarta accompanied the Iceni council to the meeting with Togodumnus. They arrived the morning of their second day of travel and were greeted formally in the throne room. Togodumnus sat up on a dais flanked on the right by Caractacus and Llyn on the left, there as a demonstration that the new king had the full support of the Druids. Togodumnus listened as Anted pledged the Iceni to a new treaty, then rose and descended to shake the forearms of each member of the delegation. Caractacus and Llyn subsequently joined the group as formality quickly faded into fellowship and conversation.

"Togodumnus has been recognized by nearly all of the tribes," Llyn said, his hand on the new king's shoulder. "I'm very pleased."

"Nearly all?" Saenu asked. "Has anyone stood against him?"

"We've yet to hear from the Atrebates," Caractacus responded. "We know they've been shipping slaves to Gaul from their own ports and the Dobunni have formally asked us for protection from them."

"But we haven't heard from them yet," Llyn quickly interjected in order to quell the potentially inflammatory discussion. "Let's keep in mind that these may be points of negotiation once Verica comes to Camulodunum."

"He's not here yet, eh, Llyn?" Caractacus asked a little too loud then proceed to show a full mouth of clenched teeth. "Would you like me to go and fetch him? You can be assured I'll ask him nicely."

"We'll give him another week," Togodumnus said, taking back control of the discussion, then quickly turning to address the Iceni. He extended both his hands to an impressively wide span. "Friends, spend a few days at the palace with us and avail yourselves of the hospitality of the Catuvellauni."

As the group began to disband to various parts of the palace, Caractacus walked up to Ceridwen. "I suspect you're anxious to locate Donogh, young lady," he said. "Believe me; he's anxious to see you."

Ceridwen blushed while nodding vigorously. "Oh, yes," she said. "Where might I find him?"

"Come, I'll take you to him. He's at my house."

Caractacus' home was not as she imagined. Expecting a continuation of the opulence of the palace, she unthinkingly blurted out, "this is it?" as they rode up to a small, almost utilitarian farm. Caractacus responded with a friendly laugh, fully anticipating her reaction. "I still hold to some of the Druid influences," he told her, "but you'll find we're quite comfortable. I prefer it here and only stay at the palace when I'm needed."

Ceridwen could feel the heat from her cheeks. "I didn't mean—" she began, but Caractacus raised his hand to stop her. "It's all right. It happens to everybody that I bring out here."

Donogh eagerly greeted her but with a contained hug. They were, after all, in front of others. However, after sharing a midday meal of vegetable stew and bread with Caractacus and his family, he quickly suggested the two of them go out for a ride. As soon as they were outside and heading for their horses, Donogh turned and whispered to her, "Don't worry, Ceri. The king of the Ordovices is required to live in the palace."

She grinned and punched his upper right arm. "He'd better be," she responded jovially.

Donogh grabbed her by the shoulders, holding her in front of him. "Or what?" he said, still grinning, then leaned to kiss her but she quickly grabbed him by the chin before his lips could connect. "You promise that you won't be going all Druidy on me," she said sternly but, unable to restrain herself, released him and they fell into an enthusiastic kiss before he was able to answer.

"I've learned so much from Caractacus, Ceri," Donogh said as they cantered together across the open meadow. "He's showing me how to analyze your surroundings before a fight and be able to pick the most advantageous position so your opponent has to use more energy than you."

"Has he shown you any way to make your sword lighter?"

"In a way he has, yes."

Ceridwen looked curiously at him. "How?"

"Keep it up high and rest the hilt against your shoulder. Then when you swing it's always a downward motion."

"What a good idea." Ceridwen was impressed. "So there are real reasons for why he's one of the best warriors in Britannia."

"It's more than just fighting skills. He's developed the Druidic ability to read people to a level where they accuse him of being inside their heads. It enables him to anticipate what someone's going to do next. That's why he's convinced that Verica will come out against Togodumnus."

"What's that?" Ceridwen suddenly asked, pointing at a fast moving object in the distance.

Donogh squinted and raised his hand over his eyes. "Riders," he said. "And it looks like they're heading for Caractacus' house."

Ceridwen and Donogh immediately galloped back to the farm and when they arrived Caractacus was already mounting his horse. "An Atrebatean delegation just arrived at the palace," he called out to them. "Come along. Verica's not with them."

Ceridwen and Donogh met up with Anted at the Palace and the three of them waited in an antechamber while Caractacus joined Togodumnus and Llyn to greet the delegates. It was a brief meeting, the throne room door being angrily flung open and Atrebates leaving rapidly after only a few minutes. Caractacus and Llyn emerged soon after.

"What news, Llyn?" Anted called out, striding up to them.

"The Atrebates will not support Togodumnus as king of Britannia." Llyn answered. "They recognize Adminius as the rightful heir of Cunobelin."

"How can they recognize a coward who fled Britannia?" Anted protested.

"Apparently, he's back." Caractacus added, "He's staying at the palace in Noviomagus as Verica's guest."

After dinner that night, Ceridwen ran down the hallway laughing, hand-in-hand with Donogh to her room in the Catuvellauni palace. She closed the door behind her and leaned against it, her hands above her head, and quickly moved her head back and forth as Donogh tried to force his lips onto hers. He gripped her head in his hands in order to execute the kiss, then slid them across her shoulders and up her arms, clasping her hands into his. He leaned his head back slightly to speak. "To the bed?" he asked.

"Make me," she said stubbornly, meekly trying to wrest her hands free from his grip. He held her carefully against the door and tried to kiss her again but she playfully turned her head to the left saying "no," while pushing back with only enough pressure to ensure that she wouldn't free herself. Still holding her hands in his, he moved them back to the sides of her head, immobilizing it, pushed his lips onto hers and separated them with his tongue. She closed her eyes and relaxed her mouth and as his hands released their grip she slid her arms around his neck to prolong the kiss. Without breaking lip contact he gently turned her sideways, placing his right arm around her shoulders, then suddenly swung his left into the back of her knees and scooped her up in his arms. "Now to the bed," he announced as he carried her, kissing her again as he moved.

Ceridwen eased away from the kiss as they approached the bed and, arms still around his neck, whispered into his right ear , "Very good, Donogh, but you still have to get my clothes off."

Donogh tossed her onto the bed then in a single movement had her dress pulled up to her waist and planted himself between her legs. "No I don't," he said, once again holding her hands above her head. She feigned a struggle but as his mouth came down on her, her brief play at resistance subsided. He moved her hands together and clasped them both in his right hand while his left stroked down the side of her face, down to caress her right breast, feeling her excitement through the thin fabric of her dress, then down between her legs. He rapidly unfastened the leather tie from the front of his breeches, pulled it completely out, then inched closer to Ceridwen. She began her fake struggle once again in an attempt to coax him into a bit more aggressiveness and continued to feign her wriggling until she finally allowed him to pin her down and penetrate her in a single movement. Perhaps, with continued coaxing, Donogh may yet get it right.

Their naked, intertwined bodies were awaked by the morning light streaming in through the open window. "I seem to have had no problem at all taking your clothes off," Donogh observed, tracing a line with his fingertips down her side from her neck to her knees.

Ceridwen pulled his face close to hers. "Last night was wonderful," she said softly and opened her mouth to meet his, then snuggled back onto the pillow after the kiss. "I can stay in Camulodunum for a few more days if you'd like."

"I'll be leaving today, though," Donogh answered. "I'm going to go with Caractacus," he added excitedly.

Ceridwen sat upright. "I'm proud of you, Donogh," she said. "You'll show those Belagic Atrebates a thing or two. Wait there." She slid off the bed, opened a drawer, and quickly returned holding a pendant. "I have a gift for you and I want you to wear it at all times." She tied the thin leather behind his neck as he picked the pendant up in his hand to study it. On one side of the silver disc was the stylized Iceni horse and on the other were two crescent shapes touching. "So I'm always with you."

"Always," Donogh repeated, then leaned over to connect with her freshly licked lips.

All the members of the Iceni delegation joined the rapidly growing crowd of well wishers gathering at the edge of the field just outside Camulodunum. Ceridwen stood with Andarta, Blyth and Prasutagus to watch as Donogh rode up to join Caractacus and over a hundred Catuvellauni warriors on horseback and 400 on foot as they assembled for their attack on the Atrebates. Many felt that this was the excuse Caractacus had been waiting for in order to escalate his long running feud with Verica but no one doubted the positive effect of having the last of the Belagic tribes under the control of Camulodunum. A successful campaign would cement the Druids plan for a unified kingdom in the southern half of Britannia and make it a formidable stronghold. Cheering rang out from the crowd the instant the army began to move forward. Men on horses, masses of foot soldiers with their spears glistening in the sunlight, and war dogs being freely permitted to bark made a truly impressive spectacle.

"They're all men!" Andarta observed.

"That's right," Prasutagus said. "Catuvellauni women don't join the warrior ranks." He put his arm around Andarta and gave her a quick hug. "What do you think of that?"

"I think it certainly has its merits." She put her head on his shoulder and peeked up at her friend. "How about you, Ceri?" she asked teasingly. "What do you think of that idea?"

Ceridwen turned her gaze from the departing army, smiled at Andarta cuddling up to Prasutagus, then turned again to wave to Donogh as he jubilantly rode off. "I'm glad to be Iceni," she said.

Chapter Six: Invasion

"Excuse my intrusion, Emperor; I know you told me you were not to be disturbed." Narcissus had dared to enter Claudius' study during his quiet time. "But this may beg an exception."

Right hand holding his position on the page, Claudius' eyes rose slowly from his reading

"King Verica of the Atrebates seeks an audience with you."

"Here?" Claudius looked bewildered.

"Here!"

Claudius gripped the arms of his chair and stiffly pushed himself up onto his feet. "Then you had better show him in."

Narcissus returned a few minutes later with Verica and proceeded with the formal introductions as befitting a visiting head of state.

"Welcome to Rome, King Verica," Claudius said while he poured three goblets of wine and handed him one. "Please have a seat." He gave another to Narcissus and the three of them assembled on the couches facing one another.

"Thank you for your hospitality, Emperor Claudius," Verica began. "I bring news of an unprovoked attack on the Atrebates by the Catuvellauni that threatens our ability to continue to provide tin and slaves. I also bring you this message from Adminius." He produced a sealed scroll, which he gave to Claudius, who immediately handed it to Narcissus. "Open this and read it aloud," he said.

"This letter details three secure landing sites in Cantium," Narcissus read. "Awaiting times."

"Most of Cantium and all of the Atrebates are pro-Roman and would welcome being included into the empire," Verica said. "So far Caractacus has only taken the northern third of my kingdom and he's being forced to commit more and more of his men as my forces fight hard against him. Strike quickly and he won't be able to mass his army in Cantium."

"Do you wish to return soon?" Claudius asked.

"I have no desire to do so at all," Verica answered. "I wish to cede my kingdom to you to make it a province of Rome in exchange for my family and I being granted asylum to settle in this wonderful city."

Claudius stood up and extended his hand. "Then you and your family are heartily welcomed, Verica. I grant each of you full citizenship of Rome."

Two days later Claudius addressed the senate. The invasion had been planned for over a year now and four legions had been upgraded and transferred to Gaul to be ready for the crossing. The Catuvellauni were distracted and not expecting an invasion; it was time.

"In command of the invasion forces is Aulus Plautius," Claudius began as he spoke to the excited senators. "He's demonstrated outstanding military leadership in suppressing the slave revolt at Apulia, oversaw the building of a major road from Triesta to Rijeka, and for these past years has been governor of Pannonia. He's clearly up to the task of both taking and then establishing control over Britannia. He has legions two, nine, fourteen, and twenty massed in Gaul, prepared and ready to leave. With direct control of the tin mines in the south we'll not be draining Rome's coffers for that metal and the fertile farmlands of Britannia are more than sufficient to support our troops. Plus, there's a large native population over there to draw on for slaves and gladiators that we won't have to pay for."

Immediately as Claudius finished speaking, the senators leaped to their feet, applauding a clearly well thought out campaign. A much-needed military victory would be a significant boost to Rome's ego and its coffers, as well as making the senators look good to their constituencies. Riders were sent right away to Aulus Plautius with instructions to begin assembling the troops and Narcissus was sent to the coast to coordinate with the Roman navy. Claudius himself began preparations to leave Rome in order to meet the troops on the Gallic coast.

In Gaul, Aulus Plautius paced anxiously back and forth outside his tent on the hill overlooking the coastline. "Is there any word at all on those boats?" he called out to his aide, then after a negative response swung around to continue his pacing, shaking his right fist and looking up at the sky while muttering to himself. The weather had been stormy for the past week and he suspected for that reason they might not even be close yet. Vespasian, legate of the second legion strolled up to him. "I hear Claudius is on his way," he said.

"Well we're not waiting for him to arrive. We've got almost 50,000 men down there ready to cross and there's no way we can keep that a surprise for long. I'll bet spies are already in Britannia telling about it." He turned to Vespasian. "How's the morale of the troops."

"The cavalry and engineers are fine but you know the legionnaires, they're a nervous lot when it comes to naval crossings. Combine that with the history of Britannia that Caesar wrote about and the problems he encountered over there and I'd say that the infantry could use a boost. Sitting here in the mud doesn't help, either."

"We have a thousand boats due to arrive at any time." Aulus looked up again at the swirling clouds overhead. "Or will be here as soon as the weather clears." He turned back to Vespasian. "I'm certain their fears will be overcome once they see the flotilla and we can get them moving. In the meantime have your engineers put on demonstrations of the scorpions. Caesar didn't have any of those. I'll instruct the other legates to do the same."

"HAIL TRIBUNE OSTORIUS," Marek called out as he approached. "I remember being in a similar situation to this three years ago."

Ostorius remained in his seat. "It's somewhat different now, though, decurion Marek. This time it's to be a full invasion and we're not being led by a madman." He pointed his chin up at his protégé. "Are you nervous?"

"A little. I just wonder how the horses will behave during the crossing. I hear each turmae will be in a separate boat so that's 34 horses all together in a very confined area that's going to be prone to rocking back and forth."

"You'll each be with your horses to keep them calm, though. Just hold your head up and act like you do this every day and your men will follow you." He stood up and stretched. "Have you seen the scorpions fire yet?"

"No, I haven't."

"Then come along, lad. You're about to see something that will instill fear into the heart of every Briton." He patted Marek on the back as they walked along together. "Not to mention giving a huge shot of confidence to every Roman soldier."

The Roman navy had taken shelter for the past week at a port only a day and a half's sailing south of the loading site and it was there that Narcissus caught up with them at the same time that the storm finally abated and the prevailing winds finally shifted to southerly. He was able to board the lead ship just in time for the rapid departure, the admiral justifiably concerned that they were to be at least five days late and realizing how agitated Plautius must be getting. With steady winds behind them, though, the fleet was able to run north at unusual speed and to the Roman observers along the shoreline who saw the sky clearing from the south it was as if the mighty fleet of a thousand sails was pushing the storm out of its way.

Prior to docking, Narcissus changed from his normal city garb into his Druid robes, stood prominently at the prow as the lead boat pulled in toward shore and was the first to debark. Word spread like wildfire throughout the legions of how a Druid had cleared the weather ahead of the ships and was coming on the crossing with them to assure safe passage. The spirits of the men soared at the sight of the tall, fair skinned man in black flowing robes as he strode rapidly up the hill to Plautius' camp. Thousands of soldiers gathered along the roadside to both see for themselves and to loudly cheer him on.

"You make quite an entrance, Narcissus," Plautius said, rushing up to shake his arm. "It's good to see you again. Did Claudius come by sea also?"

"No, he's traveling here with the detachments from the eighth legion."

"Ah yes, the siege engines. They'll be making the crossing later if needed." He looked quizzically at the Druid. "The troops seem convinced that you can control the weather."

"We both know that's ridiculous, Aulus Plautius," Narcissus responded with a smirk. "No man can control the weather."

"They think you can." Plautius nudged his chin upward toward the encampments.

"If that's what they believe." Narcissus shrugged as he answered, "Then truth becomes irrelevant, doesn't it?"

The army rapidly broke camp at daybreak and the troops made their way down to the port to their designated ships. Marek had his alae stand in a row on the beach, riders tightly holding the reigns of their horses, until they were called on to board, then led them single file along the short pier to the gangplank. "Walk backwards looking confidently at your horse at all times," he instructed, then was the first to board, demonstrating the technique. The horses were grouped in the center of the boat and, right before the loading plank was taken in, Ostorius strolled on board casually leading his horse behind him. He handed the reins to one of the soldiers at the top of the gangplank and joined Marek who stood transfixed by the casualness of his commanding officer. "I promised your father I'd keep an eye on you, lad," Ostorius said to him in a friendly, slightly teasing tone.

The crew scurried rapidly, pulling and throwing ropes in what seemed like multiple directions, yet the boat seemed to gracefully just drift away from the dock as the sails caught the wind and quickly picked up speed as it locked into its course. "Well, my boy," Ostorius said, slapping his right hand down on Marek's shoulder. "We're off. Your first campaign as an officer of the fourteenth legion."

"How long should the crossing take?" Marek looked nervously back at the horses.

Ostorius stared up into the sails. "The wind's nice and steady," he said. "Ten, twelve hours maybe. Relax! And don't worry about the horses. They'll be fine."

Marek nodded and studied the activity of the sailors, watching in amazement as each craft rapidly left the shore. There were sails in every direction he looked, all ships initially on the same heading, but after several hours of sailing it became clear that a group of them were heading further south. Marek walked to the port side of boat to where Ostorius was sitting. "I see the boats are splitting up. How many landing sites are there going to be?" he asked.

"Two. We're going to Rutupiae with the ninth and the twentieth. Vespasian is taking the second to land at Bosham." He smiled. "You should get some rest, Marek. There'll be a lot to do the instant we land."

Completely unable to rest, Marek spent the remainder of the journey at the bow of the boat staring at the vastness of the sea and the other ships spread out over its surface. For hours he strained to catch the first glimpse of land, delighted that no-one else had come up front to disturb his solitude. Was he the only one who couldn't sleep? He knew that once they had landed such times would be rare. Then, after he saw the white cliffs looming prominently off the port side, he began to wonder about the inhabitants of this place. Worthy adversaries, no doubt; they have even bettered Julius Caesar. Soon he was able to pick out green forests, then individual trees. The crossing had been uneventful with the weather calm as promised and, despite the lack of rest; he felt a surge of enthusiasm as the sailors began to make preparations for the landing. He went below and joined his men at their horses. Each animal had been freshly bridled and watered for the landing and the reins of his were handed to him as he entered the hold. From this position he could no longer see the shore and the only indication of activity was from the shouting and splashing as troops went ashore. Were they fighting? Was the enemy waiting for them? He couldn't tell. He looked at the faces of his men knowing the same thoughts were rushing through their heads, and smiled confidently at them. "Everyone ready?" he asked cheerfully. "Good. As soon as we disembark, lead your horse through the water toward the shore, mount as soon as you're able and make formation behind me on the beach."

The side of the boat suddenly hinged down and formed a ramp into the water. Marek immediately shouted, "Let's go," and for the first time he became aware of the movement of the sea, rocking the boat back and forth as it held its position in the shallows to allow the men and horses to leave. He led his horse down the ramp and was quickly immersed in the cold, chest deep water. His men followed rapidly, one by one, horses resisting only slightly as they entered the sea. When the water was only knee deep, Marek jumped up onto his horse and rode the rest of the way onto the beach. He made sure to keep well out of the way of all of the others coming ashore. Within minutes his entire alae had formed behind him, ready for action. He quickly looked around but there was no enemy. He looked back toward the water at the spectacle of the landing. In addition to the soldiers there were hundreds of local men on the beach but they were helpers, not warriors. They waded in and out of the water assisting as needed, particularly with the large boxes and disassembled scorpions accompanying the engineers. Ostorius, now on horseback, galloped back and forth assembling his division then led them up off the beach where they were grouped together with the rest of the fourteenth legion in standard battle formation. To the right of them the ninth and the twentieth were doing the same thing. There were furious sounds of hammers from behind them as the scorpions were assembled on the back of carts and brought up in groups between the formations. Finally, Plautius rode slowly past each of the legions accompanied by Adminius, congratulated each of the legates and announced that there was no enemy anywhere near their location. The surprise landing had been a complete success and they were now all to travel a mile inland to establish a fortified camp and build a stores depot. Villagers from Rutupiae were already standing by there with carts loaded with meat and vegetables. Marek looked back at the sea as the troops began to move out to catch a last glimpse of the boats as they disappeared over the horizon, then turned his head forward toward inland.

Half an hour later most of the legionnaires were at work felling hundreds of trees while the rest dug a huge trench outlining the edges of what was to be the fortified enclosure. By nightfall the surrounding wall was complete; ten feet high all around with guard towers every fifty feet and in each of the four corners. Camps were set up inside the compound in neat rows and as darkness fell the light from the crackling fires lit up the whole encampment. Marek was impressed, having never seen anything built so rapidly and with such precision. Only a few hours ago they were standing soaking wet on the beach but now his turmae had fed and groomed their horses and were cooking the evening meal over a fire in front of their tents. The entire army was in high spirits and three completely intact legions were ready to move against the Catuvellauni as early as the morning. He walked over to the fire where the men were gathering with their spoons and bowls ready to eat.

"That smells wonderful, Felix," he said to the man standing over the pot holding a ladle.

"It's fresh meat, Sir. From the locals. I think it's either sheep or goat. I've got carrots and turnips and grain in there too. It'll be ready soon."

"What are they like?" Marek turned to look into the young face of Varius who nervously asked the question; this was his first campaign. "The Britons, I mean," he added. This was, perhaps, the primary question on everyone's mind. Caesar had written in detail about the terrifying aspect of the tall, long-haired warriors with pale skin painted blue that he had encountered and, in spite of their training, it was clear to Marek that his men were very nervous.

"They're very much like the tribes we fought in Germania," he began, noticing how the men immediately begin to gather around him and were listening intently. The responsibility of command was suddenly, strangely appealing to him. "Get your food, men," he said. "We'll all sit together and while we eat and I'll tell you everything I know."

The men formed a line to fill their bowls then collected together on the ground around him. Felix brought a bowl to Marek and he sat down on a log to eat and address his alae. "We know the most about the Belagic tribes since they're a branch of the Celts that inhabit Gaul. These are the tribes closest to the coast and for the most part they're pro-Roman since we've been trading with them for the past two generations. These are the people you saw today, the ones that provided this food. The tribe we'll be fighting are called the Catuvellauni and they've occupied the Belagic territories for years so their warriors are all over these lands. Now they're a different branch of Celts, like those in Germania. They're fierce and brave but they don't have the order that we do. They fight individually, not in units." He took a spoonful from his bowl and ate it, then gestured with his spoon. "That's where we have them, men."

"Is it true you led a charge against the enemy in Germany," one of the men asked.

Marek nodded as he took another mouthful of food. "That's right, Rufus. They were about to attack the legion's flank so we charged and scattered them while at the same time alerting the legionnaires to their presence. That's something else to watch for. They're sneaky. They'll jump out of bushes or creep up on you in small groups, so always be vigilant and when we're on patrol make sure you immediately call out if you see anything."

"What about the other Briton tribes?" a voice called out from the back of the group.

"Not a lot is known about them. What we do know has come through trade since no Roman has ever been that far north. I will tell you this, though." Marek leaned slightly forward and lowered his voice. "It's said their women go into battle and fight alongside the men." He sat up and took another bite. "Of course, men and women alike will be running away as hard as they can when they've got scorpion bolts coming at them followed by all of you galloping with your swords drawn, eh?" He held up his spoon triumphantly. Confidence in their leaders quenches fear amongst the troops and, as Ostorius had told him, confidence also breeds competence. Marek determined that he would be a very competent leader, indeed

Chapter Seven: Serencleddyf

Donogh burst noisily into the dining room as the Druids and students were enjoying their evening meal. He was seemingly oblivious to the piece of twig caught up in his hair, and the jagged remnants of the left sleeve of his drenched tunic did nothing to conceal a large scab surrounded by a purple bruise. "I must speak to Devyn immediately," he managed to blurt out between irregular breaths.

Ceridwen instantly jumped up from her seat and ran to him with arms outstretched; ready to throw herself around his neck, but seeing the exhaustion on his face, instead eased him onto a chair as the rest of the group gathered around.

"Bring water," she called out.

A goblet appeared and Donogh grabbed it with both hands, greedily chugging half of it down before looking up to acknowledge the bearer with a smile of thanks. He wiped his lips with the back of his right hand, gazed at Ceridwen through red streaked eyes, then feverishly looked around and began to rise up from the chair. "Devyn," he repeated. "Where is he?"

"He is right here!"

The students moved aside as the senior Druid walked rapidly over. "Stand back," he instructed them. "Give him air. Bring food." He eased Donogh back into his seat then sat next to him.

"Deep breaths," Devyn told him. "Have some food and drink."

"I have news from Caractacus." Donogh quickly scanned the crowd then stared at Devyn.

"You may speak freely."

"Thousands of Roman soldiers have invaded from the south. They completely overwhelmed us at Noviomagus. Reports from Cantium tell of an even larger force establishing a fort there and planning to advance on Camulodunum. Caractacus has issued a call to arms and is pulling our forces together to intercept the Romans at the river Medway. He's sent riders to Togodumnus to bring the rest of the Catuvellauni army to meet with him there." Donogh took another large draught of water and caught his breath. "He sent me to tell you. That was three days ago." He looked up at all of the faces staring at him. "Caractacus and Togodumnus will meet them with 50,000 men at Medway," he proudly announced to the crowd, "and they'll drive the Romans back into the sea, just as their grandfather did to Caesar."

Devyn stood up, put his right hand on Donogh's left shoulder and stood silent while he pondered for a few minutes, then called out, "Llyn."

"Right here."

"You'll leave immediately to join up with Togodumnus." Devyn then waved his outstretched index fingers over the body of students. "The rest of you begin to make plans to return to your tribes. I'll give each of you instructions in the morning."

Devyn left to confer with the other Druids and the crowd closed in again around Donogh, anxious to hear more about the Romans and what he had seen. Ceridwen, who had been sitting behind him rubbing his neck and shoulders, now clasped her right hand onto his left forearm as he spoke. "The Romans don't fight anything like the Atrebates or anyone else," Donogh began. "They march in rows of a hundred soldiers each and every soldier has spears and a sword and carries a shield almost as big as he is. When they fight they stay in rows and the shields form a wall that protects them so you have to knock some of them over just to get to them."

"Do they have horses?" Andarta asked.

"Some do, but even the soldiers on horseback stay together." Donogh answered. "No individual attacks by himself." He smiled. "It makes it easier for our archers and spear throwers that way, though."

Ceridwen leaned over and lightly brushed the wound on his arm. "How did you come by this?" she asked.

Donogh dropped his nonchalant demeanor. "That happened before we even engaged them," he said, slowly shaking his head as he spoke. "Imagine a huge bow lying sideways that fires arrows as long and as fat as your leg, one right after the other. They had over fifty of them and they shot these huge arrows at us as we advanced. If a bolt hit someone it went right through them. There were bodies impaled to buildings and trees all around before we even reached the Roman line." He nodded at Ceridwen who was still staring at his wounded arm. "One almost got me."

"So the Catuvellauni weren't able to beat the Romans?"

"There were so many of them Caractacus called for us to retreat and just let them take the city."

"And that, my boy, was a very smart move on his part," said a voice from the doorway.

Ceridwen rapidly turned. "Llyn!"

Llyn walked into the room and sat on the edge of a table. "Donogh, you've had enough excitement for a while so go to your hut and take some rest." He wiggled his right index finger at Ceridwen who was still clutching Donogh's arm. "You and Andarta are to leave with me right away. There's an important message for you to deliver to King Anted and since I'm going the same direction I'll see you across the Menai straits and through the pass."

"We're going to cross the straits at night?" Andarta asked.

"There's no time to lose." Llyn stood up and made for the door. "Be ready in an hour," he called back as he disappeared back through the doorway.

Donogh patted the back of Ceridwen's left hand. "It will have to be next time," he said. Ceridwen reached up, grabbed the back of his neck with her right hand and forced his lips to hers for several minutes before she pulled her head back again, her hand still entwined in his hair. "It had better be soon, Donogh." She smiled at him as she rose, then quickly turned and scurried out of the door.

Several hours later Llyn, Ceridwen and Andarta had already reached the mainland and were descending from the pass as a full moon rose in the early morning sky. Uncharacteristically, Llyn was on horseback rather than foot, necessitated by the need for speed. "We'll rest here for a few hours until its light," Llyn said. The trail's not as clear in the forest ahead and the horses could use a break too. He gathered some sticks and they were soon warming themselves by a fire while munching on bread and cheese. Ceridwen, clearly bothered since they left, finally asked, "What were those giant arrow throwers that Donogh was talking about?"

"They call them siege engines," Llyn answered. "Those particular ones were a type of ballista that the legionnaires affectionately call scorpions. I suspect they'll have other types too." He shifted on the rock he was sitting on to fully face the girls. "Claudius has upgraded all of the Roman legions to include such things."

"Who is Claudius?" Andarta queried.

"He's the new emperor. Unlike the old one, he's an intellectual." Llyn leaned back slightly and chuckled, rubbing his chin. "No one ever expected old Claudius to even be of influence in the governing of Rome, not even Claudius himself, but there was an assassination and the old emperor, his wife and child, nearly the whole ruling family was killed. Claudius might have been killed too but he's smart." Llyn tapped the side of his head. "The guards found this unassuming looking man hiding behind a curtain in the palace and he offered them a huge sum of money for them to name him emperor. Well, since he was probably the last person of the imperial line left alive and the Praetorians couldn't maintain order without an emperor, they accepted." Llyn smoothed his beard while he continued the story. "At first the senate thought they could just treat him as a figurehead and do what they wanted but he cracked down and started governing in such a positive way that they had no choice but to stand behind him. In a very short time he's expanded civil liberties, upgraded the army and earned the respect of the citizens at large."

"How did he know how do that without ever intending to be the emperor?" Ceridwen asked.

"As I said, he's an intellectual. Very smart and very well read. He's written several well thought out works and," Llyn looked serious, "for many years he's had a Druid as a close advisor."

"What?" Ceridwen was aghast. "What's a Druid doing in Rome?"

"Oh, there are many Druids there." Llyn looked amused at Ceridwen's wrinkled up face. "You've learned to associate Druids with what you've seen on Mon but you must keep in mind that there are people of all types with ambition. Even Druids. Now, while the great majority of Druids turn that ambition into continued learning and educating others, some seek to apply themselves for other means of satisfaction. Take Caractacus, for example. He feels his Druid knowledge can directly serve people on a day to day basis so, rather than simply teach a select few, he's chosen to be an active leader of his people." Llyn tore off another chunk of bread. "Now, some people, like you two for example, enjoy the niceties that great civilizations like Rome can provide: Fine clothing, perfumes, tasty delicacies and spices." He bit into the bread then looked at the remaining piece in his hand as he chewed. "Well, if you were to be a Druid who harbored these same tastes, then Rome would have a tremendous appeal and, since your skills would be highly marketable, you could find yourself well rewarded in such a city."

"Doesn't this make Claudius much more of a threat, then?" Andarta squirmed uncomfortably as she asked her question, finally sliding off the rock she was awkwardly sitting on and stretching out in the ground.

"On the contrary, it enables us to understand his motives. We feel his intention is most likely to want to directly control just the Belagic tribes and replace the Catuvellauni as the major power in the region. This way he'll both stabilize trade and earn a lot more from it. We suspect that, if he succeeds, he'll be out to make treaties with the rest of the tribes rather than conquer them. I've studied Claudius. He believes in decentralized government and realizes that it costs much less to have friendly trading partners than to maintain occupied territories."

"Ha! To do that he'll have to beat Caractacus," Ceridwen exclaimed.

"He'll have to beat both him and Togodumnus," Llyn added. "And that's Claudius' big gamble." His eyes flitted back and forth between the girls and the cloth bundle he'd been carrying since they left. "Now he's begun he needs this victory in order to maintain his position as emperor but, as you're both thinking, they're going to be hard pressed to beat the Catuvellauni."

"What is that?" Andarta quickly rolled over and teasingly made to grab the package. Llyn quickly snatched it up before her fingers could reach it. "This," he said, rapidly untying it, "gives Togodumnus an even bigger edge." He reached into the fabric and produced an incredibly shiny sword. "This is Serencleddyf."

"Star sword?" Ceridwen was confused.

"Yes, a star sword." Llyn confirmed. "When a star falls to the ground what remains is a small piece of metal so hard that no one can do anything with it." He turned the sword's blade back and forth to reflect the firelight. "No one, that is, except certain skilled craftsmen on Mon. It took many pieces and over a year's work to produce Serencleddyf, but it's thin and so light that it can easily be wielded single-handedly, even from a galloping horse." He held the sword at arm's length and turned it on its side. "It's incredibly strong, will never loose either edge or shine, and it can slice through any known metal. A king carrying Serencleddyf will appear to be invincible on the battlefield and his army will eagerly follow him anywhere."

"May I hold it?" Ceridwen's eyes had been affixed to the blade since Llyn had first removed it from the cloth.

"I don't think that's a good idea, Ceridwen."

"Touch it?" Her hand tentatively reached out but Llyn jumped to his feet and quickly glanced up at the sky. "Look, its becoming light already," he said, furiously bundling the sword back into the fabric. "Get the horses, girls; it's time to go."

Llyn refused to discuss Serencleddyf further and happily changed the subject when Andarta asked him his opinion of Prasutagus.

"He's level headed, a natural leader and excellent warrior," Llyn said approvingly. "He'll be a fine Iceni king one day." He looked over at Andarta's beaming face. "The two of you are well matched; you'll be an excellent queen. You have a nurturing spirit."

"Oh, please," Ceridwen exhaled loudly, eager to express her displeasure from no longer being able to talk about the sword. Llyn snapped his head toward her. "Don't confuse nurturing with weakness, Ceridwen. I see Andarta as a bear, and bears are fiercely protective of their own in the face of danger."

"And what animal would Ceridwen be?" Andarta asked, grinning at her sulking friend.

"Humph!" Llyn snorted. His face became expressionless and he rocked back and forth before carefully wording his answer. "I see Ceridwen as a wolf."

"A wolf," Andarta repeated triumphantly before looking quizzically at Llyn and asking, "Would a wolf make a good queen for the Ordovices?"

"Ceridwen doesn't choose to look at future roles for herself. In fact, she knows in her heart that she's not even able to." Llyn spoke as if Ceridwen wasn't even present but he was keenly aware of the fact she was now listening intently to his every word. "You, Andarta, see yourself as future Iceni queen, wife of Prasutagus and also a mother, whereas Ceridwen has no vision of her future at all. She even questions if she'll be happy married to Donogh."

"What do you mean?" Ceridwen was indignant.

Llyn slowly angled his face in her direction, an annoyingly knowing half smile on his face.

"When he's completed Druid training he'll be more like Caractacus," she added, staring alternately at both Llyn and Andarta. "He will, won't he, Llyn?"

Llyn shook his head. "Oh, he'll certainly grow, but in his own way."

"But he's still better than anyone else," Ceridwen's voice faded as what she thought were her deepest secrets were being openly revealed. Llyn placed his left hand gently on her right shoulder. "It's all right Ceridwen. You're unique in that you don't seek future comfort and security that drives most people. You desperately seek the flame of passion and you need it so intensely that your need sets you apart, or, more accurately, forces you apart from others. Without that need fulfilled you're unable to see beyond it to any future role for yourself." He slowly withdrew his hand. "Until that time comes you'll live opportunistically as a wolf, always in the present."

"Where," Ceridwen started to sputter then looked down as she spoke. "Who? How will I know?"

Llyn answered immediately with a reassuring, "You'll know."

"That's no answer," she snapped back, face trembling and eyes wide.

"You can't seek it out," he explained. "Oh yes, he'll be strong." Llyn knew this answered one of her unasked questions. "He'll be courageous too; but those qualities will be obvious to everybody. You'll know only when you see in him a different kind of strength. A special strength combined with a courage the likes of which you can't possibly imagine. It will overwhelm you but you'll only have an instant to act on it. Make the right decision at that time and you'll instantly know satisfaction." He smiled broadly at her. "After that you'll be able to both plan and realize your future."

"You're saying it's not to be Donogh?" Ceridwen was desperate for an answer.

"I'm saying, Ceridwen, that when the time comes you'll know with certainty."

Ceridwen was quiet and thoughtful for the remainder of their ride together. *"It might be Donogh,"* she kept thinking to herself but the only honest answer she could summon was an unconvincing, *"Maybe?"*

Later that day, having finally left the forest, Llyn turned south and headed for Camulodunum leaving Ceridwen and Andarta to continue west by themselves toward Venta Icenorum to deliver the Druids' message to king Anted.

"Why did you want so much to touch that sword," Andarta asked in order to break Ceridwen's brooding.

"I don't really know. It just seemed so, so prefect." She sat upright and shrugged her shoulders. "Maybe because I had such a hard time mastering Glynu," she patted the hilt in front of her. "In fact, I still do. Even now it's a bit too heavy for me." Ceridwen looked directly at Andarta. "You didn't want to hold it?"

Andarta shook her head. "I've no interest in swords," she said, then smiled. "Of course if it was absolutely necessary, I think I'd want a star sword."

In spite of his Druid intuitiveness, Lynn was surprised by the unexpected reception he received at the palace. "No, Llyn. No, I won't." Togodumnus pounded his fist on the table next to Serencleddyf where Llyn had ceremoniously placed it a few minutes before.

"You're the king defending your lands," Llyn insisted, his voice loud and authoritatively steady. "You must wield it."

"I fear the berserker too much. Even now I sometimes have to fight my passions and force myself to use logic in making decisions for the country. I can't afford to loose control of that." His impassioned eyes glared at the Druid. "Give Serencleddyf to Caractacus," he pleaded. "If he should fall to the berserker I can use my power as his king and older brother to control him and save him from himself." He grabbed Llyn by his arms and spoke directly into his face. "I know it's my responsibility Llyn, but Caractacus is the better choice to be the one to carry it. I beg you."

Lynn swallowed, then, without expression, stared back into Togodumnus eyes, their faces only inches apart. "As you wish, Togodumnus. Then we must leave now."

Llyn rapidly bundled up the sword again and the two of them left the palace together and leaped onto the horses being held for them outside. They rode swiftly without speaking to each other until they were outside the city, up on a hilltop where they could see the 30,000 men assembled on the great commons waiting for them. "Look at them Llyn," Togodumnus said, pulling his horse up to a stop. "I have to always be certain I'm leading them through reason," he continued, still trying to convince the Druid of the appropriateness of his decision. "They depend on me for that. They trust me."

Llyn finally spoke, reaching over and patting Togodumnus on the back as he did so. "It's a wise leader who recognizes his own potential limitations Togodumnus. Their trust in you in not misplaced."

Togodumnus snorted then trotted his horse down the hill and through the mass of cheering men until he was at the front. He turned his mount sideways, drew his sword in his right hand and raised it high above his head. "We go to drive the Romans out of our lands, back to where they came from," he shouted as the men cheered even louder, waving their weapons in response and causing the war dogs to bark furiously. Togodumnus nodded proudly, sheathed his sword, and nudged his horse to begin the march south.

The river Medway was still another half day's journey when Togodumnus ran into the first of Caractacus' forces fleeing north. The Romans had made their move far sooner than expected and attacked before the main Catuvellauni army had arrived. Rather than face certain massacre, Caractacus chose to head north to meet up with his brother with the idea that the combined army could then drive the Romans back across the river from that point. Certainly, a force 50,000 strong would be enough. Especially now, now that Caractacus had earlier met with Llyn and eagerly accepted stewardship of Serencleddyf.

Chapter Eight: Occupation

"You've received another message from Aulus Plautius." Narcissus called out, waving the scroll in his right hand as he ascended the hill to Claudius' tent. After the invasion he had crossed back to Gaul with the returning boats and was now with the emperor and the rest of the Roman army assembled on the coast. He walked up to where the emperor was sitting. "Shall I read it?"

"Yes, do. Perhaps he's finally ready to cross the Thames and take Camulodunum for me."

Narcissus broke the seal, unrolled the scroll and began to read aloud. "Caesar," he began. "After three months of heavy fighting we have successfully secured the river Thames, built a bridge across it and have it defended by two manned forts on the north side and a major fortress on the south. Casualties to date have been high and we have lost half of our cavalry, mostly to sneak attacks from the enemy in ambush situations. Spies estimate a combined remaining Catuvellauni and Trinovantes force in excess of 30,000 men. We are, however, now ready to cross the river and advance on Camulodunum and request your presence for the siege and taking of the city. Aulus Plautius."

Claudius rocked back and forth in his seat, his fingers preening his face. "The Britons didn't run from our scorpions after all, did they?"

"On the contrary," Narcissus responded. "They've been shooting flaming pitch at them from the bushes and setting them on fire. The engineers have been kept busy just building replacements."

Claudius slowly rose to his feet and stretched. "Let's see what the Britons do when they have our siege catapults outside their main city," he said. "Although," he turned his head to one side to listen to a loud bellowing from the huge enclosures at the bottom of the hill, "the sight of those things alone should be enough to have them quaking."

"The boats have been ready for weeks," Narcissus said. "Shall I give the order to load?"

Claudius turned to face him, plopped his right hand on the Druid's left shoulder. "Yes. Let's go Narcissus." He gave his secretary's shoulder a firm shaking. "Let's go and take Britannia."

It had, indeed, been hard fighting for the Romans on the front line; especially for the cavalry. Marek's current assignment was to map out a route for the next phase of assault but accomplishing it was exacting a high price. "Come in, Marek. Sit down and refresh yourself with some wine," Ostorius said, pulling out a seat as a tired Marek came into his office to give the latest scouting report. "What news from across the river?"

"Mission accomplished, Ostorius. We can stay close to villages where the farmers have cleared the forests just about all the way there," Marek announced triumphantly, then eagerly guzzled the offered wine. "It will be hard for the enemy to ambush us without the cover of trees so they'll have to meet us out in the open."

"Excellent." Ostorius leaned over with the amphora and refilled Marek's goblet. "How are your men holding up?"

"Their spirits remain high. We almost made it this time without casualties but ran into some action on the way back when we chased a group of Catuvellauni into the marshes. I lost another one of my original turmae." He downed his wine then found himself staring at the design on the empty goblet in his hands. "His name was Varius."

Ostorius stood up, silently walked over to Marek and clamped a reassuring hand on his shoulder. "You're rising through the ranks fast, Marek," he said, "but no matter how high you go you'll still feel the loss of anyone in your command. And that's how it should be, it keeps you sane. You're one of the best cavalry officers we have. You handle your alae well and your men respect you. I can see you as a sub Praefectus by the end of this campaign."

Marek sat up straight and put his wine goblet down on the table. "Word is that Claudius himself will be leading the advance to Camulodunum."

"That's correct!" Ostorius refilled Marek's goblet and poured one for himself. "He's already landed at Rutupiae with half the eighth legion and some heavy siege catapults. Thanks to your scouting forays we now have the course to follow so I suspect we'll all be leaving in a matter of days." He sat against the edge of the table and took a long drink. "We'll have to cross the bridge fast," he said thoughtfully. "The Catuvellauni will try to hit us hard before we can organize. Their commanders learned a lot about our tactics when we routed them at the Medway and they've been using that knowledge against us ever since. It was a long hard drive to push them back over the Thames and they've had plenty of time to regroup while we've dug in here." He picked up the amphora and held it above his head, gesturing to Marek with a nod toward it.

"Yes, please." Marek picked up his empty goblet and held it out for Ostorius to fill.

"Of course," Ostorius continued, "there's a growing rumor that the only reason the Catuvellauni even retreated across the river was that their king had fallen."

"Killed?"

Ostorius swallowed a mouthful of wine while rapidly shaking his head. "I don't think he was killed, but there's more than one report of several men seen helping him across."

Ten miles north of the Thames Caractacus stood alone, hands on his hips and feet apart, unflinchingly staring into the flames; the heat from the pyre causing profuse sweat to stream from his head and drench his face and neck. Aware of the rustle of someone approaching from behind he nevertheless chose to ignore it and didn't even move his head as a robed figure moved up and stood silently at his side. "He should have been carrying Serencleddyf, Llyn," Caractacus finally barked out without looking at him. "If he'd been carrying the sword this wouldn't have happened."

"But it has happened," Llyn said, his volume as loud but his tone flat. "And that now makes you king."

"Then as king I'll make sure that the Romans never make it to Camulodunum." Caractacus spoke angrily, his right hand slowly moving up and down in front of him. "Not one of them. They're all going to die along the way." The fingers of his hand began pulsing between a claw and a fist as they worked their way to his left side, reaching toward Serencleddyf.

"And every one of your men is willing to stand with you, even to their deaths, if that's what you choose to ask of them."

"As king it's what I must do." Caractacus swiveled around, his wide red streaked eyes glaring at Llyn as his hand clasped onto Serencleddyf's hilt. "Besides, I carry the sword of invincibility."

"I can see that," Llyn responded calmly without moving. "Do you mean to strike me with it, Caractacus?"

"What?" Caractacus looked down quizzically at his right hand clutching the sword, now half out of its scabbard. He immediately thrust the sword back, cocked his head to the right and quickly opened his hand wide as if dropping a hot coal.

"Togodumnus as king refused Serencleddyf," Llyn told him. "He bade me give you the sword so he could override you with reason if it became necessary."

"What reason is to be found here, Llyn?" Caractacus pointed out into the dark as he shouted at the druid. "My brother and 15,000 others have died at the hands of these invaders who've come to take our land."

"Look at the land, Caractacus, "Llyn bellowed back at him. "Look there for your reason. It's been four months since you made the call to arms and now the fields sit overgrown. Less than one in ten of the men in your command are warriors. Most of them are farmers and the villages need them back before it's too late to build food stores for winter."

Caractacus glared angrily into the Druid's face. "We've already killed so many of the Romans. We can win this."

"After Medway you've learned how to successfully fight against them so you know full well you can't win in a direct confrontation," Llyn's voice became quieter and calmer. "Yet that's the only way to bring this to a rapid close before your supply lines run out. If that happens, not just your army but your whole country starves."

"Then perhaps they would rather die than be conquered." Caractacus snarled back through clenched teeth.

"These are your people." Llyn's arms stretched out behind him and he seemed to gain several inches as his voice once again boomed out. "They're blacksmiths and merchants and farmers. They are not warriors. Life for them will go on the same as it has always been, whether under your rule or that of the Romans. Take the warriors to the hills and wait for a more opportune time, for I seriously doubt that this is it."

"You're telling me to retreat? To, to abandon Camulodunum to the enemy?" he stammered.

Llyn raised his right index finger in front of his face. "Come with me. There's something you need to see."

Llyn led Caractacus east through the woods for an hour before turning south and in two more hours they arrived at the riverbank. "We'll cross there," Llyn said as he pointed to a small wooden bridge. They then proceeded downstream toward the blazing lights from the campfires on both sides of the river. Hidden by the woods they were soon close to the walls of the Roman encampment. "What's that sound?" Caractacus whispered.

"Climb this tree and have a look." Llyn patted the trunk of the large oak they were standing next to.

Caractacus began to unbuckle his belt then froze, staring askance at Llyn.

"Shame on you," the Druid glared directly at Caractacus as he whispered loudly. "Do you really think to accuse me of some underhanded trick? I give you my word I won't take it."

"Of course." Caractacus swallowed and nodded. "Forgive me." He then quickly finished unbuckling the belt, slid Serencleddyf under a bush and rapidly ascended the tree. Less than five minutes later he dropped back down, wide eyed, ashen faced and seemingly unable to close his mouth. He just stared at Llyn.

"They're called elephants," Llyn said. "There are 38 of them. You know the damage your war dogs can inflict, but can you even begin to imagine what 38 charging elephants would do to your army in a frontal assault?"

Caractacus sank to the ground, grabbed his sword and placed the tip on the ground between his spread legs, then, holding onto it, bent over and leaned his face against the hilt. Llyn quietly sat next to him and placed his right hand on Caractacus' shoulder.

Word spread fast and only days later the leading Iceni were called to council. The room immediately became silent as the doors were closed behind them and all eyes focused on Anted as he rose from the table with the announcement, "Togodumnus has fallen."

"How is that possible?" Ceridwen leaped to her feet and banged her fists on the table top as she spoke. "The Druids gave Serencleddyf to Togodumnus. He was invincible."

Anted placed his hands flat on the table top and leaned toward her. "Togodumnus did not carry the sword," he said. "He refused it in favor of Caractacus."

Ceridwen was stunned. "Why?" she whispered, her voice breaking as she sank back into her seat, slowly shaking her head in disbelief. "Why would anyone refuse Serencleddyf?" she quietly asked herself. "Why?"

"Caractacus has withdrawn," Anted continued, "and, by the taking of Camulodunum, the Romans claim rightful victory over Catuvellauni lands as well as those of the tribes of the Trinovantes, Cantium and Atrebates that they now occupy."

Saenu rose slowly. "Caractacus brought this on them all by deposing Adminius in Cantium and attacking Verica," he said. "The treaty that we've lived by for years clearly forbade such conflict between the tribes. He violated it and the Romans have obviously moved to enforce it."

"What do the Romans want of us, Anted?" Aesu interjected impatiently.

Anted raised his hands and slapped them onto the table top. "Everyone, sit down," he said, watching as they did so. "The Roman chief, Emperor Claudius, has called for the kings of all tribes to meet with him in Camulodunum." Anted slowly sat down himself and continued. "This is all as it should be. The Romans have resolved the conflicts and now they wish to reestablish order and resume trade by seeking treaties."

"Do the Druids recognize Claudius as the new king of Britannia?" Saenu blurted out. "After all, they forbade us to go the aid of the Catuvellauni when the Romans first landed."

"We have yet to hear from the Druids on this," Anted replied, "But since Cunobelin's bloodline no longer rules from Camulodunum I doubt there is an official king of Britannia any more." He nodded his head up and down eagerly. "That was only a Roman construct, anyway." Anted rubbed his hands together. "It seems to me there may be opportunity here."

Aesu moved to speak. "I'm not sure we should trust the Romans," he said. "We know so little about them."

"Agreed," Anted nodded. "So I propose to go to Camulodunum with only a small detachment and meet with Claudius alone. Let Aesu and Saenu remain at the Iceni border with the majority of our warriors, just in case things are not as they seem."

"I disagree," Saenu said. "We should all go and take 500 warriors each with us as a show of strength."

"I'm not sure we should be making that sort of showing just yet, Saenu. Besides, what if this does turn out to be a trick? Our main force could be obliterated."

In spite of Saenu's initial objection, it was finally agreed that he and Aesu would remain behind. Early the next morning Anted and thirty armed Iceni warriors including Prasutagus and Ceridwen mounted up and left for Camulodunum.

The Roman legions had expanded the Camulodunum city walls to include their encampment but Claudius insisted that the elephants be kept in the courtyard outside the front of the palace he was now occupying so they would be seen by everyone who approached. As word of these giant beasts spread they attracted a constant stream of people from miles around. Since there had been such little resistance against the legions as they marched through Trinovantes land Claudius proclaimed there would be no pillaging of the capitol city and that the Romans be perceived as liberators, not conquerors. The townspeople, naturally hesitant about them at first, soon welcomed the Roman soldiers. The soldiers in turn were only too eager to part with the money they brought with them in exchange for the fineries unavailable to them during the campaign. Within days of the Roman arrival Camulodunum was bustling with such robust trade it was like a major holiday.

Prior to the arrival of the delegates from the neighboring tribes Claudius insisted on meeting the officers of each legion and personally presenting promotions and commendations where due. Since Titus had now completed his three years as legate of the fourteenth and was to return to Rome to take his place as a ranking member of the senate, Claudius took this opportunity to create a fanfare and promoted Ostorius to commander of the legion. Ostorius then presented Marek to the emperor who was delighted to award him the title of sub-praefectus thereby placing him in command of a thousand troopers. Having non-Roman born officers played perfectly into Claudius' plans and he had hoped to stay and chat with Marek but the news of the impending arrival of the Iceni called him instantly back to the palace.

On advice from Narcissus who had explained how the Iceni were a very proud and strong nation with no experience with any tribes other than local Britons and Belagics, Claudius decided to meet with them across a table in the war room rather than flaunt the pageantry of the throne room. The elephants outside served to make enough of a statement and he wanted to make Anted feel as if he were being treated as an equal in spite of the clear Roman advantage. Anted was surprised at the almost diminutive stature of the emperor as compared to the tall Iceni, wondering to himself how this runt could be the leader of such a mighty empire, but said nothing and after cordial introduction immediately began vigorous discussion. The Iceni were offered the relationship of client kingdom, a friend and trading partner of Rome while remaining a completely separate, sovereign nation. This was a very different treatment to what Claudius was giving the Belagic territories; they were to be set up as civitas, or administrative units, under the control of Aulus Plautius who had been named governor of the captured territories. Ceridwen secretly smiled. She liked the fact that the Belagics were to be subjugated and was impressed with the levels of order and administration the Romans were putting in place. Farmers would be offered outlets for all of their excess crops since the legions were in constant need of food and wherever they were stationed the local villages would reap the tremendous opportunity to supply them with numerous goods and services. More efficient trade was to be established with mainland Gaul through the creation of a seaport at the site where the Romans had built the large bridge across the Thames and a town by the name of Londinium was rapidly growing there.

It took very little time after arriving at Camulodunum for the Iceni delegation to realize that having the Romans as neighbors to the south would be a major boon to both trade and regional stability. Prasutagus took things one step further and traveled to Londinium to meet with some of the importers already streaming in from the mainland to directly establish trade relationships with them rather than going through the middlemen in Camulodunum as they had in the past. He was astounded by the demand for Iceni merchandise and, realizing the opportunity that stood in front of him, eagerly negotiated a contract with one of the more astute businessmen who had come to town. "The Iceni are going to be rich, Ceri," he told Ceridwen excitedly on his return to Camulodunum. "I've negotiated a loan of a million sesterces, enough to purchase all the gold and silver our craftsmen can handle to continuously make jewelry and then I'll sell it at huge profit to be shipped to customers in Rome."

"Who will buy that much jewelry?" Ceridwen was astonished. Precious metal such as silver and, especially, gold had previously been available in such limited quantities that a craftsman could previously only hope produce a few pieces a year. Prasutagus was now talking about one a week.

"The same man who made the loan also guarantees to buy everything we produce." Prasutagus was almost delirious with his excitement. "Think what this will mean for us."

"Can you trust this man?"

"Of course," Prasutagus said indignantly. "I checked around quite thoroughly before making this deal. He's one of the most established merchants in the whole of the Roman Empire. His name is Seneca and he's not just going to loan me money, he's promised to teach me how to most effectively reap the benefits of this exciting new occupation."

After finishing his series of meetings with Claudius, Anted decided the Iceni should spend several more days in Camulodunum to mingle and learn more about the Romans before returning home. The group eagerly agreed and quickly dispersed throughout the city. Ceridwen was particularly interested in doing some shopping so, after changing out of her leather tunic and into a dress, she rode to the center of town. There were large throngs of people crowding the shopping district so she dismounted and slowly led Kelpie through the main street, excitedly looking at the merchandise lavishly displayed on the stalls along the side. She had quite a fondness for imported delicacies and was seeking out a fruit stall in anticipation of feasting on cherries, oranges, apples and sweet chestnuts. Stopping at a particularly well stocked one she smirked and blushed to herself as she realized she had also better purchase another supply of pomegranates.

Suddenly she heard a foreign accent exclaim out loud, "what a magnificent creature," and, curiosity overcoming her, stepped in front of Kelpie and peered across the road. The voice belonged to a Roman officer sitting alone at a small table. The instant he saw her he began to rise to his feet, simultaneously knocking over the table as he attempted to put his mug of ale on it and causing it to spill onto the ground. He smiled awkwardly, attempted to right the table, then chose to ignore it and briskly walked over to her. "And she has a very fine horse, too," he said directly into her eyes.

Ceridwen blushed slightly as she returned his smile. "You're taller than the other Romans I've seen," she said, coyly stroking Kelpie's neck.

"And you're more beautiful than any Roman I've seen."

Ceridwen reached up with her left arm and hugged Kelpie's neck causing her head to tilt to the right. "You've just been away from home so long that you've forgotten what women look like," she said.

"Believe me," he quickly replied, still smiling and gazing into her eyes. "If the women in Rome looked like you I'd have thought long and hard before leaving. Are you one of the Trinovantes?"

"No, I'm Iceni." Suddenly aware of a need to fidget with her hands she patted Kelpie lightly, then held onto his reins with both of them to the right side of her face. "And you? You're not a Roman then?"

"I'm from a country called Egypt." He cocked his head to the left. "Have you ever heard of it?"

"I sleep on cotton sheets every night," she said proudly.

"Really?"

"It's true," she said, then giggled. "Well, Roman soldier from Egypt, my name is Ceridwen and this 'magnificent creature' as you called him is Kelpie."

"Hello Ceridwen and Kelpie, I am so delighted to meet you both. Ceridwen," he gestured to the table, now righted by the merchant, "please sit with me, join me in something to eat and tell me more about yourself. My name is Marek."

Chapter Nine: Time Off

Ceridwen watched the merchant as he poured from the amphora, filling her goblet for the second time with excellent Roman wine, but as soon as he left she flitted her attention back across the table to Marek. "Tell me about the women in Rome," she said.

"Which ones?" he replied playfully.

"Tell me about the aristocrats in the ruling classes." She looked at him sheepishly. "The ones a man like you would know."

"They shop incessantly in order to be dressed in the latest fashions and they wear perfume and adorn their lips and eyes with color imported from Egypt." He watched Ceridwen's eyes drop down to focus on her goblet as he spoke, then reached across the table, hooked her chin in his right index finger and gently picked up her face so she was looking directly into his. "And you'd put every one of them to shame."

Ceridwen instantly beamed. "What's in fashion in Rome?"

"That dress you're wearing, for starters. Linen, isn't it?"

"That's right. The farmers from our village grow the flax themselves."

"Well, Iceni clothing like that is now considered the height of fashion, especially when it has those abstract details in the weaving, along with Iceni jewelry." He nodded at Ceridwen's golden arm band. "It only became available in Rome a couple of years ago and it's now all the rage amongst the women there."

Ceridwen reached across herself and gently touched her arm band with the fingertips of her right hand causing her hair to cascade over her face. She quickly flipped her head back, then using her right hand, brushed her hair across her forehead and behind her right ear, then blushed at Marek's approving gaze. "Now that's a sight that's sorely missing in Rome," he sighed. "Roman women insist on imprisoning their hair. They spend hours at a time having it tied up or braided like a rope and affixed to their head so it has no freedom at all. I much prefer it long and natural as you wear it."

"I like to feel the wind blow through it as I ride," she said, peeking at him over the top of the goblet as she sipped her wine. "Do you ride a horse Marek?"

"Oh yes." He nodded. "I've been riding all my life and I'm an officer in the cavalry." He looked at her quizzical expression and added, "We're the equestrians, the horse soldiers."

"I see." Ceridwen leaned to look past Marek and down the street, then turned and looked behind her. "So where, then, is your horse?"

Marek laughed and drained his goblet. "He's enjoying his time off." He put the goblet down and stared at her. "As am I."

"Me too," Ceridwen replied instantly, then buried her again blushing face in the goblet to finish her wine. Slowly, she lowered the empty vessel from her lips and rocked the base of it back and forth on the table top. "Would you like to go for a walk?" she asked quietly, seemingly speaking to her hands before cautiously raising her eyes to meet with his nodding smile.

Half an hour later they'd strolled away from the bustle of the market area and were walking together down a quiet street, approaching the edge of the city with Kelpie silently in tow behind. Ceridwen held his reins loosely in her right hand, which caused her to walk ever closer to Marek as the street narrowed. Without any break in the conversation, her left arm brushed up against his right and her hand simply, quite naturally, slid into his. He gave it a reassuring squeeze.

"Why do you serve in the army Marek?" she asked. "Wasn't it hard to leave Rome?"

"All big cities are very easy for me to leave. I'd always felt as if I didn't belong in Rome and when I traveled on business with my father to Alexandria I realized I didn't quite fit there either. Believe it or not I prefer the frontier. My dream is to one day settle down with a large villa in the countryside and set up a trading business. That is, once I've served my time with the legions."

"How long will that be?"

"Quite a while," he sighed. "At least another fifteen years. But if I complete it with high rank and good service I'll be offered land and a villa in occupied territory." He looked over at Ceridwen. "And that," he said, "has great appeal to me."

"I'm impressed. You seem to have a plan for your life all thought out."

"What about you Ceridwen? What are your dreams for the future?"

"I'm not sure that I have any." She spoke lightly with a far-away expression. "I already have land with twenty farmsteads managed by peasants and their families who've been with us for generations. A nice house too," she leaned her head briefly on Marek's arm, chuckling. "My father was a minor king so I grew up calling it a palace but it's just like one of the larger houses in Camulodunum and nothing at all like the palace here."

"It seems like you're all set then."

"It would seem so, wouldn't it?" Ceridwen stared at the road ahead as she spoke. "I have this friend, Andarta, whose father is Saenu, one of the Iceni sub kings. She's like you, all set with what she's going to do with her future." She briefly shook her head.

"Andarta's going to complete her studies on Mon and then marry Prasutagus, the son of the king, and then have children and be a mother and be queen of the Iceni." Ceridwen shrugged. "I like studying on Mon, but I can't get all excited about it the way she does, and I don't ever see myself as a mother." She took a deep breath and turned her head to Marek. "I just like to enjoy each day as it comes."

"No plans to marry, then?"

"Perhaps one day." She smiled coyly and, to change the subject, quickly pointed down an intersecting street. "Let's go this way," she said eagerly. "We can walk across the commons."

They increased their pace, briskly walking around the corner toward the green area in the distance. "Tell me about that sword you carry on your horse, Ceridwen," Marek asked. "Is it functional or ceremonial? It looks almost ornamental with all those jewels covering the scabbard and the hilt."

"It's a family heirloom," she answered proudly. "It has a name: Glynu. It's carried by the warrior head of my family and came to me three years ago. Three years ago," her eyes fell to the ground and she stared at her feet as she continued, "When my father was killed," she added softly, swallowing hard at the recollection of that day. Marek slowed his pace to match hers and they walked together in silence for the next minute until Ceridwen suddenly flung her head up again. "And yes," she said cheerfully, firmly squeezing Marek's hand. "It is quite functional."

"But you're much too pretty to wield a sword."

"What do you mean?" Ceridwen stopped walking and abruptly pulled her hand from his.

Marek raised both of his hands shoulder height and palms toward her. Stunned by her reaction he looked at her quizzically. "What did I say?"

"Since when does 'being pretty' have anything to do with handling a sword?" She was indignant.

Marek lowered his hands and attempted to defuse her with a smile and a slow shaking of his head. "My apologies Ceridwen, I'm clearly out of my element here. Women in Rome don't carry swords."

"Well they do here," she shouted at him, then added, "what?" as she saw him smirk.

"Forgive me," Marek apologized with honest sincerity in his voice. "It's just something that my commanding officer once said to me. He told me there would be women warriors in Britannia but," he swallowed, successfully suppressing another smile, "he joked that they'd all look like the men." He looked at her with wide eyes. "And you, Ceridwen, look absolutely nothing like a man. You're the most beautiful woman I've ever seen."

"I'll have you know I killed an enemy with that very sword," she tried to maintain her voice but was unable to continue to shout at him, "When I became a warrior." Whatever anger she had only moments before had melted and her expression fell flat as the memory of that horrible day once again became vivid. "Three years ago," she whispered. Her face began to wrinkle.

"Three years ago?" Marek repeated after her, a calm understanding somehow contained in his voice. Ceridwen's eyes trembled. She bit her lower lip and nodded, her hands limpid at her sides. Marek took a step forward and wrapped his arms around her, then gently eased her face into his shoulder, stroking her hair as she sobbed. Suddenly all the praises and complements of how she had achieved warrior status at such an early age, how impressed people were that she was able to serve on the war council, all that simply had melted into the empathy and tender words of this stranger. Her hands awkwardly moved up his back and she nuzzled her face into the nape of his neck, feeling very much as if she were once again a little girl. Three years of unreleased, pent-up tears flowed freely and unashamedly for several minutes and when they finally subsided she wiped her face back and forth on his tunic, then looked up at him with large, red eyes. "Thank you," she whispered, hugged him with her face flat again against his sodden shoulder, then slowly pulled away. She placed her hand back in his and they continued walking as before to the end of the street and into the open grassy area beyond. It took only a few more silent steps before Ceridwen was back to her cheerful self again. "Tell me about your horse, Marek," she said. "Did you bring him on the boat with you?"

"Indeed I did." He laughed at the recollection of his first time walking a horse into the hold of a boat. "Although," he motioned toward Kelpie, "all our horses are much smaller than yours."

Ceridwen nodded as Kelpie's head appeared over her shoulder and she reached up to scratch it. "I know," she said. "Kelpie's the tallest horse I've ever seen."

Even amongst Iceni horses Kelpie stood out as an impressive animal: almost pure white with a gray mane and tail and towering a full head above the other mounts. He and Ceridwen moved seemingly as a single unit when she rode him, almost flowing, yet they were able to separate instantly when she dismounted in the Iceni style of jumping to the ground without stopping. Their bodies worked together in unbroken rhythmical undulation at a gallop, her arms around his neck and head to his ear when they jumped. The interaction of Ceridwen with Kelpie was much more than mere horse and rider. She described it as the edge of will. Kelpie performed with such ease that he tended to lull Ceridwen, almost seductively, into releasing her control over him while she in turn maximized that edge, diligently paying attention to every detail and maintaining absolute control. It was a partnership that confidently took on any challenger.

"Where does his breed come from?" Marek asked.

"I'm not really sure of his breed, but I met him on Mon."

"Mon? You mean the Druid Island?"

"That's right." She cocked her head to one side. "What do you know of the Druids?"

"They're mystics and sorcerers, nearly everyone fears them, and they have strange religious rites where they make human sacrifices."

Ceridwen at first looked stunned then exploded into laughter, her head dancing around as she almost doubled over in uncontrollable mirth. "Oh that, that's good Marek." She tried to stand up straight but as soon as she looked at him her guffaws began again. Finally gaining control of herself she slapped her hand on the back of his shoulder. "You know how to make a girl laugh, that's for sure." She patted his shoulder as he turned to face her. "Human sacrifices indeed." Her grin extended from one rosy cheek to the other as she shook her head. "How did you come up with that?"

"It is common knowledge," Marek replied quizzically, feeling the need to add, "seriously," in response to Ceridwen's jesting.

"Where would a ridiculous idea like that be common?" she blurted.

"The, the whole world knows it to be fact."

"Have you ever even met a Druid?"

"Not really, but I saw the emperor's Druid once when he calmed the seas for our crossing from Gaul and he looked quite fierce."

"This is a Druid who lives amongst 'civilized,'" she smirked, "society in Rome?"

"Yes. He's very well admired."

"So you don't know him as some sort of bloodthirsty religious zealot?"

"I suppose that living in Rome must have caused him to change his ways." Marek looked at Ceridwen and couldn't help himself from matching her infectious smile. "Why is this so funny to you?" he asked.

"Because," she released her grip on Kelpie's rein and sat down on the grass, patted the ground next to her and waited until Marek was sitting there before continuing. "A Druid could never needlessly harm another being, never mind sacrifice one. Their most central tenet is to respect all life. The only way I could ever envision a Druid killing anyone would be in defense of self or others. Never unprovoked."

"What about in their religious ceremonies?" Marek was holding firm. "Surely they make exceptions for their sacred rituals."

Ceridwen leaned over and tentatively stroked the stubble on the right side of Marek's face causing him to directly face her as she spoke. "Druids have no religion Marek. They study and learn from the world. Their only calling beyond that is to teach and help others."

"We're taught from childhood that everybody needs to believe in something," Marek said. He brushed Ceridwen's hair back from her face with the tips of his right fingers, pausing with them lightly touching her just behind her ear. "So who are the Druid's gods?"

Ceridwen dropped her hand from his face to the ground and leaned on it. "No gods," she said moving her head slightly to push his fingers further into her hair. "Druids have no need for such constructs. Gods are just for peasants and the unlearned. It makes understanding the world easier for them."

"You realize you'd be including the majority of the inhabitants of Rome amongst that group with such a generalization," Marek said. "Everyone I've ever known has a god that they worship." He moved his hand slowly down her neck and began to gently massage the top of her shoulder with his fingertips. She slowly rotated her head in approval of his touch.

"I've studied on Mon for the past six years," she said, almost in a whisper as she leaned closer to him. "Everything that is, is. Once you understand that you see that there's really no need for gods, unless you want to use their names to control others. I believe they call that religion." She partly closed her eyes and brushed her face against Marek's hand and he slid it from her shoulder to beneath her chin then caressed her cheek with it. Ceridwen opened her eyes and looked directly at his face. "I don't believe in gods, Marek."

Marek's hand slid behind her neck. "Neither do I," he replied, leaning forward and pulling her face to his. "But you're the only person I've ever admitted that to."

Ceridwen's free hand moved up and grasped the top of his shoulder, her lips willingly parting as they made contact with his for the first time. She closed her eyes and all that existed was the kiss. No thought. No other awareness. After a too short long time their faces slowly drew apart radiating at each other an identical expression of delight and amazement. Neither had words each only saw the others eyes, merely inches apart, before their mouths drifted together again. Neither knew how long they remained like that, but it was Marek who first noticed the rain when he reached his arm around her and realized her dress was soaked. They laughed together, water streaming down their faces and helped each other to their feet in what was now a muddy, sodden field. Ceridwen whistled for Kelpie who simply appeared from somewhere and, one hand on her horse's rein and the other clasping onto Marek, made haste to the palace.

As soon as they entered the courtyard a stable hand appeared, took the reins from Ceridwen and led Kelpie way to a dry him off and put him into a stall. Ceridwen wrapped her arms around Marek's waist. "I'll still be in town tomorrow," she said.

Marek beamed. "Can you come by the exercise area next to the barracks in the morning?" he asked, stroking his hand over her drenched hair. "The troops will be running drills first thing, but after that you and I can ride through the countryside for the rest of the day."

"I'd like that." Ceridwen nodded eagerly.

Marek teasingly gave her a quick peck on the lips then backed away from her. "Go inside and get dry," he instructed, "and I'll see you in the morning."

Chapter Ten: Minerva

C eridwen was up early the next day, and in spite of a low cloud cover that normally would have cast a pall over her morning, she was in high spirits. As she rode Kelpie away from the palace the clouds had already begun to dissipate and by the time she reached the cavalry training area the sun was breaking through making bright streaks across the sky. She brought Kelpie to a stop at the edge of the field and strained to pick Marek out of the crowd of over a hundred horsemen until she realized he was out in front of them, clearly their commander. She grinned delightedly and said, "Well, well," loudly to the air around her while slowly nodding.

She watched the disciplined precision of the troopers as they rode in formation before collectively attacking the row of figures made of straw at one end. "Look at that," she said to Kelpie while, patting him on the side of his neck. "They don't dismount. They're either all very strong or those swords must be much lighter than Glynu, eh?" She chuckled. "If I tried to use my sword like that I'd go flying right off your back."

She watched intently as Marek had the troopers perform several series of precise maneuvers before finally ordering them to disband. As they slowly scattered in various directions she leaned forward, placing her face close to her horse's ear as she watched a solitary rider coming toward her. "Here comes Marek," she whispered excitedly, then sat up straight and tried to look calm.

"Good morning Ceridwen," Marek called out riding directly up to her then, before she had time to answer, grabbed the back of her neck, leaned over and gave her a long kiss while the horses stood side-by-side. They slowly separated and he withdrew his hand and asked, "so what do you think of our cavalry?"

Ceridwen quickly contained her breathing. "They're certainly organized," she said. "Do they always fight from their horses?"

"Of course they do. That's really the advantage of being mounted isn't it?"

"We don't fight from our horses. We use them to deliver a warrior rapidly into the middle of battle."

"What do you mean?"

"Watch, I'll show you." She called out, "Ha," and Kelpie instantly bolted in the direction of the row of straw men. Marek immediately galloped behind in an attempt to keep with her but had to quickly veer off to the side when Kelpie suddenly pulled up. Before her horse had even stopped Ceridwen swung her left leg across him and in simultaneous motion drew Glynu from its scabbard and leaped off. She landed softly on the ground in front of one of the straw effigies, her legs bending to absorb the shock, her sword raised high above her right shoulder. She immediately swung down and cleaved the figure in half, the momentum carrying her completely around, and as she spun back she swung Glynu in an upward sweep and lopped the head cleanly off before the trunk had even hit the ground. Turning toward Marek she shouted out, "Something like that."

"Impressive," he called back.

Ceridwen gave a shrill whistle and Kelpie rushed up to her side. She sheathed the sword and then with a single, seemingly almost effortless jump was again on horseback. She trotted up to Marek sporting a wide grin.

"I've fought against men from several Celtic tribes," Marek said, slowly nodding his head, "but I've never seen anything like that. Is that the way all you women warriors ride?"

"It's the way the Iceni ride." Ceridwen glared directly at him. "Why do you make a distinction between men and women?"

"Sorry." Marek forced a quick smile. "Please bear with me. I'm still learning about the people here."

"You can't just lump us all together, Marek; there's no other tribe that fights like the Iceni. We're known as the horse people. You Romans have only encountered the Belagics and the Catuvellauni."

"We're not all Romans," Marek began, but caught himself. He winced, then nodded and nudged his horse forward at a slow walk.

"Exactly," Ceridwen answered and coaxed Kelpie to walk to keep up and when Marek looked over at her she cocked her head to one side. "Perhaps it's fortunate for you that your commanders decided to make a truce with us." She giggled. "You never know, I might have had your head."

"I'm not sure that the Iceni fighting style would be all that effective against a Roman army. To do battle your way you'd first have to isolate individual legionnaires and they're trained not to break rank. Plus, if you made it past the spears you'd be riding into a wall of shields."

"How can soldiers fight bunched up like that? Don't they need room to use their weapons?"

"They fight as a unit and jab their swords from between the shields." Marek rapidly stroked his chin then turned to Ceridwen. "You know, one thing I have noticed as a principal difference between Roman soldiers and the Celtic warriors I've encountered is that the Celts tend to fight individually."

"Well of course we do. A warrior is defined by courage and fighting skills."

"And it's an admirable trait." Marek's upper body rocked back and forth, his face went blank, and he spoke introspectively. "When the fourteenth was stationed along the Rhine my turmae broke formation and we rode individually against the Chauci to stop them from making a sneak attack on our flank. It was like riding alone, without any restriction." Marek's eyes were almost shut as he recollected and his face made an involuntary smile. "My senses were so sharp that day and I felt so powerful. I sincerely believed I was invincible." His eyes opened to Ceridwen's understanding gaze and Marek shook his head to clear his thoughts. "The Roman army places little value on individualism, however. It succeeds through teamwork."

Ceridwen leaned over and stroked her right hand down the side of his face. "Then I pity Roman soldiers Marek. They die in battle without any chance of glory."

"They share the glory of victory. Don't forget, the legions invariably win."

"Glory isn't something that you can share." Her eyes were deep chasms that seemed to pull Marek inside her. "You feel that truth, don't you Marek?"

"I do," he quietly responded while remaining motionless, not wanting to break the eye contact that communicated the volumes he was unable to put into words.

"Perhaps you've come to Britannia in search of it," she whispered.

Marek drew a deep breath then released it with a sigh. "But an officer must think of the men in his command. Lead them to victory as a unit." He spoke as if he were reciting the code from training camp.

"You can lead them to win, but you alone will feel the glory." Ceridwen sat up straight, almost leaning back on Kelpie. "It's in your blood," she nodded knowingly.

"They can share the spoils, though. A legionnaire in the front lines can accumulate a good deal of wealth to retire on."

"You're a strange people." Ceridwen shook her head and laughed. "Fighting only for material gain? Why, without the chance of personal glory driving them on I'll bet your legionnaires wouldn't fare well at all against an Iceni warrior in a fair one on one fight."

"I don't doubt you're right. One of your warriors could very well overpower a single legionnaire. He looked at Ceridwen's proud expression and added, "Possibly even two of them." Marek stretched to sit tall. "But give me ten legionnaires acting together and they'd defeat twenty or more of your warriors any day."

"Oh, really?" Ceridwen's instantly argumentative expression involuntarily broke into a bright smile as she and Marek made eye contact again and, her face blushing, she quickly turned away and nodded toward a copse of trees on the horizon. "Shall we go for our ride?" she asked, tossing her raven hair over her right shoulder with a flick of her head.

"Lead the way," Marek gestured with his chin, and then quickly dug his heels into his horse's sides as Ceridwen rapidly took off.

By the time he reached the trees Ceridwen had already dismounted and was leaning up against a large oak, her hands behind her back. He stopped his horse just a few feet in front of her. "Do you need a rest already?" he asked playfully.

"Not at all," she replied in a similar tone. She shook her head but remained in the same position, watching Marek slowly dismount without taking his eyes off her.

"I'm so glad," he said as he approached her. "But your breathing does seem a little hard." He again stroked her luxurious hair, tracing the fingers of his right hand from the top of her head and down the side of her neck, pressing gently as he leaned toward her. "Your blood flows rapidly too," he said, his lips only inches from hers.

"What do you propose to do about it?" she asked.

"Hmm." He moved his face to her left side causing their cheeks to brush together and whispered into her ear, "Perhaps a kiss might help."

She began to respond with, "perhaps," but Marek overwhelmed her opening mouth with his before any words could escape, while in the same movement enveloping her trim body in his arms and pulling her tightly against him. Several minutes into the unbroken kiss they sank to the ground together, continuing obliviously as they lay side-by-side beneath the tree, Ceridwen firmly in Marek's right arm. Her hands slid up his back and clutched onto his broad shoulders while his free left caressed her right thigh through the soft fabric of her dress. Their lips slowly parted. Marek moved his hand up her body and began to ease the neck of her dress from her shoulder but she slipped her hand over his and squeezed it. His eyes adopted a quizzical expression and she buried her face into his shoulder. "I don't want to disappoint you," she murmured.

"What do you mean?" he asked softly, giving her a reassuring hug while trying to move his head down to look at her face.

"You're used to women with perfect bodies."

"And this isn't?" He massaged her back with long strokes, then rolled her back into his arm so she was facing him again. "What's the matter Ceri? You're too free of a spirit to be self-conscious?"

"I never have been." She flopped her hand across her bodice and chuckled. "Quite the opposite, in fact." Her voice hesitated. "I've always been proud of a scar I received in a fight with an enemy, but with you, like this," she leaned into him, burying her face once again in his chest, "but right now I feel," she bit her lower lip, "diminished by it?"

Marek leaned over and kissed her cheek. "Do you really find me that superficial?"

Her eyes tentatively peeked up at his reassuring smile.

"Honestly, Ceri," he said, easing her to a sitting position in front of him. He moved his hands to the sides of her face then slid his fingertips down to the nape of her neck. She took a deep breath through parted lips but remained completely still as he slowly, sensually, untied the leather lacing in the front of her dress. As he pulled it open the fabric slid from her shoulders and he continued smiling into her large eyes as it cascaded around her. He leaned forward, teasingly avoiding her lips and planted a gentle kiss on her forehead while easing the sleeves from her wrists and sliding them across her unresisting hands. He then took her hands firmly in his and moved them slightly away from her torso, leaned back, and for the first time gazed in obvious delight at the creamy flesh of her topless body.

"Is it all right with you?" she asked nervously. "You can't even see the scar if you look from one side, you know."

"Do you know of Minerva?" he asked, his eyes slowly moving up her until they smiled into hers.

"Is she a friend of yours?" The uncertainty in her voice belied a sudden pang of jealousy.

Marek slowly shook his head and laughed, instantly dropping her hands and wrapping her up in his arms. "A goddess," he whispered into her right ear while squeezing her tightly. She reached her arms around his back, hugging him as he spoke.

"To the Romans she is the patron of the arts," he pulled his head back to look into her face. "And she's also their goddess of war. If I believed in gods, I'd be calling you Minerva in the flesh. Look at you." He leaned further back, his expression clearly demonstrating his appreciation of the firmness of her naked breasts. "Beauty that any artist would spend his entire life in a vain attempt to capture, adorned with the proud mark of a warrior." He smiled broadly, unable to close his mouth. "You're perfect." He sighed, moving closer to her again. "Absolutely," he pulled her against him with his right arm, their faces almost touching, "perfect."

Ceridwen spread her lips as Marek's descended onto them. They rolled across the ground together, arms rapturously exploring each other's backs. Ceridwen's dress slid off her legs and she kicked it away as Marek's tongue traced a line down the side of her neck and encircled her pert left nipple; his right arm still caressing her shoulders, his left supporting the small of her back. She flung her head back, eyes closed and gasping through a wide-open mouth while her impatient fingers tore away at his tunic until she was finally free to run her fingernails across his bare chest. Her eyes opened and she smiled mischievously at him while she moved her hands down across his firm stomach. Marek slid his right arm from under her shoulders and entwined his fingers in her hair, turning her face to his and once again pressed down with a kiss while his left hand joined both of hers in unbuckling his stiff leather belt. Once free of clothing she took him in her hands. Marek placed his palms onto the ground on either side of her shoulders, supporting himself, delighting in the excitement on her face as she caressed him, then with lightning speed he slid his hands up either side of her body, forcing her arms above her head and positioning her wrists together. He clasped them firmly in the grip of his strong right hand, holding them still while his left hand moved to her right breast, teasingly squeezing the erect nipple between thumb and forefinger. She writhed, gasping as his teeth first engaged her left ear then bit at her neck and shoulders as he rolled on top of her, pinning her beneath him. His wild face appeared in front of hers, enabling him to watch the pleasure dominate her eyes as he repeatedly slammed his hips back and forth. She strained against his grasp, delighted by the fact she was actually unable to break free and thrilled by the intensity her attempts to do so added to his penetrations. Even with her feet planted on the ground on either side of his legs and straining with all her might she was unable to arch her back as he held her down, burying his face into her shoulder as one last thrust preceded the most delicious and delirious moment of immobility either of them had ever experienced.

"That trip to Camulodunum must have really been something." Andarta slowly shook her head while staring at an ebullient Ceridwen, recently back from Camulodunum with the rest of Anted's party to report to the council in the Iceni capital. "Prasutagus hasn't stopped talking about how the Iceni are going to become rich supplying the Romans with clothing and craftwork and you," she laughed, "you of all people, come back with stars in your eyes about a man you met there."

"Not just any man; he's a..."

"A Roman?" Andarta quickly interjected, her head cocked to the left.

"Actually, he's not."

"No?"

"No. He's from Egypt."

"Egyptian, eh? Maybe he'll bring you some nice new sheets." Andarta grinned as she teased but Ceridwen burst into laughter, looking up at the ceiling and stroking her chin. "That would be wonderful," she said wistfully. "Of course, he'd have to try them out with me."

"Ceri!" Andarta slapped her hand to her chest in a fake display of shock.

"He could be the one, Andarta," Ceridwen excitedly blurted out while nodding rapidly to reinforce her words.

"You said that about Donogh a year ago."

"But Donogh can't really handle me." Ceridwen's sudden, stark response astonished them both and her face instantly flushed crimson. Andarta stared at her with saucer eyes, but Ceridwen quickly recovered and briskly added, "Besides, Llyn told us that Donogh wasn't to be for me."

"I don't remember him saying it quite like that, Ceri." Andarta spoke slowly and deliberately. "But what makes you think you'll even be seeing this 'man who can handle you' again?"

"Oh, I'd say the chances were quite good." Ceridwen teasingly held out on the most exciting news.

"Come on, Ceri." Andarta's expression of admonishment easily caved into curiosity. "What aren't you telling me?"

Ceridwen jutted her face toward Andarta and grinned. "His legion's going to be in charge of building a road that's going to pass just west of Iceni lands." She excitedly clasped her hands onto her friend's shoulders, shaking her as she jumped up and down. "He's going to be garrisoned close to us here."

Chapter Eleven: Positioning

Their role in direct conflict finished, the fourteenth legion under the command of Ostorius was assigned to build a road system to provide the client kingdoms with easy access to and from the major trade centers of Camulodunum and Londinium as well as two Roman forts. Marek, anxious to see Ceridwen again, had hoped to be able to take leave and visit Toftrees before the equinox when she was to leave for her continuing studies on Mon, but building a road is not a rapid process. Even though it was his responsibility to lead the surveyors and he was therefore out in front of the legion it was mid winter before they even crossed out of Trinovantes territory and into the Catuvellauni lands where the road would run parallel to the Iceni border. All the same, his body rocked back and forth lightly as he sat on his horse, delighting in the airy snowflakes that had been falling all day as they continued to dust the naked boughs of the surrounding trees. He would most happily wait here until she returned in the spring; a warm thought indeed.

Spending the winter indoors, studying without reminders of the weather, Ceridwen, nevertheless, shared Marek's warm thoughts as she was also looking forward to the spring equinox. Although she had said nothing about it to Andarta prior to arriving at Mon, she had been tormented by how she might react to Donogh, how he would clearly see through her. But on arriving and learning that he would not be attending this year, she was immensely relieved; an attitude that both puzzled and clearly annoyed Andarta.

"Aren't you concerned that Donogh's actively fighting the Romans, Ceri?" she asked, somewhat aghast. "That he's out there on the front line?"

"He's with Caractacus. He'll be safe." Ceridwen smiled back at her friend. "Doesn't it work out wonderfully that now I'll be able to spend time with Marek in the spring and sort things out with him before I have to see Donogh again?"

"Your lifelong friend, the person to whom you're pledged to marry, is delaying his Druid training and out there risking his life," Andarta stood up and very deliberately pointed her finger to the southeast before adding in a loud voice, "and you're telling me how convenient it all is?" She dropped her hand and glared. "Ceridwen, what's come over you?"

Ceridwen pushed out her lips. "You don't really think Donogh's in danger, do you?" she asked meekly.

"Of course he's in danger." Andarta sat next to Ceridwen and clasped her hands firmly. "They say that Caractacus suffers from the berserker and that those around him try to match his daring."

Ceridwen looked up with large eyes. "I'm just not ready to deal with it. I don't know what to say. I don't know if I should say anything." She buried her head in her hands. "I don't even know how Marek feels, if he feels anything at all. And I do care for Donogh, Andarta. You know I do." She looked up and spoke firmly, accusingly. "I'm not callous. I'm just," she stared past her friend into open space, "Just very, very confused right now." She rapidly turned back to Andarta and shouted, "Oh, why do they even have to fight?" She glared, her fists clenched in frustration. "The Romans are good for us. The Ordovices could make a truce just like we did."

"I think we can expect that to be addressed in some detail at the assembly. Word is that Llyn recently arrived from the front with up to date news."

Students and residents of Mon alike eagerly streamed into the main hall at sundown and quickly filled the seats while Devyn, surrounded by the council of the twelve traveling druids, stood motionless at the front. As soon as he moved his right arm to indicate he was about to speak the room fell silent, all eyes trained on his every expression. He first scanned the faces in the room, then slowly nodded and began. "As the future leaders of your respective tribes it's important you acknowledge the big picture perspective regarding recent events. The Romans invaded in force but are only occupying the captured lands of the Catuvellauni and the Trinovantes." He smiled and continued his slow nodding. "Their landing was enabled by the Belagic tribes of the Cantium, where Adminus has been reinstated as king, and the Atrebates. It was well planned and they have achieved their goal of taking the capitol. Had the Britannic tribes joined Caractacus, as many of them were anxious to do, and stand in the way of that goal the Romans would have continued to reinforce their legions and I dare say we'd now be looking at a much larger occupying force and most of your lands being civitas." He turned his left, then right, looking at the Druids around him. "It's a credit to your leaders that they heeded our advice and avoided untold thousands of unnecessary deaths." He turned back to the crowd. "As a result, nine Britannic tribes have since established treaties with the Romans as independent client kingdoms and continue to remain in direct control of their territories," his smile widened into a broad grin, "complete with friendly relations with the Romans." He paused to enjoy the matching smiles emerge on the faces of his audience before continuing. "That marked the completion their first phase. After spending only sixteen days in Camulodunum, Claudius left with his elephants for a triumphal return to Rome leaving Aulus Plautius, the commander of the invasion, as the governor of Britannia. It's up to Plautius to take care of the second phase of their mission, which is to grow and protect trade while securing the borders of what they consider to be their newly acquired province. Roads are already being built in the Catuvellauni lands to provide tribes such as the Iceni with direct links to market towns and since the majority of trade is going to be for the much needed food and sundries for the legionnaires, wherever a fort is established it will be an instant boon to whatever region it's in. You'll see new towns rapidly spring up around them with the local inhabitants more than eager to provide whatever might be wanted by the soldiers. This will serve to further cement the positive relationships between the Britons and the Romans and will, clearly, be to everyone's advantage. They still, however, have yet to secure their western border. Llyn." He nodded to the Druid to his right and stepped back.

His eyes having been thoughtfully focused downward all the time Devyn was speaking, when Llyn finally looked up to address the assembly it was clear to all those in attendance that he was most certainly not smiling. "While your peasants and compatriots are enjoying the benefits of commerce with the Romans, Caractacus and his army of over 2,000 warriors continues an ongoing orgy of death and destruction against them," he began. "Armed with Serencleddyf and still mourning the loss of his brother, he's balanced on the knife edge of berserker and has exacted a terrible toll from the Romans."

A new voice burst out from the audience and all eyes turned to Andarta as she asked the question on everybody's mind, "Do the Druids recognize Caractacus as king of Britannia?"

Immediately, before Llyn could even open his mouth to reply, Devyn interjected a resounding, "Yes, we do."

A murmur rose throughout the hall until Llyn cleared his throat and everyone once again fell silent. He made a quick nod to Devyn then turned back to address the crowd. "Notably absent from the delegations who met with Claudius were the Ordovices who've since made it very clear they not only recognize Caractacus as the legitimate king of Britannia, but actively stand with him in opposition of the Roman invaders. They sent a thousand additional warriors to join Caractacus' Catuvellauni army in the lands of the Dobunni, and the combined forces completely disrupted tin exports from that region. This caused the Roman commander Vespasian to call for the twentieth legion to reinforce his severely depleted second in order to push the defenders back and secure the tin mines. Knowing better than to challenge two legions in open frontal assault, Caractacus has fallen back into the Ordovices lands and with the advantage of their numerous hill forts they now occupy a position to not only stop further Roman advance but perhaps to even drive them back. The Ordovices' rivers and the mountains undisputedly form the western front for the Romans."

Devyn once again stepped forward, placed his right hand on Llyn's left shoulder and stood next to him as he once again spoke to the assembly. "As far as Claudius is concerned the conquest of Britannia is over and he'll soon turn his attention to further expansion of the empire elsewhere. The legions used for this invasion were a significant portion of the Roman army and now that they're here as an occupying force it's unlikely that they'll ever be reinforced. As the legionnaires retire, they'll either settle in here or return to their homelands. This attrition and assimilation works in our favor," he patted Llyn's shoulder, "and an active front will speed up the process of reducing their numbers significantly. The Briton tribes, meantime, will continue to learn and profit from the advances the Romans have brought us. These are things that will be useful to us and make us stronger until," Devyn brandished his clenched fist in front of his chest, "we decide it's time to take back control as a unified Britannia."

As the assembly dispersed Ceridwen made her way to the front, anxious to corner Llyn before he left again. Seeing her pushing through the crowd he motioned for her to go to the far corner and before she could even ask he raised his right hand and said, "Donogh's all right, Ceridwen." For the first time all evening he broke a smile. "In fact, he's doing himself proud under Caractacus' tutelage. He's transforming from bard into a very fine warrior."

"Really?" Ceridwen was intrigued.

"Indeed!" Llyn said proudly. "But he's still Donogh." Llyn leaned forward to make sure he had full eye contact with her. "And as much as you'd like to see him become something else, he'll always be Donogh."

"What are you saying?"

"No matter how skilled a warrior he becomes, he'll never incite your passion to the extent of a certain sub-praefectus I've heard about."

Ceridwen bit at her lower lip as she instantly turned her gaze to her feet, uncomfortably aware of the fact that her face had suddenly become crimson. To make matters worse Andarta walked over to join them and Llyn greeted her with a, "Hello Andarta," followed by, "I actually believe that Ceridwen here thought the exploits of an Iceni princess in an occupied city would go unnoticed by the Druids." His grin stretched almost the width of his face. In spite of her desire not to further embarrass her friend, Andarta joined his mirth and burst into uncontrollable laughter.

"Come," Llyn put his arms around both of the girls' shoulders, "I'll walk with you back to your rooms. I want to have a talk with both of you."

The three walked out into the night. The cloudless sky and three-quarter moon provided ample light for them to follow the trail and as they walked slowly toward the buildings in the distance while Llyn began to share his thoughts. "Of all of the tribes who established client kingdoms with the Romans, I'm most concerned about yours," he said. "Although Anted entered into a pact with the Romans on behalf of, and for the benefit of, all the Iceni, I know for a fact that Saenu," Llyn looked at Andarta, "your occasionally very hot headed father, and Aesu," he nodded at Ceridwen, "your uncle, are both quite vocal about their opposition of what they're calling the invaders and are refusing to trade in Roman coinage. They've even been melting Roman sesterces down and using the gold to stamp their own coinage. Prasutagus has tried to explain the necessity for uniform coinage throughout the country but they insist it's just a ploy to undermine tribal identity. They're skeptical of Prasutagus' efforts to bring wealth to the Iceni and it's beginning to cause a rift between them and Anted."

"We've always felt strongly about the Iceni way of doing things," Andarta explained, understanding Llyn's concern while trying to justify her father's position. "Our uniqueness is ingrained into who we are."

"Yes," Llyn agreed, "your tribe in particular has always keep itself isolated from the rest of the world, which was fine before Rome found out about you and since developed a taste for Iceni clothing and craftwork. Times have changed, Andarta, and the Iceni are being pulled into the wider world, whether they like it or not. I'm afraid there'll be no going back."

"And you want us to take that message back with us," Ceridwen chimed in.

"It would sound better coming from the two of you than as a dictate from a Druid," Llyn smiled at them both. "Don't you agree?"

Andarta's furrowed brow and partly closed eyes belied her concern with what the Druid was telling them. "My father is no longer getting along with Prasutagus?" she asked quietly, her teeth suddenly biting into her lower lip.

Llyn put his arm around her slender shoulders and gave her a quick hug. "Prasutagus is the bright future for the Iceni," he said cheerfully, "and with his shrewdness for trade one day you and he will be the rulers of the wealthiest tribe in all of Britannia."

Andarta looked up with her eyes now wide and smiling. Llyn nodded vigorously. "Change is always difficult and it's just going to take a bit of time before some people realize it's all for the better, that's all."

"Are you saying that we should accept that the Romans will always be here then?" Ceridwen asked.

"Well, they're here for a while." Llyn's head was turned slightly to the left and he rocked back and forth as he spoke.

"But the Druids recognize Caractacus," she added. "Will he drive them out?"

"Caractacus is holding the frontier," Llyn forced a large smile. "He's doing his bit in preventing any further incursions." He rubbed his beard. "It's going to take several years before things unfold enough to bring Britannia together. In the meantime, let's benefit from having the Romans here."

Andarta burst out laughing. "Oh, Ceridwen's definitely doing that," she said while Ceridwen glared at her, face glowing and desperately trying not to laugh also.

"I would like to offer a word of caution in that area, Ceridwen." Llyn said. "Please be careful."

"I shouldn't worry, Llyn." Ceridwen was smug. "I can tell he already likes me a lot and we seem to share a sort of bond. It's hard to describe."

"So you do like him, yes?"

"Hey, you were the one who said that Donogh might not be the right one for me."

"And you feel this man may be more like what you have in mind."

"He could be." Ceridwen beamed and nodded. "We'll find out."

"Indeed we will," Llyn nodded back in agreement, "but let me tell you something you need to take to heart. When a man joins a Roman legion he makes a pledge of allegiance, an oath that binds him for up to twenty years while he remains in service. It's not rote words either; that allegiance is absolute. So much as questioning the order of a superior officer could result in immediate execution and, even worse, disgrace upon his entire family. Roman soldiers have been ordered to kill their own comrades in the past; so be mindful, Ceridwen. No matter how your Roman officer may care for you, he'd kill even you without flinching if he were ordered to. Duty and honor always trumps emotion in the legions."

Before either Ceridwen or Andarta were able to give sound to their objections, Llyn beckoned with his head toward the door in front of them, wished them a "good night girls," then rapidly disappeared into the night. Ceridwen and Andarta scurried indoors.

"Can you believe that?" Ceridwen shouted, throwing her cloak onto the chair as soon as they entered her room. "He tried to make Marek out as some sort of mindless idiot."

Andarta eased onto the edge of the bed. "I think Llyn was trying to have you keep in mind that Marek is a Roman officer."

"But the Iceni have never had a conflict with the Romans. They're our friends and trading partners. What does Llyn mean by him being ordered to kill me? That's really overreaching his point." She flopped onto the bed next to her friend and looked up. "Absolutely ridiculous," she shouted at the ceiling.

"He bothered me too," Andarta said. "I'm troubled about how he spoke of my father."

Ceridwen sat up and put her hand on Andarta's shoulder. "Don't worry about that. We're bound to have a council meeting when I return and I'm sure these disagreements will be brought up and taken care of. We can always trust Anted to act in the best interests of the Iceni as a whole.

Chapter Twelve: Insurrection

"Legate Ostorius, welcome." Plautius extended his right arm as the fourteenth legion's commander entered the occupied palace in Camulodunum. "I understand your road building is ahead of schedule."

"The weather has been favorable for us, Plautius. The winter here isn't as harsh as we were led to believe."

"Ah, you like Britannia, then?" Plautius poured two large goblets of wine and handed one to Ostorius.

"Indeed, I do." He took the goblet but didn't drink, holding it a few inches below his chin while is eyes remain affixed on the governor.

"I'm pleased to hear that." Plautius said. "Since you're about to become much more intimately acquainted with it. You're being promoted to governor. Congratulations." He tilted his wine in salute then quaffed half of it back.

"Governor?" Ostorius sputtered.

"Governor!" Plautius deliberately placed his goblet on the table. "Now that the borders here are secure, I've been recalled to Rome. It's good politics for Claudius to have me active in the senate again." He poured more wine. "He's pulling in as much support around himself as he can and there's talk of a new campaign."

"So soon?" Ostorius' eyebrows furrowed into his brow. "More glory ahead, eh?" His forehead relaxed and he drank heartily from his goblet. "Here's hoping your next conquest will be as exemplary as this one was."

"I can only hope for commanders as able as you and Vespasian."

"How is Vespasian? What's the word from him?"

"Since he called for the twentieth legion to be combined with the second, he's secured the tin trade again and there are now only border skirmishes with the Ordovices. It's pretty much a stalemate over there." Plautius became expressionless. "And I suggest you leave it at that, Ostorius." He froze until Ostorius moved the empty goblet away from his lips. This advice would certainly run contrary to the incoming governor's ambition. "Don't get any fool ideas to push further west. The risks are too great." He held up the amphora. "More?"

"Please." Ostorius' response was quiet. He held out the empty goblet.

"Besides, as governor your role will be primarily to promote the peace. Although," Plautius cocked his head to one side, "there is one matter that might need your attention in the near future. We're hearing rumblings about dissent amongst the Iceni. Here," Plautius tossed two gold coins onto the table. "Have a look at these."

Ostorius picked them up and examined them. "What interesting designs? This one represents a horse and, what's this one, a boar?"

"They're both recently minted by the Iceni."

Ostorius dropped the coins individually into Plautius' outstretched hand. "I thought king Anted accepted the client king treaty?"

"Which forbids the production of coinage," Plautius was nodding as he responded, "he did." He held the coins up in a clenched fist. "These were made by two Iceni sub-kings named Aesu and Saenu. We've been treating the Iceni as a civilized race governed by a single king but they act like a damned republic. If any of the tribes are going to give you trouble it's going to be them."

"But aren't they getting the lion's share of trade?" Ostorius drained his goblet and plopped it on the table. "I hear that everything Iceni is all the rage in Rome."

"Why, Ostorius." Plautius laughed as he poured more wine. "I had no idea you kept up on fashion." He picked up his drink. "But you're right. Anted's son, Prasutagus, has set up an office in Londinium and through his efforts the Iceni are coming into a great deal of wealth in exchange for their goods. The heir to their throne is definitely on board with us."

"Sounds like an ideal situation."

"It will be down the road." Plautius guzzled his wine and poured more. "But Prasutagus isn't king yet."

As soon as the news reached Saenu that there was to be a new Roman governor in Camulodunum, he assembled ten of his closest warriors and rode hard for Venta Icenorum. Immediately upon his arrival in the Iceni capitol he burst into the palace and called for Anted. "We now have a chance to correct things," he shouted as the king appeared, rapidly continuing while still in the hallway with, "Well, what do you think? Are you with me, Anted?"

"This is a discussion for the council, Saenu," Anted said sternly. "We should also only be speaking of this behind closed doors."

"I don't care who hears me," Saenu bellowed. "Since you established the treaty with the Romans, you're the only one that's had any standing with them. Now there's a new governor we can explain things to him and set that right." He stepped closer to Anted, their faces only inches apart and glared into his eyes. "That is, unless you disagree with me." His right hand slid across his torso and rested on the hilt of his sword. "From the way you've been acting these past few months I'm suspecting that you might be taking a liking to being the only recognized king."

Anted remained motionless and spoke without breaking eye contact. "How can you say that?" he replied with a growl, the intensity of his voice greater that what Saenu's had been. "My negotiations with Claudius and Plautius resulted in peace between us and the Romans. If it had been you there, we'd probably both be dead now and Iceni lands occupied territory." He softened his voice. "Besides, how was I to know they were only going to pay lip service to the roles of you and Aesu? I agree it is unfortunate that they only recognize me as king but considering how things might have turned out, how bad is that?"

"It could be better, but you don't seem to have felt it necessary to go back to them and explain how things really are here." Saenu moved his hands to his hips. His breathing was loud.

"Come." Anted coaxed Saenu into the war room where only their guards and warriors were allowed in. The door slammed shut leaving the hallway full of palace staff and others who, drawn to the shouting, instantly fell into a roar of chatter before dispersing within minutes to spread the word about the dissent.

"Look around the land," Anted said as soon as the door was closed. "Look how our people are benefiting from that treaty I negotiated for us. Plus, with Caractacus still out there the Romans are going to be extremely sensitive. The timing just hasn't been right to suggest any modification of the agreement."

Saenu grinned. "Until now," he said, sliding his hand across the edge of the table. "Look, we really don't need all this trade, Anted. Let's cut it back; in fact, we could even cut it out. We Iceni have always kept ourselves to ourselves and it's worked for hundreds of years."

"I'm afraid isolationism isn't a luxury we have any more in the modern world," Anted pulled on his beard while he responded, "but I will agree with you that we might have got into things a bit too fast. Since Prasutagus secured that cash flow he has been like a whirlwind."

"How about if you and I and Aesu pull our warriors together and go meet with this new governor. We can explain to him the Iceni don't have a single king but govern from a council. We can tell him we don't need all their Roman money and that our people are fine without all those fancy imports." He jumped to his feet and put his hands on Anted's shoulders. "Let's do it now, Anted," he pleaded. "Let's do it before the Iceni people lose their sense of who they are."

The men stared into each other eyes for a long thirty seconds before Anted broke the silence with, "Of course you're right." He slapped his right hand on Saenu's shoulder and nodded briskly. "But as you so aptly point out Saenu, the Iceni operate by the decision of council. I'll call a meeting as soon as possible and ensure that we're all in agreement on this before we act. Ceridwen can be here from Mon within a week, and I think my son should be here also. Agreed?"

"Agreed," Saenu slowly moved his right index finger up and down in front of Anted's face, "but only for the sake of form. The council meeting's entirely moot."

"Oh? So you're confident that Ceridwen will side with you, then?"

"I was confident that you would." Saenu snatched his hand back and laughed at Anted's bewildered expression. "But, just in case you'd become too Romanized, my son Blyth has 200 loyal warriors quite close by and ready to march, along with forty charioteers. Plus, Aesu has assembled an additional 300 of his own and is probably less than a day away from here."

"So the two of you planned to overthrow me by force?" Anted's chin trembled.

"Only if it were necessary, Anted. Only if you'd chosen not to act in the best interests of our people." Saenu's toothy grin shone through his beard. "If you'd done that, I'd have had no choice, would I? I'm not one to ignore the moral obligations in the governance of the Iceni." He slowly bobbed his head, his teeth still showing, then briskly added, "But I much prefer you as the true king I've always supported. Now all our warriors can accompany us to Camulodunum in a display of might. Just in case this new Roman governor needs a little encouragement in seeing how things really are with the Iceni."

Anted turned to give his orders for riders to immediately leave for Londinium and Mon then, as the room cleared, he looked back at Saenu and burst into hearty laughter. "Come on, you crazy old boar," he said. "Let's eat."

The Roman spy who also witnessed the interaction in the palace hallway was in Camulodunum within a day and only hours later Ostorius and his guards left at full gallop, heading north for the camp of the fourteenth legion.

"The legion's spread out over a hundred miles of partially built road," Marek explained to a clearly frustrated Ostorius who had just rushed into camp. "It will take the best part of a fortnight to pull them back and organize them."

"We don't have time for that." Ostorius slammed his fist onto the table, "We need to act, and we need to do it now. The Iceni are about to either overthrow their king or move in force on Camulodunum, or possibly both. We know for certain that the two sub kings' armies are gathering outside Venta Icenorum, so whatever is going to happen is going to happen very soon. With an active western front and potential sympathy for Caractacus amongst the tribes we can't be seen as tolerating any form of armed outbreak anywhere inside Britannia. I don't care if it's an insurrection or outright civil war; we have to deal with it now." He shook his head then looked up at Marek. "What do we have here in camp?"

"Most of the cavalry's here, along with a couple of hundred legionnaires."

Ostorius' eyebrows rose. "The full cavalry, eh."

"Thirty turmae," Marek responded without expression.

"Hmm. Nine hundred men and horses?" A huge smile appeared on his nodding face. "Well Marek, you've always tried to convince me that cavalry should be used in an assault."

"Do you really mean to march on the Iceni without infantry?" Marek repeatedly smoothed his right hand over his chin.

"I mean to display Roman might to them and get them to stand down. We can then deal with whatever it is that's bothering them." He looked squarely at Marek. "Not to worry, I'm sure we can work out a diplomatic solution. After all, I'm governor now." He chuckled. "Spread the peace, you know." He looked at the amphora sitting on the corner table. "Pour some wine for us, lad."

Marek stared at his hands in silence as he filled the two goblets and didn't look up as he handed one to Ostorius, but found his voice after the first sip of wine. "The Iceni will certainly respect cavalry," he said. "The horse is central to their culture."

"Then tomorrow they're going to be really impressed. At first light we'll take the entire cavalry north and hold at the Iceni border." He took a large draught of wine, slammed the depleted goblet on the table and wiped his mouth with the back of his right hand. "That'll send those dissidents the right message, eh?"

"Indeed, it will." Marek said quietly, saluting Ostorius with the wine. Slowly drinking it back he realized how grateful he was of the timing, that it was not yet the vernal equinox.

"What?" Anted shouted as he was awoken the next morning with the news of almost a thousand Romans advancing from the south on horseback. "Bring Saenu and Aesu here. Now!"

He needn't have bothered with that order. Having received the same information independently they were already furiously on their way to the palace and within minutes the three were assembled around the table in the war room. "Peace with the Romans, eh Anted?" Saenu was standing and pointing south as he shouted. "It looks like that now Caractacus has dug in and they can't go any further west they're pushing north and they mean to take our lands."

"We don't know that, Saenu," Anted rose, his fists resting on the table top. "We have no idea what their intent is." He leaned onto his trembling forearms.

"It's pretty obvious it's not for a friendly visit, Anted," Aesu calmly broke into the discussion. "It looks like the new governor is wasting no time in expanding Roman territories."

"I don't think so," Anted said sternly, watching Saenu as he continued to respond with carefully selected words. "You were eager to visit him with a contingent of warriors, a display of might as you put it. Perhaps he's simply providing us the same courtesy."

Saenu's eyes widened and his teeth again appeared through his beard. He took a step toward Anted. "It seems to me to be a bit too coincidental that he might be doing that just now," he snarled, making direct eye contact. "Where did your messenger really go, Anted?"

"How dare you." Anted bellowed, his right fist instinctively reaching across his chest.

"Oh, I do dare," Saenu interrupted him. "You agreed with what I said to simply placate me and give you time to call for Roman aid. As the king they recognize they'd feel obligated to assist you in putting down a civil insurrection." He quickly reached for his sword as Anted did the same while Aesu backed out of their way. "You sold out your people, Anted," Saenu screamed as he raised his weapon and attacked.

Anted raised his sword to block the swing and sparks flew as the blades crashed into each other. "This is madness, Saenu," Anted pleaded. "Send riders to the Romans to find out their real intent."

"And to buy you more time as they get closer?" Saenu swung again but Anted quickly dodged to the side, avoiding it. The tip of the sword gouged into the floor next to him.

"Then what can I do to convince you they're not coming at my behest?" Anted took several steps back.

"A true Iceni king would send out warriors and annihilate any invaders at the border." Saenu replied, both hands gripping his sword, resting it on his right shoulder. "That is, if they truly were uninvited invaders," he stood sideways, adding mockingly, "Oh king."

Anted stood with the tip of his sword resting on the floor between his feet, his eyes unflinching as they glared at Saenu. "You propose to directly attack the Romans, eh?" He made a mocking chuckling sound. "They'd make mince out of us."

"Who says?" Saenu snapped back. "I've never known you to be a coward, Anted." He began to raise his sword off his shoulder. "And that answer confirms you as a traitor to your people." Anted instantly picked up his sword and lunged. "Aesu will bear witness to my sword proving you wrong," he roared. "You've gone too far this time Saenu."

Saenu kicked a table over to clear the way as he avoided Anted's attack. They were yelling loudly, their blades sparking each time their swords met, while Aesu, his back against the locked door, watched. He watched Anted hold his sword high above his head ready to swing down on Saenu but, instead of backing off or blocking, Saenu charged forward driving his sword ahead of him until the tip protruded through Anted's back. Anted's weapon slid from his hands and clanged on the floor as he first looked down, then up again. His mouth opened as he stared at Saenu but no words, only blood sputtered out before he collapsed. Saenu pushed the body over with his foot then kept it there for leverage as he withdrew his sword. "Proof, eh, Anted," he panted gripping his sword in his vibrating fist. "I give you proof by the sword that you betrayed your people." He then looked over at Aesu. "We need to organize our warriors fast and hit the Romans before they can cross our border. They won't be expecting to engage us until they reach Venta Icenorum."

"This Roman leader is shrewd," Aesu replied. "He's using horses for speed rather than regular foot soldiers. Clearly, he was planning to take us by surprise."

"Indeed." Saenu wiped the blood from his sword as he spoke. "But from what we know of the Romans they rely heavily on their infantry. Without their main strength we should be able to turn things on them with a decisive, unexpected blow."

Ostorius squinted in the midday sunlight and pointed to a series of forested hills rising in front of them. "Those hills mark the Trinovantes/Iceni border," he told Marek, on horseback next to him, as he slowed his mount to an easy walk, "and not one outrider from Anted."

"I don't see any movement ahead at all." Marek held his right hand to shield his eyes while he surveyed the tree line. "Odd. I'm certain by now they know we're here."

"Right you are." Ostorius nodded in agreement. "It makes we wonder if we shouldn't have waited and brought infantry after all."

"As you said, there wasn't time." Marek looked resolutely at him. "The cavalry's well trained, though. If it comes down to it."

"I have the feeling it just might." Ostorius stared into the distance trying to scan the horizon. "Since it looks like we have open meadow for the next few miles at least, let's proceed with a grand showing. Have the troopers form into five formations side-by-side." He stroked his chin, turning to eyes the countryside on either side of them. "And make sure to keep them well clear of those trees."

Marek raised his right arm to stop the advance then fell back to the column as the decurions rode up and assembled around him. "Five formations of six turmae side-by-side," he told them. "Your men are all well trained and experienced but keep in mind this one could be very different; no Roman army has ever engaged the Iceni. If we do end up in a fight, they'll probably come at us fast on horseback. Order your men to charge right at them with swords drawn and hit them before they can dismount. Iceni swords are heavy, which makes them not very maneuverable while the warriors are mounted, but once on the ground they'll be formidable." He smiled reassuringly. "Then again, the Iceni have never encountered Roman cavalry either. Dismissed."

Marek watched his decurions as they rapidly and efficiently arranged the troopers into the designated formation. Once ready, he raised his right hand and with a slashing motion brought it down in the direction of the hills, called out, "slow walk," then clicked his tongue and trotted his horse to join Ostorius again in front. They proceeded quietly for half a mile when something appeared in the distance ahead. At first all they could make out were just flashes, sunlight reflecting off something moving. Suddenly, a black cloud of arrows arose from the flashes. Marek immediately shouted, "Forward fast," and kicked the sides of his horse into a gallop. The closest troopers were at once behind him and Ostorius while the extreme right and left turmae galloped even faster to create an advancing, curved formation. It was only an additional ten lengths before the descending arrows flew only feet overhead and landed behind them. Directly ahead at least fifty chariots were bearing down on them, archers at the ready standing in the wicker cockpits behind the drivers. Ostorius drew his sword and held it aloft to signal the troops to prepare for battle but as they galloped closer a voice from one of the horses next to Marek yelled out in astonishment, "They're women."

"And they mean to kill you, Felix," Marek shouted an immediate reply. "So you'd better hit them first." Then as loud as he could he called out, "Attack."

In spite of the thundering of 900 horses at full gallop Marek, once again, felt the familiar sense of freedom and solitude that came to him in these situations, as if he were about to engage his adversary completely alone rather than at the head of the fourteenth's cavalry.

Oblivious to the arrow bouncing off his breastplate, he raised his sword above his right shoulder and closed on the lead chariot, intoxicated by feelings of his own invincibility. Mentally prepared for women warriors he still he had to consciously override an involuntary twinge of apprehension as he swung his sword at the blonde, long haired driver. His Roman sword was too short, she sidestepped the tip, and in the split-second decision that followed he elected to use it to wrench the bow out of the archer's hands rather than take off her head as she was aiming her next arrow at his neck. The innocence of this young archer's face, perhaps not even ten years old, adorned with a smear of woad on each delicate smooth cheek would live forever in his head. She should have been at play. She should have been anywhere but here on a battleground. He instantly imagined a young Ceridwen riding a chariot into battle; did she acquire her taste to be a warrior even then? Did she kill at that delicate age?

He snapped himself out of his thoughts and pulled his horse up to turn in pursuit of the chariot but overcompensated for his speed causing it to suddenly stop and rear up on its hind legs. As he looked behind, he realized his troops were scattered and that the chariots were deliberately leading them in multiple directions. He quickly turned back to witness the hundreds of mounted Iceni warriors forming in a row stretching completely across the meadow and moving toward the battle. "Forget the chariots," Marek shouted furiously. "Charge the riders. Charge!"

Completely out of formation but heeding his command the cavalry galloped, swords at the ready, against the Iceni. Many of the Britons were carrying spears but without having time to dismount before the cavalry reached them threw them ineffectively while still mounted. The Romans rapidly broke through their line, dispatching many of them in the confusion while they either attempted to get away or dismount to draw their large iron swords. Those that did make it safely to the ground held their swords in both hands and began to rush at the cavalrymen in a strategy to knock them from their horses and engage them on foot. "Good," Marek said to himself as he heard his decurions calling out for their men to regroup and fall in behind them, making ready to attack again as they had done so many times in drills. That sense of order would keep the trooper's confidence high. As for himself, he continued through the middle of the battle alone until he saw a warrior staring at him, standing in the challenging pose of holding his sword high up over his right shoulder. Marek kicked the slats of his horse and held his gladius at the level of the warrior's neck as he thundered toward him, then quickly pulled it away as the enemy roared and swung his huge sword down, causing him to dash it onto the ground. Before the warrior was able to raise it again Marek had turned his mount and, as the warrior turned to see where he had gone, Marek brought his gladius down on the left nape of his neck followed by a quick second chop to the right side of his neck before the man's head lurched unnaturally back and his body collapsed.

Gasping, Marek turned completely around. The remaining Iceni were scattering, several of them being chased down by well-heeled turmae, the remainder already disappearing into the distance. He saw Ostorius off his horse and fighting in close quarters with a tall Iceni woman but, before Marek could arrive to assist him, Ostorius had thrust his sword up through her solar plexus. She spewed blood over his breastplate while crumpling to the ground before him. Ostoruis withdrew his sword and looked up at Marek. "The day is yours, my boy," he said proudly. "Excellent work!"

Marek stared at his superior officer, his panting mouth partially open and his head cocked to one side.

"Haven't you noticed the enemy leaving the field?" Ostorius asked. "It's over. You just killed their leader."

Three hours later the cavalry reassembled and Ostorius lead them in formation across the border into Iceni territory to march on Venta Icenorum. Both Saenu and Aesu had been killed in the battle; the Iceni were now without an identified king and potentially subjects of the Romans. The future of their kingdom now depended on Ostorius' first decision as the new Roman governor of Britannia.

Chapter Thirteen: Home

The messenger that Anted sent to Londinium had a considerably shorter ride than the one sent to Mon, resulting in Prasutagus' hurried arrival in Venta Icenorum only hours behind Ostorius and more than a day before Ceridwen had even received the summons. With potential conflict implicit in the urgency of Anted's message, Devyn instructed Llyn to also make haste to the Iceni capitol and Andarta, now even more concerned about her father, insisted on accompanying them. They rode hard and were exhausted by the time they rushed up the steps into the Iceni capitol building, the presence of Romans throughout the city adding confusion to their anxiousness.

Inside the palace they were met by Prasutagus who rushed up to them, threw his arms around Andarta and pulled her close, keeping her next to him in a tight hug. "Your father and Blyth are dead," he told her, his hold restraining her while the side of his face pushed on the top of her head. "They were killed doing battle against the Romans."

"No!" Andarta screamed, desperately trying to push him away while her fists flailed against his chest. Ignoring her pummeling he held tightly onto her shoulders and, when she looked up, gazed compassionately into her tear drenched face. His eyes confirming that he spoke the truth, Andarta's strength failed and she collapsed back onto him, sobbing into his arms. Prasutagus looked up at

Ceridwen and Llyn, his right hand on the back of Andarta's head holding her against his left shoulder. "Anted and Aesu are also dead, along with over 300 of our warriors."

"Fighting the Romans?" Ceridwen was aghast.

"Tell what has happened?" Llyn's booming voice demanded.

"The details aren't entirely clear; there are several conflicting reports. Apparently, the ongoing disagreements between Saenu and my father had escalated into such open hostility that the Iceni were on the verge of civil war. When the Romans heard about it they sent a detachment of cavalry to try to defuse the situation, but," Prasutagus took a deep breath, partially closing his eyes and looked up at the ceiling while exhaling before he continued. "Their approach was interpreted as an invasion and our warriors attacked them at the border."

"And were summarily defeated," Llyn added harshly, his hands resting on his hips.

Prasutagus nodded slowly. "Exactly."

"There are Roman soldiers in the city." Llyn pointed toward the door while glaring at Prasutagus. "Have Iceni lands been declared occupied territory?"

"Absolutely not," said a loud voice and all eyes instantly looked up at the Roman officer emerging through a doorway from a side room. Prasutagus motioned with his head. "I'd like you all to meet Ostorius, commander of the Romans you see around you and also the new provincial governor of Britannia." He removed his right hand from Andarta but kept his left tightly around her as she turned to look. "Ostorius," he said, "may I introduce princess Andarta." He then motioned with his free hand, "And this is princess Ceridwen and our trusted advisor, Llyn."

Ostorius stepped closer to them, his open palms low on each side of him as he moved. "We deeply regret the misunderstanding, which has resulted in tragedy here," he said. "Let me assure you that

Rome has no design on Iceni lands. Rather, we seek to maintain and expand upon the relationships put in place by the efforts of Prasutagus." He stood next to Prasutagus and placed his right hand on his shoulder, "The man we now recognize as your king." He turned to him and smiled proudly. "A favored client king of Rome." Andarta's eyes instantly shot up to Prasutagus' face.

"So I'm to take it you have no plans to leave any forces here then?" Llyn asked.

"Certainly not," Ostorius quickly responded. "We're simply here at the moment as guests and in hopes of further securing the peace."

"Come," Prasutagus pointed to the dining hall. "Let's sit down and talk comfortably."

Bread, wine, fruit and cheese were immediately brought in as the five of them settled around the table. Llyn smiled skeptically at Ostorius then turned to Prasutagus. "Is there still the treat of civil war between the remaining factions?" he asked.

"No one wants that. The real friction was between Andarta's father and mine," he turned to Andarta and continued to look at her as he spoke. "So it now falls to us to mend that rift." He took her left hand in his right and barely able to contain a broad grin burst out with, "Marry me."

Andarta gasped, simultaneously shocked and thrilled, managed to sputter out a gushing "yes" without closing her smiling mouth before leaning over to him, her arms around his neck. "Oh yes, yes, yes," she repeated.

Llyn rocked back and forth in his chair while Ostorius reached for the wine and filled the goblets. "A toast," he called out, picking one of them up and raising it. Everyone eagerly followed suit. "To the king of the Iceni and his soon to be queen. We wish long life and prosperity to you both."

Llyn and Ceridwen instantly repeated, "Long life and prosperity," and all drank heartily. Clearly, with the two major subtribes joined in marriage and the demand for Iceni goods promising continued wealth for all there would be no more cause for dispute. The new Iceni king would embrace the influx of things Roman, but balance would undoubtedly be ensured with a queen who harbored deep roots to tradition and the old ways.

Conversation between Llyn and Ostorius, who each seemed eager to learn more about the other, dominated the remainder of the mealtime. Prasutagus and Andarta focused their attention on each other while Ceridwen sat thoughtfully until the nagging question in her head caused her to blurt out, "Which cavalry?"

"What?" Ostorius asked with his left hand at his ear.

"Which legion are your cavalry from?" Ceridwen replied, a bit impatiently.

"The fourteenth," Ostorius answered and then turned back to his conversation with Llyn.

Ceridwen bit her lower lip. "*He's here*," she said to herself. "*Marek's here*." She took a deep breath and tried hard to concentrate on the rest of the conversation going on around her when a sudden thought caused an involuntary shudder. "*Did he survive the battle? He could be dead?*" Her heart beat faster and faster while she listened through the ongoing dialogue, impatiently waiting for the meeting to be concluded. *What more could there possibly be to discuss? Everything's fine now.*

As soon as Prasutagus announced that they would reconvene the council in three days Ceridwen hurried outside but, standing at the bottom of the palace steps, it occurred to her she had no idea how to go about searching for Marek. Would he be looking for a drink in the main shopping area of town? Maybe she'd begin there. Had the cavalry set up a temporary barracks somewhere? She was so simultaneously energized and immobilized by her confused thoughts that a friendly, "Hello Ceridwen," caused her to almost scream as she jumped. A huge, open mouthed smile of happiness and relief took over her face when she turned to see Marek standing next to her, his arms reaching for her. She rushed to him and gripped his neck, holding onto him tightly as he effortlessly lifted her from the ground and provided the much-needed reciprocating hug. The sides of their cheeks brushed together as each pulled their head back, presumably to speak, but their mouths communicated directly, unnecessary words remaining unspoken in the fury of engaged lips. They finally, slowly pulled apart and gazed into each other.

"I'm leaving soon for Toftrees," Ceridwen whispered. "Come with me. I want you to see my home."

"Well, I do have a few days leave coming." Marek teasingly tried to answer in a matter-of-fact manner but his uncontrollable smile betrayed his delight. He pulled her to his side, his right arm snug around her shoulders. "Do you have things here to take care of first?" he asked.

"I just need to pick up Kelpie." Ceridwen partially closed her eyes as she nuzzled her head into the nape of his neck. They slowly walked together along the pathway behind the palace, stopping in front of the palace stables. Marek kissed the top of her head and said, "I'll meet you in front of the palace in two hours," then quickly disappeared while she dreamily floated inside to retrieve her horse.

"There you are," said a voice from the shadows. "I thought maybe you'd forgotten to say goodbye before you left."

Ceridwen turned quickly to face her friend who had just followed her inside. "Of course not Andarta," she leaned back slightly and raised her eyebrows. "I, umm, just had a couple of things to take care of first."

Andarta was grinning. "Yes, I noticed."

"So you'll be queen soon." Ceridwen deftly changed the subject. "Have you set the date?"

"Not yet. Prasutagus and I haven't even had a minute alone since you and I arrived here." Andarta was beaming. "But I'm so excited,

Ceri. I never expected it to happen so soon, so suddenly." She looked down. "I know I should be mourning for my father and Blyth." Her voice flattened and she stared at the ground, "But they did die honorably," she looked up rapidly, almost panicked, "Didn't they?" Her eyes began to well.

Ceridwen wrapped her arms around Andarta and pulled her close, gently patting her back as she tried to muffle her sobs. "It's all right Andarta," Ceridwen cooed softly. "They died warrior's deaths, defending Iceni land. They died well. You can be proud."

They walked together to a small bench where they sat in silence, Ceridwen comforting her friend until Andarta's crying abated and she was able to sit upright. She pushed her mussed red hair behind her ears, away from her swollen eyes, and forced a smile. "I'd better go and find Prasutagus," she said. They stood up and Ceridwen headed toward Kelpie's stall while Andarta made for the door. "See you in a couple of days," she called out.

"See you then." Ceridwen toyed with the edges of her eyes as she turned back. "Did I tell you Marek's coming to Toftrees with me?" She grinned, enjoying Andarta's stunned expression.

"No, you did not." Andarta stormed back to the stalls. "Are you serious?"

Ceridwen nodded briskly. "Absolutely!"

"How long," Andarta began but was interrupted by Prasutagus calling her.

"I'll tell you all about it when I return," Ceridwen promised.

"Oh, you'd better." Andarta scurried toward the door, eager to be with her fiancée.

Ceridwen, laughing and shaking her head as she walked, continued to where Kelpie, freshly fed and groomed, waited for her in the stalls reserved for aristocrats' horses. She carefully loaded his back up with blanket and bundle for the trip home then lifted Glynu down from its hanger on the sword wall. Instead of strapping the belt around her horse's neck, though, she sat down with the scabbard resting across her lap. She wrapped her right hand around the hilt and drew the blade out an inch, then quickly re-sheathed the exposed iron. "The Iceni fought against Romans, Kelpie," she said quietly, then looked up at him. "And they were routed." She stood up and attached the sword to him. "Let's hope there's no more of that, eh?" She nuzzled against his head and whispered in his velvet ear, "After all we're friends with the Romans," then giggled. "In fact, we're very, very good friends."

Finally loaded for the ride she led Kelpie to the courtyard in front of the palace to wait for Marek. But, before she even made it to a bench to sit, he came cantering up and pulled to an impressive, almost instant stop only a few feet away from her. She stared, temporarily speechless, having never seen the splendor of a ranking Roman officer's battle armor before. Marek immediately dismounted, wrapped his left arm around her shoulders, pulled her to his breastplate and forced a kiss to her still stunned lips. He slowly drew his head back, still holding her tightly, and simply said, "Hello."

Ceridwen, still stunned, smiled back through her quizzical expression causing Marek to burst into loud laughter. "Since we have no local camp I have to carry my things around with me," he explained. "And without a cart the only way to carry armor is to wear it. That is," he reached up to the pack on the back of his horse and produced his helmet, "except for this." He brushed his hand over the bright red crest, grinned, and plopped it on Ceridwen's head. "As you can see, it's not particularly comfortable but it does its job when needed."

Ceridwen lifted the helmet back off her head and handed it back to him. "I'm so glad you have it then," she said. "I don't want anything happening to you." She suddenly looked down and blushed having not intended for such thoughts to become words. Why was she always doing that around him? Marek hooked his right index finger underneath her chin and eased her face up with a sincere, "don't worry."

"Ready to ride?" she asked, not moving her head from the embrace of his crooked finger.

They quickly mounted their horses and within minutes were free of the city and heading at a canter for Ceridwen's estate, arriving as the late winter sun just started to disappear behind the naked trees. Several peasants rushed to them to care for the horses and to welcome their mistress home, as well as to gawk at the curious stranger she had brought with her. She was gracious to her people but rapidly maneuvered Marek past them and into the main house. "Thank you Garth," she said holding the door as peasant hurriedly left after making up the fire. She leaned with her back against the door as soon as it closed and, with an open-mouthed smile to Marek, announced, "You can put your armor anywhere you like."

Not taking his eyes from her, Marek unbuckled his belt and allowed his sword to drop to the ground. He took a step toward her and without breaking his eye lock loosened his breastplate, tossing it to one side while he continued to slowly cross the room, kicking off his caliga just prior to reaching her. Breathing heavily with her hands at her sides, Ceridwen gripped at the timbers in the door. Marek reached out with his right hand, brushed the hair from Ceridwen's face and in a continuous motion, his fingers firmly entwined in her hair, held her head still and forced his lips down on hers. His free hand slid around Ceridwen's waist, simultaneously pushing her hips against him while his fingers walked her dress up to where he was soon able to squeeze her exposed buttocks. His lips and tongue similarly ravaged her mouth. She released her grip on the door and slid her arms across Marek's shoulders, pulling herself closer to him. He released her hair, giving her the freedom to more hungrily participate in their ongoing kiss while his right hand worked its way down her back. After grinding her against him with both hands on her buttocks, Marek then slid his hands up to her waist, up her back, pressing her against him at all times. He then, finally, eased back from the kiss. Ceridwen, panting, raised her arms as Marek's hands continued to slide upward and her dress flew away from her fingertips to somewhere over their heads, somewhere behind him. He scooped her naked body up into his arms as easily as if she were a child, turned, and carried her off to the adjacent room where an oversized bed had been immediately obvious to him when he first entered the house. He gently tossed her onto the soft coverings, and she giggled as she bounced, then immediately rolled over to watch Marek toss his tunic onto the floor. He climbed onto the bed next to her and she instantly slid on top of him, straddling his chest. She leaned forward with all of her weight pressing down with her hands around his wrists on each side of his head in an attempt to pin him down. Marek stared at her aroused breasts and ran his tongue across his top lip. "Think you've got me?" he asked playfully.

"Yes, I have you now," Ceridwen nodded hard.

"I'm so glad," he said, then in a single motion arched his back and quickly flipped her onto her back next to him. Before she could even respond he was on top of her. She gasped and closed her eyes in response to his mouth on the side of her neck while his hips worked their way between her thighs. She grabbed at his back as he penetrated her, holding tighter with each successive thrust to the point that her fingernails gouged into his back. Rapid breathing becoming laborious, her head suddenly lurched back and she screamed, her fingernails drawing blood while Marek bit the top of her shoulder as their bodies shuddered in simultaneous ecstasy.

After an hour in each other's grips, exhausted, they sprawled out on the bed and remained motionless until they were slowly wakened by the brightness of the morning sun. Ceridwen stirred first but kept perfectly sill, not wanting to disturb Marek, delighting in just being next to him and watching him sleep. She first thought about

Llyn's earlier warning of how Roman soldiers were so disciplined that they would kill anyone on command but, surely, she reasoned, this Egyptian Roman soldier must be the exception. How could this man who gives so deeply into his own passions ever follow a command that went against them. She smiled, dismissing the Druid's warning as not applicable in this case and choosing instead to think of the more recent discussion he had with her and Andarta. Llyn had explained how the Roman forces were stretched thin and without reinforcements they stood to become assimilated over time. At some future point Britannia would be able to take back self-rule with the remaining invaders successfully incorporated into the various tribes. She looked affectionately at Marek and whispered, "But I plan to assimilate you much sooner than that," then leaned over and lightly kissed his forehead. "Everything you ever wanted can he found right here, Marek."

Chapter Fourteen: Repositioning

"What was the ruin of Sparta and Athens?' Claudius posited. The senators listened intently as the emperor personally took the role of censor at the lustrum. "As mighty as they were in matters of war," he enunciated slowly, "it was that they spurned those whom they conquered." He scanned his audience, absolutely delighted to see how many of them were nodding thoughtfully. "Our founder, Romulus, was so wise that he fought as enemies then hailed as fellow citizens several nations on the same day. From its earliest foundations Rome has been made up of strangers. That non-Roman born men should be entrusted with public office is not, as many wrongly think, a sudden innovation, but was a common practice in the old republic and Rome benefited greatly from it. Everything, senators, which we now hold to be of the highest antiquity was once new and the practice of permitting free men from the provinces to sit amongst us as senators and lawmakers will establish itself this day as a day of precedent."

Claudius remained silent, watching the senate vote in the decree that the Aeduni, a tribe from Gaul, were to be the first to obtain the right to become senators of Rome. The senators cheered the positive outcome, but Claudius just smiled to himself and thought, *take that, Seneca*, as the final piece of the plan he began years ago fell into place. Certainly, there were still many in the senate who, like Seneca, wanted to keep Rome run by "pure" Romans, but they had fallen to the minority since his banishment. The consul Vipstanus excitedly moved that Claudius should be henceforth called "Father of the Senate" but Claudius intervened, calling the consul's flattery as extravagant. He closed the lustrum and eagerly departed Rome for what he felt was a well-earned respite at the port city of Ostia. A place to spend bliss filled hours with Calpurnia, his favorite mistress.

For three days Claudius relaxed and basked in his victory but on the fourth day of his vacation he was notified that his mistress had arrived unbidden and was anxiously seeking an audience with him. Curious by the breach of protocol, Claudius immediately assented and Calpurnia was permitted entry. The instant she came in she threw herself at the emperor's feet and, crying for forgiveness at bringing him such news, told him that his wife Messalina had, in his many absences from Rome, been having an affair with consul-elect Silius and had just married him. "Why are you telling me this?" Claudius' face cocked to the left and he grabbed her by the hair, turning her face towards him.

"I know it is not my place to do so, but I felt it important that you knew so I told Narcissus." All she could see was Claudius' increasing reddening neck. "He ordered me to come and tell you directly."

Claudius tossed her to his left, took two huge steps and flung open the door. "Guards. Bring Narcissus here. Now!"

"I am here," Narcissus said calmly from across the hallway. "I felt it important that you heard the news directly from the horse's mouth." He walked through the doorway, directed by Claudius' pointing index finger, adding, "But there is more." He indicated to Calpurnia to stop covering on the floor and get on her feet. Terrified, she ran out of the room.

"More?" Claudius slammed the door shut and swung back around to face Narcissus, continuing with his booming voice, "What more?"

"Do you know," Narcissus swallowed, "of your divorce?"

"What do you mean?"

"The people, the army, the senate all witnessed the marriage of Messalina and Silius. You must act at once or the new husband becomes master of Rome." Narcissus watched Claudius take it in as he leaned against the back of a chair. "That is why I had Calpurnia tell you as soon as she had told me."

Claudius took a deep breath, slowly, thoughtfully disconnected himself from the back of the chair and looked up at his secretary. "Bring Lusius Geta to me."

"At once," Narcissus eagerly answered as he made for the door and within minutes returned with Lusius, the commander of the Praetorian Guard.

"Lusius, do you know of the marriage of Silius?" Claudius asked him directly.

"I do, Sir." Lusius remained in perfect posture. "Rome is a city that knows all and hides nothing."

"Is he," Claudius licked his lower lip, struggling for words. "Am I still in command? Is he still a subject of Rome?"

"The Praetorians await your command, Sir."

Narcissus stood tall but with his palms pointed down. "May I suggest we proceed immediately to the Praetorian camp?" He studied Claudius who was still reeling from the news of the attempted coup. "And take them with us into Rome."

"Yes. Yes, of course." Claudius' response seemed disconnected.

"Emperor," Narcissus's urgent tone snapped Claudius back to paying full attention. "Under the circumstances I recommend you transfer control of the army to me until this matter is resolved."

Claudius glared at him.

"For your own protection, you must trust me to make the correct decisions on your behalf."

As soon as messengers began to stream to them with news that Claudius knew everything and was headed for Rome, bent on vengeance, and the army officers that had been loyal to them had been summoned to report to Narcissus, Messalina and Silius knew their dreams of ruling the empire were over. To conceal his fear, Silius went to his business in the forum while Messalina gathered Octavia and Britannicus onto a cart and left to meet her ex-husband on the road. It was her reasoning that he may be lenient on the mother of his children, especially in their presence. Her plan, however, was thwarted by the fact that Narcissus kept Claudius surrounded by the Praetorians and refused to let her through. She vainly tried again outside the house, but Narcissus had both her and her children promptly removed from the grounds.

With Claudius now back in Rome, Narcissus immediately assembled a tribunal before which he led the clearly furious emperor. Claudius spoke a few words to the assembly at the dictation of Narcissus and then the procession of conspirators and their accomplices began. First was Silius, who walked unaccompanied by the guards and stood alone in front of the emperor. "I offer no excuse," He said, "and ask only for a quick death for my failed ambition."

Claudius looked up at Narcissus who make a small nod, then back to Silius. In spite of the raging anger inside he simply uttered, "Granted," and Silius was taken away to be strangled. The same fate befell the following stream of former officers regardless of whether or not they pleaded for mercy. Bettius, Pompeius, Saufellus, Decius, Sulpicius, Juncus and Mnester were all summarily executed that night. Throughout the proceedings, Claudius seemed to preserve a strange silence. Everything was under the control of Narcissus.

The emperor was then taken home for a celebratory banquet with his loyal officers, and it was only after several goblets of wine that he finally asked the whereabouts of Messalina. Narcissus sat down next to the emperor and quietly told him that she had gone to her mother's home.

"Poor creature," Claudius said, matching his secretary's almost whisper. "Tell her to come to me tomorrow and plead her case."

"I understand, Emperor," Narcissus proclaimed so loudly that everyone in the room heard him as he jumped to his feet. "It shall be done." He grabbed Lusius by the arm and the two of them rapidly left the banquet hall, Narcissus vigorously giving the Praetorian commander his orders. Lusius gathered a dozen men and rode off leaving Narcissus standing outside, alone with his thoughts. He took a deep breath and slowly shook his head as he exhaled, then went back inside.

When Lusius found Messalina she was all alone and huddled in a corner of the garden, clearly terrified. Her blood stained hand was holding a dagger with which she had repeatedly tried to stab herself but, unable to accomplish the task, she was covered in superficial wounds and bleeding profusely. Messalina's crying eyes looked up at the Praetorian. "Please, will you help me?" she pleaded.

Lusius smiled warmly and reached out toward her, then rapidly punched the flat of his hand against the handle of the dagger, forcing it through her heart. He watched in silence during the three long minutes it took for her body to cease its convulsing and, when it became motionless on the ground, he ordered his men to deliver the corpse to her mother. They took Messalina's body away and he quickly remounted his horse to return to the banquet. It had been Narcissus' instruction that he was to report Messalina's suicide as soon as possible.

With the rapid execution of all parties having anything to do with the attempted coup the normal day to day activities of Rome soon fell back into place and the name of Messalina was not mentioned again except by one person: Agrippina. She was granted an audience with her uncle a week after his return and brazenly announced how his former wife was stupid to squander her position the way she did. "An emperor needs a wife he can trust," she continued. "And one who is also well connected."

"Now why do I feel you have someone in mind?"

"Well, you can't deny that since Crispus died last year, I'm not only the richest woman in Rome but I'm also the most influential. Influence that, as my husband, would be yours to direct as you might see fit."

"True indeed, but why would I want another wife?" Claudius asked, and then laughed. "Surely I've learned my lesson there."

"What about your succession?"

"I have Britannicus."

"Of course you do, Uncle." She tilted her head to the left and forced her eyes wide open. "We both know how faithful his mother was to..."

"Stop it." Claudius slammed his fist onto the table and leaned forward as he glared at his niece. He slowly raised his right hand and began to shake his index finger at her. "There'll be none of that talk here."

"All right," Agrippina cooed. She wrapped her hands around his angry fist and rubbed his still pointing finger against the side of her face as she sat on the couch next to him. "But it must have crossed your mind."

Claudius' anger subsided as Agrippina playfully licked his finger, and then ran it across her parted lips. "You do realize, don't you," she teasingly nibbled on the side of his finger, "that Nero is of pure Julian blood," Agrippina smiled at Claudius' quizzical expression. "Oh, don't give me that look, 'uncle," she tossed her head back then grinned and put her arm around his shoulders. "Did you never wonder why your favorite niece married her first husband at such an early age?" She rubbed her hand lightly across his thigh. "It wasn't that I didn't like our 'special games,' you know." She smiled and slowly enunciated, "uncle," then ran the tip of her tongue across her upper lip. "Marry me," she said softly. "Marry me and don't doubt that you have a son who is really yours."

Cautious after recent events, Claudius decided he would never again venture outside Rome and paid intimate attention to the affairs of state, no matter how mundane they seemed to him, in order to ensure that no one would ever usurp him again. Narcissus' status was elevated even further with the additional title of magistrate bestowed on him in recognition of his loyalty, a move that made many senators nervous that a Druid was now in the position of lawmaker, but none dared to speak out disapproval. Agrippina became a frequent visitor to the emperor's palace and over the span of a few months managed to successfully wear Claudius down, offering not only her influence but promising to assist him with some of his minor duties. Their wedding was held the following New Year's Day whereupon she was named empress and Claudius officially adopted Nero, recognizing him as co-heir with Britannicus.

All things from Britannia continued to be the rage in the city and the volume of trade had very rapidly made Londinium one of the busiest ports in the empire with a population in excess of 50,000 and growing as merchants continued to stream in to capture their share of the wealth. Equally important was the vast quantity of grain imported from the island nation; Britannia had very rapidly become a breadbasket for Rome. Along with goods and grain, however, also came stories of the bravery of the renowned cult figure Caractacus, unofficially considered king of the Britons. His influence was underscored to Claudius when he overheard Nero and Britannicus at play each arguing that they be Caractacus in their game. The fact that Ostorius was simply maintaining a stalemate at the border and there was very little actual conflict did nothing to detract from the growing image of a warrior king, invincible due to a reportedly magical sword, holding the great empire at bay. The whole world was aware of the events in Britannia and, if even Romans romanticized such a figure, then leaving him in place clearly posed a danger. Claudius couldn't afford to have his inaction perceived as weakness.

"How stable is our relationship with the occupied tribes and client kingdoms in Britannia?" Claudius asked, taking the floor in an open session of the senate, "For I don't wish to divert additional resources over there unless it's absolutely necessary."

Plautius, having been called back from the Germanic front by Narcissus to serve in the senate as one of Claudius' most loyal supporters, immediately jumped to his feet. "The only engagement our troops have had, other than with the Ordovices," he announced, "Has been in quelling the Iceni civil war just over a year ago. Since then all has been quiet."

"What is the situation with the Iceni now," called out an anonymous voice.

"It's very stable." Plautius replied. "The old king was killed in the conflict and the new king, Prasutagus, is a staunch supporter of trade with Rome. In fact, he's become very wealthy by it and has since married and has a young child. The Iceni pose no threat at all."

"Are we in a position to focus our forces in Britannia on the western front?" Claudius asked.

A series of affirmative grunts and nods from throughout the hall followed with no one standing in dissent. Roman victory overseas would make them all look good.

"Very well, then." Claudius stood tall. "I will instruct Ostorius to move on Caractacus."

That evening, in his study, Claudius carefully dictated his instructions to Narcissus. "Ostorius will have to be especially careful not to disrupt relations with other tribes or put trade at risk. Furthermore, his mission is not to expand the occupation to include the territory of the Ordovices, but simply to remove Caractacus. Kill him if necessary but," he leaned back in his chair with his fingers locked behind his head. "Ideally capture him and have him delivered to directly to me. Right here in Rome."

Chapter Fifteen: Caractacus

"**I**t can't continue like this, Llyn. It's madness. Absolute madness." Caractacus, disheveled and covered in mud after the battle, called out through the relentless rain to the Druid who was just arriving at the fort.

"Madness, you say?" Llyn's expression was accusingly comical. "They tell me you attacked ten Romans by yourself and had three of them down before your men caught up with you."

Caractacus restrained his wild expression. "Come inside and get dry," he grunted.

Llyn tossed back his hood as soon as they entered the main building and unfastened his cloak as they walked to the warming fire at the far end. Caractacus was out of character; unsettled. "The Romans keep attacking but we're holding them at the border every time," he continued. "Today's battle was harsh but still nothing's gained and both sides keep losing men. Good men."

"But there's something else?" Llyn posed his question with flat assurance, reading Caractacus' wild eyes.

"The Romans have captured Tegas." Caractacus screamed loudly and crashed his fist onto the top of a nearby table, the vibration knocking two goblets to the floor. "While our warriors were at battle today a squad of Roman horsemen entered the camp and took them. They took all the women and all the children; even Teon."

"Where's Gwathford?" Llyn asked while simultaneously grasping at the reason behind Caractacus' reckless behavior toward the end of the day.

"Captured during the battle." Caractacus groaned through clenched teeth. "They took my son in the field and I come back to learn they also have my wife and my daughter." He deflated onto a bench, held his head in his hands and slowly pushed it from side to side. "We all know I've been berserker under the spell of Serencleddyf since Togodumnus' death. It's served our cause well. But now, now that the Romans have my family, I realize that control really lies with me." Blood streaked eyes appeared as Caractacus dragged his fingertips down his face. "I can finally override the berserker, Llyn, but at a time when I need that ability to disconnect the most." He slapped his thighs. "Serencleddyf is a curse!" He glared at the Druid as he shouted, "A curse, I tell you." He snatched one of the goblets from the floor and stood up in a single motion, spun around and lunged at the nearby barrels. He filled the goblet with ale, guzzled it wildly then slammed the empty vessel onto the tabletop. He looked to the Druid with wide pleading eyes. "I want to be with my wife and children, Llyn. I need to know that they're safe."

Llyn remained silent, looking at him with the same professorial expression he used when drawing answers from his students. Caractacus took a slow, deep breath then released it with a sigh of understanding as he sank onto the bench. "It's me they want, isn't it?" He said looking up then quietly snorting at Llyn's affirming nod.

"The Romans have no designs on these lands, but your berserker ways have turned you into a legend. They can't allow legends, Caractacus. They carry the potential to undermine the empire."

"These people will follow me even to their own destruction and I can't be taken in battle. I'm responsible for them but they're needlessly dying on my account, to be at my side in order to hold a stalemate. How do I pull me out of this and leave the Ordovices intact? I can't possibly surrender."

"Will you return Serencleddyf to me?"

"You gave it to me!" Caractacus' shouted, rising to his feet while right hand seized the sword. He almost had it fully drawn before he looked down quizzically to where his fist was wrapped around the hilt then sheepishly pushed Serencleddyf back into its scabbard. "What need do you have of it?" he demanded of the floor by his right foot, unable to look up at Llyn.

"Absolutely none." Llyn's voice seemed to reverberate through the hall. "But how well is it now serving the people of Britannia?"

Caractacus turned his head slowly until he was looking over his left shoulder at the unflinching, unblinking Druid. "If I do," he barked, but then his eyes made contact with Llyn's and the remainder of his sentence failed to materialize. He licked his lower lip, eyes partially closing as he began to nod. "Of course," he whispered and began the painstaking process of unbuckling his belt. No words were exchanged as he held the sword in both hands, his eyes affixed to it as he slowly walked across the room to where Llyn was holding out a large piece of cloth. Caractacus gently placed Serencleddyf onto the cloth and Llyn quickly wrapped it up then concealed the bundle in a sleeve inside his cloak.

"Do I leave now?" Caractacus asked.

Llyn made a deep nod. "Go to the Brigantes. Their loyalty as a client kingdom will be absolutely affirmed when Queen Cartimandua hands you over to Ostorius and you and your family will then be transported to Claudius in Rome. It will be Britons, not the Romans, who will deliver you."

"What happens to the Ordovices? What about all of the killing?"

"Leave that to me." Llyn slapped his right hand onto Caractacus' left shoulder and shook it firmly. "The hills and the river Dyr form a natural border and the Romans will have no more reason for incursion. Now, no more questions. You must go."

The men stared silently into each others faces until Llyn firmly nodded. Caractacus swallowed hard, darted back a quick lip curl, then immediately turned around and disappeared through the doorway. Llyn stood alone, remaining motionless until well after the sound of hoof beats had faded away into the distance.

"Is it true?" Agrippina called out, rushing across the room to detract Claudius' attention from the papers on his desk. "Is it true that Caractacus has been captured?"

"Captured and on his way to Rome as we speak. Ostorius has done well." Claudius stood up and stretched. "There'll be a parade as he and his companions are marched through town. It will be a magnificent," he said grinning. "The public will love it, the king who stood against the empire finally vanquished."

"It's the leading citizens you need to appease, husband. While the senate voted with you to allow foreigners to hold positions of power many of them are still very nervous about the long term implications for Rome. Now that such a renowned foreign king is at your mercy, they're looking to you to assuage these concerns by respecting custom and having Caractacus executed right away."

"I see." Claudius stroked his chin. "And what are your feelings on the matter?"

"Oh, don't get me wrong. He has to be killed. I just don't feel that he should receive a standard execution."

"No?"

Agrippina slid onto into a sitting position on the desktop and rubbed her foot against the side of Claudius' leg. "I'm sure the senators would be just as pleased if you sent him to the Circus Maximus?" she cooed. "Wouldn't it be a much better use of him to have him die in the arena?"

Claudius stroked Agrippina's left cheek with the back of his right index finger. He was well aware of the antics of his young wife. "So you suggest a more interesting way to have him dispatched, eh, my dear? One that's, perhaps, more fitting with your interest in gladiators?"

"He's been a thorn in your side for these past nine years and since he's going to die anyway why not let the people have some," she smiled sheepishly and raised her eyebrows, "Entertainment?"

"Putting aside your personal interests, Agrippina, you do raise a good point about keeping the senators in line. They'll always acquiesce to the will of the crowd if for no other reason than to keep their own fat arses in their comfortable seats." Claudius turned away, ignoring his wife as he proceeded to wander about the room muttering and caught up in his thoughts.

It was mid-morning when riders galloped through the streets heralding the approach of Caractacus and his captors, summoning the people of Rome to assemble and witness the promised grand spectacle. Surrounded by Praetorians under arms, first came a procession of Britons displaying ornaments and the spoils of war that the king had gained over his years in power. Next came his wife and children and, last, Caractacus himself, bound in chains but walking erect, his eyes wandering about as he took in the grandeur of the surroundings. Excited crowds cheered as he passed by and he occasionally nodded to them in acknowledgment, each time earning a rebuff from the nearest guard. The people then rushed to fill the seats in the Circus Maximus as the procession entered into the arena and immediately fell silent once the prisoners were lined up in front of the emperor's dais. Taking part of what Agrippina had said earlier to heart, Claudius had determined to hold his tribunal here in front of the masses. He slowly perused the group of people assembled in front of him. Tall, long-haired men were standing silently and looking at the ground. Tegas, Caractacus' wife, was clearly frightened but still held protectively onto one child under each arm. Teon was biting her lower lip and holding onto her mother while Gwathford stole peeks of the assembly as his eyes darted about nervously. Only Caractacus looked up. The guards removed his chains and, after stretching his arms out to each side, he stood with his feet firmly planted a cubit apart, hands on his hips, and he stared directly at Claudius. "Emperor of Rome," he shouted. "May I be heard?"

"Indeed, Caractacus, king of the Britons," Claudius called back. "You may speak your case."

"Emperor Claudius," Caractacus responded with a crisp, booming voice, then turned slightly to face Agrippina, sitting next to her husband on a separate throne, and with a slight bow added, "Empress." He then turned back to Claudius. "My lineage has been acknowledged by Rome for generations. Had I instantly yielded to your forces I no doubt would have entered this city as your friend rather than as your captive." He gestured with his open right hand out in front of him. "You would have received me, under treaty of peace, as a king descended from illustrious ancestors and ruling many tribes," he slowly drew his hand back and laid it flat across his chest, "but very few Romans would have been interested and we would have met quietly in your chambers instead of this magnificent arena." He paused and rested his hands back on his hips. "As it is, my present lot is as glorious to you as it is degrading to me. I had men and horses, I had arms and wealth." His voice increased in both volume and intensity. "You wonder that I parted with them so reluctantly? Does it really surprise you that I am sorry to lose them?" He pointed his right index finger at the dais. "You Romans choose to rule the world, but does it necessarily follow that the world should eagerly accept slavery?" He snatched his hand back and held it as a fist only a few inches from his chin. "If I had surrendered without a blow neither my downfall nor your triumph would have become famous. Look," he shouted while throwing his arms outstretched and rocking from side-to-side, gesturing to the throngs surrounding him. "Preserve your fame, great Emperor. If I am executed all of this will fade into oblivion. But, if you spare my life, I shall be an everlasting memorial to your clemency." Caractacus dropped his arms to his sides and stood silently staring at Claudius while the crowd burst into deafening cheers around him. Were they cheering for him or for their emperor? It mattered not. Caractacus fervently watched the interactions on the dais. Agrippina was glaring at her husband, speaking though her clenched teeth while he smiled and appeared to be indifferent to her. Instead, he was leaning back in his chair and paying attention to someone sitting behind him. He finally nodded and pushing down with his arms, rose to his feet and raised his right hand to silence the still cheering mob. He looked down to the prisoners. "You speak well, Caractacus. I am moved to restore your wealth and freedom and have you and your family live here with us with all the rights of a citizen of Rome." He raised his hand again, correctly sensing the enthusiasm of the crowd and wanting to keep them quiet until he had finished. "I do impose one provision, however. You may not leave Rome for a minimum of seven years."

Caractacus bowed graciously and Claudius again took his seat while the crowd exploded into a frenzy of cheers and applause. Agrippina rose, shaking her right index finger menacingly at Narcissus who was sitting behind the emperor, then rapidly left the dais. She rushed out of the Circus and immediately on arriving home proceeded to write a letter, whispering the words to herself before committing them to paper. "I'm becoming very scared for the integrity of Rome," she began. "Claudius' astuteness in pulling the populace to his side makes him immune from criticism from the senate and the city is being more and more influenced by foreigners. His druid, Narcissus, has been made a lawmaker and now that we have a Briton king, also a Druid I've since found out, at liberty amongst us with the rights of a citizen. I fear that the future direction of the empire itself may soon be out of the hands of true Romans. We're in dire need of your influence back in Rome and I hereby resolve to do everything in my power to find a way to have your banishment revoked." Agrippina's desperate letter was immediately sent to Seneca by means of her most trusted slave well before Claudius had even left the Circus Maximus.

"Let me see if I'm hearing you correctly," Claudius said, looking quizzically at Agrippina after she had presented her proposal to him. "You're asking me to recall your old lover to Rome; the same man that I personally banished?"

"I'm asking you to recall a man who was once your best friend and who is arguably the greatest mind alive today."

"Are you forgetting that it was that fine mind and powers of persuasion that got Seneca banished in the first place?" Claudius jutted his chin toward her. "You do remember how he threatened to openly oppose me in the senate?"

"Of course I do, but since he's been gone you've handily won the senate to your side and after this Caractacus incident it's clear that you also have the mob behind you. You're untouchable." She placed her hands on each side of Claudius' face and spoke directly into his eyes. "Besides, Seneca's more interested in business than politics now and I doubt he would even think about taking you on."

"That much is true." Claudius gently nodded to free his head. "His investments in Britannia have made him very wealthy." He stared at the wall over Agrippina's right shoulder. "And I will admit that I do miss my debates with him."

Agrippina pushed the fingertips of her right hand against Claudius' cheek, turning his face back and enabling him to see the well-rehearsed sincerity on hers. "I'm only asking you to allow him back to be a tutor for Nero, not to be a force in the senate." She shook her head as she implored. "If our son is to be emperor one day, we owe it to him to give him every advantage. What better advantage than to receive tutelage from Seneca? Would you deny him that?"

"You make good points," Claudius cocked his head thoughtfully to the right but then leaned against his wife. "If I allow Seneca, though, there must be balance." He wagged his right index finger. "If I permit Seneca's return as tutor, Nero must also spend equal time studying with Narcissus."

"What is it with you and these Druids, Claudius?" Agrippina pushed away and spun around, turning her back to him. She stared out of the window. "They're flooding into the city and causing people to turn from our gods. They scare me, Claudius. I don't like them, and I especially don't like Narcissus."

Claudius moved behind her, placed his hands around her waist and turned her around to face him. "Those are my terms, my dear wife," he said calmly, shrugging his shoulders.

Agrippina paused, then slid her arms around his neck and leaned her head on his shoulder so he couldn't see her face, her play of anguish melting into a victorious smile. What could Narcissus try to teach Nero that Seneca couldn't simply undo? "So be it," she said to her husband with her best feigned sigh.

Chapter Sixteen: Peace

With Caractacus out of the country and the Ordovices maintaining their tentative pact of non-aggression, the Romans were free to focus on building roads and towns throughout the occupied territories. Even further enhancing their already positive relationships with the adjacent client kingdoms. Pax Romanum, the Roman peace, had finally become a reality in Britannia.

To the north, the ever increasing wealth amongst the Iceni due to continued Roman desire for their manufactured goods and excess grain had served to make Prasutagus a well loved king, placating even the most ardent holdouts of the old ways. For the first time, the Iceni were a unified nation versus a collaboration of three sub-kingdoms.

Equally dear to the hearts of the Iceni people were their queen Andarta and the two princesses, the precocious three-year-old Camora and her two-year-old sister, Tasca. So when it was announced that the royal family intended to travel to Camulodunum for the festival of Lammas, hundreds of Iceni gathered outside the palace to make the trek to join them. Ceridwen, also planning to attend the festival and to meet up with Marek in the capitol city, rode from Toftrees to Venta Icenorum first for a visit with her old friend and to continue from there to Camulodunum with her, her family, and the Iceni procession.

"It's been years since I've been to Camulodunum, Ceri," Andarta said as the two of them relaxed on couches in her spacious receiving room. "I hear it's changed so much."

"You two won't believe it," Prasutagus chimed in as he entered the room carrying another tray of drinks for the three of them. "The palace has been replaced with a huge administrative building made out of stone. They call it the forum." He handed goblets to Ceridwen and his wife then sat down with them. "But even that pales next to the Temple of Claudius." He raised his wine to the women and quaffed a mouthful.

"The Temple of Claudius?" Ceridwen asked. "What's that?"

"It's where the Romans go to worship their gods. It's a magnificent building, Ceri, and apparently rivals any temple in Rome itself. There's a huge statue of Claudius in front made out of bronze and the building itself is decorated with green and black marble brought in from all over the empire."

"And Prasutagus tells me that the shopping is even better than it used to be," Andarta chirped excitedly.

"That's right," he said. "As the Roman soldiers complete service most of them are settling down with local girls and putting their savings into businesses. Shops are springing up everywhere and you can buy things imported from all over the world."

"So what are Marek's plans when his service is complete?" Andarta teased, looking directly at Ceridwen. "You said he came from a family of merchants. Is he going to set up a shop too?"

Ceridwen could feel her cheeks glowing. "I don't think so," she said, looking into her wine with a twisted smile. "He leans more toward a country life than a city life."

"Ah," Prasutagus joined in. "So you've had discussions along those lines, eh?"

"We've talked about his goals, yes." Ceridwen looked up. "But he's still in service for the next ten years."

"He spends all of his free time with you though, doesn't he?" Andarta said.

Ceridwen smiled gleefully and briskly nodded. "Oh yes."

"Whatever happened between you and Donogh?" Prasutagus asked. "Andarta tells me the two of you once had plans."

"Oh, that was a long, long time ago." Ceridwen clearly preferred to dismiss this subject. "Back when we were children."

"He's not aggressive enough for her," Andarta added before bursting into uncontrollable giggles.

"Andarta!" Ceridwen glared, trying to look angry but, unable to quell even her own smirk. She continued to speak into her half finished wine. "Now that the Ordovices have finally given up on their attacks against the Romans I'm sure Donogh is back on Mon studying to become a druid." She drained the goblet. "That was more important to him anyway."

Despite Prasutagus' vivid description of the city, Ceridwen still stood in awe when she first laid eyes on the new center of Camulodunum. "Is this what Rome looks like?" she asked Marek as they stood in front of the temple. "This truly is spectacular."

"You can't imagine the splendor of Rome," he said, squeezing her to his side as they looked up at the statue of Claudius. "But perhaps one day you'll be able to see it for yourself."

"You think so?" she said in gleeful surprise. "Will it be with you?"

"I'd like that," Marek kissed the top of her head, "but I'm in service here for at least another decade you know, so it might be a while."

"And then?" Ceridwen had both of her arms around him and she hugged his side as they slowly strolled.

"And then," he repeated her words playfully, "I see myself settling down here in Britannia with a local girl."

"Hmm, anyone I know?"

"You just might. She has this magnificent horse." He swung Ceridwen in front and fully embraced her and their parted lips hungrily feasted on the kiss that had been building up. They drew apart slowly. "We are in public," he said.

"That's all right.' Ceridwen tossed her head causing her hair to cascade obligingly down her back without her having to let go of Marek. "It's festival time."

"But not a festival involving gods; is that right?"

"Correct." They slowly released each other and continued their walk holding hands. "Lammas celebrates the end of last year's harvest and the beginning of this year's harvest."

"Then who or what do the people credit for the harvest?"

"No credit is needed. The Druids track the seasons and tell the people when to plant but the harvest is due to the efforts of the peasants themselves. Lammas gives them a few days off for some fun and games: overindulge in food and drink and maybe get a little wild before they have to get back to the fields."

They turned a corner at the top of the hill and looked out over the expanse of new houses laid out in orderly rows with paved streets between them. "Wow!" Ceridwen exclaimed, stopping abruptly to take it in.

"That's the Coloma Claudia Victricensis Camulodunesium, essentially a Roman town or what Romans refer to as a colonia," Marek explained. "Not only are retiring Roman soldiers living there," he turned with a quivering smile at Ceridwen who was squeezing his hand, "With their Briton wives," he said, a little louder. "But the locals themselves are finding town life very attractive. Especially those who work in the city."

"Last time I was here this was all meadow and farms," Ceridwen said. "What happened to the landowners?"

"They're very wealthy people now." He laughed at Ceridwen's expression. "They've been paid many times what the land was worth and I know for a fact that several of them are living in some of the larger town houses."

"It just goes on and on, and no city wall."

"No need. All the neighboring tribes are at peace, and Roman presence will continue to ensure that."

They continued to saunter through the streets and took in the expanded shopping district where they lunched on exotic imported foods before arriving back at the room Marek had rented for the time they were together at the festival. The combination of constant teasing over the past several hours combined with frequent kiss breaks and recent wine prompted Ceridwen to virtually attack Marek as soon as he'd closed the door behind them. He initially enjoyed the rough removal of his shirt and eagerly reciprocated her aggressive kissing, but when her fingernails drew blood from his back he pushed his arms apart and gripped her wrists tightly in his hands, holding her away as she leaned forward in repeated attempts to bite the top of his shoulder. "So you want to play rough, eh?" he asked.

"I want you," she cried out and attempted another lunge with her ravenous mouth but was held at bay by Marek's firm grip.

"But I'm going to have you," he said teasingly. He quickly flipped her around, pushed her hands together above her head and held both her wrists in his left hand while his right arm secured tightly around her waist. In spite of her writhing and struggling against him, he picked her up like that, carried her toward the bed and forced her onto it face down. His left hand now pinning her wrists down to the bed above her head, he used his right to pull up her dress to expose her milky smooth behind. "I like it rough too," he said as he slapped her. She was defiantly silent and tried to push and roll in every direction while he continued his spanking. "And I'm going to keep this up until you behave," he said, increasing both the vigor and the frequency of the slaps.

When Ceridwen's writhing finally subsided Marek moved his tingling right hand from her bright, warm bottom and began unfastening his belt. Ceridwen lay quietly, panting, but still trying without success to free herself from Marek's vice grip on her wrists. Sensing an opportunity to break free she screamed and pushed when she felt him move onto the bed next to her, but he maintained the tight hold of his left hand. She gasped as his right hand slid forcefully between her legs, exhaled through a wide mouth as it moved up, them murmured almost contentedly as he spread her moistness over her burning flesh. She was able to offer only slight resistance when he pushed against the inside of her right knee to spread her legs apart, and when his body slid on top of hers she simply closed her eyes. More than ready to be penetrated, Ceridwen attempted to push her hips upward but Marek forced her to remain flat. He slid his free hand beneath her, teasing her with his fingers while he maneuvered into his desired position on top.

Ceridwen, flooded with a combination of conflicting feelings of excitement and helplessness, made a desperate last ditch attempt to wriggle free but in doing so caused Marek's erection to penetrate her behind while his fingers simultaneously entered and inch into her. He gently squeezed and whispered into her left ear, "You're mine to do with as I wish," then began to rub his fingers against her while he pushed his hips forward; slowly but resolutely. She flailed her head back and forth but, ignoring her protestations, he systematically and completely entered her then stopped moving his hips as she screamed in the climax brought about by his dexterity. "Good girl," he whispered to her. "Now it's my turn." He slid his hand from underneath her and traced a line with the back of his fingernails up her side, across her neck and to her lips. She instantly turned her head the other way but when he moved his head to that side of her in what appeared an attempt to kiss her she immediately flipped it back. Anticipating that move, he roughly shoved his soaked fingers into her mouth. She clamped down with her teeth but he pushed back, making a fist in her mouth while he proceeded to pull back with his hips. She continued the pressure with her teeth for his first two thrusts but then eased off as his rhythmic pumping ground her against the bed and she was soon panting ecstatically, her now compliant body passively yielding to his growing demands. Suddenly both bodies become rigid together, delightfully frozen for the moment while Marek exploded inside her until, spent, he finally released her wrists and simply lay on top of her. They were silent for several minutes before he slowly rolled off to the side then turned her toward him and held her tenderly. He kissed her forehead and looked into her eyes to drink in the warmth of temporarily satiated passion that she was exuding. "Rough?" he asked.

"Mmm, rough," she cooed, nuzzling up to him. "I love it when you force me to do what you want."

They slept until late afternoon then dressed again. It was unfortunately necessary. Ostorius had been away from the city for several weeks and Marek had been summoned to join him and catch up over a meal that evening. Ceridwen, wanting to take advantage of that alone time, decided to visit some of her old haunts. When Marek left to dine with Ostorius at the forum she walked over to the older parts of Camulodunum, the areas of the city that she remembered her father bringing her to at festival times when she was a child. Soon she was away from the plaster and marble and was absolutely thrilled that so many of the individual little wooden buildings with their stone walls had managed to remain unchanged in spite of the occupation. Caught up in her thoughts she walked obliviously past a hooded figure sitting causally on one of the short walls and would have continued without giving him a thought but he called out to her. "Hmm, perfume too," he said.

Ceridwen stopped dead at the familiarity of that voice. She spun around and ducked down slightly to try to see the face inside the hood. "Donogh?" she asked.

"The same," Donogh announced, tossing back the hood to reveal a face that transported Ceridwen instantly back to her childhood. He jumped off the wall as she ran up to him. "It's so wonderful to see you, Ceri. Look at you, dressed up in city finery, all pretty and perfumed, but," he looked around, "without your horse. Where's Kelpie?"

"Stable," Ceridwen replied flatly, so stunned that Donogh was standing in front of her that she was unable to construct even the simplest sentence. For his part, Donogh couldn't stop grinning. "Well, at least he's still with you."

"What? What are you doing here, Donogh?" Ceridwen blurted out. "I mean, it's wonderful to see you too, but..."

"I came to see if the stories I heard about you were true, and having been watching you for the best part of a day now I can see that they are." His head bobbed about as he spoke as if it were a toy on a string. "And I'm so glad for you, Ceri." He enveloped her in a bear hug then slowly released her and leaned back against the wall. "I'd have given anything for you to look at me the way you look at him, but seeing you that way I know he's able to make you happy. Believe me, I can't tell you how wonderful it is to know you have that." His exuberance suddenly flattened. "It also explains why you never came back to Mon."

Ceridwen's face turned crimson. "I didn't know what to tell you."

"Your absence told me all I needed to know."

"I really wanted to, Donogh, but..."

"Hush." Donogh gently laid his index finger across her lips. "I understand." His smile was quite genuine. "And it's all right."

"Really?" she whispered.

"Really."

Ceridwen reached with both hands outstretched, grabbed Donogh's cheeks and stared into his eyes. "Thank you," she said to his face. "But tell me the truth now." She dropped her hands to her sides. "What were you really expecting to find here."

"I was expecting," he cocked his head to the right, "hoping, actually, to find the old Ceridwen here, horse in hand and carrying her sword."

"Swords aren't allowed in the city during Lammas." She looked down to see the hilt poking from beneath Donogh's cloak as he pulled it to the side. He laughed, hopped back on top of the wall that sat there looking at her slowly shaking his head. "I will tell you the truth, Ceri," he said brazenly. "I came here with plans to ask you to come back with me, away from all this, this," he snapped the fingers of his right hand repeatedly, mentally struggling for the right word, then blurted out, "this, Romanism."

"Is that so?" Ceridwen leaned against the wall next to him and folded her arms.

"It is!" He made a single quick downward movement with his chin. "But it's clear to me now that you've become a part of it." He took a deep breath and reached into his pocket. "So," he held up the pendant she had given him years before, dangling it from his right hand, "I resolved a bit ago that I'd better return this to you."

"It's yours, Donogh; always will be. It's a symbol of our friendship."

"I took it to mean more that that, Ceri," he said knowingly, his voice now deeper. "Do you remember when you gave it to me?"

Ceridwen looked down and bit into her lower lip. Donogh reached over, took her chin in his right hand and forced her face up to his. "Don't worry, that's all in the past," he said gently. "We're dealing with the here and now. Tell me. Does he love you?"

"Oh yes, yes he does."

"But he's a Roman soldier. I've seen them in action, Ceri, they're disciplined and obedient."

"So?"

"So what if he is ordered to march against the Iceni. Would he do it?"

Ceridwen looked quizzical. "The Romans are our friends, Donogh. They're our allies. Look at how much we've developed with their help. The battles are done and we're all at peace." She tightened her folded arms. "How can you even come up with something like that?"

"Indulge me." Donogh raised the flat of his right hand. "Consider it hypothetical. Would he blindly obey orders if it put him into conflict with you?"

"He's from Egypt, not Rome, and he thinks more like us. He's much more of an individual than the rest of the Romans."

"So you're saying he'd let his feelings for you override his orders, eh?" Donogh cocked his face to the right and held the pendant up high. "If you're certain that he'd defy his superiors because of his love for you and risk execution for himself and shame for his family, then I want you to take this token back and give it to him with my blessing."

Neither of them as much as flinched during the long minute that followed. "I don't for an instant doubt how he feels for you Ceri," Donogh said softly, but he is a trained Roman officer. How much longer does he have in service?"

"Ten." Ceridwen's voice was barely a whisper. "Ten years." She looked at her old friend with uncertain eyes.

Donogh jumped down from the wall and returned the pendant to his pocket. "Then perhaps we'll do this again at another time, eh?" he said jovially. "When you're more sure of things." He took Ceridwen's shoulders in his hands and gave her a quick kiss on her lips. "Until then, I'm going to hang onto it." He tapped his pocket. "On the off chance that some hope remains for me down the road."

Ceridwen opened her mouth to speak but, not sure what the words were to be, simply remained quiet while Donogh disappeared amongst the trees.

Meanwhile, at the forum, Ostorius had been briefing Marek about a growing concern. "But the Trinovantes have always been pro-Roman," Marek objected. "Even before the invasion. I remember when we marched in how they came and greeted us as liberators."

"All true," Ostorius agreed. "They even continued their support when we occupied their territory and chose to govern Britannia from here. Their discontent comes from the colonia. We took hereditary lands from them and gave them to our retiring officers."

"Weren't they paid well for the land?"

"Mmm." Ostorius nodded while finishing a mouthful of meat. "Quite handsomely at that. But we all know the reality was that they had no choice but to sell to us. The fact that we then took their peasants as slaves didn't seem to sit quite right with them either."

"They didn't see the peasants as coming with the land?"

"Apparently not, although I doubt it matters much to the peasants whether they're called serfs or slaves, the work's the same. Anyhow," he wiped his mouth with the back of his hand, "as I was saying, these discontented Trinovantes are being recruited to join with some Ordovices prince who's stirring up nationalistic sentiment amongst the Silures. It seems this person was quite close to Caractacus and talks of re-establishing a native king." Ostorius furrowed his brow. "After they've driven the Romans out." He poured more wine. "This could mean big trouble for us down the road. I've got the 20th legion heavily fortifying the base at Glevum, just in case."

Chapter Seventeen: Seneca

"Ah, I've so missed Rome," Seneca exclaimed as he and Claudius finished their sumptuous dinner. "Let me thank you again, Claudius."

"Behave yourself, Seneca, and you're welcome to stay."

"I wouldn't worry about me. Even if I wanted to, you've so adroitly manipulated the city to your will that there isn't anyone left who'd join me in standing up to you. I salute you." Seneca raised his wine, drank a mouthful and relaxed back against the cushions. "Besides, your banishing me caused my focus to move onto business instead of politics and has resulted in extremely good fortune. Why would I want to disrupt any of that?"

"Why indeed! You've become very wealthy with your Iceni partnership. I wasn't able to spend much time with them after the invasion, tell be what they're like."

"They maintain their isolationism culturally and view themselves as superior to the Belagic tribes. King Prasutagus envisions himself to be your equal. On the other hand, the Iceni are spending the wealth they are gaining through trade on imports so they are beginning to be pulled into the world at large."

"It sounds like things are progressing nicely with them."

"On the surface it would seem so, but there are those amongst them who voice concern about the potential loss of Iceni identity. A sentiment that is actually fueled a bit by the queen, Andarta. She only enjoys imported fineries as occasional luxuries, not daily needs, and is very traditional Iceni. The people look up to her. Take her lead." He reached for a date then leaned back and nibbled on it as he spoke. "The Iceni as a whole have no animosity to the Romans, though. In fact, Prasutagus and Andarta have even been guests of the governor in Camulodunum."

"Excellent! I'm very pleased to hear that. I understand Ostorius is well liked by the natives over there, too. You know I awarded him the Triumphal Insignia for capturing Caractacus."

"Oh, yes, he is well liked indeed. Especially when word got around that Caractacus was set at liberty in Rome instead of being killed." Seneca's stare moved slowly from the date pit he was holding to Claudius. "Not a wise move at all, in my opinion."

"And why not? You just said it served Ostorius' popularity well."

Seneca tossed the pit into a nearby bowl. "The empire has always secured rule by its might. It's better to be feared than liked." He twisted his mouth. "Even 'well liked.'" He reached for another date. "So now adding to all the Britannia fever that was here in Rome to begin with, by setting Caractacus free you've also created in influx of Druids setting up their schools."

"I'd think that you of all people would encourage the citizens to open their minds to new things."

"Not at the risk of undermining the framework of our society."

"Oh, that's too far over the top, even for you, Seneca."

"You think so? Already I hear contributions to the temples are down. Soon you're going to have to face the senators when they're bombarded with complaints about how these pagans are taking money away from the true Roman gods."

"If the druidic ideals have a greater appeal than gods to some of the citizens then we should be welcoming the diversity. There are so many religions out there now I fail to see how adding another will create such grave danger to our society."

"Oh, that's very good, Claudius." Seneca rocked back and forth, slowly clapping his hands and nodding with his entire upper body. "Those arguments will most likely work well on the senate, especially when the priests end up considerably leaner." He laughed. "But we both know that druidism isn't a religion. They are atheist; they don't even have gods." He shook his index finger directly at the emperor. "And that fact can undermine us."

"Not if the Druids are integrated into our societal structure, Seneca. We have the opportunity to gain tremendous benefits by incorporating the best of other cultures."

Seneca held himself at bay and only his nostrils belied what might have been running through his mind. "We're supposed to civilize the world, Claudius," he said tightly, cautiously. "Not lose ourselves in it."

Immediately after his tutoring session with Nero the next morning Seneca rapidly rushed away to his prearranged meeting with Agrippina. Now that he'd been working with Nero for a week, Agrippina wanted his initial assessment and to hear his plans to develop her son into the future emperor. Seneca had more serious concerns to discuss, however, so as soon as he and Agrippina were out of earshot he grabbed her left shoulder. "I knew your concerns about foreign influences were well founded," he said with uncharacteristically wide eyes. "But until my conversation with your husband last night I hadn't grasped the full extent of what's going on." He looked at his hand as if noticing for the first time where it was, released his grip and backed away to sit on the couch. Agrippina rushed to sit at his side.

"Claudius fully intends to support the rise of druidism in Rome," he said, deliberately withholding emotion from his voice.

Agrippina took his hand in hers and rapidly rubbed the back of it. "But how many Romans do you actually think will be swayed by a bunch of mystics? Surely all we have to do is prevent him appointing them to office to keep that contained."

Seneca took a deep breath and exhaled while he slowly turned to face her. "Don't you ever dismiss the Druids as mere sorcerers or mystics. Their message has great appeal to the intellectual elite, and that alone will cause it to spread like wildfire through the streets. Since most of our leaders nowadays tend to follow what's popular with the people, rather than stand for something that might make them unpopular, that's a formula for potential disaster."

"You're the epitome of the intellectual elite and yet you don't support the Druids?"

Seneca closed his eyes tightly while rubbing his fingertips into his hairline. "You don't get it," he said, slapped his hands down in his lap and once again looked up at her. "I can't openly support them because I'm committed to preserving Roman society. Intellectually, I fully agree with just about everything they say." He smiled at Agrippina's stunned expression. "Look," he continued. "One of the tenants of druidism is equality amongst all living things. Let's say for practical purposes that means one human is no better than another. How would you feel if being a Roman no longer made you better than a pagan?"

"That's a ridiculous assertion, Seneca." Agrippina snarled.

"Is it?" he said calmly.

"Yes it is. Romans rule the world."

"Because they are inherently better humans? I don't think so." He slowly shook his head and twisted his lips together. "Now, imagine that thinking becomes pervasive in the city. The next logical step will be the realization that slavery is unjust."

Agrippina sat bolt upright.

"Now you get it," he said with a flourish. "Question slavery and you question our whole way of life."

"But once Nero is emperor we can take care of all that. We can just ban Druidism."

"Just because you're married to Claudius doesn't automatically line your son up to succeed him. Britannicus would be a more widely accepted choice."

"I've already got him to name Britannicus and Nero as co-successors." She smirked. "Britannicus can be dealt with later."

"Still, you should cement things as tightly as possible." Seneca scratched his chin. "How old is Octavia now?"

"Twelve."

"That's old enough. Work on Claudius. I want to see her married to Nero as soon as you can arrange it."

Claudius was also interested in Nero's development. "Tell me what you observe in Nero, Narcissus," he asked, relaxed in the privacy of the couch in his study. "In your opinion, do you find him as good a prospect as Britannicus for future emperor?"

"I hope for the sake of the empire that you live many, many more years." Narcissus diplomatically shook his head. "Neither of the boys is particularly mature. Britannicus shares your intellectual curiosity but, like you probably were at that age, he doesn't demonstrate any ambition. Nero is more personable and outgoing but isn't as intelligent and, if I may say so, due to his mother's influence he carries with him a strong sense of entitlement."

Claudius' face couldn't contain his laughter. "Narcissus," he said, "You call him a spoiled brat so eloquently." He patted his secretary on the back. "What else can you tell me about him?"

"I was surprised to find he has a tremendous aptitude for poetry. If he were a Celt he'd be identified right off as a potential bard."

"I'm sure that thrills his mother." Claudius was once again laughing out loud.

"Nero confides in me that she's always telling him what to do and he has to report to her every day about what he and I talk about.

The fact he knows how angry she'd be if he did tell her about my encouraging him to develop his natural talents actually causes him great consternation."

"But he does pursue it in spite of his mother. Now, that's very encouraging."

"Indeed. In fact, you'll be pleased to learn that he's receiving similar advice from both me and Seneca in that regard."

"Hmm?" Claudius twisted sideways.

"To be less dependent upon his mother."

"Good for Seneca."

"Nero also told me that Seneca was critical of some of your decisions."

"Hardly a surprise there."

"This one might be. He said that you shouldn't have named his mother empress, that women have no place being in a position of power."

"Oh? I'll bet Nero didn't tell his mother that one either, eh?"

Their conversation was interrupted by a loud banging on the door and the arrival of an urgent dispatch from Britannia. Narcissus opened it immediately.

"There's been trouble on the on the western front," he summarized aloud. "Not from the Ordovices but from the Silures. An expeditionary squad was sent out from Glevum to investigate reports of a new gold find inside the Silures territory and to establish trading if it were the case. They were ambushed and slaughtered. Ostorius responded by moving the twentieth legion in force against the Silures but, due to the treacherous character of the country, they were unable to maintain formations and were subsequently defeated. The Silures drove them back across the Severn and," Narcissus lowered the scroll and looked directly at Claudius. "Ostorius was killed in the battle."

Such news couldn't be contained; later that night Seneca was awakened by frantic knocking. He stumbled to open his front door and on doing so was visibly shocked when Agrippina burst her way in. "The Silures routed the twentieth legion and the governor of Britannia has been killed," she announced. "I assumed you'd want to know immediately."

"Has Claudius named a replacement? I believe Vespasian is still over there in command of the second."

"Vespasian completed his tour last year, he's somewhere in Gaul now. No, Claudius has appointed Aulus Didius Gallus. He's already left for the coast."

"Gallus?" Seneca shouted, stretching his eyes upwards. "Gallus is a diplomat. We need a seasoned military man in charge. How does Claudius expect someone like Gallus to subdue the Silures?"

"He doesn't."

"What do you mean, he doesn't?"

"Gallus' orders are to secure the border. Fortify the garrisons, but that's it."

"No reprisal?" Seneca seized an amphora from the table, held it up until Agrippina quickly nodded, and then poured two glasses of wine. "Julius Caesar must be rolling over in his grave" He handed a glass to Agrippina then took a large mouthful from his. "Still, Claudius is consistent. He'll make this work to his advantage, too."

"Why wouldn't he want to attack? Too much risk of losing more troops?"

"No." Seneca drained his glass and poured another. "He's differentiating the civilized parts of Britannia, Roman occupied and client kingdoms, from the tribes like the Silures. By providing protection and insulation to the civilized part and denying the benefits to those outside, the peace is secured. Across the board he ignores the fact we're an empire, while single handedly he's taking us back to being a republic."

Agrippina sipped her wine thoughtfully then, with a sudden realization, stated, "You were sleeping and you answered the door yourself."

"Of course I did. I live alone, you know that."

"Yes, but—" She looked curiously. "Don't you have any slaves?"

"I don't believe in slavery, Agrippina, so, no, I don't."

"You really confuse me, Seneca. You're the most pro-establishment Roman there is, yet you outright disagree with mainstream Rome in so many aspects of your personal life."

"My personal life is just that." Seneca snapped out at her. "What I'm committed to publicly is preserving the Roman way of life and I'll fight with all of my strength and powers of persuasion to defend the empire and what it stands for. Claudius knows what he's doing and, in all honesty, I admire him for it." He glared at Agrippina and enunciated the word, "personally," then grinned. "If this were utopia and we could live in the idealistic world that he proposes, he'd have my full support." He guzzled back another glass. "But this is Rome. And that, my dear, is why he must be stopped."

Chapter Eighteen: Integration

"**I** come from Camulodunum," Llyn announced loudly as he entered Prasutagus' main reception hall in the palace at Venta Icenorum. As he moved across the room to greet the king he continued with, "after having enjoyed several days with the new Roman governor, Gallus." He slapped his hands onto Prasutagus' arms and looked directly into his face. "You look well, Prasutagus."

"And you too, Llyn. Please, take a seat and tell me about our new governor. I had plans to travel to Camulodunum myself to meet him but the Brigantes civil war broke out so I sent an emissary with my apologies. Queen Cartimandua requested our aid."

"He quite understands. Cartimandua sent an appeal to Gallus also." Llyn rapidly rubbed his chin and sighed. "We underestimated her husband's anger when she turned Caractacus over to the Romans."

"Perhaps," Prasutagus added. "But Venutius never has been content with the title of prince consort so more than likely this just gave him an excuse to stir up some residual anti Roman sentiments and make his move."

"Good point. He was able to gather the support of maybe a third of the Brigantes nobles, but he also went back to the Carvetii to raise a full army. He intends to overthrow Cartimandua and sever the client kingdom relationship." Llyn looked up at Prasutagus rapidly. "So you did send aid?"

Prasutagus nodded. "Five hundred warriors and fifty chariots went directly to Cartimandua's palace at Isurium," he said proudly.

"Good." Llyn made a satisfied fist out of his right hand. "They'll make a formidable addition to the Roman troops. I'll go there also."

"Which legion did Gallus send?"

"For a rapid response he sent the auxiliaries from the fourteenth."

"Auxiliaries?"

"Cavalry," Llyn clarified. "The main force he's sending is the ninth legion, but it will be a week before they get there."

"He's committing an entire legion?"

"It's imperative to Gallus that allies know they can count on the full support of the Romans. Besides, after the debacle with the twentieth legion and the Silures he also needs to show a decisive Roman victory."

"So he sent the fourteenth cavalry, eh?" Prasutagus couldn't contain his seemingly inappropriate yet contagious smile.

"What is it?" Llyn asked, twisting his mouth.

"Ceridwen." Prasutagus began to laugh. "Ceridwen is among the warriors we sent to Isurium."

As they rode north from their base at Viroconium Marek found his mind drifting back to the events of the past few weeks. He had so wanted to take his vengeance out on the Silures, as if doing so would in some way make Ostorius' death easier to bear. He vividly recalled his protestations when Gallus explained that, on orders from Claudius himself, there would be no reprisal, that the western border would simply be sealed. Perhaps the upcoming action would help. He stretched his shoulders and shook himself awake then turned to look back at the almost 800 men and horses following him. This was his command. Every one of them well trained, battle seasoned and anxious to make up for the twentieth legion's recent defeat. "We're well inside Brigantes territory now," he said to the officers riding behind him. "We'll make Isurium before nightfall." Then turning back he scanned the trees in the distance ahead of them and began to think about the upcoming assignment, how serving in conjunction will allied forces was going to make this a unique adventure. The cavalrymen would certainly fight according to their tried and true methods, but for himself came a curious realization. He was relishing the idea of fighting alongside the Brigantes warriors as if he were one of them.

It was nearly dusk when the cavalry arrived outside the walls of Isurium. Marek raised his right hand to stop the column then, flanked on either side by his decurions, he rode to within earshot of the main city gate. "This is praefectus Marek in command of the fourteenth Roman cavalry," he called out. "Here to provide aid to our ally, queen Cartimandua."

The sounds of furious scurrying immediately came from within the city and the gates slowly creaked open. At Marek's silent signal the cavalry moved up and each turmae fell in two abreast behind their respective officer. "Slow trot," he said and led the way into Isurium as each of the cavalry units followed in turn. The Brigantes lined the streets to cheer and wave at the hundreds of horses and their smartly uniformed riders as they trotted in deliberate precision though town and made formation on the commons in front of the palace. A delegation rushed out to greet them; inviting them to make camp on the grounds of the commons and requesting their commander come inside to meet with the queen. Marek ordered a general dismount, gave instructions to his officers and, after handing the reins of his horse to an attendant, entered the palace. Queen Cartimandua personally greeted him, ebullient in her thanks for the cavalry's speedy arrival, and ushered him into an antechamber already laid out with a table of food and drink. "Please take refreshment," she said, waving him toward a seat, then sat across from him and poured two flagons of ale. "Meat and ale is also being taken out to your men."

"Thank you your majesty," Marek said after downing a large draught of ale. "Tell me, where are the enemy forces now?"

"Less than a day north of here. My ex-husband and 10,000 Carvetii intend to storm the city tomorrow."

"How strong is the Brigantes force?"

"We have 6,000 warriors at Isurium." She grinned at Marek. "Venutius knows the ninth legion is on its way here so his plans must be to take the city first, but he doesn't know of your arrival. Your men will remain hidden within the city walls until the battle is ready to be joined."

Marek nodded in agreement. "A sound plan. The surprise of the cavalry will throw them into disarray."

"You will, of course, be our guest here in the palace tonight," Cartimandua held up the jug of ale as she spoke. Marek picked up his mug for her to fill, saying, "I thank you, but I'll be fine staying with my men."

"Are you sure about that?" A familiar voice sounded from behind him. Marek spun around in his seat to see a grinning Ceridwen emerging from a curtain. Speechless, he simply stared at her blue eyes. "After all, I'm staying in the palace," she added.

Cartimandua vibrated with laughter. "I wondered how long she'd be able to remain behind that curtain," she said, delighting in Marek's perplexed expression. Marek leaped to his feet as Ceridwen rushed up to him and grabbed her, picking her off her feet and whirling her completely around as they tightly embraced with abandon in spite of the presence of the queen. Attempting to re-establish a sense of palace decorum they pulled apart and a thrilled but bewildered Marek managed to sputter out "Ceridwen. What, what are you doing here?"

"The Iceni sent 500 horse warriors to assist in driving back Venutius," Cartimandua replied in her stead.

Ceridwen looked up into Marek's eyes. "We ride against them together," she said exuberantly.

They quickly took their leave from the queen and as soon as the door to Ceridwen's room in the palace was closed behind them Marek placed his hands on the sides of her shoulders and gently pulled her to him, then slid his arms around her back to cocoon her. Her eyes and lips partially closed, she turned her face up to his to engage in the long, passionate kiss each had been anticipating. The sounds of the cavalrymen in revelry with the locals around their campfires, so vividly clear even inside the castle, quickly faded away for Ceridwen and Marek as they simultaneously caressed each other as if this kiss were both their first and last. Their clothes somehow floated aimlessly to the floor and they stepped out and over them, moving to the bed that Ceridwen had prepared with the finest cotton sheets and pulled back prior to his arrival. Reaching down without breaking eye contact, he scooped her into his arms and tenderly placed her onto the sheets. His mouth moved to her neck as he joined her on the bed and she tilted her head back, breathing through parted teeth as his amorous lips made their way to her aroused left breast, his hands massaging her hips. His tongue snaked down the front of her body, stopping only to tease between her legs, before moving up again to be buried in the nape of her neck. With a series of small kisses Marek eased his way back to her mouth as he slid his body on top of hers, simultaneously penetrating both her wetness with his rigidity and her mouth with his tongue. Tight in each others arms, they rolled back and forth across the bed, each taking turns on top and each desiring nothing else in the world but giving to the other. After more than an hour and completely exhausted they remained intertwined, holding onto each other. "You've never been so tender Marek," Ceridwen whispered before burying her cheek into the sweat on his chest. "And I've never needed tenderness so much before."

Marek caressed her head with his left hand, holding it in place while cushioning it under his chin. He knew they were now both thinking about tomorrow, both aware that their respective armies were outnumbered and that many would not survive the upcoming battle. He kissed the top of her head and held onto her even more firmly so she couldn't move and, more importantly, couldn't see his teeth controlling his trembling lower lip. He closed his eyes, his confused brain tormenting him that the only woman he could love was also the only woman he was unable to protect.

Ceridwen was the first to stir, gently awoken by a thin beam of morning light squeezing through a space between the closed curtains and becoming an ever brightening sliver on the opposite wall. She squirmed to turn without breaking Marek's embrace and kissed his eyes awake, watching as they fluttered into recognition. "Time to get going, sleepyhead," she said softly, cheerfully. He moved to speak but she placed her finger across his lips. "Shush," she said. "No words." She forced a smile.

He briskly nodded, rolled out of the bed and left to ready his troops. Daylight demanded bravado. At mid morning, however, the battle plans disseminated and horses at the ready, Marek elected to yield to his need to see Ceridwen one more time and mounted his horse for a short ride to the east gate where the Iceni were gathered. The city was strangely quiet as he rode through the almost deserted streets, the townspeople either at the walls or huddled in their houses, so when he heard the sound of children at play he was naturally intrigued and diverted his horse in the direction of the jubilant shrieks. There must have been a hundred girls and boys running around in the large courtyard, chasing each other and playing games tossing objects to and fro. Marek smiled broadly, their innocence a welcome diversion from harsh reality elsewhere. A young girl, perhaps eight or nine years old, walked up to him and said, "Hello. Would you like to play with us?"

"Not today," Marek replied with a smile. Certainly, he wasn't about to explain to her why not. He laughed as she skipped off to rejoin her friends but then something caught his eye at the other end of the courtyard. "No," he said quietly through a complete exhale, his jaw dropping while he stared, staring at the row of chariots, the horses being tended and attached by the women drivers. These children were with them; their own children. He turned again to the cherubic faces beaming with glee and fought to close his mouth. They were going into battle. These were the archers. He coaxed his horse for a closer look at the vehicles, each unique with brightly decorative wheel bosses and emblazoned with abstract animal motifs, the most prominent being that of a running horse. Except for the wheels they all looked so flimsy, really not much more than braided wicker such as might be used to make a basket.

Marek moved his horse along the row and the women dressed in sleeveless earth toned woolen dresses smiled and greeted him pleasantly as he went past. Each of them were adorned with at least one silver or gold arm band, the Iceni jewelry that was so highly prized in Rome. If only Roman women knew what occasioned the wearing of them, he chuckled to himself, and then quickly pulled up, suddenly aware of a large white horse in front of him. "Come to wish us luck?" Ceridwen asked as she trotted Kelpie up alongside him.

Marek leaned over to quickly kiss her lips. "Indeed, I have," he replied then leaned back to look at her. She was wearing a short leather tunic, her bare arms and legs were intricately decorated with blue woad and around her neck was a magnificent golden torque. Marek had never seen Ceridwen in battle attire before, and after being initially taken aback, was so pleased he had come to find her. Before him was a warrior who would need no outside protection on the battlefield.

"Listen," Ceridwen said sharply. There was a barely perceptible commotion in the distance, but it was growing louder as they sat there. It was the sound of 10,000 advancing Carvetii banging their swords on their shields as they approached. Ceridwen calmly reached into the pouch she was carrying, produced a small iron woad grinder and ran her right thumb along it, then smeared a blue streak under each eye. The children began to gather around the chariots to receive their war paint and, as Marek watched them, Ceridwen leaned over and gently stroked his cheekbone with her still blue thumb. They exchanged silent smiles, expressions that spoke so much to each other. Marek quietly donned his helmet and rode back to his men.

Cartimandua's battle strategy placed the main Brigantes force outside and to the northwest of the city so Venutius' army would be compelled to cross in front of the north gate as they attacked. The Roman cavalry would leave via this gate and charge them directly at the flank while the Iceni were to leave from the east gate and strike the enemy from the rear.

Marek waited with his men just inside the gate. The sound of the approaching Carvetii was so loud one could imagine they were immediately outside the wall, when they suddenly fell quiet. The enemy had reached position. He looked up at Cartimandua standing above the gate, a green cloth held in her outstretched right arm. She opened her hand and the cloth fluttered away, tossed about gently on the breeze while the gates opened simultaneously to the deafening shouts and roars of the opposing armies running headlong toward each other. Marek drew his sword and held it above his head, called out, "forward," then rode through the gate first and cantered into the field while the twenty six turmae fell in behind him. He quickly looked around, nodded to the decurions on each side of him, pointed the tip of his sword forward, yelled out, "charge" and galloped toward the melee.

Once aware of the Romans bearing down on them, many of the Carvetii turned to face the charging cavalry and ran at them with spears to try to knock them from their horses. Marek and his men slashed wildly with their swords as they pushed through the teeming mass in an attempt to divide them, a standard Roman strategy to force a large group of enemy away from the main battle. As Marek successfully emerged from the other side of the Carvetii army he quickly turned to see the Iceni engaging them from behind. While the Carvetii had superiority in numbers, they were now surrounded and the Roman turmaes were dividing them up into smaller units and spreading them about the field. He prepared to charge back when a chariot moving at full gallop collided with a group of men on the ground only a few yards in front of him. The driver had attempted to run them down but they grabbed hold of her horses and, despite the arrows from the archers, they managed to make the horses stop suddenly causing the chariot to twist and fly up into the air to the right of them. Marek dug his heels into his horse, gladius at the ready, and decapitated one of the Cavetti in a single stroke. Turning for another pass, it was clear from the grotesque positions of their mangled bodies that the driver and one of the archers were dead. The surviving child was injured and holding onto her left arm. Marek quickly sheathed his sword and, without stopping, dismounted right next to her, holding tightly onto the reins of his horse as it abruptly halted and kicked its back legs out. "Quickly," he called to the clearly confused girl, and as she turned to him he effortlessly picked up her small frame by the waist and placed her on his horse's back. "Get back to the city," he said, grabbing his small shield from the back of the horse then slapping it to make it move. He slid the shield onto his left arm and immediately drew his gladius again as a Carvetii warrior emerged from behind the wreck. Their swords clashed, but due to the lighter nature of his weapon Marek was able to recover faster and ran his opponent through the side. Using his left foot for leverage he pulled his bloodied sword out of the body as it fell to the ground and then turned with the broken chariot behind him to face three more enemy warriors. Three against one, this was going to be tough.

Suddenly there was a flash of white as a horse leaped over the chariot and Ceridwen was instantly behind the men while Kelpie disappeared. Glynu sliced through one of them at the waist as Ceridwen spun around and the distraction enabled Marek to stab another through the torso. He made after the third, but at the sound of horns in the distance the remaining Carvetii ran off as fast as he could.

"They're calling a retreat," Ceridwen panted. "It's over." Her top lip was drawn back as she spoke and her eyes were completely gray.

Bonfires blazed on the commons that night as the Brigantes, Iceni and Roman cavalry celebrated their victory together with revelry and ale. Ceridwen, dressed once again in a fine long dress and the woad washed away sat cuddled up to Marek on a bench in front of a fire as they nibbled on cheese and sipped their ale. "You know," she said thoughtfully, looking directly at him. "We even fight well together."

Marek gazed into her wide blue eyes. "We do everything well together, Ceri. You're the most incredible person I've ever known. We're going to have a great life together, you and I." He gave her a quick squeeze and they stared contentedly at each other in the firelight until they were distracted by a figure moving in front of them. "Llyn," Ceridwen said excitedly as she recognized him. She and Marek both began to get up, but Llyn raised his hands and told them to remain seated. "I just wanted to check how the two of you were after the battle," he said.

"Then have a seat and take a drink with us Llyn," Marek insisted as he jumped to his feet, dragged a stool in front of them, indicated for the Druid to sit down, then handed him a flagon of ale as he did so. "The battle went our way, but when the ninth legion arrives in a few days we'll really have at them."

"Oh, I doubt you'll be seeing more action here," Llyn said. "Venutius realizes that his opportunity to overthrow queen Cartimandua has passed."

"But he's still out there," Marek protested. "And he's with a large force of Carvetii warriors."

Llyn nodded as he gulped ale. "Indeed!" he said. "So now you're about to appreciate Claudius' wisdom in sending over a governor who is a diplomat instead of a military man."

"What do you mean?" Ceridwen asked, unashamedly snuggling under Marek's right arm.

"It's like this," Llyn leaned toward them as he spoke, a little quieter than before. "Venutius has no quarrel with the Romans; he just wants a position of true power with the Brigantes instead of the fancy title of consort. Cartimandua now owes the Romans a debt but she's not thrilled about a permanent encampment here, and the last thing Gallus needs is a northern front to defend." Llyn's eyes darted back and forth between the attentive Marek and Ceridwen. "So the ideal solution is for Cartimandua and Venutius to agree to be co-rulers of the Brigantes and have the Roman troops return to their home bases."

"Well that's quite a tall order," Marek slowly shook his head as he exhaled through pursed lips.

"Not at all," Llyn sat upright again and spoke into his ale. "Gallus bade me act on his behalf. I met with Venutius earlier this evening and I just left Cartimandua." He drained his mug then grinned exuberantly. "It's done," he said, holding the empty vessel out for Marek to refill.

"That's wonderful news, Llyn." Ceridwen's voice was full of admiration.

"Gallus is an excellent administrator," he replied. "Already he's integrating local Britons into positions of authority and has them working alongside their Roman counterparts. The Druids are most supportive of his efforts." His mug filled, Llyn raised it in toast toward Marek and Ceridwen. "I look at the two of you before me and I see the future of Britannia," he said as the three mugs clicked together. "The best of both worlds."

Chapter Nineteen: Nero

The northern border protected by the client kingdoms of the Iceni and the Brigantes and the western border secured by the walled Roman towns of Deva, Viroconium and Glevum, Roman Britannia, as this area was now commonly called, provided its inhabitants with a tremendous feeling of stability and security. With governor Gallus empowering more of the local populations to self-administration, the Romans were viewed significantly less as occupiers and more as active participants in the development of a newly developing blended culture. Since the Britannia experiment was so successful, many considering it almost idyllic with the allure of wealth combined with friendly foreigners and their curious ways, it resonated with tremendous appeal and by the year 54 immigrants from all parts of the empire were braving the crossing to participate in the seemingly unlimited opportunities available in the rapidly growing settlement of Londinium; a city which, with a population of over 70,000, had become one of the busiest ports in the world.

The direct benefits of increased flow of wealth and grain into Rome were touted as a grand achievement by Claudius who used it both as a model of how to manage the provinces as well as a compelling argument in support of his continuing efforts to have both the military and senate run by representatives from all parts of the empire. Seneca, however, arguably one of the richest men in Rome as a result of his early investments in Britannia, was not at all happy with this seemingly unstoppable trend away from the well established, and what he considered should be inviolate, Roman ideology: Rome run by pure Romans. Behind the closed doors of the houses of old school senators, he tirelessly railed against Claudius' ideology and in the just two years since his return to Rome he had discreetly both regrouped all of his old followers as well as recruiting several new. "My silent majority," he confided to Agrippina, "For if they ever have the opportunity to speak out then the remainder of the senate would surely fall in line behind." He held his chin and pondered this last statement, partially closing his eyes. "The real Roman ones, that is," he added. "I don't include those long haired Gauls."

"Then you'd better hope that time comes before they're in the majority." Agrippina looked stoic. "He's intent to induct two more at the next opening, you know."

Seneca slammed his fist onto the table and rapidly pushed himself to his feet. "Damn him!" he shouted in a rare outburst belying the passions he always concealed. "The very essence of our empire is being destroyed by the republican dictates of its own emperor."

"I've tried to convince him to slow down but he's listening less to me nowadays."

"And more to Narcissus, I'll warrant," Seneca added.

Agrippina glared at him. "There's someone else with too much power."

"Jealous?" Seneca asked, looking at her over his shoulder as he leaned on the table. "It seems you're now empress in name only, eh?" He turned and placed his hands on her shoulders. "Claudius played you for your influence," he smiled at her, "And now he has it you seem to be expendable. You do have to admire him, you know."

Agrippina reached with her right hand and touched the side of Seneca's face with her fingertips. "We have to stop him," she said, lightly tickling his cheek. "With Claudius gone you and I can rule Rome through Nero." She slid her arms around his neck and pulled him into a kiss while his hands moved down her back and held onto her waist. He walked backwards to the couch, pulling her with him without breaking lip contact, then sliding her body on top of his as he reclined. She slowly eased her mouth from his and smiled as her right hand navigated between their bodies.

"It seems you want to act soon," Seneca said, pushing lightly on the top of her right shoulder.

"Very soon," she replied, easing herself down the couch until her head was level with his waist. She looked up, dreamily toying with her lips on his fingertips.

"You'll need my complete involvement to pull it off," he told her. "Or you and Nero might find yourselves being dragged through the streets by an angry mob." He entwined his fingers tightly in her hair. "Certain things need to be put into place first."

"You tell me when," she whispered with a breathy voice, then closed her eyes as she parted her lips.

There was a treat for Claudius at dinner the next evening. The palace cook had discovered a patch of Amanita Caesarea, the mushrooms famously named for Julius Caesar since they were his favorite delicacy, on a walk through the forest that morning. He had meticulously prepared them and presented them with pride, bowing to place the silver plate before the emperor and empress and walking backwards as he left, thrilled by the smiles his efforts had produced. Claudius smiled in anticipation of the upcoming taste sensation. Agrippina was smiling since she recognized the mushrooms to be actually Amanita Muscaria and she couldn't believe the fortune that had just befallen her.

"Please help yourself my dear." Claudius graciously motioned to the plate and watched as Agrippina reached for one of the deadly mushrooms, took a bite of half of the cap, then rolled her eyes up into her head as she beamed. "Delicious," she gushed, then leaned forward and slid the remainder into her husband's mouth, watching with glee as he thoroughly enjoyed it. She reached for her wine and discreetly spat the piece of mushroom from under her tongue into it as she pretended to drink. The small amount she had ingested would have no affect on her since she had taken milk thistle as part of her daily regimen for years, a precaution she considered to be quite necessary for a woman in her position.

"Are you sure you won't have another?" Claudius asked while gobbling his third mushroom.

Agrippina immediately reached for another then looked into his eyes and grinned. "Why don't you enjoy them," she said, letting go of the mushroom she had first grasped and picked up an item from the platter next to it. "I'm rather enjoying these lamb's kidneys." She took a large bite and slowly chewed. "In fact," she added, "I might even prefer them."

"Splendid!" Claudius was genuinely appreciative of her sacrifice as he dove into the remainder of the Amanita.

Most of the emperor's household was woken before dawn by Claudius' apparently delirious screaming. "I've been poisoned," he yelled out at the top of his voice. "Bring Narcissus to me. Bring him now."

Agrippina rushed into his room, sat next to him on the bed and took his hand in hers. A sleepy Nero followed her, unbeknownst to her. "We're looking for him," she told Claudius with a soothing voice. "We'll bring him to you as soon as he is located."

"Then bring any Druid," Claudius demanded.

Nero scurried out of the room before his mother noticed him and rushed down the hallway, the sound of Claudius bellowing for a Druid echoing behind him. He ran to Narcissus' room and banged furiously on the door. "Are you in there?" he called out. "Claudius needs you."

"I'm locked in," Narcissus answered through the door. "I haven't been able to get out or raise anyone since yesterday evening."

The key was conveniently hanging on the wall next to the door. Nero stared at it and, immediately realizing its context gritted his teeth together and closed his eyes while he silently punched his clenched fist at the air around him. He then exhaled, slowly reached for the key, unlocked the door and entered. "Claudius has been poisoned," he said dispassionately but, unable to contain himself, violently slammed the key onto the ground. "Poisoned by that disgusting, manipulative whore we call my mother," he shouted. He looked wide eyed at Narcissus. "She means to blame you."

"A double coup," Narcissus reached for the key and swirled it around his right index finer, understanding immediately the circumstances in motion. "Making her son emperor and disposing of me at the same time." He dropped the key onto the desktop, his desperate attempt to force a smile managing only a grimace.

"You've always been my friend, Narcissus," Nero clasped the druid's hands in his and shook them. "I implore you to take poison, quickly, before she gets to you. I don't want you tortured. She'll have you die horribly." He looked up with saucer eyes. "Please."

Narcissus swallowed hard, then released his hands from Nero's and opened the drawer on his desk. He removed a small vial, tossed the stopper onto the floor and held it up. "I thank you," he said, then guzzled the contents.

There was shouting coming from down the hallway and Nero ran out of Narcissus' room to see his mother and Praetorian guards rushing toward him. "Is that murderer in there" Agrippina demanded.

Nero stared back through the open doorway at the body of his favorite tutor lying on the floor. He pointed and calmly announced, "Narcissus has killed himself."

Agrippina's deed complete, Seneca immediately capitalized on his position as Rome's leading intellectual. Free now to openly argue against the policies that Claudius had so ardently striven to institute, Seneca gave impassioned oratory on both the senate floor as well as in the forum before the general populace of the need for Rome to refocus back, back to the building blocks that made the empire. Claudius' last utterances, the frenetic repetitive screaming of the word, "Druid," played particularly well into Seneca's hands. It made it easy for him to convince those in positions of power, especially after the confirming interpretation by Agrippina at the funeral, that the much-loved emperor spent his final breaths accusing these mystics of his murder. After all, wasn't Narcissus, a Druid in a position of trust, the one who killed him and subsequently committed suicide rather than face trial? Clearly, Druids couldn't be trusted. Do we really want them in positions of authority? Should we really be putting them on the same level as pure, honest Romans?

"You once told me you admire the Druids," Nero challenged Seneca when they met to resume their daily tutoring sessions.

"Indeed, I do." Seneca's response was immediate and his brow furrows belied his pleasure in Nero's quandary.

"We both know it was my mother who murdered Claudius but everyone is blaming the Druids. How is it then that you're out in the middle of it all encouraging them?"

"How would it serve the empire for the truth to be known?" Seneca was famous for answering simple questions with deep, thought provoking ones. "Not only would your mother be killed but your own position would then be quite precarious too, you know."

"But why foist the blame on a whole group people whom you know to be completely innocent?"

"You really think they are innocent?" Seneca swooped his head sideways, presenting Nero with a crooked smile. "You know very well that left unchecked they stand to undermine the empire itself."

"But they're innocent of this crime," Nero protested. "And they had no reason to assassinate Claudius, he was their biggest advocate."

"Again, you're absolutely correct," Seneca said calmly in an attempt to settle Nero down. "And that's also the reason why you should want them to take the blame. When Claudius brought Britannia into the empire he also dreamed of bringing cultural growth and intellectual enrichment to the citizens of Rome, hence his encouragement of the Druids. The masses don't want that," Seneca sneered, shaking his head from side-to-side as he spoke. "They're too shallow. They want the new fashions and the pretty jewelry. They don't want to think. They want to be entertained." Seneca waved his index finger at Nero. "Learn this. A new gladiator in the arena is always going to be more popular than the most intelligent of Druids in the forum, and a leader who plans to be here for the long term will give the people what they want rather than what he thinks will benefit them." He brought his finger back. "Blaming the Druids for Claudius' death gets rid of them both and restores the status quo."

"But it, it's not right." Nero's fumbling thoughts spilled out of his mouth.

"And how would you define 'right'? Hmm?"

"Equality? Truth? Umm, respect for others?"

Seneca raised his hand to stop Nero's blabbering. "You spent too much time listening to Narcissus, boy," he said.

"Then you tell me. What is 'right'?" Nero demanded impatiently.

"Right is that which serves the greater good."

"What do you mean, the greater good?"

"That would be civilization. More specifically, it is Roman civilization." Seneca stretched his arms out dramatically. "All of this around us. The job of the emperor and the intellectual elite is to protect the Roman way of life and whatever needs to be done to do so is, by definition, the right thing to do. The lesson to take to heart here is that your greatest tool is pragmatism."

"So you're saying my mother did the right thing."

"The right result, yes." Seneca grabbed his chin with a troubled expression and muttered, "But her motivation I find suspect."

"Not the 'greater good?'" Nero said mockingly.

Seneca looked up with stern eyes. "The greater good was served," he said, his tone causing Nero to shrink back.

"What do you mean about her motivation then?" Nero asked quietly, politely.

"She purports to hold to Roman traditions but flaunts her empress title. Your mother is highly skilled at manipulation, but her ambition far exceeds her intellect. I suspect the reason she wants you to be emperor at such a young age is so she can govern through you."

"Britannicus and I are to be co-emperors and she has little influence over him. Besides," Nero looked indigent. "Are you saying I can't make decisions independently of my mother?"

Seneca answered with a simple raised eyebrow; no words were necessary.

Succession was clearly outlined in Claudius' will and with Agrippina standing behind them, one hand on each of their shoulders, the fifteen-year-old Britannicus stood next to the sixteen-year-old Nero to take the oath of joint governorship of the empire that next day. The empress/mother would selflessly assist and guide the boys in their development for the benefit of all Rome. Nero looked first at Britannicus, then his mother, before turning to the assembled crowd in front of them. I should be the emperor, he thought as he dreamily looked over the top of crowd. Not merely a figurehead co-emperor with the power in the hands of the empress. In fact, I would be a good emperor. I'd govern for the benefit of the people of Rome with help from trustworthy advisors like Seneca. He shook his head to clear his thoughts and turned to look at his mother, loving son smile concealing his inner distain. It was true that her motivations were always pure self-indulgence. As emperor he would have much bigger concerns to attend to than heeding the bidding of this manipulating woman. After all, what was a woman doing in such a position of power in the first place? Yes, he would become emperor, and he knew what he had to do to accomplish it. Nero whispered his new motto under his breath, "Pragmatism." What a wonderful word. It contained action, it served the greater good, and it was delightfully inaudible to the others on the podium.

Seneca's guidance served Nero well during his rise to power, and the sudden death of Britannicus due to some mysterious illness only a few months later was effectively played down with Seneca's influence over the key senators. Shortly afterwards Nero ascended to the position of emperor without question and he immediately began to shun his mother, completely excluding her from official functions as he grew confident in his own ability to make decisions. Decisions previously approved, of course, by his closest mentor and advisor.

Agrippina was furious that she was not only out of the limelight but that her influence over her son had so rapidly waned. The loss of power was more than she could bear and caused her to desperately resort to the only method she had ever known for achieving her goals. Laden with Egyptian makeup and perfume, her hair freshly treated with henna, she waited until Nero was drunk after dinner one night then slid onto the cushions next to him. The other dinner guests appeared to pay no attention as she played with her son's hair and gently nibbled at his ear, blatantly allowing her left breast to fall free of the flimsy covering she was wearing. Seneca, however, was keenly observing the proceedings; this was a situation he could turn to advantage. He looked quickly around the room until his eyes fell on Acte, a young slave girl, and he beckoned her over. "You will seduce the emperor away from that woman," he told her. "Remind him, on my authority, that the old woman next to him is his mother."

He looked into the girl's frightened eyes and stroked her hair, then placed his hand on the back of her neck, pulled her close and whispered something into her ear. Acte abruptly pulled her head back and, trembling and vibrating her head from side-to-side looked pleadingly at Seneca.

"Don't worry, my dear," he told her. "Do my bidding and I'll buy you your freedom." He smiled and nodded at her. "Now, go."

Agrippina glared as the willow slave girl, a third her age and half her size, slowly walked over to where she and Nero were sitting. "Go away," she hissed.

"I cannot, empress," the slave replied quietly, "For I have been instructed to please the emperor." She unashamedly lay next to Nero, her half-naked body gyrating against him while she maneuvered her mouth to his ear and whispered, "Seneca begs me to remind the emperor that soldiers would never endure the rule of an impious sovereign."

Nero suddenly looked up at Agrippina, but his bleary eyes were unable to bring her into focus and he was therefore deprived of the look on her face. The message, however, had been delivered clearly. Without a word, Nero turned his back to Agrippina and his arms and mouth fully embraced Acte.

Agrippina, visibly humiliated, rushed out of the room. Two hours later a decree was issued banishing her from the palace, and less than a year later she was dead. Seneca, now the undisputed power in Rome, was free to focus Nero on, as he put it, "correcting the mistakes of Claudius."

Chapter Twenty: Suetonius

Britannia initially seemed immune from the turbulence that occurred in Rome following the ascent of Nero, and with governor Gallus following the policies established by Claudius, trade continued to flourish as it had for much of the preceding decade. It was almost two years after Nero became emperor before his first decree impacting the governing of Britannia reached Camulodunum. In response to complaints from the priests at the temple of Claudius about declining offerings, Gallus had been ordered to impose a tax on the Trinovantes and give the proceeds to the temple. Although on the surface this was a seemingly minor issue since taxation to raise money was standard procedure in most Roman provinces, it nevertheless troubled Gallus greatly. He asked Amergin, the leading Trinovantes landowner, to join him at the Camulodunum forum.

"At the time of the invasion we welcomed you Romans as liberators," Amergin snarled through his unruly beard. "But instead of our getting our lands back from the Catuvellauni you've systematically taken them to build your Colonia." He slammed his fist onto the table and leaned toward Gallus. "Your soldiers are marrying our women and settling down here, which you encouraged them to do, yet because they're choosing to accept our ways and are no longer contributing to your temple you're now telling me you want to have us pay for the temple's upkeep." A huge toothy grin appeared in the middle of Amergin's beard as he straightened up. "Good luck collecting," he said, his voice breaking into raucous laughter.

"I've already written an appeal to Nero," Gallus said. "But I'm not hopeful of the outcome."

"Listen," Amergin wagged his right index finger. "Not all of the discontented factions have left to join with Donogh, you know. The majority of us want to stay in our homeland and get along peacefully, but I'll give you this warning," his finger slowly curled back into a fist. "It won't take much to bring a lot of pent up anti-Roman sentiment out into the open and, believe me, I tell you with assurance that it would be very ugly."

"Come now, Amergin. Look how the Trinovantes have benefited from the Romans. Look how many of you are living in the city that Romans have created."

"There are no true Trinovantes living in Camulodunum any more, Gallus," Amergin pushed his flat right hand away from his body and walked toward the door, turning back just as he exited through it to add, "It might well be in your best interests to keep that in mind."

Amergin, muttering under his breath with his head swinging wildly from side-to-side as he stormed out of the forum, crashed into a man just entering, inadvertently striking him in the stomach and sending him tumbling backwards down the steps. He instantly rushed down to where the fellow had fallen. "My apologies," he said, offering his hand to help the winded man back to his feet.

The man slowly looked up. "What prompts such a hasty exit, Amergin?"

"Why, it's Prasutagus!" Amergin quickly pulled back his hand. "Great king of the Iceni," he said mockingly and pretending a bow, "Here to consult with your Roman overlord in there no doubt," he beckoned with his head back to the building. "Take my advice and don't trust a thing he says."

"Gallus has always dealt fairly with us," Prasutagus protested.

"Until he's told not to," Amergin looked serious. "Listen to me, please," he said, taking Prasutagus by the shoulders and looking directly into his face. "The Belagics came to this island from Gaul all those years ago to flee Roman occupation. We thought it would be different when they came here, but the empire doesn't change. They're taking our land, taxing us and taking our peasants as slaves, just as they always have. Beware, Prasutagus." Amergin's wide eyes exuded both honesty and desperation. "The Iceni will be their next conquest."

"You're speaking nonsense." Prasutagus stood unflinching. "The Iceni are an important client kingdom."

Amergin bared his teeth in an open mouthed, sideways smile as he slapped his hand against Prasutagus' left shoulder. "You keep on believing that, Prasutagus," he said, then dropped his hands to his side and disappeared rapidly down the steps.

Prasutagus went into the main business area of Camulodunum after his meeting with Gallus, eager for the meal and conversation he had previously set up with Llyn. He arrived early and relaxed at a table at his favorite imported foods emporium, munching on olives and dates, waiting for the druid to arrive while contemplating the concerns that Gallus has shared with him. It seemed the new emperor, unlike Claudius, was a staunch believer in centralized government and was not at all happy about the way Britannia had been 'so loosely' administered. Prasutagus sat slowly chewing on dates, caught up in his thoughts about the possible impact this might have on business, until he saw Llyn walking toward him.

"Greetings Prasutagus," Llyn began as he took a seat. "How are the girls?"

"Growing like you wouldn't believe. Andarta's personally training them in archery and Camora's already talking about learning to use a sword." He chuckled. "That's due to the influence of Ceridwen. Camora idolizes her."

"I take it you see Ceridwen often then?"

"She's around the palace quite a bit. She even comes over with Marek from time to time. They're really looking forward to when his time with the legion is up. They have plans, you know."

Llyn nodded approvingly. "I'm pleased to hear it," he said. "Many of those who came with the legions have much to offer the future of Britannia. The integration's going well."

"There are a couple of sore spots around here regarding that, you know." Prasutagus looked up and moved his head from side-to-side.

"I do know." Llyn picked up an olive and studied it as he spoke. "The Trinovantes have not been dealt with well; I've just been speaking to Amergin." He popped the olive into his mouth.

"I ran into him earlier. He warned me about Roman imperialism."

Llyn reached for wine and took a gulp before responding. "Depending on the political climate in Rome we may be forced to act sooner than I'd prefer," he said. "Building a nation may end up being a bit more involved than just passively waiting for the Romans to be assimilated."

Prasutagus' stroked his right ear, eagerly waiting for Llyn to elaborate, but they were interrupted by an, "Excuse me, are you Llyn?"

They both immediately turned to see two tall men in dark robes standing next to the table. Llyn rose to look directly into the face of the Druid speaking to him. "I am," he replied.

"I am Senias," he said and pointed to his companion. "And this is Calatin. We just arrived from Rome with an important message from Caractacus."

Excusing himself from Prasutagus, Llyn left hurriedly with the two druids to adjourn to a more private location. As soon as they were behind closed doors Senias began telling Llyn how druidism had been declared illegal by Nero and that practicing Druids had been ordered out of Rome.

"What of Caractacus?" Llyn interjected. "Must he also leave?"

Since he's a foreign king he's considered a celebrity." Senias laughed. "Plus, he never overtly taught or engaged in such debate so, no, Caractacus is quite safe. Besides, the agreement he made to secure his liberty compels him to remain in Rome for several more years. He's bound by his word."

"He's very concerned about things here in Britannia, however," Calatin added.

Senias nodded. "He has insider knowledge that Nero means to do away with the client kingdoms. By directly occupying these territories there will be more wealth for Rome and the emperor needs more revenues for his immense building projects."

"I heard the income from Britannia was considered exemplary," Llyn twisted his lower lip. "Why would Nero risk disrupting that?"

"He's being manipulated by a very shrewd advisor by the name of Seneca who advocates a return to the traditional ways of empire. He's also pushing for campaigning to the west to capture the tin and gold mines."

"I know that name. Seneca is also the financier for the Iceni, isn't he?" Llyn asked.

"He's the one," Calatin said. "He's one of the richest men in Rome and with the control he has over Nero it's clear that he's the person really running the empire."

Llyn stroked his hands down the sides of his face as he rose to his feet. "We must leave for Mon immediately. Devyn needs to hear this as soon as possible."

Although he had initially sloughed it off, Amergin's warning continued to play over and over again in Prasutagus' head and he found himself quite needing to discuss the changing state of affairs with his wife when he returned to Venta Icenorum. "The Iceni are in a unique situation," he explained to Andarta. "We're allies of the empire and in business with a leading Roman citizen, yet we're completely independent politically."

"A business partner that I don't like," Andarta interjected. "You know how I feel about Seneca."

"Nevertheless, it was his investment and direction that's made us rich." Prasutagus spread his arms wide and turned from side-to-side. "We really are rich, you know."

"Keep in mind that if he ever pulled that investment all of these riches would grind to a halt."

"And so would his cash flow," Prasutagus made a knowing smile. "I'm not concerned about Seneca, but it would seem that Nero doesn't rule quite as loosely as Claudius and I'm afraid the independence we've enjoyed might become a bit precarious down the road unless Britons can gain independent rule."

"What do the Druids say?"

"With the changes in Rome, Llyn told me they may be forced to move the timetable up. The Trinovantes and the Catuvellauni are becoming increasingly restless and the new taxation to support the temple doesn't sit well at all."

A month later Llyn was back in Camulodunum to deliver a bold proclamation to Gallus: the transition of administration of Britannia to elected Britons. In exchange, there would be a guaranteed increase in production of grain along with the opening of the lands of the Ordovices and the Silures to export the copper and gold they mined. The Romans would gain more goods and significantly increased revenues while being able to re-deploy the majority of their four legions to locations outside Britannia. Those who wished to remain would be free to do so and the Colonia would be left intact. Gallus listened politely and intently to Llyn but then slowly rose to his feet while shaking his head from side-to-side. He stood in front of Llyn and took the druid's left shoulder in the firm grip of his right hand and stared into his eyes. "I'll personally deliver your proposal my friend," he said. "I'll even take it to Nero himself, if I'm able." He took a deep breath while his arm dropped to his side. "But you must know that current politics are against independent provincial rule." He turned to his desk, picked up a scroll and handed it to his guest. "As you can see, Llyn, I've been recalled," he said with a weakening voice. "And I suspect my replacement is well aware of those copper and gold mines you spoke of."

"Do you know who the new governor is to be?"

"Oh yes! His name is Paulinus Suetonius, a seasoned and very capable Legate. It was his command that suppressed the revolt in Mauritania and he was the first Roman to cross the Atlas Mountains. He's highly ambitious and his military prowess gives him license to pretentiousness." Gallus rubbed his chin while staring at Llyn. "I don't see the two of you getting along well at all."

The abrupt departure of Gallus came as a surprise to most Britons and, since he had been so popular, everyone was curious about whether the new governor would have a similar disposition. The fact that Suetonius came from a military background as opposed to being a career diplomat was a growing cause for concern to some; most especially the Iceni.

"Tell me about Suetonius, Marek," Ceridwen quizzed as she rolled over next to him, propping her head up with her hand. Marek, exhausted having arrived at Toftrees only a couple of hours before and being taken immediately to bed by a very playful Ceridwen, lay flat on his back and at first moved only his eyes. "Ah," he puffed teasingly. "You actually want to talk."

She rubbed the side of her face across his shoulder and slid her hand across his chest. "Just for a bit," she whispered, playfully nibbling at his ear before pushing her head back and pouting. "But only if you're able."

"Well," he said turning onto his side. "He's made a lot of changes in the six months he's been here."

"I know that," Ceridwen made a quick slap across Marek's thigh. "I want to know about him." Her eyes became slants and she licked her top lip. "I hear he has a young daughter."

"Yes, her name is Julia and she's about seventeen. He's very protective of her, most likely due to the fact her mother died when she was very young."

"Is she beautiful?"

"She looks like a horse," Marek answered in a matter of fact voice.

"Good," Ceridwen said as she flopped onto her back and spoke to the ceiling. "Just make sure you don't find her attractive."

Marek loomed over her. "Impossible," he said while sliding his hands up her abdomen and firmly caressing her breasts. "No one dare even try to compare to my Ceri." He took each nipple between thumb and forefinger and squeezed until she gasped then moved his hands up to her shoulders, holding her down while he slid his body on top of hers. He buried his face just below her left ear, kissing and passionately biting the side of her neck while she engulfed him, her arms and legs wrapped tightly around his back. There was no more talk of Julia.

Marek had intended to stay with Ceridwen for several days but early the next morning Rufus, one of his officers, delivered an urgent dispatch. He was to leave right away to rendezvous with Suetonius in Camulodunum. Arriving that evening after a full days ride, Suetonius greeted him with a sumptuous meal and newly imported wine while briefing him on the reason for the summons. "My predecessor," he began, pacing the room while alternatively waving and biting into a roast chicken leg, "did nothing to extend our territory and caused these Britons to become far too familiar with their conquerors. Now, as a result of that, they've developed a mutinous spirit."

"Has something happened?" Marek put his wine down on the table.

"The tribes have come together into something they call vergobretos, which basically means all decision making has been relinquished to the Druids." He took the final bite of his piece of chicken, tossed the bone onto a metal plate and ignored the fact if bounced off onto the table while he reached for a goblet of wine. "It seems the whole of Britannia is being pulled together as a unified nation and the most obvious reason for it is that they mean to drive us out." Suetonius guzzled his wine and slammed the goblet back onto the table. "So we're going to strike first and subdue the Druids directly."

"We're going to attack Mon?"

"That's right." Suetonius refilled both of their goblets. "And it's not just the Druids that we'll encounter there. We have intelligence that disaffected Trinovantes and Catuvellauni have been gathering there, creating an army." He wrapped his fist around his goblet with a flourish. "Of course, we'll have to subdue the Ordovices first in order to get there, so I've ordered 2,000 legionnaires from the twentieth to Viroconium to join up with the fourteenth legion." He took a large gulp and with his free hand beckoned Marek followed suit. "Drink up," he said. "You and I leave together for Viroconium in the morning and we'll take the reinforced fourteenth up to Deva for the crossing."

"Ah yes, right at the ford in the River Dyr." Marek nodded and guzzled his wine. He knew the place: a well-fortified crossing between civilization and the mountainous unknowns that filled even the most seasoned legionnaire with trepidation.

"Correct. Now then, you've been here since the invasion so I want you to fill me in on everything you've learned about these Britons." He picked up the amphora and refilled Marek's goblet. "I need to know what I might expect before we do battle with them."

"Well," Marek began. "Each tribe has some unique features, but as a whole they're very much like the Germanic and Gaul Celts. They fight as individuals, not as a cohesive group."

"That's good." Suetonius scratched the underneath of his chin. "Do we have anything specific on the Ordovices?"

"We've only had border skirmishes with them, but they were headed for some time by Caractacus. He originally came from the Catuvellauni so I suspect they'll use familiar tactics. We had many encounters with the Catuvellauni after the landing so the cavalry, especially, has a lot of experience."

Suetonius sat smiling at Marek. "Ostorius' notes were filled with praise and commendations for you, you know. Do you realize you may be the highest ranking non-Roman in the army?"

Marek cocked his head to the left and returned the smile.

"It's true," Suetonius continued. "Your leadership has been noticed by some very august people, indeed. I consider you one of my biggest assets here in Britannia."

"Thank you, Suetonius," Marek responded, a little uncomfortable with the praise. He quickly buried his face in his goblet.

Suetonius waited until Marek had taken his drink then added, "There is one thing I want to make clear to you, however."

"Yes?"

"My daughter, Julia, has told me that you've caught her eye. Ordinarily I'd be delighted that she fancied such a fine officer but, as I just said, you're not a Roman. You're in this army due to a crazy whim of Claudius when he was emperor and, as your commander, I wouldn't trade you with a real Roman officer for a second."

Suetonius turned and glared directly at Marek. "But I'll not tolerate so much as a thought of a mixed marriage for my daughter so you'd better keep far away from her. I want that well understood."

Chapter Twenty One: Battle

Marek sat on a rocky outcrop overlooking the River Dyr and stared into the swirling water until the raucous sounds of the army melted away and his brain was clear to think. He was pleased the men were in such high spirits on the night before the crossing but at these times he much preferred his solitude to joining them in their revelry. The new weapon that Suetonius introduced to the legion had been a tremendous confidence booster, especially to the legionnaires from the twentieth who had fared so poorly the last time they ventured across the western border, and had served to assuage many a fear. This campaign was a chance for redemption for them. All the same the shrine of Minerva, a stone's throw from where Marek was sitting, had been solemnly visited by an unbroken flow of legionnaires all evening. The shrine was the reason he had chosen this place to sit since it took him back to when he first met Ceridwen and he had compared her with the goddess. It seemed like only yesterday that he was telling how the scar on her breast labeled her as a true warrior and how she was the perfect woman. He closed his eyes dreamily. She truly was his perfect woman. He rocked back and forth for a few peaceful moments of recollection then slowly opened his eyes to stare at the land across the river. Tomorrow the half finished invasion would continue and soon there would be no more western front. In a few years this entire island would be reaping the benefits of Roman peace with every tribe either a conquered province or a client kingdom. He could then retire, Ceridwen would certainly marry him, he'd settle down with her in Toftrees and together they'd enjoy the richness of colonial life. They were almost there; only a few more years to get through.

Only a few hours after sunrise the next morning nearly 7,000 legionnaires and 2,000 cavalrymen had forded the Dyr while a hundred scorpions were shuttled across using the ferry. The majority of the cavalry already across, Marek rode toward the river, mentally readying himself for leading them in the march toward the hills looming in the west. Obviously the Ordovices knew they were coming and, more to the point, they would certainly be ready.

Suetonius, however, was ready also. An experienced commander he had full knowledge of the terrain ahead and had pre-selected several sites for possible battlefields. Shortly after midday with scouts urgently reporting enemy sightings both ahead and to the south he was consequently quite at ease ordering standard formation in the first place he had chosen, a wide open meadow. Scorpions were quickly lined up behind the first row of legionnaires and the cavalry were split into two groups to protect the flanks. The Ordovices did not disappoint. Unseen initially amongst the trees ahead, their shield bashing and traditional shrieks easily gave away their location and Suetonius had his men prepare for them. The Ordovices conveniently became louder and louder as they drew closer, so as soon as upward of five hundred spear throwers emerged from the forest the scorpions were in the ideal position and released their deadly bolts, instantly impaling scores of their naked bodies to the trees while many more were skewered to the ground. Suetonius, on horseback just behind the infantry, yelled, "Turtle," as the remaining spear throwers released their projectiles. Each cohort completely encased itself in a shell made up of their large shields and the spears fell ineffectively down on them, most simply bouncing off as the naked Ordovices disappeared once again into the forest. Suetonius called out, "Re-form," and the legionnaires rapidly resumed the previous line formation, a few of them having to pull spears out of their shields first. Marek, at the head of the cavalry on the right flank, held tightly onto the reins of his horse and watched Suetonius' calm confidence as he kept the legion at bay to draw the enemy into the open. Ordinarily the cavalry would have charged the spear throwers, certainly they were anxious to do so, but orders were to hold position.

The din from the hidden Ordovices increased in both volume and frequency until 10,000 screaming enemy warriors, all waving their swords and shields, were disgorged from the forest and ran as fast as they could toward the legion. The scorpions fired and while they were being reloaded Suetonius yelled, "Ready javelin number one." Every legionnaire held the longer of the two special spears they had been issued behind their heads and immediately after the scorpions let go their second round Suetonius gave the order to throw. Marek, trying to ignore his racing pulse by taking controlled breaths, watched a cloud of 7,000 javelins rise from the line and rain down on the enemy as they scrambled for cover beneath their stretched leather shields. The effectiveness of this new weapon was immediately apparent as he watched the Ordovices frantically struggle to remove them from their shields. The heads of these javelins were so sharp and light that as soon as they penetrated their target they bent, remaining mangled and stuck. As expected, most of the Ordovices discarded their now useless shields in order to continue their charge, leaving them unprotected from the second javelin volley that came down on them with deadly accuracy only seconds later. A full third of the enemy didn't even make it as far as the Roman line.

As soon as Suetonius gave the order to advance Marek drew his gladius and quickly looked back at his men. He raised the sword high above his head them brought it down decisively with a swift straightening of his arm. Yelling out "Charge," he galloped a thousand men and horses into the middle of the approaching enemy to further reduce the number that actually reached the Roman infantry. Without shields the enemy vulnerability was dramatically increased but they still fought fiercely and successfully dragged many cavalrymen down from their horses. In spite of heavy losses the cavalry managed to hack their way through the center of the Ordovices and as they approached the edge of the forest Marek signaled for them to regroup. They then begin the drive to push the remaining enemy toward the approaching line of legionnaires. This not only required the Ordovices to fight both in front and behind of their lines but also effectively cut off their ability to retreat back into the woods, which is what they tried when the second wave of cavalry joined the fray from the left. Since a few of the enemy did manage to make it through the cavalry line Marek called for the turmae in his command to begin the mop up, but as he pulled his horse around it stumbled and, rather than be thrown, Marek quickly dismounted. There was no time for him to retrieve his shield so he quickly drew his dagger with his left hand while nimbly jumping backwards to avoid the blow of a large iron sword. Marek swung his gladius at the Ordovices warrior to block the second stroke and pushed into him in an attempt to knock him down. The warrior stood his ground, however, and the two men stood face-to-face, a foot apart with their crossed swords between them. "You've lost the battle," Marek told him through gritted teeth as the two men groaned, pushing their swords against each other. "Surrender and live."

The Ordovices warrior opened his mouth wide in a half roar and quickly took a step back and to his right hoping to cause Marek to stumble forward. Instead, Marek leaned back slightly to keep his footing and brought up the dagger in his left hand, stabbing his opponent in the side. Roaring from the pain, the warrior attacked wildly, successfully knocking Marek's gladius from his hand, but the momentum also crashed his own sword against the ground. Quickly switching his dagger to his right hand, Marek rushed at him and drove the dagger upwards into the center of his opponent's abdomen. The Briton stood erect, defiantly staring into Marek's eyes; his beard soaked from the blood streaming from his mouth, and spat before collapsing to the ground, his right hand still firmly clenching his sword. Panting, Marek looked down at the fallen warrior and noticed something; something shiny, silver and delicate. It had been around the warrior's neck but as he fell it had flopped out of his tunic and was lying on the ground next to him. Marek scooped it up then quickly went to retrieve his gladius but, looking around, it was clear that he would need it no more today. Small groups of captured enemy were being escorted away with the majority lying dead on the field. This was the decisive win Suetonius had wanted.

By nightfall a palisade had been erected and tents set up in orderly rows within the safety of the enclosure. The aroma of meat roasting on spits over the cooking fires soon permeated the camp, adding to the anticipation of the upcoming victory celebration where Suetonius had promised each man his fill of the finest imported wine. They eagerly gathered to hear his report on the battle, his congratulations on their brilliant success and the body count: 6,000 plus enemy dead compared to only 600 Roman losses, only 56 of them being from the all important infantry. Amid the loud cheering that followed, the ecstatic men eagerly opened the promised casks of wine, filled their goblets and proceeded to laugh and share tales of the day while sitting around the crackling fires. Marek, goblet in hand, made sure to spend time with each turmae as he walked amidst the cavalrymen, joining them in both remembrance of the glory of those fallen as well as celebrating the joy of victory.

"It truly was a great victory," Suetonius announced as he walked up to where Marek was standing gazing into a fire.

"Indeed, it was." Marek turned to look at his commander. "The Ordovices were perhaps the strongest adversary we'd face in Britannia and you've all but completely taken them out in a single blow." He raised his wine. "Congratulations."

"The congratulations belong to you, Marek. You were right about the fierceness of the Ordovices, yet in spite of taking heavy losses right away you kept the cavalry charge going." Suetonius raised his goblet in a salute. "Your tenacity and leadership saved many a legionnaire today."

"Thank you." Marek glanced downward as he replied, then took a deep guzzle of wine to momentarily conceal his face. A wonderful victory, certainly, but at a cost of the largest loss of men he had ever experienced.

"You'll be in need of replacements to bring the cavalry back to full strength before we go on." Suetonius waited until Marek moved the goblet from his mouth and looked back up at him before continuing. "I want you to enjoy the feast tonight and take tomorrow for rest, but then the next day you'll ride to Verulamium and meet with Petilius Cerealis, legate of the ninth legion. You'll be carrying orders for him to relinquish 500 of his cavalry to your command." He made a quick, snapping nod with his head. "That should about do it, don't you think?"

Since Toftrees was only a few short hours northeast of the road to Verulamium and his last leave had been cut short, Marek had no trouble convincing himself that he was perfectly justified in taking a half day detour from his assignment. He excitedly galloped the last stretch, thundered into Ceridwen's estate without slowing, then pulled up abruptly in front of her house and rapidly dismounted. The front door flew open before he reached it and there she was rushing to him and beaming. Marek immediately pulled her body tightly against his, his left hand behind Ceridwen's head pressing it under his chin, his right firmly around her middle while her hands instinctively locked around his waist. He held her in silence for several minutes then slowly moved his head to caress the top of hers with his right cheek before kissing it. He eased his grip, tenderly watching her eyes emerge before they closed, only seconds later, as their mouths yielded to the need for an overdue, impassioned kiss.

When their lips finally, unhurriedly, separated, Ceridwen whispered, "Come inside," into Marek's right ear and they scurried through the door, still holding tightly onto each other.

"I can't stay long, Ceri," Marek said while he quickly removed his breastplate and eased it onto the floor. "I'm not supposed to be here at all, but I just had to see you."

"We heard about the fourteenth's drive west and the battle with the Ordovices," Ceridwen clasped her hands around the back of his neck and pulled him forward to kiss her again. "I wasn't expecting to hear from you for months." She slid her hands down his torso and slid them back up under his shirt with her fingernails dragging across his back.

"I'm to pick up reinforcements from the ninth, otherwise you wouldn't have," he said as she pulled his shirt off over his head. He gripped her shoulders and grinned at her then, in one swift motion slid his hands down her arms, down to her ankles, then up again pushing her dress up with them. His fingertips caressed the back of her naked legs while his lips moved up the front with a series of kisses, pausing to pleasure her with his tongue between her creamy muscular thighs before continuing to push her clothing upwards. He traced a line with his tongue from her abdomen to her breasts, sucking her left nipple first to arousal, then exciting the right even more with his teeth. As he straightened his body he finally slid his hands along her upward reaching arms to toss the dress somewhere over his head. Her arms came down across his shoulders and around his neck as he squeezed her now naked body against his. Ceridwen moved her right leg up the outside of his left and slowly rubbed it up and down, gyrating against him as his tongue frantically probed her mouth, sharing her taste with her. He leaned forward and, without breaking lip contact, dropped onto his left knee and eased her down onto the rug, forcing her to straddle his thigh while he reached for her arms and pinned them to the floor above her head. She attempted to push against him but doing so only ground her inflamed moistness into his thigh, and as Marek broke away from their kiss, Ceridwen was panting through a wide open mouth while her body writhed beneath him. "Take me," she eked out, her breathy words almost pleading.

Marek pulled his right knee over her left leg, and then used it to push against the inside of her thigh. "Spread your legs," he instructed as he slowly leaned forward to cause the bulbous tip of his erection to just touch but not enter her. She thrust her hips wildly but only succeeded in spreading her moisture over his engorged tip. "Spread them wider," he ordered. Suddenly Marek released her arms, grabbed the backs of her knees and pushed them up and out, forcing her wide open. He leaned forward and slid his arms across the backs of her thighs to force her legs to remain up and spread as he once again pinned her arms down, then entered her completely with a single steady thrust. She managed a loud gasp before turning rigid, her only movement being the quaking of her mouth until, devoid of sound or breath, she was forced to inhale. Marek buried his face into the nape of her neck and almost completely withdrew before rapidly shoving himself back inside hard. After only five subsequent sound poundings with his hips he quite willingly released Ceridwen from her contortion, first to remain ecstatically motionless on top of her and then, several minutes later, to lie contentedly next to her as they intertwined in each others arms on the floor.

After half an hour on the hard floor Ceridwen slowly sat up and stroked Marek's hair back off his forehead. He didn't move, happy to continue to lie there looking up at her. "So, is it Suetonius I should thank for sending you on this mission so I could see you," she asked playfully.

"You could," Marek replied, stretching and putting his hands under his head, "but it wouldn't register with him. He's focused solely on his mission."

"His mission to be an effective governor?"

"Oh it's much more than that. Suetonius means to subdue all of Britannia in order to advance his clout in Rome. He's an extremely ambitious man."

"What about you, his star praefectus?" Ceridwen asked proudly. "Does he mean to have you rise to glory with him?"

"Hardly." Marek sat up straight and had to consciously stop himself gritting his teeth. "He praises my skill as a commander but I'll be getting no recognition other than in the field." He swung his head to look directly at Ceridwen. "Everything's gone back to 'Rome for pure Romans' and there's no more place for us foreigners." He snorted.

"Well that's not a problem at all," Ceridwen said, smiling and stroking back the hair that had once again flopped forward into his face. "Your place is right here with me."

He grabbed her hand, kissed it and rubbed it against his left cheek to enjoy the softness of her skin. "I think about that constantly," he said, rubbing his lips across her palm. "With the new direction in Rome I've completely lost my taste for being any part of it whatsoever," he pulled her hand with his to his chest. "But I'll smile and serve my time, even under a racist commander." He slowly shook his head. "When I pledged my allegiance there was a real future with the legions. Now, more than ever, I just want to hurry through the next few years and be done with it." He looked at Ceridwen, sitting quietly and watching while he ranted, then smiled and wrapped his right arm around her. "Listen," he said, squeezing her to his side. "Next time you go to see Andarta I want you to warn her and Prasutagus that Suetonius is also looking for any excuse to crack down on the tribes. As governor he doesn't like the concept of client kingdoms."

"No?" Ceridwen asked, wrapping her arms around Marek's chest and cuddling up to him. "Why is that? I thought Rome benefited as much as we did."

"Simply put, he feels they keep too much revenue. With an occupied territory all generated wealth belongs to Rome."

"I'll certainly pass your concerns along," Ceridwen smiled happily up at him, "But I wouldn't worry. Prasutagus is a born diplomat and he's done very well with the Romans so far."

"True," Marek said, nodding in agreement. "But warn him for me anyway. Things are changing very rapidly and I don't like the new direction at all."

A few hours later after his third 'goodbye for now' to Ceridwen, Marek was back in armor and astride his horse but, just before he rode off, he remembered something. "I think some Ordovices mercenaries as well as the Carvetii must have partnered with Venutius when he tried to overthrow Cartimandua," he said while rummaging though his side pouch. He then produced the item he had retrieved right after the battle. "Many Iceni fell that day and one of the Ordovices I killed was wearing this." He dangled the silver coin pendant. Ceridwen immediately recognized the stylized horse and grabbed it, speechless.

"Obviously it was taken as a spoil from a fallen Iceni," Marek continued as Ceridwen stood transfixed, staring in disbelief at the coin in her hand. "Perhaps you can find out who it should rightfully go back to."

Ceridwen looked up, tears streaming down her cheeks as she tried desperately to exert control over her wavering mouth. Marek extended his right hand and tenderly stroked the side of her face with the back of his fingers. "I know; I'll miss you too," he said softly, "But don't worry." He then quickly turned and galloped off as a wailing Ceridwen dashed inside the house.

Two hours after Marek left, a rider arrived in Toftrees with an urgent message from Andarta. Prasutagus had been taken ill, would Ceridwen please come to Venta Icenorum at once.

Chapter Twenty Two: Passings

"He's dead, Andarta," were the first words Ceridwen blurted out on greeting her friend. More than a day had passed since Marek had left but her conflicted brain had yet to come to terms with this horrible turn of events, let alone put it into any perspective. She looked helplessly at Andarta through swollen bloodshot eyes. "Donogh is dead."

"Donogh?" Andarta gasped in surprise then, realizing what must have happened, asked, "He was with the Ordovices that took on the Romans?"

Ceridwen swallowed hard while vigorously nodding. Andarta took her friend's hands and led her to a nearby couch, then sat next to her. "Donogh had become a warrior of renown," she said. "So I don't doubt that he died well." She squeezed Ceridwen's hands. "But we'll still miss our friend."

Ceridwen forced a half smile. "I know," she whispered. "And I should be celebrating his life, but," she rapidly rubbed her lips in a desperate attempt to control her wrinkling mouth and managed to eke out, "But it was Marek that killed him!" She suddenly wrapped her arms tightly around Andarta's neck for support as her body convulsed with her wailing.

Andarta was clearly confused but, holding back her questions, she responded instead with a comforting hug and silently rocked Ceridwen back and forth until her tears finally subsided and she became able to straighten up again. Ceridwen smoothed her eyes with the tips of her index fingers and transformed back to her natural sparkly demeanor. "Thank you," she said warmly to Andarta. "I needed to get that out and you're the only one who could have understood."

"Donogh was killed by Marek?" Andarta asked.

"Yes, but it was in battle so it was fair, and Marek doesn't know who he was. Oh, I miss him so much, Andarta," Ceridwen responded ebulliently to the sound of Marek's name. "As sad as I am about Donogh's death, it really isn't Marek's fault, is it? Oh, I wish he and I could just run away from this ridiculous world right now and spend the rest of our lives together." She spoke to the ceiling. "Soon," she sighed wistfully as contentment flooded her previously anguished face. She then slowly dropped her eyes to look at Andarta. "Please forgive me for being so self-absorbed," she said. "You asked me to come here as comfort to you because Prasutagus wasn't well. How is he feeling? Better, I hope."

"My husband is dying, Ceri."

It only took three days for Marek and the replacement auxiliaries to catch up to the fourteenth legion that had, with very little opposition, already completely crossed the Ordovices territory and was now camped in a fortified enclosure on the shores of the Menai straits. He promptly reported to Suetonius.

"I can't imagine Cerealis was too pleased to relinquish most of his cavalry to you, was he?" Suetonius asked jovially.

"He wishes you every success," Marek responded flatly.

Suetonius slowly turned to look directly into Marek's face and began to chuckle. "The legions are definitely the place for you, Marek," he said as his grin grew. "You'd make a lousy diplomat."

"My taking these left him with only 300 equestrians. You can't expect him to be happy about it."

"He's fine." Suetonius flapped his right hand in front of his face. "He still has over 2,000 legionnaires; more than enough to control that part of the province." He nodded toward the shoreline where there was an ongoing flurry of activity. "What do you think of this idea?" he asked rhetorically. "I've got the engineers building a hundred shallow draft boats."

"To carry the scorpions over?"

"No, they'll be staying here. Scorpions are big and bulky and the new javelins are much more effective against an attacking army anyway. No, these boats you're looking at are for the legionnaires so they can cross in full armor and strike as soon as they land." He nodded at Marek. "You and the cavalry can walk and swim your horses across." He looked back admiringly toward the boats. "We'll be making the crossing at first low tide tomorrow and by nightfall I expect to have a garrison established."

Marek stared at the island shore on the horizon. "For holding the prisoners?" he asked, scratching his bristled chin with anticipated understanding. It was standard procedure when assaulting an urban population to take as many slaves as possible, as opposed to moving as a killing machine when engaging an enemy in the field.

"No." Suetonius' snapped response caused Marek to turn abruptly and notice how his commander had set his jaw. Suetonius drew a deep breath through clenched teeth, exhaled, stood up straight and slowly shook his head from side-to-side. "No," he repeated emphatically. "My orders, directly from Rome, are to slaughter them." He looked to Marek, unafraid to have his cavalry officer read the disagreement so pronounced on his face. "It seems that Druids are dangerous, even as slaves." He, too, then looked out toward the sea before explaining. "Apparently, in the few years that Claudius had them running rampant in Rome, the Druids managed to subvert a significant portion of the population and Nero is purported to fear them and their influence." He forced a laugh. "Not that Nero's actually running things."

"He's not?" Marek turned and cocked his head to the right.

"Nah! He's just a figurehead reveling in the glory of the office. Nero actually likes the Druids." Suetonius pulled at his chin with obvious irritation. "Seneca's the real power in Rome. Seneca's the one who gave these orders."

An eerie silence fell over the Roman camp with that evening's sunset. Flames shooting up from Mon were accompanied by bloodcurdling screams and shrieks. The word quickly spread through the ranks that the Druids were preparing dragons for battle. In spite of their decisive victory over the Ordovices, the legionnaires were quickly becoming terrified about the upcoming crossing; no army in history had ever fought against the all powerful, mysterious sorcerers known as the Druids. By midnight Suetonius was sufficiently concerned that he ordered every officer down to the rank of centurion to assembly.

"Listen to me." Suetonius voice boomed as he stood before them, his feet firmly planted a cubit apart and his hands squarely on his hips. "The occupants of Mon are flesh and blood men and women, the same as each of you, the same as the numerous enemies that we've dispatched in the past." He scanned his silent audience. "Many of them are actually treasonous Trinovantes and Ordovices who have already fled before you and who will soon die on your swords and, yes," he bounced his head. "Some of them are, indeed, Druids." His teeth shone in the firelight. "If Druids were as powerful as some people make out do you think we'd even be in Britannia? If they're so powerful, how is it that they have so easily been driven out of Rome?" He raised his right hand and held it clenched in front of him. "We're the Roman army. We don't give quarter to barbaric superstition." He flung his arm outstretched behind him. "That's for the Britons: The people whom we've conquered."

The officers immediately cheered in unison, their uplifted voices echoing into the night.

"Tell this to your men." Suetonius returned his hand to his hip. "I know they're afraid, but their fears are unfounded. Come on," he laughed loudly. "Half of the Britons over there are women." He nodded as the contagious laughter rippled through the crowd. "Tomorrow your men will be looking to you. Are you going to let them feel the disgrace of yielding to a troop of women and a band of fanatic priests?"

Brave faces were also being donned in Venta Icenorum that night as Andarta, Camora, Tasca and Ceridwen gathered at Prasutagus' bedside. The ailing king, his head supported by pillows, was hardly able to move his hands but nevertheless clenched as best he could onto those of his wife and daughters. "I've had a good life," he said with forced breath. "And before I leave you," he awkwardly licked his lips, "I want you to know the reasoning behind my will." He fixed his eyes on a scroll sitting on a small table next to Ceridwen. She pointed at it and, when he made a single nod, she quickly picked it up and handed it across the bed to Andarta.

"Read it," Prasutagus ordered.

Andarta's fingers fumbled with the will but, once unrolled, she quickly read it then looked quizzically at her husband. "You'd have an outsider own Iceni land?" she asked him, then turned to Ceridwen. "Prasutagus has named Nero a joint heir with Camora and Tasca," she explained.

"It's a token." Prasutagus strained as he spoke. "This way," he took three short breaths and tried to lick his lips. "This way the Iceni will be safe because Nero will be earning a percentage of the profits."

Andarta put a cup of water to his lips and he attempted to sip from it but most ran down the side of his mouth. She wiped it away and forced the corners of her mouth up at him and he continued his struggle to speak. "Profits from my lands. He's bound to make sure nothing happens to that." He made a feeble attempt to again squeeze his wife's hand. "It's not taking much away from the girls since they're only giving up a third, and they'll inherit your lands anyway," he leaned back as he exhaled, "Andarta." He clenched his teeth and forcefully pushed the back of his head into his pillow.

"Come girls," Ceridwen said quietly. "Give your father a kiss and let's let your mother spend some time alone with him." She kept one hand on each of the girl's backs as then bent over to kiss Prasutagus then, holding their hands, quickly led them out of the room. Looking back through the partially open doorway, Ceridwen watched as Andarta's right hand first went to her mouth then across Prasutagus' eyes. As Ceridwen pulled the door closed, Andarta collapsed in tears onto the bed.

At the Menai straits the next morning the sun rose to a bleak drizzle which offered no promise of abating even as Marek assembled the cavalry along the shoreline over two hours later. Sitting astride their horses the men all stared silently into the strangely quiet sea; it was as if, as low tide was reached, some unseen force had simply flattened out the waves. Mon was barely visible through the rain, just a shadowy outline of a shape in the unperceivable distance.

First off were the boats, each laden with fifty fully outfitted legionnaires ready to release a collective 10,000 javelins once they hit the beach. The cavalry were to cross closely behind them. Marek shouted to his men, enthusiastically confirming once again that for most of the way the water would barely reach their feet as he cantered along the beach between the row of horses and the water's edge. He pulled up, turned toward Mon, raised his right hand and yelled out, "Forward," as his horse's hooves disappeared beneath the dark water. He instantly recalled Ceridwen telling him how she would never attempt to ride Kelpie across the strait and always led him as she walked ahead, something that had always struck Marek as an odd thing to do. Right now, though, he was willing to concede that there was much to be said for having your feet on something solid when surrounded by so much water.

They were three quarters of the way across before the water reached a depth where the horses were compelled to swim, the same time that the previously quiet natives of Mon began horrific screaming and the flames of a thousand torches gathered on the foreboding beach ahead. "Stay together," Marek called out and, as soon as his horse found footing less than a minute later, quickly followed with, "It's already getting shallower." Looking beyond the row of boats he focused his eyes on the movement on the beach. Enemy archers were getting ready for them.

The boats landed amidst a hail of arrows and rocks but, protected by their oversized shields, the legionnaires simply marched up onto the shore and systematically made formation as if the missiles were nothing more than mildly bothersome insects. The Britons quickly fled the beach and disappeared amongst the distant sand dunes as the last boat, the one with the praetorians, Suetonius, and his horse, came aground. The commander walked his horse off the boat, moving to dry ground before mounting it, and once the cavalry was ashore and lined up behind the legionnaires, he ordered the troops to advance. It was only then that Marek realized it had finally stopped raining and that a warm wind from the south was rapidly clearing the clouds overhead.

The legion was not even as far the high tide line when the enemy reappeared, a mixed company too numerous to count completely covering the crest of every sand dune in front of them. Some were certainly warriors armed with swords and shields, no doubt the bulk of the renegade Trinovantes, but the majority of them were men and women armed only with a single spear or a sling. Suetonius immediately halted the advance and the legion waited, fists wrapped around their javelins, ready for the enemy's inevitable charge. The screams from the Britons signaled the beginning of their attack and, as they swarmed off the dunes to charge the legion, Suetonius called out for the first deadly throw. The second javelin barrage only seconds later produced such confusion in the enemy ranks that only half of the survivors continued the charge while the rest turned around and ran away back up the beach. It was time for Marek and the cavalry to engage them. The equestrians galloped forward to the dunes, running down and rapidly massacring those attempting to flee, then turned and reassembled at the top of the beach in a single line. At Marek's command they moved forward to corral the remaining enemy, either driving them onto the legionnaires' swords or dispatching them if they attempted to get past the horses. It was soon over, and except for a lucky few who somehow managed to evade the slaughter, Mon's entire defense force lay as a mass of bloodied, mangled bodies. The fourteenth quickly fell back into formation and, while a screaming flock of carrion birds swooped in over their heads to partake of the fresh feast on the beach, they systematically began their march over the dunes toward the main Druid stronghold. With the crossing behind them and the morning skirmish a resounding success, the legion's confidence was clearly buoyed. Suetonius sat proudly on his horse, ahead of his jubilant army. "I don't remember seeing any dragons on the beach," he said loudly and jovially. He turned to the officer riding to his right. "Did you see any, Marek?"

"Not one, Suetonius."

"Then dragons must just be another myth, eh?" He projected his voice so it was clearly audible to the entire army. "Just like the so called power of the Druids themselves." Suetonius, taking deep breaths through his open mouth, ran his tongue behind his lower teeth as laughter rippled through the ranks. With the taking of Mon he'd be showing the world that nothing stands in the way of the Roman army.

It was only a short while later when Suetonius raised his right hand to stop the column. He stared at the strangely quiet forest ahead of them, squinting and scanning it several times from side-to-side. Finally, he turned to Marek. "Ride with me up that hill," he said, and the two of them quickly ascended for a better view of the path ahead. The army remained still and incredibly alert.

"Just as I thought," Suetonius said, rubbing his left cheek with his right hand. "There it is."

The two men looked down on the now clearly visible Druid town. There were over a hundred buildings, the largest making up the town center in an area where the forest had been cleared, but the majority of them were nestled amongst the trees. There was a raised mound in front of what appeared to be the main building. The cleared area was filled with activity as the occupants prepared for the siege. "Move half the cavalry into the forest to surround those buildings and cut off any escape," Suetonius pointed with his right index finger. "I'll then have the legionnaires move in." He turned his head rapidly with a jerk before Marek could respond. "But I don't want you in there with them, Marek. You and I will watch the action from up here."

Marek, his questions quelled by Suetonius' expression, elected to bite his tongue, simply nodded and left to deploy the cavalry. Half an hour later the two men were back on the hill to watch the assault. It was now close to dusk and the wind that had earlier cleared the sky was increasing in intensity to the point of occasional howling and driving in menacingly looking thunderclouds. Oblivious to the changing weather, Marek and Suetonius watched the legionnaires march unimpeded through the forest and fall into formation at the edge of town. At the town center a tall figure in a long blue robe that billowed and fluttered behind him took to the mound and six rows of men and women carrying spears lined up in front of him. They were all naked, their bodies intricately painted with blue swirling designs and their long hair tossed randomly by the breeze.

"I've seen this before," Suetonius said. "Why do Briton spear throwers always go naked into battle?"

"Two reasons," Marek replied. He'd asked that same question himself so many years before. "First, so their throw is unimpeded, but the second reason is more important. If they fall they're ready to return to the earth." He turned his head slowly to look at his commander. "They are, and always will be, part of the land."

Suetonius nodded thoughtfully, almost respectfully. He jutted his chin toward the Druid on the mound. "That has to be their chief."

"Devyn," Marek said quietly.

Devyn raised his staff above his head and one of the Roman officers suddenly yelled out, "Turtle." As Marek and Suetonius looked on, archers suddenly appeared on every rooftop and in every doorway. The legion, protected by their cover of shields, quick marched into town. Cohorts broke away as small turtles moving toward each building, but the main force, besieged by continuous arrows, pushed on to the town center. The wind was growing fiercer and the now almost constant howling was accompanied by flashes of lightening and rumbles in the distance as the Romans flooded into the square. Devyn turned his face to the sky and, following a quick movement of his hand at his neck, his robe was taken by the wind. His lean body, like the spear throwers in front of him, was painted in woad. He stretched his arms above his head and with both hands clenched around his staff he roared up at the sky. In hundreds of places throughout the town the ground suddenly exploded into flames. Every building was on fire as were many of the frantic legionnaires, rolling on the ground to extinguish themselves amidst panic stricken screams of, "dragons." Before the Roman officers were able to regain order the spear throwers moved forward and charged the invaders. The Druids had never stood a chance in this encounter, but they took many Romans with them. More than even Suetonius had anticipated. While it was true that Devyn and his followers came to their deaths on the swords of the Romans, they fell amidst the flames of their own design.

The rain from the thunderstorm doused the fires during the night, and when morning finally arrived, there was nothing left of the Druid city. Suetonius kicked into the muddy charred earth where the main building had once stood. He and Marek were surveying the site, confirming that nothing of value remained. "Over 400 legionnaires dead and almost a thousand injured." Suetonius was attempting to mentally reconcile the cost of this victory. He took a deep breath to fill his lungs with the fresh air that was already displacing the smell of the extinguished fire then rapidly shook his head. "We'll stay out of action for a month or two to let the men recover. The Ordovices have been defeated, the Druids are no more, and the Silures are in the vice grip between us and the twentieth legion. We'll take care of them in due course, they aren't going anywhere." He nodded sharply towards Marek. "I dare say we'll have the conquest of Britannia all wrapped up within another three months."

Marek scanned his eyes over the ruins, still in disbelief that the Druids would allow themselves to come to such an end. Surely this was somehow a facade, an elaborate diversion. But he'd witnessed their total annihilation with his own eyes. Or had he? While Mon had always been their home, Llyn had told him on more than one occasion that the Druids had no allegiance to any particular geography, that the only important thing was continuing education, the passing of oral tradition, and providing guidance to the tribes of Britannia. More than guidance; they'd basically taken control of the country through the recent declaration of vergobretos. Plus, they surely knew well in advance that the Romans were coming and had more than ample time to prepare for them.

Marek's right hand reached to scrape across the stubble on his chin to conceal the treasonous thoughts that were suddenly taking control of his mouth, allowing him to resist telling Suetonius that things may not be quite as straightforward as the mighty Roman commander believed them to be.

Chapter Twenty Three: Boudica

The battle decisively won and after a few days of uneventful patrols across Mon, Suetonius left a contingent of 500 legionnaires from the twentieth legion at the fort and pulled the remainder, along with the fourteenth legion, back across the Menai straits to the mainland where he ordered the construction of a fortified town overlooking the coast. Segontium, a symbol of Roman occupation as well as a garrison of sufficient means to quash any local resistance, was completed within a month.

Marek had just returned from a late afternoon ride in the countryside and was alone currying his horse outside the stables when a sultry voice from behind him cooed, "Hello Marek." He turned with a start. "Julia!" he exclaimed, raising his eyebrows as he looked at his commander's' daughter as she stood smiling at him. She was an incredibly attractive girl in spite of the fact that her eyes and lips were lined with dark color and her hair was too perfect. If he had his way he'd wash her face and give her a tussling, but then he'd probably be unable to resist that mussed look and end up bringing on the wrath of her father. He quickly glanced behind her, but she was alone.

"Tell me what you think of my new dress, Marek," she asked, swinging her hips to cause it to flutter around her legs while she spoke. "It's Iceni; I just picked it up at the market in Camulodunum. There's so much more selection when you buy locally than what you find in Rome." She stepped toward Marek and brushed the hair from his forehead, but he grabbed her wrist and held it away. "You shouldn't be here," he told her.

"No?" she pouted, easing her hand away and allowing it to drop to her side. "What do you think my father do if he found us together," she smirked. "Make you marry me?"

"He'd more likely have me flogged."

"Oh, I don't think so." She slowly moved her head from side-to-side, her lips parted while her hand toyed with the pendant hanging between her half exposed breasts. "He says you're the most capable officer in his command."

Marek turned back to his horse and resumed brushing it. "Did he also tell you I'm not a Roman?" he said tersely.

"Yes, he did." Julia moved behind him, slid her hands around his waist and whispered, "I've heard forbidden fruit tastes sweetest," into his ear before playfully biting at it. Marek's fumbling caused him to drop his comb. He quickly leaned down to retrieve it while Julia stepped back and giggled. "I have to go check in with my father," she said, walking backwards. "I came to Segontium with a delegation from Rome and I have all sorts of things to tell." She beamed and waved at him with the fingers of her right hand. "I'll see you later, Marek."

It turned out to be only a few hours later when Marek saw her next because, as soon as he had finished meeting with the emissaries from Nero, Suetonius called for the senior officers to dine that evening with him and his daughter. Marek relaxed comfortably on the pillows provided and enjoyed the roast venison and fine wine while attempting to avoid Julia's wide eyed smiles and silently mouthed messages, until the governor dismissed the serving slaves and rose to speak. "It seems that several things of importance have occurred while we've been campaigning," Suetonius began, "so I've brought you here to fill you in. There are some directives that I've received from the emperor but," he turned and smiled at Julia, "my daughter can undoubtedly provide the most pertinent information."

His smile disappeared as he looked back to his officers. "On a potentially disturbing note I've just learned that our long time ally, King Prasutagus of the Iceni, has died."

Marek instantly put down his goblet and stared, almost in disbelief, listening attentively as Suetonius continued.

"The Iceni recognize succession by his wife, Queen Andarta, who apparently is also from the Iceni royal bloodline."

"Do we know the cause of his death?" Marek asked.

"Some disease," Julia interjected casually. "I don't think he was an old man but I hear he failed rather quickly."

"I see," Marek said, then looked down and swallowed.

"What's significant about this," Suetonius added, "Is that he named the Emperor Nero as heir to his lands."

"But he had children!" Marek involuntarily blurted out, then sank back into the pillow when the room went silent and he realized everyone was staring at him.

"Two girls," Suetonius said slowly while glaring at Marek. "Who were listed in his will as heirs." He looked back to the room again. "Nero was named as a co-heir but I suspect that that was just intended as a show of loyalty. I'm quite certain Prasutagus didn't expect anything to occur as a result of it." Suetonius paused and reached for his wine leaving the unsaid, 'however,' floating in the air and fully enjoying how it was tormenting Marek in particular. He finally nodded to Julia, beckoning for her to speak.

"About fifteen days ago, Seneca arrived in Britannia and immediately headed for Venta Icenorum." She clearly enjoyed having the full attention of the officers. "What I gleaned from those traveling with him was that Nero has changed a lot recently. Realizing that Seneca is seen as the real power in Rome, Nero is pushing him into the background and making more decisions on his own. He also fell out of favor with many Romans when he had his mother killed, so when Prasutagus' will was brought to Rome, Nero seized it as an opportunity to increase his popularity." Julia grinned. "Since women can't inherit property under Roman law, Nero first declared the Iceni lands to be his personal property. Then, since he was, by that reasoning, Prasutagus' only legitimate heir, he proclaimed that he was necessarily now king of the Iceni." Julia, still smiling, looked around at the wonderfully shocked faces of her audience and she even giggled when she laid eyes on Marek's expression.

"Anyhow," she continued jovially. "In an effort to increase his popularity, which worked very well by the way, Nero immediately turned around and ceded the Iceni territory to the citizens of Rome." She was so animated, as if she were delivering a story at one of the elaborate parties she was accustomed to, and the lightness of her delivery made it clear that the subject matter was of secondary importance to her.

"My orders," Suetonius chimed in, "are to inform the Iceni they are now a province and to take whatever steps are necessary to secure them as part of Roman Britannia."

"And that's why Seneca was so anxious to get there first," Julia added with glee, eager to retake the limelight. "He wanted to get his money back from Queen Andarta before she found out the Iceni weren't going to profit any more from trade and that their business was worthless."

Marek buried his face into his goblet to conceal his horror. While everyone else in the room enjoyed laughter he was desperately hoping that Ceridwen had taken his warning to heart and was able to convince Andarta not to provoke the Romans.

"More wine all around," Suetonius boomed loudly. "I've already issued orders for Petilius Cerealis to send representatives from the ninth legion to notify the Iceni of their new status. In the meantime we have an enemy, the Silures, to prepare for."

Andarta stood defiantly blocking the doorway to the palace at Venta Icenorum while the Roman centurion stood out in the courtyard and read the proclamation aloud. When he had finished he rolled it up, tied it, then walked up the steps and handed it to Andarta, who remained with her arms folded and refused to even look at it, never mind take it from him. "I don't care what it says," she said with a calculated calm in her voice. "The Iceni are a free and independent kingdom and I'm ordering you and your men to leave it at once."

The centurion half smiled and once again held out the scroll to her. "Perhaps you weren't listening when I read this," he said, tapping it against her left arm.

"I heard you quite clearly," Andarta snarled back, glaring at him with unblinking eyes. "And since your emperor considers himself a member of the Iceni royal family, do you imagine he'd take lightly your intrusion into our home?"

"Oh, he would absolutely approve!" The centurion answered. He was clearly enjoying this. "Perhaps you don't know about the emperor? He killed his mother, and the last time he had a step-sister he married her." He leered at Camora who was standing behind her mother while adding, "Maybe I'll continue that tradition as his proxy."

Andarta slapped his face with as much might as she could muster, but immediately after the blow had fallen he had her wrist in the firm grip of his right hand. He roughly dragged her out of the doorway with one hand and tossed her to the soldiers behind him, then slowly turned around as she struggled to no avail against them. "Tie her between two of those trees," he nodded toward a stand of oaks. "I'll be out to flog her as soon as I'm finished with her daughter."

Andarta could see nothing as she was dragged to the trees and all she could hear was the laughter of the Roman soldiers as they pillaged the palace, loading carts with whatever valuables they came across within. The ropes dug into her wrists as she pulled and strained against them and they were thoroughly soaked with her blood when the centurion returned and stood in front of her brandishing a leather whip. "It was such a wonderful surprise to find you have two daughters," he told her, playfully slapping the coiled leather into his open hand. "I'd have you too, but after them I'm afraid I'm all used up."

"Or maybe you're just not man enough for a real woman," she spat at him.

The centurion walked behind her, grabbed her dress in both hands at the neck and in a single move ripped it in two leaving just a piece of it hanging in tatters from the shoulders of her now almost naked body. "Your girls refused to scream for me," he said as he readied the whip. "I do hope you won't disappoint me too."

The loud crack of leather against flesh followed by a back arching sting forced Andarta to dig her fingernails into the palms of her hands to suppress her vocal chords, but she successfully endured twenty lashes through clenched teeth before the centurion spoke again. He walked back in front of her, shaking his head as he gathered up the whip. "There must be something wrong with you Iceni that prevents you from screaming, eh?" He cocked his head to look into her eyes but instead of the face of a broken woman he met a stoic glare.

"Remember this face, centurion." Andarta slowly enunciated every word. "For the next time you see it will be the instant before you die."

"You really are quite the feisty little bitch, aren't you?" The centurion laughed dismissively as he straightened up, then walked away to assemble his men. "The next time a Roman comes by you'd be well advised to show a little respect," he called out to her as he led the soldiers away with the spoils from the palace. "We're going to recognize you as the administrative head of this Roman province, but if you want to keep that position you'd better learn how to act the part."

When the sounds of the Roman soldiers had faded safely into the distance Camora and Tasca cautiously emerged from the palace and, seeing the way was clear, ran to their mother and cut her bonds. She collapsed onto the ground but found the strength to pull the girls to her and, with one arm around each, held onto them for a few silent moments before nuzzling into Tasca's, then Camora's disheveled hair. "I promise both of you the vengeance you deserve," she said, squeezing them to her sides before painfully rising to her feet. Hand-in-hand the three of them walked back into the palace and anxiously made for the hiding place where Prasutagus' sword had been concealed after his death. The Romans had not discovered it. They rapidly opened the secret compartment, and as soon as her trembling hands become fists around the scabbard of the heavy sword Andarta's face broke into a resolute, teeth baring smile. Seemingly unable to take her eyes from it she slowly raised the sword up. It had passed to her with Prasutagus' death, but she'd not even wanted to look at it until now.

It was dusk when the peasants who had earlier scattered before the Roman soldiers returned to the courtyard, accompanied by seven warriors they had roused from the closest farms. "Queen Andarta, Queen Andarta," the peasants called out anxiously as they gathered outside the palace, but their meek, worried voices gave way to a raucous cheer when she emerged wearing a leather tunic, a large gold torque around her neck and the former king's sword hanging to her left side. She walked to the top of the steps flanked by Camora and Tasca, each wearing leather and holding her bow. "Prepare my chariot," she called out, and as four peasants promptly scurried away she descended the steps and extended her right hand to the warriors, calling out each of their names as they came forward. "Camma, Veleda, Gaine, Emrys, Tages, Ono, Dubhtach. My friends, will you ride with us?"

Her question wasn't necessary. Each warrior quickly took turns first clasping their queen's hand then mounting their horse, and when the peasants led two horses pulling Andarta's chariot into the courtyard they immediately fell into a row behind it. Clenching her teeth against the pain of the wounds on her back and struggling against the weight of the sword she, nevertheless, stepped up into the chariot without making a sound. As soon as Camora and Tasca were on board she took up the leather reins and, after a quick glance to the riders, quickly disappeared into the now dark forest with the small band of warriors close behind.

It was still night when they emerged from the trees into the vast meadow that marked the southern border of Iceni territory. The fires from where the Romans had made camp almost a mile in the distance were quite visible under the clear moonless sky. Andarta pulled to a stop and struggled to draw the sword from its scabbard but quickly realized her intention to hold it aloft as they galloped against the Romans was not going to be possible; it was simply much too heavy for her. Instead, she used all of her strength to hold it above her head with both hands, called out, "attack," and with one hand on the reins quickly re-sheathed it as her horses leaped to gallop. Her long red hair streamed like flames behind her, fluttering over the heads of Camora and Tasca as they readied their bows. Their arrows silenced the sentry with deadly accuracy only moments after he had called the alarm. Andarta charged her chariot furiously through the camp then quickly pulled up the horses at the other end while the warriors leaped from their mounts to engage the now awakened legionnaires. Andarta put one hand on each of her daughters' shoulders. "Stay close to me," she told them, then clambered down from the chariot and began a fast walk back into the Roman camp. Her right hand gripped the hilt and her left held the scabbard of her sword, enabling her to simultaneously wear and carry it. Immediately in front of them was the centurion fighting against one of the Iceni warriors. "Leave him to me, Tages," she screamed out.

Tages instantly, obediently, broke off the engagement and backed away and the centurion swung around ready to face his new challenger. "You?" he laughed broadly, holding his gladius slightly angled away from his right hip. "Come on then, woman."

Andarta held her sword directly in front of her with both hands and ran screaming at him while an arrow zinged from each side of her, one hitting him in the chest and the other deeply embedding into his neck. The tip of heavy Iceni sword disappeared into his middle, and as he stumbled backwards, Andarta fell forward, still clutching the hilt, and with her own weight impaled him onto the ground. Temporarily winded, she first gasped to gain her breath then crawled up on top of the centurion's body, hands on his shoulders as she stared down onto his face. Blood was gushing from his mouth and he attempted to spit it at her, but his energy was already gone and his attempt barely registered more than a feeble gurgle. Andarta glared unblinkingly into his eyes with the desperate need to watch life completely drain away from him. Camora and Tasca, their bows half drawn, stood protectively over her. Finally satisfied that the centurion was dead she slowly looked up at her daughters. "Just as I promised you," she announced triumphantly and then quickly turned to Gaine who had just run up to them. "Are they all dead?" She asked her in a strangely calm, matter of fact voice.

"All dead," Gaine answered as she sheathed her sword. "And you dispatched their leader yourself."

Andarta rose to her feet as the victorious warriors gathered around and silently formed a circle around their queen and princesses. They seemed to be waiting for something. Andarta looked puzzled.

"Your first kill, my queen," Emrys said, nodding toward the centurion's body as a means of explanation. Andarta was unable to conceal the inappropriate delight she suddenly felt as she turned and, both hands on the hilt, pulled her sword out of the limpid corpse. No one noticed the figure walking silently toward the group as Andarta raised the sword above her head and brought it down to decapitate the body with a single blow. It was only when she wrapped her fingers into the hair and held the severed head aloft, the blood from it streaming down her arm while her audience cheered, that she saw the approach of the Druid. "Llyn!" she called out in surprise.

"Hail, warrior queen," he called back. He solemnly looked around at the twenty scattered bodies. "Did any Iceni fall?"

"Not one!" Camma instantly responded.

"I see." Llyn slowly walked up to Andarta who was still clutching her prize, proud proof of her entry into the company of warriors. "Tell me, queen. Who did these men kill to deserve this level of retribution? And what happened to the peace loving Andarta?"

Blood still boiling Andarta stared defiantly back at the druid. "They killed Andarta," she said flatly and held up the head. "And victory exacted this price."

"Victory, is it?" Llyn stood his ground.

"Yes, Llyn. Victory. Andarta tried to live at peace with the Romans and they killed her. Here on out I take the name of victory itself and, as warrior queen, will return the Iceni to the old ways. Andarta is dead. My name is now Boudica."

"Do you realize the consequences of what you've set in motion here, Boudica?" Llyn asked, his voice loud but not angry. Llyn was actually proud of her. "We'll have to drive the Romans out of Britannia now, or they'll exact a terrible revenge," he warned.

"Then it's time for the Romans to leave." Boudica stood tall.

"It most certainly is!" Llyn quickly nodded with approval at the band of warriors. He then looked directly at Boudica again. "Return to Venta Icenorum and assemble your army," he said earnestly. "I'll be there in a day with Amergin."

"But Amergin is Trinovantes?" Boudica looked askance.

"The Trinovantes have a thousand warriors at the ready. We were developing plans for them to take back Camulodunum and I was on my way to ask the Iceni to support them." He made a slow, sweeping side-to-side motion with his head across the dead Romans. "But it seems more likely that they'll be now joining you, Queen Boudica."

Chapter Twenty Four: Berserker

C eridwen squirmed uncomfortably, her conflicted brain racing in multiple directions as she sat at the war room table with Boudica, Amergin and Llyn. The four of them were charged with the task of bringing about a free Britannia. She stared at the transformation of what used to be her best friend. She'd known Boudica all her life as Andarta the pacifist, the one who had disdained the very idea of handling a sword and would never even contemplate becoming a warrior. Yet, here she was, Iceni queen, proudly displaying a severed head and unhesitatingly issuing a general call to arms to make war on the greatest army in the world.

Ceridwen moved her eyes to Amergin sitting in the next chair. She'd despised the Trinovantes ever since they'd ambushed and killed her father, always looking down at them and considering them below the status of true Britons; especially since they'd so easily given up and became a Roman territory. Yet, here was the leader of the Trinovantes underground ready to stand with the Iceni and lead a thousand of warriors against the Romans. This man even had the ear and the respect of the Druids.

She turned in her seat slightly to look at Llyn. The Druids had invoked vergobretos to contain the tribes and prevent them from rebelling against the Romans, yet he was now here instigating an all out war. Was this really for the best interests of the people of Britannia, or simply revenge for the destruction of Mon?

But most disturbing to Ceridwen was what she saw when she looked inside herself. Ceridwen, the consummate warrior and fierce defender of Iceni independence was the only one sitting around the table wrestling with how this upcoming fight could be averted; how this could all be brought about peacefully. In spite of her participation in the fervid discussion she'd been silently, secretly agonizing about it for hours, but as the group began to solidify their plans she finally bit down on her lower lip and closed her eyes in acceptance of the inevitable. At least it would be ninth legion they would have to confront. Marek and the fourteen were far away so there was no chance of having to meet him across battle lines. After all, she did have a duty here. Surely, Marek of all people would understand that. Yes, she nodded confidently as both the group resolution and her personal resolve came together. Yes, she would have no problem with this at all.

Phase one was to take Camulodunum. Llyn would enter the town the day before for reconnaissance and, as he put it, "to arrange for a few things that will prove useful." This would certainly rouse the ninth legion, and if there was ever hope of having a phase two of the plan, the Iceni/Trinovantes coalition would have to defeat them.

"As soundly as the Silures beat the twelfth," Boudica chimed in. Ceridwen was taken aback and she quizzically studied her friend. Not only had Boudica eagerly embraced her new role of a warrior but she seemed possessed, actually relishing in the idea of armed conflict. Amergin, however, looked concerned. "We might outnumber them," he said, uneasily rubbing his chin. "But our warriors know how effective the legionnaires can be and there might be more than a little reluctance to take on a battle ready legion."

"Afraid, Amergin?" Boudica, wild eyed, leaned across the table toward him.

"Practical, Boudica," Amergin said unflinchingly before leaning slightly toward her.

Llyn slammed his fist onto the table. "Enough," he shouted, glaring at both of them. "Amergin is correct, but we have the means to overcome those fears." He waited until everyone was silent and staring intently at him before fully standing and producing a bundle from inside his cloak. He placed it on the table and slowly unwrapped the outer cloth covering.

"Serencleddyf!" Ceridwen jumped to her feet, her hands flat on the table as she leaned across it, unable to take her eyes off the sword as Llyn raised it up in both hands.

"All your warriors will follow Serencleddyf," he announced. "As eagerly as they all followed Caractacus."

He backed away from the table and, still holding the sword in front of him, walked toward Boudica. "Will you wield it, Boudica?"

"Let me," Ceridwen screamed out. All eyes turned to her as she scurried around the table to stand next to Boudica. "Let me be the one to carry Serencleddyf for you," she pleaded. "I have much more experience fighting with a sword and you will lead from your chariot anyway." Ceridwen was panting, unable to close her trembling mouth as she stood just a small step away from the sword, staring desperately into Boudica's eyes. "Please. Let me carry Serencleddyf."

"It's my responsibility, Ceri," Boudica said flatly and reached out for the sword. She took the scabbard in both hands and lifted it from Llyn's grasp. "It feels so light!" she exclaimed with surprise and quickly wrapped the fingers of her right hand tightly around the hilt. The scabbard firmly in her left hand, Boudica then drew Serencleddyf and held it above her head in a single motion. "This is how we'll enter battle," she screamed out at the top of her voice. "I'll hold Serencleddyf high for all to see as we drive out the Romans and return to the old ways." Still holding the sword aloft she looked systematically at each of her companions. Llyn gave her a quick nod of approval. Amergin bowed and said, "Boudica, queen of the Britons. The Trinovantes will follow wherever you lead."

Boudica then stared directly into Ceridwen's gray eyes, eyes that were still focused attentively upwards toward the sword. "Ceri?" she asked.

"I'll be beside you all the way," Ceridwen said airily, then tore her gaze down from Serencleddyf to force herself to look at her queen.

The men under Llyn's command worked quickly and silently through the night to secretly dig a tunnel under the huge statue of Claudius in the square at Camulodunum, shoring it up with heavy timbers to prevent it from collapsing under the weight. Still dark when the task was completed to his satisfaction, Llyn then had the men collect dry brush and bracken from the edge of the forest and stuff it into the cavity until it was over half full. As the faint glow in the eastern sky signaled early dawn he then set the brush alight and ordered the men to quickly cover the tunnel opening with the sheets of turf they had so carefully removed at the beginning of the venture. The small amount of smoke that seeped out mixed into the early morning fog and raised no suspicion from the townspeople as they began their day.

By mid-morning Llyn and his band had completed their next project at the estuary, and as the tide receded, he casually asked a couple of passers by what they thought the odd shapes in the sand were. Since news of any kind travels fast through a Roman town it wasn't long before hundreds of people were rushing to witness the shapes of human corpses being exposed by the ebb tide. The resultant wave of unease that rapidly spread through Camulodunum turned to outright panic when, at late morning, the massive statue of Claudius mysteriously tumbled face down into the ground and word spread of a rebel army bearing down on the city. Faced with such ominous signs of impending doom even the retired Roman soldiers became caught up in the pervasive sense of hopelessness and desperation.

Amergin and his thousand Trinovantes warriors were the embodiment of the settlers' worst fears. Free to let vent their years of pent-up frustration and anger they brutally slaughtered every Roman they encountered as they systematically ransacked, then burned, all of the villas north of Camulodunum while awaiting the arrival of the Iceni army. With bloodlust fully boiling, the Trinovantes eagerly followed Boudica's 5,000 mounted warriors when they arrived, even running alongside and keeping up with them as they cantered south to Camulodunum. By midday the city was surrounded. The aspect of Boudica, her height accentuated by her standing in chariot, brandishing Serencleddyf above her head with her long red hair streaming behind her in the wind was absolutely terrifying. Word spread throughout the Britons of a sorceress to lead them to freedom and a restoration of the old ways, words that instilled unbounded fear in the Romans as they interpreted this to mean she was a living deity. More importantly, it was clear that Boudica was the Druid sanctioned queen, the new leader of all of the tribes of Britannia.

The end of the capital came swiftly. Without city walls there was no way Camulodunum could be effectively defended and even the most stalwart soldier who tried to stand his ground was simply swept away as the army systematically smashed everything in its path, destroying every wooden building before setting it alight. By nightfall Camulodunum had been reduced to a firestorm and those who managed to survive the onslaught sought safety inside the only building not made using wood: the temple of Claudius. The veterans undoubtedly felt they could resist from here until help arrived.

Help was, indeed, on its way. As expected, the ninth legion was dispatched from its base in Verulamium as soon as word of trouble had reached them. But rather than await their arrival, Boudica led the Iceni contingent away from Camulodunum that night to intercept them. Llyn had convinced her she would fare better by attacking the Romans on the march rather than taking them on in conventional battle, so she rapidly moved the Iceni army northwest to hide out in the forest. The all too eager Trinovantes were left behind in order to finish the job in Camulodunum. They waited patiently through the night and when morning arrived the fire had sufficiently subsided for them to storm the magnificent temple. They annihilated every one of the veterans inside and then completely smashed the ornate marble into unrecognizable rubble.

At the same time that the Trinovantes were obliterating the Temple of Claudius, the central symbol of Roman occupation in Britannia, the Iceni were laying in wait to ambush the other symbol of Roman authority, the mighty ninth legion.

Ceridwen's left hand held tightly onto Kelpie's reins as she leaned through the bush for an unimpeded view of the road below. Leading the column were the auxiliaries. She had to be patient and quiet as these men and horses passed since her assigned target was the first group of legionnaires. These cavalrymen would meet Boudica's chariots head on. It was important to rout them quickly since cavalry were the legion's best defense in an ambush situation and 500 rapidly moving, chariot based Iceni archers was the best way to accomplish that. A sudden, odd thought caused Ceridwen to break out in a warm smile as it occurred to her that Marek had significantly helped the Iceni with this battle. Single handedly he'd previously taken away the majority of their cavalry, a force that would have made them much more formidable, reducing them to only around 300 horsemen. "You see," she whispered to Kelpie. "He's always looking out for me." She hugged her horse's neck and quietly watched as the last of the cavalry went by.

Next in line came the standard bearers of the ninth legion, and as they passed in front of her Ceridwen silently slid up onto Kelpie's back. "This is it," she said taking a deep breath, and then howled loudly as she rode Kelpie down the slight incline to the road. The battle hardened legionnaires instantly drew their swords but were unable to make any formation on the narrow section of road and were forced to stand individually as the Iceni swarmed down on them from both sides. The din of the chariots charging into the cavalry added even more confusion to the Roman ranks.

Ceridwen leaped off Kelpie with Glynu firmly in both hands and engaged the lead centurion with a furious swing. He blocked the blow with his shield, jarring Ceridwen and causing her to take several steps backwards in order to lift Glynu up over her shoulder so she could swing again, but the centurion rushed at her with the tip of his gladius before she was able to complete the move. Her sword dashed onto the ground. She jumped to the right just in time to avoid being stabbed and, stumbling, somehow summoned the strength to swing Glynu in an upward motion. Her opponent avoided it by taking a step back but doing so gave her time to move her sword again up over her right shoulder and stand face-to-face with the centurion. He grinned and attempted to goad her into making the first move, but Ceridwen was resolute and kept her focus on his eyes. When he finally made his lunge she nimbly leaped toward him, swinging her sword rather then backing off. Glynu first sliced the side of his neck, and when she completed her spin around she thrust it deeply just below the Roman's armpit. The gladius fell to the ground as the Roman dropped to his knees.

Ceridwen pushed him away with her foot in order to quickly retrieve her bloody sword from the convulsing body. She looked around. The deed was done and the victorious Iceni were busily taking spoils from the vanquished. She sheathed Glynu then reached down to pick up the fallen Roman's sword, the gladius that had come so close to running her though. It was so light and easy to handle; no wonder the cavalrymen could use them from horseback. She would keep this; in fact she might even use it.

The opportunity to do so came that very afternoon. Only a few auxiliaries had escaped the carnage and they scattered with chariots in pursuit rather than make an orderly retreat back to their base.

Without any army to defend it, the city walls of Viroconium were now useless against the Iceni, and capitalizing on their sky high morale, Boudica ordered an immediate attack. They battered down the main gate and swarmed through the streets killing all they encountered, but the goal here was not one of destruction. Rather, it was to capture the vast storage buildings intact. Llyn's smile grew broader and broader as he went from building to building, mentally tallying the take. A Roman legion's mandate was to maintain a sufficient supply of provisions for an entire year, and Llyn concluded that Cerealis had done his job very well. There was now no need for the late spring planting. Here was enough food such that the entire Iceni population, every farmer and peasant, could be taken from the fields for a season to assist in phase two, the most ambitious undertaking ever attempted against Rome. With the ninth legion destroyed, Londinium was defenseless.

The strategy was sound. Londinium was a Roman creation, set up as a huge port and trading center to exploit the wealth of Britannia. There was no fort or standing army there, just 70,000 traders and merchants and bankers; 70,000 foreign exploiters. With them gone there would be nothing left to protect, and faced with a hopeless situation, it followed that the remaining Romans would simply leave Britannia to avoid their own annihilation. The main Roman force, the combined twelfth and fourteenth legions, was down to only 10,000 men and the second legion in the south couldn't have more than 2,000. Romans as a rule never withdrew, but there was a precedent. The Teutoberger forest over fifty years ago was the only other place where an entire legion had been destroyed and that incident resulted in a free Germania. Llyn's intent was for the channel to be the modern equivalent of the Rhine.

By nightfall the Iceni were settled in and around Viroconium and their ebullient voices carried across the trees with the smoke from their numerous celebratory fires. Ceridwen chose a site away from the others and sat alone, thoughtfully watching the reflection from her small campfire dance on the blade of her newly acquired sword. She had eaten earlier and Kelpie was settled for the night but, in spite of the intense activities of the day, what should have been a much needed sleep remained elusive. A slight rustle from behind suddenly startled her and she instinctively grabbed the gladius tightly in her fist and jumped to her feet, only to encounter Llyn's calm countenance standing in front of her. He looked down at the sword. "I noticed you using that while mounted today, Ceridwen," he said. "You were very impressive!"

"It's a superior weapon," she said, holding it away from herself, turning it back and forth so it could once again reflect the firelight.

"And you, ever the wolf, eagerly seize new opportunity."

"That's how we grow, Llyn. You taught us that." Ceridwen resumed her seat next to the fire and Llyn sat opposite her.

"Do you still feel Serencleddyf should have gone to you?" he asked.

"Boudica uses it to inspire the people," Ceridwen answered cryptically. "Waving it about from that chariot of hers is all very well, you know." She stared into the fire. "But as a weapon it's seeing very little action." She forced a smile. "A shame, really. It's such a fine sword." She peeked sideways at Llyn to try to read his expression.

"Boudica's role as queen is to lead," he said in a matter of fact tone. "Do you think she's being effective?"

Ceridwen turned quickly, ready to tell him that wasn't the point but, as Llyn's teeth flashed, she realized that it was exactly that. Unable find fault with his argument, she wordlessly conceded the point. Then, after a little thought, Ceridwen waved her index finger to recapture Llyn's attention. "She's fallen to the berserker, you know," she said.

"Oh, she was there well before I gave her Serencleddyf."

"But you gave it to her anyway?" Ceridwen snatched her finger back.

"At this time, Ceridwen, Britannia is in need of the berserker." He looked at the ground and broadly caressed the lower part of his face with his right hand while he slowly turned his head from side-to-side.

"But she wants to throw away everything we've gained since the Romans arrived," Ceridwen protested. "All Boudica talks about is returning to the old ways." She turned deadly serious. "What became of your concept of growth through assimilation?"

"Our hand has been forced and we have to take Britannia first." He tightened his fist around his beard he then looked directly up at Ceridwen. "And I'm afraid that our best chance for Britannia to be free is to allow Londinium to fall to a demonstration of our resolve."

Ceridwen gulped as she understood the gravity of what the druid was telling her. "So you're condoning her invocation of the old ways?"

"It's the only way." Llyn slowly nodded as his hand released his beard. "And it's going to take a berserker to do what needs to be done now."

It took only a matter of days for the Iceni to organize nearly every horse and cart and every able body into a force of over 100,000, ready to accompany the 10,000 mounted warriors for the upcoming assault. Ceridwen felt chills run down her spine as she watched the berserk Boudica, completely unrecognizable now from the friend she had been a mere month prior, stand in her chariot brandishing Serencleddyf in her raised fist. "To Londinium," Boudica furiously screamed out to the cheering horde. "For Britannia, for freedom, for the old ways."

Chapter Twenty Five: Old Ways

Two months after returning from the conquest of Mon and having finished building the city of Segontium, the fourteenth and twelfth legions were about to move again. This time, against the Silures. Ready for action and anxious to be free from fending off Julia's persistent advances, Marek eagerly gave orders to his decurions to ready the cavalry and prepare to leave. Time would go by faster if there was action and the focus it would provide would help divert his thoughts away from the gnawing concerns he had for Ceridwen. Plus, once the Silures had been taken care of, he'd be able to take some time away from the army and satisfy himself that she was all right. She should be. While the Iceni certainly wouldn't react well to being named a province and she might not be inclined to heed his warning not to antagonize the Romans, Andarta was now in charge. And Andarta had always been a pacifist. As queen, she'd be able to keep Ceridwen's hotheaded, reactionary nature under control. At least he hoped so.

When first word of the Iceni uprising reached Segontium Suetonius wasn't completely surprised, and confident in Cerealis and the ninth's ability to deal with local tribal unrest, he saw no reason to alter his master plan. Suetonius considered the Silures the last major threat and was supremely confident that they could be rapidly crushed with his vice-grip maneuver, thereby finalizing the complete Roman occupation of Britannia; an accomplishment certain to significantly boost his political career in Rome. When news arrived a few days later of the loss of Camulodunum and the complete annihilation of the ninth legion, however, he instantly yielded to the obvious necessity of putting this goal on hold. Angered at having to change his plans and more worried than he chose to admit about the consequences of the loss of the ninth, he gruffly ordered the army be rapidly deployed east toward Trinovantes territory.

The march had barely begun when the even more devastating news arrived; over 100,000 armed Iceni were one the move and heading toward Londinium. It would be impossible for the legions to arrive at the city before them, and even if they could, Londinium had no walls or defenses. Suetonius immediately summoned Marek, and accompanied by 500 cavalrymen, they rode to Londinium as fast as their horses were able. They arrived there a full day ahead of the rebel forces.

Suetonius was amazed at the apparent normalcy of the activities in the city so, leaving the cavalrymen assembled near the main gate, he and Marek headed directly to the office of the procurator to seek out Decianus, the emperor's agent. "Do you have any idea what's about to descend on this city?" Suetonius shouted incredulously.

"A rather large mob," Decianus answered as he sat relaxed behind his desk. "Yes, we've heard about it." He carefully studied the Roman commander's expression then smiled and casually shook his head from side-to-side. "You army types always see things from the darkest side. I don't know why they're coming to Londinium, but I can assure you the Iceni have been excellent business partners with the merchants here for years. I refuse to even imagine that they could be meaning us any harm."

"No harm?" Suetonius beat his fist on the procurator's desk. The vibrations knocked over a small vase. "They've just burned Camulodunum, slaughtered everyone there and massacred the ninth legion."

"Then they clearly have an issue with Roman military authority," Decianus glared back at Suetonius, "don't they?" He looked away to right the upset vase, then flitted his eyes back. "Londinium is not a military target. If you feel they do have hostile intentions then I would suggest they are really more your concern, commander. Not ours."

"Listen to me, you pompous idiot." Suetonius boomed out. "The fact is this." He pointed at some imaginary spot behind him while leaning forward so close to Decianus' face that he could feel the commander's breath. "There is an angry rebel army less than a day away from Londinium and I can't get troops here fast enough to defend you. If you don't order an immediate evacuation of the city I can't be responsible for the consequences."

"Consequences? Now you listen to me," Decianus shouted back without flinching. "You're too used to dealing with the barbarians across the border." He wagged his index finger. "The Iceni are a civilized tribe. I can only imagine what it is that you've done to upset them, but they've obviously got your attention with their response and it looks like they're getting into position for some serious negotiation." He smiled as he slid back into his chair. "At worst they'll probably," he shrugged, "Oh, I don't know. Capture the city and ransom it back to you?" He leaned back and laughed then shook his head from side-to-side condescendingly. "We've not done anything to them so they certainly won't be out to do any harm to us. Your suggestion that we should simply scurry away," he wriggled his hanging fingers for effect, "For the merchants to leave their shops open to pillage, is absolutely preposterous. Now, get out of here."

"What are your thoughts, Marek?" Suetonius asked as the two men left the procurator's office. "Decianus does have a point that Londinium isn't a military target and that if it were captured it would give the Iceni tremendous leverage."

"But to what end?" Marek muttered thoughtfully. He stopped walking and slowly nodded as a wave of realization came over him, then quickly snapped his head up to look directly at Suetonius. "This whole thing may be more than the Iceni just wanting their independence back, you know," he said, his eyes wide. "You've heard the stories of this mysterious Boudica who's suddenly appeared as the Iceni queen, how she's most likely a Druid. This could be the beginning of an attempt to take back all of Britannia."

"But the Iceni are a bunch of artisans," Suetonius protested. "They could never pull that off."

"That's just how we've come to know them. Historically the Iceni have been the most feared warriors in Britannia. That's how they remained so unique a tribe."

"Perhaps," Suetonius rubbed his chin. "But in spite of the fact they're rebelling, the Iceni are still integrated into the new world. You heard Decianus tell us how for more than ten years they've been active traders and competent business people." He vigorously shook his head and resumed walking. "They're not going to just walk away from that. They need their trade with Rome; it's too much a part of their lives. Capturing the city and ransoming it to get their independence back makes good strategic sense for the Iceni." He stopped and turned to look back at Marek who hadn't moved.

"You'd better be sure of that." Marek seemed riveted to the ground. "For if the Iceni have indeed reverted to their old ways then they won't be taking prisoners from Londinium."

"What do you mean?"

"They respect life too much to imprison people, Suetonius. And if it should happen that they no longer care about trade, then..." his voice faded as he watched Suetonius take his turn at being wide-eyed.

"Then that's not a risk we should be willing to take," Suetonius completed Marek's words thoughtfully. The thought suddenly coalesced and his body straightened with a start. "Order the cavalry to ride through every street in Londinium and give the alarm. Warn everyone of the imminent danger," he said. "I don't care what Decianus says, the inhabitants should flee the city."

Within the hour the cavalrymen were cantering through the streets shouting out dire warnings but, except for occasional jeering from groups of townsfolk, for the most part they were completely ignored. The entire population appeared to share Decianus mindset. As the sun began to set Suetonius made one last offer for anyone who wished to accompany them to safety to step up but, with no takers, he ordered Marek and the cavalry to march away with him to reconnect with the main Roman force.

The nonchalance expressed by the people of Londinium that evening rapidly gave way to abject fear the next morning. Panic promptly ensued when the sun rose to reveal over 100,000 Iceni immediately to the north. Without any announcement or declaration the entire rebel army simply began to stream into the city behind hundreds of fast moving chariots carrying skilled Iceni archers. Terrified screams were silenced by arrows and swords and every building was systematically plundered for the easy takings.

Although she was one of the first warriors in the city and rode ready to strike with gladius firmly in her grip, Ceridwen ignored the people screaming and running to get out of her way and galloped Kelpie through town toward the docks. In spite of Boudica's orders to slaughter without mercy, her inspired speech reminding the Iceni of Roman atrocities and inciting the most acrid form of vengeance, the fact this act bore the full sanction of the Druids, Ceridwen still couldn't do it. She couldn't bring herself to kill someone who wouldn't fight back. Perhaps there would be soldiers at the docks, ready to defend the ships and warehouses, that she could engage and maintain her personal sense of honor. An hour ago there may well have been, but by the time she reached the river the ships were already headed down the Thames for the safety of the open sea. Hundreds of people around her were leaping into the river and attempting to swim after them, but the vast majority disappeared almost instantly beneath the fast moving tidal current and only the occasional bobbing head could be seen out in the river proper. Ceridwen strained to look but failed to see anyone make it to a boat and, growing tired of fighting with Kelpie to keep him away from the water, she finally turned him away and rode back into the city. The bright morning sky was gone, completely blotted out by the dense, choking smoke from dozens of fires stretching from one side of Londinium to the other.

A chariot suddenly thundered through the street ahead of her chasing after three terrified townsfolk. She clenched her fists around Kelpie's reins and helplessly watched as two of them were picked off with precision by the archers while the third was trampled beneath unforgiving hooves. "What a grand victory, eh, Ceri?" Boudica screamed out as she pulled her chariot up alongside Kelpie. "There'll be no more exploitation from these invaders, that's for sure." Tasca and Camora both beamed with pride as they stood in the chariot on either side of their mother, bows at the ready should another hapless survivor come into view.

"The ships have fled," Ceridwen said, avoiding responding directly to Boudica's exuberant words. "And with them I imagine the majority of grain from the warehouses." She sheathed her sword. "We'd better make sure our farmers make it back to their fields quickly for the last planting or it's going to be a lean winter."

"The Romans still have three legion base towns with very full granaries, Ceri." The fingers of Boudica's right hand were strumming Serencleddyf's hilt while she spoke through dancing teeth. "That's more than enough for our simple needs."

"That may be true," Ceridwen cocked her head to the left and stared at Boudica with a one sided smile. "But it also depends on how much excess they have. What if the majority of them decide to stay in Britannia?" She shook her head tightly. "There's no way we can be sure there'd be enough for all them and us too."

Boudica raised her right hand and held it open toward Ceridwen. "I'm not going to disband the army," she said with sharp finality. "If Llyn's mission fails we're going to need it intact very soon."

"You make it sound as if you've already decided we're going to have to fight them, Boudica," Ceridwen said argumentatively. "Llyn's plan is to grant them amnesty. How can that fail? Especially after," she swung her right hand around with a broad flourish, "After all this." She bit her lower lip as thoughts of Marek flooded into her head. She'd been a part of this grand plan all along with the understanding that the Roman soldiers were to be disarmed and allowed to either leave or begin their lives anew in Britannia. Until this instant it hadn't even occurred to her that there could be another possibility. She'd been focused on marrying Marek and the two of them living happily together in Toftrees but now, suddenly, her wild imagining of them riding carefree together through the meadows was being replaced by the horrific image of him in full armor and charging right at her with his sword.

"That's up to Suetonius, isn't it?" Boudica responded rhetorically.

"But, but they can't choose to fight," Ceridwen stammered, clearly shaken. "They're so outnumbered it would be suicide for them to take us on."

"We'll know the answer soon enough. Llyn's already left to deliver the ultimatum."

Llyn stood alone near the bank of the Anker, a river flowing though an open meadow in front of the Roman camp. The early evening wind came from behind him, filling his cloak and fluttering his hair like a lion's mane around his weathered, bearded face. He intently focused on the two figures that had emerged from the stockade shortly after he called out for a meeting with Suetonius. They were now walking directly toward him. As soon as they were close enough for him to recognize who they were he raised his arms and boomed out, "Greetings Suetonius and Marek. I bring word from queen Boudica."

"Her demands for the release of the prisoners from Londinium, I assume," Suetonius barked back.

"There are no prisoners, Suetonius." Llyn slowly shook his head from side-to-side and dropped his arms. "Neither is there a Londinium any more."

"Then what became of Londinium's 70,000 inhabitants?"

"They became 70,000 corpses. Both your capitol city and your major trade center have been destroyed, along with one of your legions. Britannia has been freed from Roman domination and you and your men are now subjects of Boudica, queen of the Britons."

Suetonius, unable to contain his seething, snarled back, "Then what is her message?" through gritted teeth.

"That there is no more need for bloodshed and you and your men are free to return to your homes. It's over, Suetonius. Simply order your troops to lay down their weapons and you'll all be escorted unharmed to the coast."

"As simple as that, eh?" Suetonius began a deep-throated laugh.

"Those amongst you who wish to remain here and become assimilated as inhabitants of Britannia are encouraged to do so and are welcomed with open arms." Llyn made a quick smile at Marek then froze his face and stared directly into Suetonius eyes. "You're hopelessly outnumbered, Suetonius. I strongly suggest you acquiesce to Queen Boudica's benevolence."

"Listen to me, Druid." Suetonius leaned toward Llyn and slowly wagged his right index finger. "I've doubled the size of this province since I've been governor. Do you actually expect me to passively let a mob of uncivilized barbarians led by a woman take that away?" He stood erect and slowly placed his hands on his hips. "You go back to your so called queen and tell her that I'll return to Rome when I'm dragging her behind me with a rope around her neck. She'll be my special gift for the emperor."

Llyn half smiled and made a small bow as he backed away from the officers. "You have three days," he said, then quickly turned away and disappeared into a wall of fog that had risen up behind him.

Less than two days later Llyn was back with the Iceni. Ceridwen was the first to see him enter the camp and immediately ran up to him. "Did you see Marek?" She asked excitedly.

"Indeed I did, Ceridwen." Llyn quickly glanced at her but didn't slow his gait as he rapidly approached the queen. "But I wasn't able to talk to him since he was standing right next to Suetonius at the time."

"Didn't he say anything?" Ceridwen was scuttling sideways like a crab.

"You and I can talk later, Ceridwen." Llyn said as he walked towards Boudica. Ceridwen remained close behind him.

"So, what's your take on Suetonius, Llyn?" Boudica shouted before Llyn had even reached her. "Do you think he'll pull out?"

"My first thought was to dismiss his response as requisite bravado, something to display in front of the troops, but the more I think about it the more I'm convinced that he really is energized to bring you down, Boudica." He refused to look at the crestfallen Ceridwen. Rather, he studied the curious pleasure evident in the queen's gleaming eyes. "I believe he'd rather sacrifice himself and his men than suffer the political indignity of yielding the province." He looked thoughtful and slowly rocked his head back and forth. "But we'll know for sure in a few days."

"We're watching their movements but so far there's been no serious activity," Gaine chimed in. "We have 200 warriors close by ready to escort them to the sea if they so choose."

Emrys shook his head. "They're Romans," he said loudly. "You're all thinking it. You all know in your hearts that they're going to fight."

"Then every one of them is going to die." Boudica added in a strangely flippant, almost eager tone.

As the meeting disbursed Ceridwen ran after Llyn and once out of earshot of the others she anxiously grabbed his arm. He looked into her pained expression and stroked the hair away from her face. "I know," he said soothingly.

"But if there is a fight, do you think," she stumbled over her words due to her shallow breathing. "Do you think he might not? Is there a chance, maybe, that Marek might defect?" She forced her face into Llyn's view, her hopeful eyes pleading for comforting words of agreement. "Since they'd all be going to," she choked the words out, "To die anyway, no one would ever know he wasn't a part of it."

Llyn cocked his head to the left to look directly at her. "You know Marek much better than I, Ceridwen. Look into yourself and you tell me what you think he'll do."

The strength suddenly left Ceridwen's legs and Llyn quickly caught her before she collapsed. He eased her to a bench in front of one of the campfires where she made a futile gesture to muffle her sobs with her hands. Llyn sat next to her and put his hand gently on her shoulder. "But if it does come to that you don't have to join in the fight, you know," he said softly.

"What do you mean?" Her red rubbed face was suddenly indignant. "Of course I'd have to fight, Llyn." Then, as she looked at the Druid, she vividly remembered Marek's words the last time they were together. It was as if he were sitting right there with her. "I have no choice, Marek," she whispered apologetically as her forehead fell onto Llyn's right shoulder. "I'm Iceni."

Chapter Twenty Six: Massacre

Marek walked languidly along the riverbank. The days were much shorter now and dusk descended at the time that only yesterday would have been a sunny afternoon. Until that yesterday he'd been full of hope that the Iceni uprising would be settled peacefully and things, while not completely returning to the way they were, would be such that he could at least serve his last years of service quietly. His singular goal had been to leave this infernal Roman army with all its pretense and politics and disappear into the Iceni countryside to begin a new life; the life he had always dreamed of. The life he had joined the legion in order to obtain, so many lifetimes ago. A life in Britannia, the only country he'd ever been to where he could feel relaxed enough to consider it home. A wonderful life with the woman whom he could never stop thinking about. The woman who, by simply being herself, had shown him he was not only capable of love but actually relished in it and became larger because of it. The woman, who, due to Roman racism and the inflexibility of the Roman way of doing things combined with the stupidity of the Briton queen, may very likely have to die soon on one of the thousands of swords at his command; possibly even his own. He closed his eyes and slowly turned his head from side-to-side. The chances of her listening to his last words to her and not joining the battle were as remote as him violating his pledge of allegiance and deserting his post. He took in a cleansing breath and exhaled through a wide open mouth, well aware that no matter how intense the upcoming battle he would still be standing when it was over. Never before had his invincibility caused him such turmoil.

He turned and looked back at the palisade surrounding the camp. After more than ten years in active service he was still amazed how such a fortress could be constructed in a matter of hours through simple organization and teamwork. Of course, therein lied the real strength behind the Roman army; an organized, well trained legion conferred a ten to one advantage over a disorganized enemy. That fact was ingrained into every Roman officer and Marek vividly recollected how he had explained it to Ceridwen all those years ago. Suetonius had designs to push that advantage to significantly new heights, however. "Suetonius," Marek forced a half chuckle while shaking his head. A true genius on the battlefield and unquestionably the most effective commander that Marek had ever served with, but Marek despised him as a person. Suetonius, as he lived and breathed, was the absolute epitome of what Rome had come to stand for. All the same, his plan for the upcoming battle was nothing if not superb. Britons from the surrounding tribes were flocking to join Boudica's 'army of liberation' and it was estimated that the rebels could be as many as 200,000 strong by the time they arrived. Clearly too overwhelming for any form of conventional engagement, and if the Romans tried to take a defensive position from inside the palisade they'd soon be overrun by the sheer force of numbers. "Oh, it's going to be defensive all right," Marek said aloud, fully aware that he was alone. The Romans were going to fight from a staggered line defense but in a carefully selected spot just south of the camp. Dense woods on three sides would give the enemy only one approach from across an open plain but then narrowing into a defile just prior to reaching the Roman line. Marek rubbed his chin while shaking his head from side-to-side. "Absolutely brilliant!"

It was well past sunrise the next morning when the army marched and rode from the protection of the palisade, but the relentless drizzle had stolen the daylight and the Romans were compelled to wend their way through an eerie grayness. The low lying morning mist from the river refused to disburse and wafted around the legionnaire's ankles, hiding their feet, and the audible whispers from within the ranks about "dragon's breath" and "sorcery" were of great and growing concern to Suetonius. He turned to Marek who, as praefectus of the cavalry, was compelled to ride next to him at the head of the column. "If any of us are to survive this," he said quietly but with grave undertones, "we're going to need every man sharp and motivated, and right now they seem neither."

"I think this weather's reinforcing the rumor that the Iceni uprising is actually Druid revenge for what happened on Mon," Marek said flatly. "That the Druids are the guiding hands behind all of this."

"That could be," Suetonius said as he twisted his mouth, but then he made a snap nod and sat upright with a beaming smile. "But aren't these the very men who trounced the Druids on Mon?" he added brightly. He then pointed at what appeared to be a mile wide hole in the edge of the forest ahead of them. It looked unnatural, as if some huge tree eating beast had taken a massive bite out of it. "We're here," he said. "Get the auxiliaries into formation."

The legionnaires made their battle formation behind an unbroken row of full length shields toward the back of the hole in the trees while the cavalry fell in on either flank. Together they completely stretched from one side of the opening in the forest to the other. A hundred paces in from the plain they waited in silence. The sound of Boudica's advancing army, which had been imperceptible while the Romans were on the move, now pierced the dismal gloom and seemed to emanate from every direction before them. It was impossible to tell how near or far away they might be, the increasing volume only suggested that they were getting closer, but as much as he strained, Marek could still see nothing in the plain. Even he felt unnerved. That is until Suetonius trotted his horse into the open area in front of the line and turned to face the men.

"You hear that racket?" he shouted while pointing his right thumb back over his right shoulder. "It's the sound of undisciplined barbarians, most of them mere women and whelps, who actually think they're coming to something other than their own slaughter." He laughed loudly while broadly shaking his head from side-to-side, then turned his horse sideways and extended his arm towards the plain. "The savages who'll soon be rushing toward us are not soldiers coming to offer us battle. They are bastards, runaways, the refuse of your swords, who have often fled before you, and will again take themselves to flight when they see the conqueror flaming in the ranks of war." He turned his horse around and raised his right fist above his head while staring directly at his men. "In all engagements it is the valor of a few that turns the fortune of the day. It will be your immortal glory, that a scant number can equal the exploits of a great and powerful army." He quickly dropped his hand and pulled back on the reins of his horse before turning to see what had made it want to jump. A solid line of screaming Iceni, as far as he could see, stood at the far edge of the plain. He turned back to his men, trotting his horse back and forth in front of them. "Keep your ranks; discharge your javelins and, when the time comes, rush forward to a close attack and hew a passage with your swords. Pursue the vanquished and never think of spoil or plunder. Conquer, and victory gives you everything."

The Roman soldiers roared out warlike acclamations, and brandishing their javelins, they now clearly burned with impatience for the onset. Suetonius, his confidence in his men restored, then cantered his horse toward the Iceni and stopped halfway between the opposing forces. "I offer you the chance to spare yourselves," he called out to the Iceni. "Surrender and live as slaves."

Marek sank his head between his shoulders and broke out in a slit eyed, teeth clenching grimace as he watched Suetonius gallop back to the Roman line. "A perfect move Suetonius," he muttered to himself, realizing that the commander had firmly assured his will. In spite of the fact that Suetonius had just destroyed any chance of a peaceful solution, Marek was forced to admire the deftly placed offer. The Roman soldiers would see Suetonius as benevolent and would have no trouble killing women knowing they had been given a chance to live; if they attacked now they had willingly chosen death. Perhaps only a handful of people in the Roman ranks besides Marek and Suetonius knew that the insult he had sent to the Iceni absolutely assured an attack.

The bait was eagerly snatched. "What sort of people do they think we are?" Boudica shouted so loudly that the Romans could easily hear her words spewing to her people. "There are no cowards in the tribes of Britannia." She moved her chariot twenty paces in front of the Iceni and, stopping sideways directly in front of the opening in the trees, drew Serencleddyf and held it high above her flaming red hair, full and flowing down her back even though it was soaked by the omnipresent rain.

Gaine, mounted next to Ceridwen and Kelpie at the front of the line announced enthusiastically, "That should provoke the Romans, eh?"

"Let's hope so," Ceridwen replied, pointing her chin to the opening in the woods. "It would be suicide to try to get them out of there." She then looked around nervously at her impatient compatriots. "But our queen had better get them to attack us soon."

Boudica turned her chariot to face the Iceni. Camora and Tasca were standing on either side of her but, in spite of their determined poses, the fact that their shoulders barely extended above the front of the vehicle underscored that they were still children. Furthermore, they were not just any children and Boudica's screaming out about how nothing is safe from the pride and arrogance of the Romans caused all Briton eyes to fall on Tasca and Camora. The Britons well knew how these innocent little girls had been brutally ravished by the Romans, and Boudica's continued berserker ranting further fueled their inflammation to the point of almost boiling over. Ceridwen leaned forward and patted Kelpie's neck in an attempt to calm herself as much as her horse. "She's got to keep the people in line," she whispered nervously into Kelpie's ear while her wide grey eyes carefully surveyed the entire scene. The bloodlust in the ranks was ready to explode. "Settle them down, Boudica," she said a bit louder as she sat up, holding tightly onto the damp leather reins. "You have to draw the Romans out."

Boudica, however, was determined to further incite her people and she proceeded to gallop her chariot back and forth in front of the cheering Britons. "The vindictive gods are now at hand," Boudica yelled out. "A Roman legion already dared to face Britons and they paid with their lives for their rashness. Even now these Romans shrink back with terror."

"No," Ceridwen initially said beneath her breath, but then raised her voice. "That's not what they're doing, you fool." Ceridwen gasped, suddenly realizing Boudica's intention. "They're setting a trap," she tried to add, but her voice trailed away as she rapidly looked around to witness everyone around her caught up in the same mindless hysteria. Boudica, convinced of her own invincibility and driven by unrestrained vengeance, had become completely insane and was going to drag close to a quarter of a million Britons into a bloodbath in her berserk quest. She could have used the threat of this mass of people as clout to negotiate the end of Roman dominance in Briton. Instead, she was making her own people expendable to satisfy her own warped sense of retribution. She wanted more than just independence. She wanted every Roman dead. "Look around and view your numbers," Boudica screamed wildly at the top of her lungs. "These Romans don't stand a chance." She pulled up in front of her army and turned to face the enemy. "Chariots at the ready," she called out, already beginning to move hers forward.

Two hundred chariots with every archer on board holding a loaded bow immediately moved into the field, formed into a line of sorts, and began at a trot behind the queen. They were, however, quickly forced to speed to a gallop in order to keep up with her. Thousands of Britons, both on horseback and foot, suddenly broke forwards and poured after them. Boudica once again brandished Serencleddyf high above her head. From behind, with her bright red hair flowing back, the sword looked like it was rising up out of flames. Ceridwen cringed and turned to look at Gaine as Boudica's banshee cry screamed out the order for a full charge.

"We've got to go, Ceri. Battle's joined." Gaine shouted in order to be heard over the war cries of the charging army, then dug her heels into the side of her horse and galloped to join the fray. She was right. Ceridwen instantly yelled, "Ha," to Kelpie and followed in earnest pursuit.

Camora and Tasca, faces streaked with woad, stood expertly with bows fully drawn and one foot each under the leather strap on the floor of their mother's chariot as they neared the row of Roman legionnaires. "Aim just over the shields," Boudica told them. "Drop your arrows in on them."

Simultaneously with the girls releasing their arrows a cloud of 8,000 javelins rose from behind the shields, disappearing over their heads as Boudica pulled to the right no less than twenty paces in front of the Romans. "Keep shooting," she shrieked to her daughters as they rapidly discharged arrow after arrow while the chariot galloped to the end of the Roman line. It was only at the turn at the end of the run that Boudica saw what had happened. Every chariot was destroyed, horses were running amok in the field and the approaching swarm of Britons had no choice but to clamber over the broken bodies and wheels in order to prevent being trampled themselves by the surge behind them. The surviving drivers, carrying their heavy swords in both hands, were running clumsily forward with their children archers beside them. The Iceni warriors were desperately trying to weave their galloping horses around them. Suddenly, a second wave of javelins rained down on them and Boudica could only watch in horror as thousands of Britons and horses were impaled into the ground. The warriors who managed to save themselves using their shields immediately had to discard them to avoid being pulled down from their mounts by the spears firmly stuck in them. Without shields, the survivors still continued their mad advance.

As soon as their second javelins had been released the Romans began a forward march, but not in their traditional straight line. Some of legionnaires moved several paces ahead of the others and the line quickly resembled the edge of a saw, fully protected by body sized shields. The sound of 10,000 legionnaires moving as a single unit echoed across the narrows of the battlefield and Boudica drove to the center of the plain in an attempt to rally a group of Britons behind her for an organized charge. They ignored her. Individually they pushed forward in a disordered frenzy to avenge the thousands who had already fallen and, as hundreds streamed by her on both sides, she had no choice but to turn her chariot to ride alongside them.

"Boudica!" The shout made her turn to see Ceridwen galloping next to her.

"We have to break the line," Ceridwen shouted. "Fall back and regroup."

"They're not listening to me," Boudica protested, but quickly veered her chariot to the right and slowed down when she realized that Ceridwen had at least a hundred warriors riding with her.

The first of the Iceni finally reached the Romans and made valiant efforts to stop the advance, savagely beating against the oversized shields with their huge swords, but without means of protection and no room to maneuver due to the proximity of their comrades behind them, they were easy pickings for the Roman swords jabbing though the openings between the shields. The saw edge line moved forward in a steady march and the legionnaires were soon walking on top of the bodies of Britons that were continuously being pushed into them by even more rushing into the funnel of trees.

Marek watched the carnage with a mixture of horror and impatience as he moved 2,000 tightly compacted, mounted cavalrymen on either flank closely behind the legionnaires. "Soon," he whispered to himself. He tried to calm his breathing but nothing could affect the excited pulse he felt in his chest and neck. The tree line was approaching and a solid mass of Britons filled the plain beyond. Behind the Briton army were carts and wagons filled with supplies and on top sat infants and children too young to be able to use a bow. There were so many wagons bunched up together that it would be impossible for an army to move through them, an observation that provided Marek with his ideal strategy. As the legionnaires finally marched beyond the tree line Marek ordered the cavalry to rapidly stream out and form a line on either side of the attacking Britons, then close in. "Let no one through," he yelled out as the 4,000 horsemen collectively hacked away at the now surrounded Britons. Their war cries gave way to deafening screams of panic as the Britons started to run in every direction but ended up facing either the gladius of a legionnaire or cavalryman or else the solid wall of carts. Many attacked the horsemen in groups, furiously fighting to pull them down from their mounts and, due to the sheer numbers, hundreds of the cavalrymen were either perishing or being forced to fight on foot. Still the cavalry steadily advanced. Marek suddenly turned, startled by shouts and the thunder of hoof beats from behind him. A single chariot was racing along the tree line from the north accompanied by 200 galloping, mounted Iceni warriors. "First alae fall back," he shouted to a section of his men as he turned his horse to face them, but the cavalry wasn't their target. Boudica and these warriors charged into the northern flank, the chariot driving up over the Roman shields and crushing the legionnaires beneath while the horses leaped over. The Iceni had breached the line and the north side of the saw tooth line was faltering, enabling the Britons to push through. Marek screamed out, "Charge," and led 500 cavalry back to support the flank but slowed to a stop when it became clear that the legionnaires were handily taking care of things without them. He immediately recognized a large, magnificent white horse frantically rushing back and forth, riderless, behind the line. It suddenly turned and trampled several legionnaires under its deadly hoofs in order to punch a hole in the re-formed line and escape, galloping away the way he had come. "Ceridwen!" Marek involuntarily shouted as Kelpie disappeared in the distance. He turned back to look at where the skirmishing was, but the legionnaires had already closed the gap and were once again marching forward in their orderly, saw blade front line. Marek's face burned and he could no longer contain his breathing. He screamed as loud as he could while turning his horse back toward the mass of Britons and galloped hard directly into the middle of them, the entire alae following him in. "I warned her," he shouted wildly. "Why did you Britons have to be so stupid?" He stabbed a woman in the neck as if in response for her not answering his question. "Why?" he screamed out, hacking through the crowd. "Why? Why?" Each word accompanied another swing of his gladius. He was unaware of the chain reaction his charge caused as thousands of Britons tried to flee the advancing cavalry and crushed their own people into the carts in the frenzy. All he knew was his own unrestrained rage and he was directing it at anyone who came within striking range. He jumped off his horse as it was pulled down and continued his rampage on foot, half blinded by his own tears. "Fight me. Kill me," he shouted to the Britons, but the only remaining enemies were peasants who stood no chance against him and, eventually, most of them ran from him. "Will no one offer a fight?" he cried out, chasing after them, desperate for the battle not to be over. Finally yielding to the inevitable, he stopped running. He'd survived in spite of himself.

Panting through a wide-open mouth, Marek tore off his helmet with his left hand and held it by his side. Gladius still at the ready in his right he slowly surveyed the field. Bodies were everywhere; men, women, children and horses. Thousands of them, piled up as far as he could see in every direction. The wagons had all been overturned and broken by the stampeding Britons. Caught up in himself and completely oblivious to the wails and groans of the injured and dying around him he simply stood there, his lower jaw first shuddered then his whole body slumped. "Ceri," he wailed, shaking his head. He inhaled deeply, but something came over him and he stood tall again. His right fist tightened around his sword. "You should have listened to me," he shouted to the wind, wild eyed anger flooding in to fill the hole created by the loss of Ceridwen. He stared directly upward at the sky and noticed for the first time that the rain had stopped and the clouds were shriveling. "No one stands a chance against the Roman machine," he roared at them, waving his gladius above his head. His shouts incited a cheer that resounded amongst the several thousand Roman soldiers around him, the crescendo of victory as they rummaged through the field gathering up their well earned trophies. Marek's right hand quivered at the tightness with which he was holding his bloody sword. Crimson streaks trickled down his right arm and dripped off his breastplate, down his mud encrusted legs and into his already soaked sandals. He lowered his head and glared beyond the broken carts, into the distance where the surviving Iceni had fled. Some Briton warriors still lived. There would still be more fighting to be had.

Chapter Twenty Seven: Kelpie

B oudica sat on the forest floor with her back against an ancient oak and eased the now barely conscious Tasca into her lap while Camora stood sentinel at her side in quiet disbelief. When the chariot lost a wheel she and her mother had been thrown free but Tasca went down hard into the wreckage. In the few hours since, she'd been transformed from vibrant little sister into painfully bruised waif with a grotesquely distended belly. Camora bit her lower lip and started to ease down onto one knee but a sudden rustle from the underbrush caused her to jump back up and quickly notch her last arrow into her bow. She stood rigid with the tip of the arrow pointing into the direction of the sound, but eagerly released the tension when she saw who was approaching. "Over here Ceridwen," she called out in a loud whisper.

"It's all clear," Ceridwen replied. "No one followed. I don't think anyone even saw us enter the forest." She immediately dropped to the ground next to Boudica and ran her fingers through Tasca's hair, forcing an assuring smile when the little girl meekly looked up at her. "You were very brave in battle, Tasca," Ceridwen told her. "All the Iceni are so proud of both you and your sister." She gently placed her hand flat over Tasca's lower right side. It was hot. "How are you feeling?" she asked briskly, still smiling.

"I feel cold, Ceri." Tasca winced as she spoke and then turned to try to warm herself against her mother. Ceridwen looked up at Boudica and slowly shook her head from side-to-side.

"I have just the thing for that, Tasca," Boudica said reassuringly as she removed a small vial from the pouch on her belt. She carefully eased it open and with her left arm behind Tasca's neck poured it into her daughter's mouth, nuzzling the top of Tasca's head while she did so. "This will help you to sleep," Boudica whispered softly, cradling and rocking the helpless little girl back and forth while Camora and Ceridwen stood over them. Within minutes Tasca's eyes closed and Boudica looked up.

"Don't be so sad, mummy." Camora said, uncontrollably throwing her arms around her mother's neck then cuddling under her right arm. "She'll be fine after she sleeps."

Boudica squeezed Camora and kissed the top of her head. "And you need your sleep too."

"But I need to keep watch."

"I'll take the first watch," Ceridwen chimed in. "After all, you're an Iceni warrior now, and warriors need their rest."

Camora's eyes became saucers and her proud grin kept growing until it covered the lower third of her face. "But I'm not sleepy," she protested, her eyes flitting between her mother and Ceridwen.

"I have a potion for you too, Camora," Boudica said, reaching into her pouch then handing her a vial. "Drink this," she said, "And I promise it will make you sleepy."

"Oh, goody," Camora said. She sat on the ground and happily removed the stopper but hesitated before touching it to her lips, peering over it at Boudica. "Are warriors allowed to cuddle their mothers while they fall asleep?" she asked, cocking her head slightly to the right.

"Of course they are," Boudica replied, her right arm wrapping around her eldest daughter's shoulders. "You'll never be too big for that."

Camora eagerly downed the potion and in the comfort of her mother's arm, nuzzled into her side. There were no more words, only Boudica's tears after Camora's eyes closed for the final time. Ceridwen kept a respectful distance but only partially to give Boudica the opportunity to compose herself. The primarily reason was her own fear that she, too, would be unable to contain herself if she looked too closely into the anguished face of this woman, sitting so helplessly with a dead daughter under each arm. This was the person who, for nearly all of her life, had been her best friend. Ceridwen took a deep cleansing breath and exhaled through her mouth; it was going to be up to her to be that friend once again.

Boudica looked up with her ruddy swollen eyes as Ceridwen walked back towards her. "What have I done, Ceri?" she breathed out heavily.

Ceridwen crouched opposite her but had no immediate answer. Over 100,000 Iceni lay died in the field just a mile away from where the person who caused it was now sobbing over the bodies of her poisoned children. Any attempt at words of comfort would come across as hollow, even cruel.

"I've destroyed us," Boudica continued. "I've destroyed the Iceni with my own inflamed arrogance." She winced and shook her head, then looked up again paying no attention to the flop of red hair half covering her right eye. "Suetonius may have won the day, but we," she squeezed Tasca's and Camora's corpses, "We, my daughters and I, have denied him his prize." Her lower jaw deprived her of the ability to grin at her morbid victory. "He'll never parade us through the streets of Rome, Ceri. Never!"

"What of Serencleddyf?" Ceridwen asked.

"Serencleddyf?" Boudica guffawed from the back of her throat. "Serencleddyf makes you invincible, Ceri, but only you. It does nothing for those around you except curse them. Curse them into blindly following wherever folly you lead them into and leaves you with their deaths hanging on your shoulders. I see it all too clearly now, Ceri. You can only handle it with success while the berserker has you. Without the berserker, invincibility is an intolerable burden."

Boudica violently pulled the stopper from a vial that had suddenly appeared in her hand and, before Ceridwen could even respond, she'd downed the contents. "Return Serencleddyf to Llyn for me Ceri. Tell him I'm sorry." She feverishly latched her right hand onto Ceridwen's wrist. "Promise me this."

Ceridwen placed her free hand on top of Boudica's and nodded. "Of course," she said softly. "You have my word." She remained in that position until Boudica's smile diminished along with her grip and, as life drained away, Boudica nestled into peace with her daughters amongst the roots of the oak. She was finally freed from torment, free to join with Camora and Tasca as their bodies were resorbed back into the earth. Ceridwen leaned forward, unfastened the dead queen's belt and took Serencleddyf.

Since she didn't regroup with any of the scattered bands of surviving Iceni it took almost four days for Llyn to catch up with Ceridwen. When he did, she was standing triumphantly over the body of her kill, a decurion. She was wiping Serencleddyf clean with a piece of cloth ripped from the Roman officer's uniform. Two dead auxiliaries lay close by. As if he were encountering a wild beast he deliberately approached her from the front and made no sudden movements or attempts to conceal himself. She snapped upwards with a snarl, dropping the cloth and holding the sword at an angle in front of her as soon as she sensed movement but, once she recognized the Druid, she lowered it until the tip rested on the ground. "I was hoping it would take you longer to find me, Llyn," she called out.

"How do you feel, Ceridwen?" Llyn asked cautiously.

"Odd you should ask me that," she replied. "It's strange, but I don't feel anything. Not happy nor sad, not even angry." She shrugged her shoulders. "Nothing." She looked down at her right fist still tightly wrapped around the hilt of the star sword, turned up her grey eyes just enough to take in the concern from Llyn's brow, then quickly shoved Serencleddyf into its sheath. "Why is it that I'm denied the berserker?" she demanded.

"The berserker is not a part of the nature of a wolf. You operate from cunning and stealth and you rely on your instincts, Ceridwen. Not your emotions." Llyn remained rigid while he spoke. "The berserker simply isn't a part of you."

Ceridwen pointed her chin proudly at the bodies around her. "All the same, I'm still doing my part." she said.

Llyn bowed his head reverently. "Indeed, you are, Ceridwen."

"And I'll continue to," she added while unbuckling her belt. "Even without this." She grabbed the scabbard and laid it across the open flats of both of her hands, then extended her arms toward the Druid. "I promised Boudica I'd return Serencleddyf to you," she said flatly. "It's an excellent weapon and the tip can pierce armor but, quite frankly, I'm just as effective with a gladius."

"The power of Serencleddyf doesn't lie with it being a weapon," Llyn said, rapidly concealing it beneath his cloak. "It's a symbol of leadership, and that's something you don't aspire to." His head flitted up and spoke directly into her, now blue, eyes. "You only ever saw Serencleddyf as a sword and, in that light, you're absolutely correct." He paused to enjoy her expression. "Your gladius is just as effective a weapon."

Ceridwen stared back curiously at him, her right eye slowly closing as her head tilted to the left while she matched his growing smile. "That's all it is?"

"What's the first lesson you learned on Mon?"

Ceridwen's mind was suddenly transported to the innocence of twenty long years ago. All at once she was again riding carefree on Kelpie, racing against Donogh through the groves while simultaneously multiple years of study were so alive in her head it was as if she were also seated in class. She straightened her head, re-opened her right eye and looked squarely at the Druid. "Magic is the property of lack of knowledge." Her words were loud and defiant.

"You were the best student we had ever known, Ceridwen. These things came to you innately, but you were too self-contained to ever be a Druid. You were far too driven to personal action to ever be an advisor. You followed your calling, the calling of the warrior, the wolf, and combined with your intelligence and education you're now the most exemplary Briton in the land."

"What land, Llyn?" Ceridwen extended her arms to either side. "Look around you," she said incredulously. The entire Iceni nation no longer exists. Everything on Mon has been destroyed. The dream of an independent Britannia is over. All that's left now is to take as many enemies as we can down with us."

"Oh, it's by no means over." Llyn shook his head. "And there is much more left. These recent events are just steps along the road to a stronger, independent Britannia." He looked up at the sky. "It's becoming dark. Let's make camp and while we eat I'll tell you everything."

"Can you tell me about," Ceridwen wrinkled her face as they walked toward the trees to gather wood then quickly spurted out, "about Marek?" She swallowed and looked away. "Do you know if he survived?"

"I spied on the Roman assemblies for the first three evenings after the battle," he said. "Each morning the cavalry and auxiliaries are sent out to round up Iceni horses and capture any survivors they come across for slaves. Every night fewer and fewer return." He looked askance at her. "A testament to the effectiveness of you and the other warriors who are still lurking out here." He bent to gather firewood and, not looking at her, added, "Every officer is required to attend assembly, Ceridwen, and I've never seen him there. I suspect the worst."

"I see," Ceridwen said curtly. She took a deep breath and then quickly blew it out while she arranged a small circle of stones on the ground. "My land is forfeit, Kelpie is lost and Marek's dead." Slamming down the last stone she abruptly stood up, slapped her hands on her hips and glared at the druid with her wolf gray eyes. "And you're telling me these are just 'steps along the road'?"

"Oh, yes," Llyn answered without hesitation. He piled the wood they'd collected inside the stone circle and applied a few stokes of flint. The wood first smoldered, then a few flames licked up, but Llyn didn't speak again until the fire had become sufficient to ward off the damp darkness around them.

Almost as soon as the battle was over a jubilant Suetonius ordered large corrals to be built to contain the thousands of captured Iceni horses, and a gyrus in which to train them. Iceni horses would not only be highly valued booty for his men but hundreds of them could also be trained and sent back to Rome as prizes for the emperor. Taking advantage of his elation at the victory, Julia successfully appealed to her father for several things she'd been wanting and, astonished at the ease with which he agreed, also secured his permission that she be allowed to pick an Iceni horse for herself.

Even though the battle had been decisive and the area in the vicinity of the fort was immediately quite secure, it was still several days later before Suetonius finally acquiesced to her whining and gave permission for her to venture outside the palisade to view the captured animals. His instructions to her had been quite clear in she could only have a horse that had completed training in the gyrus. However, the sight of a white steed pacing back and forth in one of the holding corrals immediately captivated her. She rushed to the fence for a closer look. "What about one of these horses?" She asked the duplicarius who'd been assigned to assist her.

"Untrained," he replied and continued walking toward the gyrus. "The trained ones are over here."

"That's all right." She called to him, standing fast. "You can just take one from here and train him next." She smiled coyly as he turned around and added, "Can't you?"

"Which horse do you like?" He asked respectfully as he walked back.

"That white one." Julia eagerly pointed at the large mount standing a full head above the others.

"Oh no," he stopped abruptly. "You don't want that one." The junior officer rapidly shook the back of his head. "He's mean. We've taken him into the gyrus twice already and he's just too wild."

"Then what's going to happen to him?" Julia asked, leaning over the fence as the horse stopped pacing and walked toward her.

"Because of his size and strength he'll be sent to Rome for the chariot races."

"He doesn't look mean to me. Look at this." Kelpie nuzzled her open hand and allowed her to run it along the side of his head and pat his neck. "Maybe he just doesn't like men."

Several cavalrymen who had previously been unable to even get close to Kelpie gathered around to watch in amazement as he now appeared so tame and interactive. Julia was beaming; it was as if this horse was selecting her rather than she it. "Get me some rope," she ordered eagerly. "I'll walk him to the gyrus myself."

An hour later, Suetonius stopped by and broke into a proud smile when he saw his daughter expertly running her new horse through the training obstacles to the cheers and accolades of a dozen cavalrymen. "He's amazing!" Julia exclaimed, pulling up to an effortless stop in front of her father.

"A magnificent animal indeed," Suetonius nodded approvingly. "But he's so big. Are you sure you feel comfortable handling a horse of this size?"

"I'm not a child, you know." Julia wrinkled her mouth. Their discussion earlier today had certainly underscored that point. "Let me take him out for a decent ride."

"Not too far though," Suetonius warned. "Stay within the patrolled area."

"How about if I just ride him along the river?"

"Ah, the southern road, eh?" Suetonius laughed while he quickly nodded. "Very well, but please be careful, Julia." He opened the gate to the gyrus and stood to the side, watching as Julia rode Kelpie out. "All right?" He added sternly.

"Of course," she called out excitedly without looking back, already cantering toward the river. She leaned forward and whispered into Kelpie's ear. "I'll need to come up with a worthy name for you, horse," she said. "But right now we're on our way to meet someone very special. Maybe he can help me name you."

Julia was rapidly mesmerized by Kelpie's flowing movements as he effortlessly flew across the meadow and by the time they reached the trail she was completely seduced by his rhythmical undulations beneath her. Time and context disappeared into some sort of fantastic fog and she closed her eyes to more clearly listen to what appeared to be music emanating from the mist surrounding them. She stretched forward to ride him with her body in as much contact as possible with his back and wrapped her arms tightly around his pulsating neck, slowly rubbing the side of her face against it. It was the most exquisite combination of sensuality and dream state she had ever known.

Suetonius stood rigid with his teeth fixed and fists clenched tightly, veins ready to burst from his crimson neck, as the centurion finished delivering his report. The cohort of legionnaires had been on routine patrol along the river when Julia came galloping along the other side on this large white horse. She was riding extremely fast, holding onto its neck, and seemed completely oblivious to their warning shouts about the sharp bend ahead. There was no hesitation or cry out; the horse simply leaped into the river and the two of them disappeared immediately beneath the swirling waters. The ten men searched until dark but could find no trace of either of them.

Suetonius said nothing at first while his breathing grew audibly deeper then he suddenly lurched forward and slammed both fists onto the table in front of him. "Damn these Britons," he finally roared out. Then, panting like a cornered wild beast, he slowly looked up. "Bring me my sword," he bellowed with non-negotiable ferocity.

Within minutes Suetonius was at the prison enclosure with a hundred legionnaires in tow. "These Iceni won't make good slaves," he shouted fanatically as he kicked the gate open. "Kill them all." He rushed inside the compound, wildly swinging his gladius as he led the slaughter in a futile attempt to quell his blinding rage. He was still swinging his bloody sword in front of him after all the prisoners had been hacked to death, screaming repeatedly that the Iceni had murdered his daughter and that they were all going to pay. He glared through the bars of the enclosure at his officers with a crazed open mouthed grin. "Assemble the fourteenth legion," he said with a surprisingly controlled voice. "We're going to march to Iceni territory and not one of them, not a woman, not a child, not even a farm animal, is going to be left alive."

Chapter Twenty Eight: Agreement

Marek awoke with a sudden start, kicked off the blanket in a near panic and frantically flailed his arms until the dark room became familiar again. Yes, he was in Rome. Drenched with sweat he sat up and swung his legs off the side of the bed, staring blankly at the floor while waiting for his heart to settle down. It was the same recurrent nightmare or, rather, remembrance. Remembrance of the origins of his anger, a driving anger that had served him so well after the Iceni massacre and had continued to sustain him these past two years. Two years since Suetonius and the fourteenth legion had been recalled to Rome. He slid off the bed and stumbled across the room to where a jug of water sat on a small table. He first poured some directly on his head, emptied the remainder into a bowl, and then cupped several mouthfuls with his hands before washing the residue of sleep from his face. Anger was a two edged sword: an excellent coping mechanism but it deprives one of the ability to move onto new ventures. His time with the legion was up but he was unable to even imagine, let alone contemplate, any other life but that of a soldier. He cursed his invincibility. The all too familiar dream had transported him back to how, after witnessing the scene of Ceridwen's certain death, he had readily dismounted to take on uncountable enemies on foot with the glorious intent to die in action. It didn't work. Instead of being killed he was praised for his valor, given the title of 'butcher of the Iceni' and was bestowed the glory and accolades that went with it. Now he was a celebrated hero of Rome for his key role in bringing about the destruction of the people he most cared about, the people he planed to spend the rest of his days with. The Iceni were no more and the irony tormented him.

He walked to the window for the distraction of gazing at the night sky, but the strip of dawn on the horizon was stealing the stars and the crescent moon had insufficient detail to be of interest. Instead, he returned to the water for another drink, vividly remembering the admiration Suetonius had for him at the end of that battle oh so long ago. "Marek," Suetonius had said. "As the best officer in my command I'm sending you with a detail of Praetorians to the base of the second legion to represent me and to take action on my behalf."

So, while everyone else was involved in post battle mopping up operations, Marek had the auspicious honor of riding south to Durnovaria wielding the full power and responsibility of the governor of Britannia. On arriving he immediately demanded to see Poenius Postumius, the legate of the second legion, who rather buoyantly rushed up to him. "I'm so pleased to see you managed to survive," he had said. "Did many more of you escape Boudica's army?"

"We soundly defeated them." Marek responded without expression. "And her army is no more. Governor Suetonius sends me on his behalf to learn why the second legion didn't obey his orders to join with the fourteenth and the twentieth at the decisive battle."

The color immediately drained from Poenius' face and he grabbed the doorway to catch himself from falling as he staggered backwards. "Come inside," he said quietly as he recovered, his eyes flitting between Marek and the Praetorians surrounding him. "Please."

"Stand guard here," Marek said to the Praetorians, then followed the legate into his office.

Trembling, Poenius poured two goblets of wine and meekly offered one to Marek who just turned his head from side-to-side and stood with his hands on his hips. He watched the legate guzzle them both.

"Was it the legion, Poenius, or just the commander who refused to follow orders," Marek asked pointedly.

Poenius forced a smile; he was well aware of what Marek's mission had to be. If the legion were to be determined to be cowards they would be decimated: one in ten of them would be killed as an example to all legions. If Poenius alone had chosen to not follow orders Suetonius would be required to make his death a spectacle. "You have to understand," Poenius said. "We," he stopped, stood up straight and nodded firmly, then licked his lips before continuing. "I took it upon myself to keep the second legion here. I expected Boudica to win."

"I understand." There was so much more that Marek thought to say but he chose to remain tight lipped. This was not a time to engage in conversation.

"As envoy, did Suetonius grant you the full power and authority of the governor?" Poenius asked.

"Yes, he did."

"Then you have the ability to grant me an alternative?"

"I do, and will if you wish it." In that instant Marek realized why he had been sent. If Suetonius had come himself he would have had no option but to dispatch Poenius in a humiliating public display. Through Marek he was able to give this unfortunate legate an honorable way out.

"And no action will be taken against the legion?"

"That is correct. This incident will be closed if you take the fall." Marek drew his sword and held it at the ready while Poenius crossed the room to where his was hanging. The legate drew his gladius and threw down the scabbard. "Thank you, Marek," he said, positioning the tip of the blade just below his rib cage with his arms fully extended to hold the hilt. He closed his eyes and fell forward, decisively driving the sword deeply inward and upward without uttering a sound. Marek watched the body convulse in the huge, continually expanding red puddle on the floor for several minutes and, when it ceased writhing, he went outside to order the Praetorians to tie the corpse to a horse for transport back.

The other honor that Suetonius bestowed on Marek was far more personal. "Even though you're a foreigner," Suetonius had said, "You represent the best attributes of a true Roman and so I've decided to put my feelings about your heritage aside. My daughter has long favored you and after your most recent display of bravery I find myself compelled." He smiled. "No, I find myself proud to offer you her hand. You may see her with my full approval when you return from your mission to Durnovaria."

Marek closed his eyes as he recalled how he had felt at the time. His immediate reaction was to consider Julia as a spoil of war, his to do with as he pleased. He would have his way with her all right. In fact, he vividly imagined her in multiple ways. The journey back with Poenius' body was the only time since the loss of Ceridwen that his otherwise omnipresent anger wasn't at the forefront of his brain. It had been temporarily offset by intense feelings of carnal lust directed at what had always been forbidden to him: the governor's daughter.

He scooped up a handful of water and splashed it onto his forehead then looked up so it dribbled down his face while he ran his wet hand over his hair and down his neck. He'd never been able to generate any feelings of sorrow when he thought of Julia; the only thing he had ever felt was more anger. Anger about how he had been cheated out of his prize. Julia was riding out to meet him when she died.

It was obvious to Marek what had stimulated these intense dreams and recollections. Suetonius, still his commanding officer although he hadn't seen him in over a year, had summoned him to a midday meeting today. Marek thoughtfully ate his morning meal and later, refreshed and dressed in full uniform, leisurely meandered through the bustling streets of Rome on his way to Suetonius' house.

From the Roman perspective Suetonius had been an exemplary military governor of Britannia, dramatically expanding the size of the province and putting down Boudica's rebellion with a battle strategy and execution that would be studied throughout the ages. The severity with which he dealt with the Iceni after the fact, however, was his undoing. Complaints of Suetonius' brutality finally convinced Nero to replace him with Publius Petronius, a diplomatic governor who rapidly initiated a policy of appeasement toward the natives and was able to restore the all important flow of commerce. Two new legions had also been dispatched to Britannia and the fourteenth, now highly resented by the Britons for its annihilation of the Iceni, was judiciously ordered back at its camp near Rome where it had remained ever since.

Both Suetonius' appearance and demeanor had changed dramatically since the last time Marek had seen him. He greeted Marek with a cheerful, and very unprofessional, "Come in and take some wine," as soon as he opened the door and then beckoned to a couch with an overly flamboyant arm gesture. Clearly, Suetonius had already enjoyed several goblets of wine already this morning. Marek poured some for himself and sat down, a little taken aback by his commander. This was a man who had previously demanded respect simply by his mere presence but presented here was just a shell of that man, gaunt and unkempt, as if he didn't care. Suetonius sauntered across the room and plopped down in a chair opposite Marek. "Let me tell you," he said, carefully balancing his wine so as not to spill any. "It's not just Rome that's going downhill. The whole damn empire's gone soft. They've even gone back to letting locals run things again in Britannia. And they're letting foreigners," he tipped his goblet slightly toward Marek, "no offense intended."

"I understand." A drunken Suetonius was most amusing.

"Foreigners back in the senate." He unapologetically belched.

"I thought Nero was against all that?" Marek interjected.

"Oh, that was only when Seneca was the man behind Nero." Suetonius drained his goblet. "But old Seneca pushed a bit too much and he's now totally out of favor with the emperor. The real Nero is oriented much like Claudius used to be and he's even re-implemented several of Claudius' old policies. Nero also understands how to keep the mob on his side; look how he's playing up to them with all those grandiose chariot races and gladiatorial events." Suetonius leaned forward and dropped his voice to a whisper. "There's a rumor in some circles that he's taken up Druidic studies."

"I thought the Druids were driven from Rome a long time ago?"

"All but one." Suetonius continued to guzzle from his goblet. "The old Briton king was obligated by pledge to remain in Rome, and Nero spends a lot of time with Caractacus now. He apparently takes his much of his counsel to heart." Suetonius scooped up the amphora, refilled both their goblets with a flourish, and dramatically eased it down again. "But enough of politics," he said. "You didn't come here to listen to my babbling." He picked up a scroll from the table in his right hand, tapped it a couple of times into his left palm, and then handed it to Marek. "Congratulations. You've officially completed an outstanding tour of duty. You're now free to pursue any endeavor you wish but, of course, you'll remain on reserve status for the next four years." He picked up both the goblets, handed one back to Marek, and both men took a hearty swig. "So, tell me Marek. What are you going to do?" He pointed at the scroll with his chin. "As you can see, you've leaving with a good deal of money."

"I'm not really sure," Marek replied thoughtfully. "My original plan when I first signed up was to retire to a villa with an orchard or something along those lines." He knocked back the remaining contents of his goblet and swallowed hard. "But retiring officers aren't given land grants in the provinces anymore." He looked at the number written on the scroll. "It's a tidy sum to be sure. I could comfortably buy a nice townhouse with it." He chuckled. "But we both know that's not for me."

"You could always buy land in the provinces with it."

"True. But for what I had in mind I'd need three or four times that amount."

A curious moment of silence followed during which Suetonius' smile belied the fact he was contemplating Marek's last statement. "That can be arranged, you know," he said slyly.

"What can?"

"Money can." Suetonius sat up and eagerly poured more of the delicious wine. "Lots of it, if you're so inclined." He offered a full goblet. "The fact is, we have a favor to ask of you, Marek."

"We?" Marek asked as he deliberately looked about the room. "Who is it that constitutes 'we'?"

"Let's just call them a consortium of many leading citizens who share a common concern about the future of the empire."

"This sounds suspiciously like treason, Suetonius," Marek said uncomfortably. He put his goblet down on the table and crossed his arms.

"Oh no, it's nothing that grandiose. Suetonius abruptly raised the palm of his left hand above his head, then smiled and leaned forward as he slapped it onto his thigh. "Besides, you know me to be a loyal soldier, don't you? It's just that, right now, you're uniquely able to solve what they perceive to be a rather small, but growing, problem." He put his goblet down. "You're familiar with the gladiatrix?"

"Yes, they're the female gladiators. Mostly from Britannia, aren't they?"

"Correct! They're primarily surviving Iceni warriors whom Publius Petronius, the esteemed governor of Britannia, has elevated to celebrity status in the arena instead of killing or enslaving them. They began just like other gladiators but in the past year they've organized into something they call the Isis cult and they're fighting under names of various goddesses. Completely sacrilegious and making a mockery of our temples. Many have been killed in the arena, of course, but one of them in particular has become an undefeated superstar right here in Rome at the Circus Maximus."

"I'm not sure I'm following you, Suetonius?" Marek's arms remained locked.

"Well, these particular citizens I'm telling you about would like to see her out of the picture. Who better than 'the butcher' to accomplish this, while also demonstrating the superiority of the Roman military?"

"Ah, so you want me to kill her." Marek said incredulously. He slid his hands onto his hips. "And I suppose you'll want me to go into the arena to do it, right?" Marek couldn't help himself. He simply laughed.

"That's right."

"Wait," Marek's laughter abated as fast as it had come. "You're serious, aren't you?"

"We are absolutely serious."

Marek was stone faced as he stared at his former commander. "And the money?" he asked.

Suetonius grinned, reached into a nearby cupboard and produced a large pouch, which he first shook, then dropped into Marek's opening right hand. "That's gold," he said. "More than enough for the largest villa you can imagine."

"But only if I beat her?"

"Oh the money's yours for simply agreeing to fight. We know you'll win, Marek. You always win."

"When is this fight supposed to take place?" Marek's attention was focused at the heavy bag he was now holding in his right hand.

"June 19th."

Marek finally looked up from the gold. "That's just three days from now," he said.

"I'm sorry I wasn't able to give you more notice." Suetonius said unapologetically. "It's to be her final fight and if she isn't taken care of she retires undefeated and free. That's something we don't want to happen."

"A female Iceni warrior, a celebrity at that, at liberty in Rome, eh? I see how that might cause consternation amongst your 'concerned citizens.'" Marek was liberal with his amusement and decided to push the negotiation a bit further. "All right, Suetonius. But if I'm going into the arena I also want my four years of reserve duty to the legion eliminated."

Suetonius nodded eagerly. "Done." He went back to the cupboard, retrieved another scroll that was annoyingly already prepared and handed it to Marek. "You're now completely free."

"And I want to be anonymous in the area."

"No problem, that's our wish too. You'll both we wearing full head masks and your name will be withheld. It's our fail-safe, you see. In the unlikely event that you lose, we can reveal that you're not really a Roman."

"I do see." Marek rocked back and forth. "So tell me, Suetonius. What's the goddess name that this blasphemous, undefeated gladiatrix fights under?"

"Minerva."

"Great name, sort of an ultimate blasphemy, isn't it?" Marek chortled as he left.

Marek never really had a choice in the matter; Suetonius could have easily called his reserve status and made his next four years intolerable if he had balked. He fumed as he walked home. Over the past couple of years Nero had been exerting what was, in Marek's opinion, a positive influence by swinging Rome back to an era of tolerance toward outsiders which, inevitably, gave the old line citizens like Seneca cause to plot and rail against him. So, even while the majority of Roman citizens were well satisfied with Nero's policies and goods of all kind were readily flowing in from all over the world for the benefit of all, conspiracies were clearly in the works. What most infuriated Marek was the fact that he had agreed to be used by Seneca and his like to advance their position. "Still," he said to himself as he kicked a loose cobblestone down the street. "What do I care? I have my freedom and my money and in a few days I'll be out of here." In spite of all of the wine he'd consumed with Suetonius, Marek was completely sober as he swung his bag of gold back and forth while he walked down the street. His hatred for Rome had never been more intense.

Chapter Twenty Nine: Gladiatrix

M arek was so keenly focused on organizing his post fight plans that the next three days became a non stop flurry of activity and then, seemingly suddenly, it was the early morning of the big day. He leisurely ate a hearty breakfast of fish and figs, donned his comfortable, well used battle armor and headed out for the Circus Maximus, a huge amphitheater with seating for 250,000 spectators. The building itself was the center of a complex surrounded on all sides by a vast, sprawling arcade of hundreds of wooden shops inhabited by astrologers and cooks and prostitutes and the vendors of every product or service one could possibly imagine. This was the commercial heart of Rome. Marek, head down, wormed his way through the crowd of enthusiastic hawkers and, once inside the Circus itself, sought out Flavius, the head lanista, for outfitting.

"You're free to wear your cavalry armor if you wish and your gladius and dagger are fine," Flavius said as he walked around Marek, keenly studying him. "But," he pulled an item from one of the many racks adorning this fascinating fitting room, "you'll have to use this shield."

"It seems rather flimsy," Marek commented, sliding his left arm into the two leather bands on the inside. He swung his arm back and forth. "Surely it can't withstand much."

"They're usually good for two or three solid blows," Flavius replied, chuckling. He eased it off Marek's arm and stood it on the ground. "This is a show, after all, and the crowd loves it when a fighter's shield is demolished."

"I wonder that they don't use infantry javelins in the arena, then," Marek muttered, a bit louder than he intended, while he shook his head at the ineffectual shield.

"Because that might be a bit too real," Flavius responded in stride. "We wouldn't want to accidentally kill a gladiator like that. It takes months, even years, to make a good arena fighter and we have to protect them as best we can."

"How often does a gladiator fight?"

"Oh, no more than four or five times a year. The rest of the time they're either being healed from their wounds or they are in training. If a gladiator survives for three years he, and nowadays she, is then able to retire to a comfortable life." He picked up a helmet from the row he had been surveying and handed it to Marek. "Here, try this one."

While the helmet looked unwieldy at first, it was remarkably light and, once he'd tightened the two side buckles, Marek found it gave him an astonishing freedom of movement. "This is even better than military issue helmets," he said, then quickly unfastened and removed it as fast as he could. He first stared at it in disbelief, and then looked up at Flavius. "Did my voice really sound that loud and strange?" he asked.

"Indeed it did." Flavius said as he gently took the helmet back from Marek. "These are made by master craftsmen and each one is a work of art. Nothing like those mass produced military headpieces you're used to." He laughed as he turned it over to show the details. "Look. Inside, here, is a device that not only magnifies and projects your voice, but also makes it sound deeper. It lets the crowd hear what you're saying and even if you were to let out a high pitched scream it would sound to the crowd as a lion's roar." He put the helmet down on a nearby table and stroked the top. "Gladiators must always be heroic to the audience." He said, slowly straightening up and tenting his fingertips. "Even in the throes of death."

"Oh, I've no concerns in that regard, Flavius."

"No?" Flavius snapped back but then studied Marek's face curiously. If this was bravado it certainly wasn't transparent. "You do know that Minerva is undefeated, don't you?" he said emphatically, clearly trying to goad an emotional response. "Twelve times. Ten of them outright kills."

"That's why I'm here." Marek's flat voice carried no inflection. "There'll not be a thirteenth."

"Mm, like ice." The sides of Flavius' mouth rose approvingly. "You know, it's most unusual to see someone who's going into the arena be all by himself beforehand. Most of the gladiators have a close camaraderie with others in their school, like family, who are there to support him and provide encouragement before the fight. Don't you have anyone?"

"No, Flavius." Marek picked up the helmet and tried it on again. "I'm all alone," he boomed in a voice not his own.

And then it was time. The huge door swung open and Marek stepped onto the hard packed sand, squinting in the sunlight, while the loud, enthusiastic voice from the Circus announcer echoed throughout the arena. "The challenger today," the voice said. "Is a decorated hero of the famous fourteenth legion. This man has not only stood face-to-face against vicious women warriors, but he has slain more of them than can be counted." The announcer's voice became louder and louder as he continued to finally crescendo with, "I give you the butcher of the Iceni." As instructed, Marek walked to the center of the arena, holding up his shield and waving his gladius above his head while the crowd roared its approval. The eyes of so many people, thousands, all focused on him was strangely intoxicating and he instantly understood the motivation of the gladiator. Once in place in the middle he raised both his sword and shield again and slowly turned to scan the whole crowd. More cheers, even louder cheers, welcomed him to this place of death as entertainment. He grinned silently.

"And now," the announcer started up again with his effervescent voice. "The undefeated favorite! Citizens of Rome, I give you," he paused just long enough for all eyes to focus on a door now opening. "Minerva, the Iceni gladiatrix."

Marek, too, turned to look in awe as she stepped into the arena. The entire Circus Maximus appeared to shudder around him as the inflamed crowd leaped to their feet and thundered into cheers and applause. Minerva waved her sword to her fans while striding briskly toward Marek. She wore the standard leather tunic of the Iceni warrior but was carrying a Roman gladius and a painted wooden shield very similar to the one Marek himself was holding. Her helmet was jet black and in the shape of a horse's head. In a flash Marek's vision suddenly went blank and the intense state of anger from two years ago was suddenly rekindled at the sight of horse motif. He could hear the magnified sounds of his breathing and his fist tightened around his sword. He slowly re-opened his eyes to watch her approach.

"Butcher of the Iceni?" she called out, taunting him with the bellow of a lioness while playing loudly to the crowd. "You never met me in that battle."

"That was clearly your good fortune, or you would not be here now." Marek answered with the voice of a bull. The crowd screamed its approval.

Side-by-side, the contestants walked to the platform in front of the emperor's ornate marble box. Marek looked up to see who had been favored to join Nero in the most desirable seats. Suetonius was there, as he expected, right next to Seneca, but sitting to Nero's right was Caractacus. "Today," the announcer began again. "We have a re-enactment of the famous battle and the heroic defeat of the most terrifying of all the tribes of Britannia, the Iceni. Gladiator and gladiatrix, take your positions."

Marek and Minerva bowed to the distinguished company in the box and stepped off the platform. They remained side-by-side and, with military precision, took ten paces back toward the center of the arena, stopped, then turned their backs to each other. The crowd loudly counted out each of the next six steps they took as they separated, then fell instantly silent when the contestants turned to face each other. Everyone was now waiting and all eyes turned to the small white cloth held aloft in Nero's motionless fist. Suddenly cheering resumed, the cloth was fluttering away in the light breeze and Minerva was charging at Marek, screaming. Stepping forward with his right foot he blocked her swing at the cost of a chunk of his lightweight shield but she nimbly sidestepped his uppercut gladius thrust. "I'm going to make you suffer for 100,000 Iceni," she howled, half crouching two paces in front of him with the tip her sword pointing upward.

"That was your own undoing," Marek snarled back. "Only fools make a frontal attack on a legion in protected formation." He swung at her and their swords clanged together, each pushing against the other. "You Iceni brought destruction on yourselves," he continued. "You attacked us." He backed away in order to make a more effective swing, his unbound anger inflamed by the vivid memory of his last words to Ceridwen. He screamed, "Even after you were warned not to," as he crashed his sword down onto her shield. They both furiously swung and hacked away in rapid succession, absolutely delighting the audience, but the sound of the elated crowd faded into nothingness for Marek as he focused solely on his opponent. This woman who so painfully reminded him of everything he had lost that day was going to feel the full brunt of everything he could muster. This wasn't about money or glory or politics or villas. This was for unbridled vengeance. With another rage infused swing he cleaved Minerva's shield in half and forced her to stumble and back away as she shook the remnants from her arm. She quickly drew her dagger to replace the shield in her unprotected hand.

"Prepare to be undefeated no more," Marek bellowed at her, rushing forward.

"You're a long way from finishing me, Roman." She crashed her sword again down onto Marek's battered shield but this time slid into a crouching position right afterward and swung low with her dagger. Marek jumped back but his left thigh was already stinging and blood was drizzling down his leg from the superficial wound. "I've drawn first blood," she exclaimed jubilantly.

His shield hanging in two pieces on his arm, Marek wriggled free of it and also unsheathed his dagger. "Indeed, you did," he cajoled her. "Come, try for more."

Expertly defending themselves against each other's swords they nevertheless each successfully scored minor hits with their daggers at every turn and while Marek's breastplate was merely dented, the slices in Minerva's leather tunic were opening up into gaping holes. It was also clear by her evident panting and labored swings that she was not used to fights lasting this long. Marek recognized his emerging advantage and in a rapid attack drove her back into a completely defensive posture. "I'm going to cut you to pieces," he roared at her as he pushed his sword down onto hers, forcing her again into a crouching stance. "I'm stronger than you and I have more hatred to keep me going than you can possibly imagine."

Minerva ineffectively jabbed her dagger back and forth while her right hand began to falter as she desperately held her sword against Marek mounting pressure. "What gives you, a Roman, the right to such hatred?" she angrily blurted. "We didn't take your home the way the Romans took mine." Summoning a sudden surge of energy she pushed Marek back enough so she could jump to her feet, but before she could raise her sword he came down on her right shoulder with the leading edge of his gladius and sent her careening backwards. She rolled over and scrambled to her feet, backing away as he slowly advanced toward her. The brunt of the blow had fallen on the now cleaved shoulder strap and caused only a minor cut to her shoulder, although the quantity of blood suggested otherwise. Her mangled tunic half hanging off her was now a liability, severely interfering with the movement of her left arm.

"I'm not a Roman," he answered, gladius at the ready. "And your people took from me the only home I've ever wanted. Even your death isn't going to settle that."

Minerva continued to walk backwards as she frantically thrust the tip of her sword under her tunic's left shoulder strap and, with a swift upwards cut, freed herself. The blood soaked leather fell in a heap onto the sand and her naked breasts even further thrilled the already ecstatic crowd. She immediately regained her fighting pose and lunged at the approaching Marek who simply sidestepped her, but didn't strike back. He was staring at her right breast; at a scar. It was a distinctive scar, from a time so long ago. "Why do you fight?" he demanded from her, blocking her onslaught but not taking advantage of the openings available due to her weariness. "Why fight when you can't win?"

"I fight for my freedom," she cried out, her helmet successfully misinterpreting her obvious pain. "If I win I'm promised freedom and the restoration of my land."

"And that's more important to you than your life?"

"I'll be dying a good death," She screamed. "And there's freedom there too." She lunged at Marek with both her gladius and dagger. He blocked both of them with uppercut movements, locking both her weapons onto his, and forced her arms up and away from her body as he pushed her backwards.

"And I was sent here to ensure that death," he announced for the pleasure of the crowd, but then whispered, "But instead, I'm going to give you what you want," desperately hoping his words were too quiet for the infernal helmet to transmit. Marek shoved her down, hard, then, unexpectedly, took four steps backwards. He quickly unbuckled his helmet and dropped it onto the ground before she was able to scramble back to her feet. He stood facing her, weapons still at the ready. "For three years I've mourned you, Ceridwen," he said happily. Without the helmet only she could hear him. "Had I known you'd survived I would have done everything possible to find you. Yet, find you I finally have." He beamed at her with a truly grateful face. "A single blow to the neck, Ceri," he said straightening up, "and you'll have what you want the most. Let me give this to you." He stood with his weapons hanging limply in his hands. "But take off that helmet first. Let your face be the last thing I see at my death."

A confused crowd fell silent as they watched their favorite gladiatrix cautiously keep her distance from the butcher and remove her helmet. She shook out her sweat drenched long black hair and as it cascaded around her white naked flesh she took her gladius in both hands and raised it above her right shoulder. "So be it Marek," she said to him, then stepped forward with her left foot and screamed out as she took her swing. Time suddenly ceased, Marek didn't flinch, and the swing abruptly stopped with her gladius just touching the side of his neck. She watched his eyes trace a line down the length of the sword, along her fully extended arms and up to her open mouthed, tear drenched smile.

"That is the most beautiful face I have ever seen," he said calmly, his body remaining perfectly rigid.

"You, you really are the one," she gasped as she slowly lowered her sword.

"I'm so glad you realized it." Marek responded breathing an enthusiastic sigh of relief as he quickly sheathed his dagger.

"Our fates are in the hands of the emperor now," Ceridwen said, her eyes flitting back and forth as guards rushed out onto the arena and formed a row on each side of them.

"Don't go all Roman on me now, Ceri," Marek told her. "I learned from the Britons that the life a warrior is always in his own hands, never the dictates of another. There is no such thing as fate. Pick up your helmet." He reached down for his. "Carry it in your left hand like this and keep your gladius ready in your right. We have to approach the emperor with due respect, but if he decides against us we're going fight it out," he beckoned toward the guards with the top of his head. "With them."

"That's not very Roman like, Marek," Ceridwen said quietly as she picked up her helmet.

"My pledge to the legions is over," Marek replied. "I'm now free to despise Rome." He turned and looked directly at her. "But I love you." He broke into an immense grin and happily walked side-by-side with Ceridwen to the platform. "We're either leaving for Britannia together or we're dying together, fighting side-by-side, right here."

From their position on the platform it was clear there was lively dissent in the emperor's box. A furious, red-faced Seneca was standing and pounding his fist into the palm of his left hand while Caractacus, hands on his hips, was leaning forward at him from the vantage of his seat. Nero finally held his hand out to silence them and then stood up to address Marek and Ceridwen. "Such skill," he began. "Such bravery. Such compassion." Nero enunciated flamboyantly, taunting both the fighters as well as the crowd with his ebullience. "I declare you both winners, as we all have won who witnessed you in this arena today."

While the crowd cheered and applauded, Caractacus sent a slave to the arena floor with a fine Egyptian robe for Ceridwen to wear. It was only after she and Marek had sheathed their swords and she was donning it that she even recognized that she was naked from the waist up. She blushed under Marek's intent gaze. "Meet me at the south entrance at nightfall," he told her. "I have some things to take care of."

"I'll be there." Ceridwen squeezed Marek's hand, her excited eyes dancing for his. "I have a couple of things to do myself, but I'll be there."

Marek rapidly disappeared and Ceridwen sauntered back to where the other members of her Isis gladiatrix clan were waiting to congratulate her and tend to her wounds. She rested for only an hour before claiming her freedom, then rushed away from the Circus Maximus for a prearranged appointment in the main part of Rome. Along the way she chuckled to herself at the pretentiousness of the women she passed who so obviously stared down their noses at her, this fair skinned woman with the unkempt hair. She gazed in awe at the huge marble buildings and the slaves who so compliantly served their masters. Everything Marek had told her about Rome so long ago was all true and the thought of how safe and secure and superior these Romans felt made her grin excitedly. They were a people who'd never known the wolf at their door. She was about to show them.

Tegas greeted her warmly and anxiously ushered her inside almost as soon as Ceridwen had knocked on the door. "We were so worried," Tegas told her. "Caractacus said you suffered quite a wound today."

"Just a cut to the shoulder," Ceridwen answered, her left hand instinctively reaching for it as she spoke. "It'll heal with no problem."

"I'm very pleased to hear it," boomed a voice from behind. Ceridwen quickly turned and exclaimed, "It's so good to see you again Caractacus."

"For a while today I didn't think you'd be seeing anyone ever again." He cocked his head to the left and his mouth straightened. "Now, are you sure you're strong enough to go through with this?"

"Of course I am." Ceridwen pulled her eyebrows back at Caractacus' effrontery.

"That's our Ceridwen," he said, bellowing with laughter. "After what happened in the arena I just had to ask. Come then," he beckoned to a table. "Let's take some refreshment before you have to leave."

It was early dusk when Ceridwen approached the complex of wooden buildings around the Circus Maximus. The storekeepers had gone for the day and the shops were completely deserted. "Deserted and vulnerable," she muttered confidently to herself as she reached into the large bag Caractacus had given her and pulled out the bundle of five torches. Nervously looking around to ensure she was alone she proceeded to light them and, holding the ensuing blaze at arms length, walked sideways toward the corner building and tossed one of the torches through the space between the doors. It instantly exploded with a whoosh, as if it had ignited some flammable material inside, and she quickly ran away and turned the corner onto a new street, panting. "That's going to attract attention," she said aloud in an effort to calm herself. Ceridwen winced at the heat from what she was still holding. She had to get rid of the other four torches quickly. There was no one around so she shoved one into the building she was leaning against and ran further down the street counting the shops. "Caractacus said a separation of at least four buildings," she repeated to herself and as she pushed the next torch into the fifth, then another on the opposite side of the street. Eager to deploy the last torch she ran obliviously to the end of the row and leaned back to throw it into the corner building, but a hand suddenly grabbed tightly onto her wrist while an unseen arm wrapped around her from behind. She wriggled furiously but her assailant simply dragged her backwards to the side of the street and, sliding his right hand up from her wrist, easily took the torch from her. Her arm now free, Ceridwen quickly turned toward him, claws ready, but stayed her hand when she saw Marek's stern face looking down at her. "I have to do this, Marek" she pleaded, stretching for the torch that he deliberately held out of her reach.

The arm that had initially restrained her was now simply holding her and Marek pulled her to himself. "Then we'll do it together," he said softly, thrusting the flaming brand over the top of the door they were standing in front of. "Here on out we do everything together." His right hand now free he dug his fingers into the back of her hair and forced her to face him. "I've known of Caractacus' plan to burn Rome for some time," he said, staring into her eyes and relishing in her confusion. "But until a couple of hours ago I had no idea the Isis clan were a part of it."

"You mean there are others involved too?"

"At this moment, Ceri, there are a hundred fires like this breaking out all over the city."

"You, you and Caractacus?" she stammered.

"Have been working together? Yes." He nodded briskly. "In fact, I just missed you at his house earlier today. We're to meet up with him again shortly, though, since he's the one who's arranged for a ship to get us out of here." He held her rigid while he lowered his face to hers. The heat from the flaming building next to them was intense but neither paid any attention. Vengeance had been served and their passions were once again focused on each other. "You and I leave for Britannia tonight," he said. "We're going home."

Their lips came together with a hunger borne of years of emptiness and, as his grip softened, their arms locked onto each other in tight embrace as Rome burned around them. Ceridwen gushed with a delicious yet previously unknown feeling made up of the best parts of contentment and excitement. Llyn was right; she and Marek were the future of Britannia.

Did you love *The Last Iceni*? Then you should read *Love, Lust &
Passion: The Real Story of the Pirate Anne Bonny*[1] by Ronald Haines!

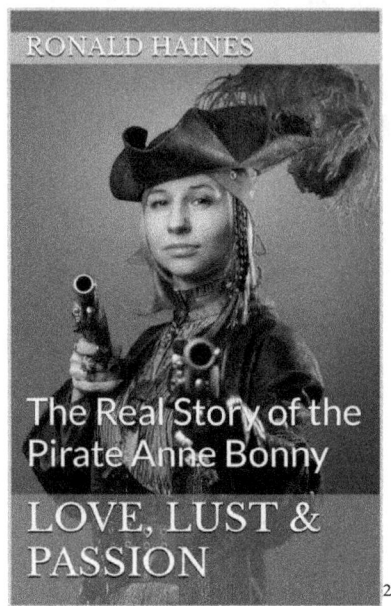

[2]

The young Anne Bonny eloped to get away from home and now she's
left her husband to sail away on a pirate ship with Jack Rackham and
Mary Read. Her days are filled with sun-kissed adventure and the
ménage without jealousy satiates her. But does she really have what
it takes to be a pirate in the Caribbean of 1720 when the world is
closing in? A cannonball from a British warship has just taken down
the mast. She is about to find out.

This second edition includes an addendum explaining some of
the history about Anne Bonny.Learn about the real life of Anne
Bonny, a novel about the teenager who runs away from the confining
life of colonial Carolina to Nassau in New Providence, Bahamas

---

1. https://books2read.com/u/mZZdaE

2. https://books2read.com/u/mZZdaE

hoping to enjoy the lust filled, idealized life of freedom as a pirate.While in the Bahamas Anne meets and becomes intimate with Mary Read, whom Anne considers to be the epitome of a woman pirate, and serves with her under the command of Calico Jack Rackham, the last of the golden age pirate captains.Numerous versions of the pirate life of Anne Bonny have been told over the past three centuries, but few of these stories have considered her from a historical perspective. Most of them simply re-visit the sensational and titillating tales of a woman serving aboard an eighteenth century pirate ship and take what is generally accepted about her at face value.When one considers the historical chronology, however, many of the stories about Anne Bonny do not make sense. After researching, it is the opinion of this author that much of what has been accepted as fact about Anne Bonny was more likely to have been about another woman pirate, Mary Read. Anne's actual story, however, not only makes for a great read, but also makes a lot more sense when one considers the fact that her entire time aboard a pirate ship was only two months.Researched historical chronology and available biographical information was used as the basis in writing this pirate adventure novel, with license taken by the author to determine the motivations of the characters since they were inferred by him from the facts, and the story line was then created to both fit and explain those facts. While interesting from a historical perspective, this book also contains both heterosexual and bisexual situations and is therefore not suitable for minors. The pages in this pirate adventure novel tell the real story (truth being defined as the most logical interpretation of the facts) of the pirate life of Anne Bonny. While Anne never became a famous pirate captain, the story of Anne Bonny and Mary Read as women pirates is well established in Caribbean and West Indies history. Were they lesbian pirates? That might depend upon your definition as you read about their circumstances.INTERVIEW WITH THE AUTHORQ. Why is the historical Anne Bonny so different from what is presented in modern culture?A. Nowadays we would call it marketing and PR. Most of the exploits attributed to Anne Bonny were actually done by Mary Read, but when you're looking for sensationalism who would you choose as your heroine? Mary, an androgynous, battle-hardened woman in her 30s, or Anne, a buxom young redhead?Q. So Mary Read was the real pirate woman?A. Exactly! Mary was a seasoned pirate while Anne spent two months aboard a pirate ship. For Anne, this was more of a coming-of-age adventure.

Read more at https://ronaldhaines.com.

Also by Ronald Haines

Pirates of The Bahamas
Pirates of The Bahamas

Real Pirate Stories
Love, Lust & Passion: The Real Story of the Pirate Anne Bonny

Standalone
The Last Iceni
Finding Out Will Change Your Life Forever: Dealing with the
Knowledge You are Face Blind
Existential Humanism: How to Live Authentically in Today's
World

Watch for more at https://ronaldhaines.com.

About the Author

Ronald Haines finds the study of history and historical people fascinating. He believes that people are really no different now than they were even thousands of years ago in terms of their motivations, desires, prejudices and biases. Ronald's Historical Fiction novels are well researched for historical fact, and through his characters readers will be put inside the heads of the people who there, living it.

Ronald is an existential humanist: goal directed, self-motivated, and a big believer in individual freedom and its requisite companion, personal responsibility. You'll find these traits expressed throughout his works.

Ronald genuinely enjoys the process of writing and can be totally immersed in whatever world he is creating for hours at a time. But when not at his desk writing, you'll find him sailing, gardening, hiking through the woods, or walking along a beach.

Read more at https://ronaldhaines.com.